PopularMMOs

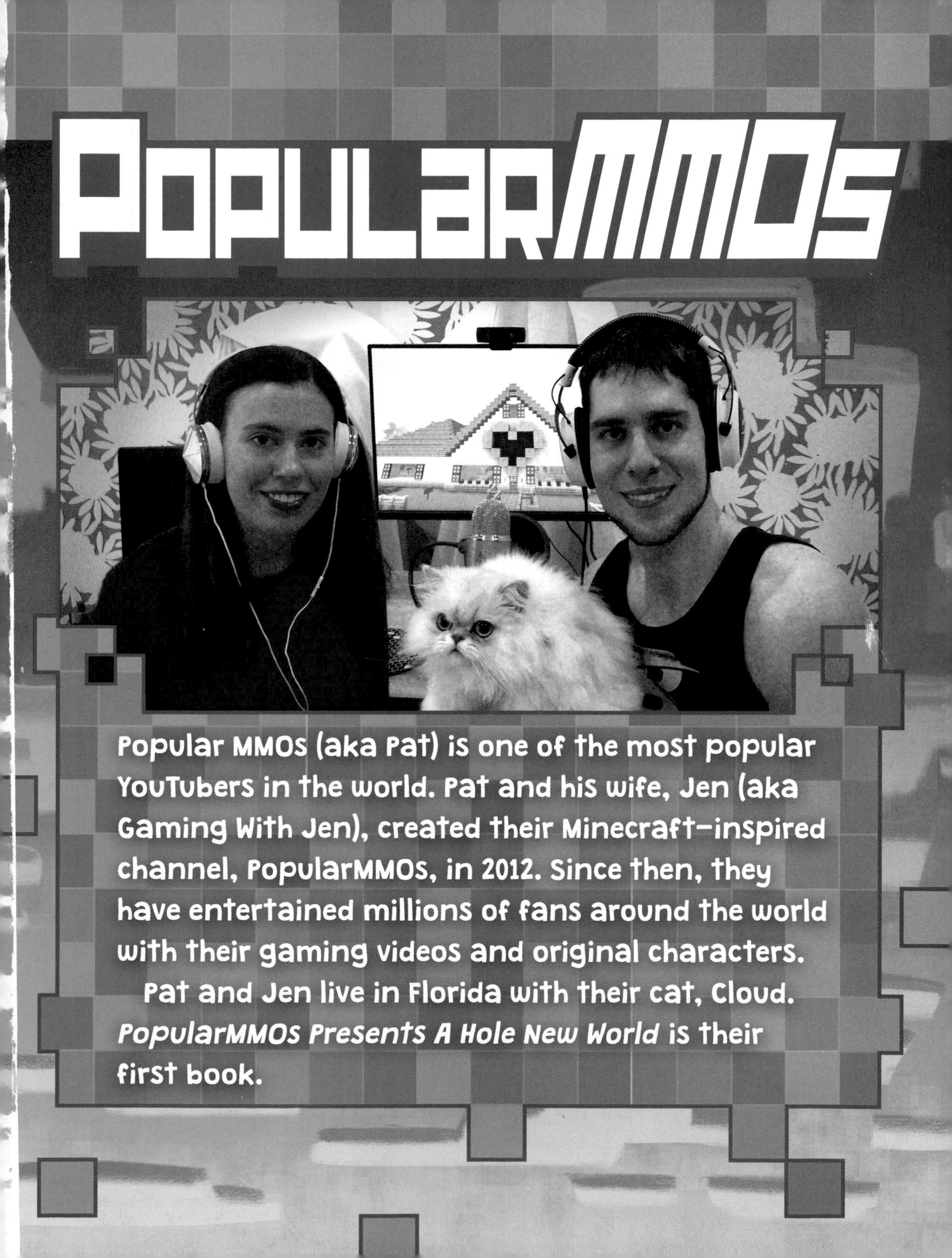

Popular MMOs (aka Pat) is one of the most popular YouTubers in the world. Pat and his wife, Jen (aka Gaming With Jen), created their Minecraft-inspired channel, PopularMMOs, in 2012. Since then, they have entertained millions of fans around the world with their gaming videos and original characters.

Pat and Jen live in Florida with their cat, Cloud. *PopularMMOs Presents A Hole New World* is their first book.

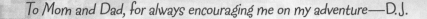

To Mom and Dad, for always encouraging me on my adventure—D.J.

A special thanks to Joe Caramagna for all his creative help!

PopularMMOs Presents A Hole New World Text copyright © 2018 by PopularMMOs, LLC. Illustrations copyright © 2018 by Dani Jones. All rights reserved. Printed in the United States of America. No part of this book may be used or reproduced in any manner whatsoever without written permission except in the case of brief quotations embodied in critical articles and reviews. For information address HarperCollins Children's Books, a division of HarperCollins Publishers, 195 Broadway, New York, NY 10007.
www.harpercollinschildrens.com

Library of Congress Control Number: 2018934063
ISBN 978-0-06-279087-3 (trade bdg.)
ISBN 978-0-06-284639-6 (special edition)
ISBN 978-0-06-287868-7 (special edition)

The artist used an iPad Pro and the app Procreate to create the digital illustrations for this book.
Typography by Erica De Chavez 18 19 20 21 22 WOR 10 9 8 7   ❖   First Edition

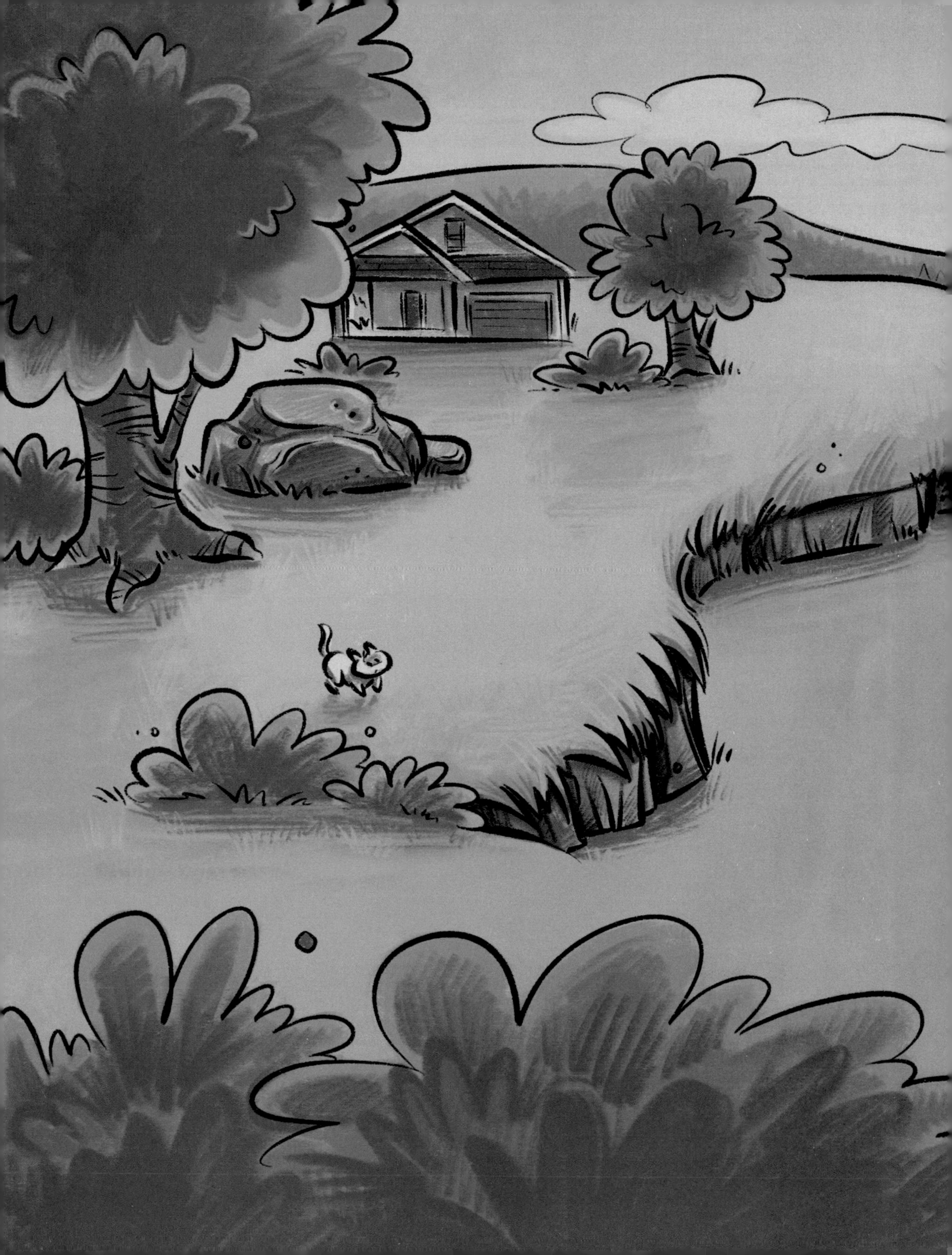

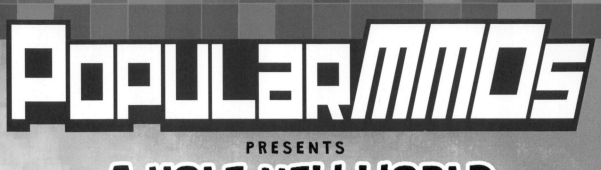

PopularMMOs

PRESENTS

A HOLE NEW WORLD

By PAT+JEN from POPULARMMOs

Illustrated by DANI JONES

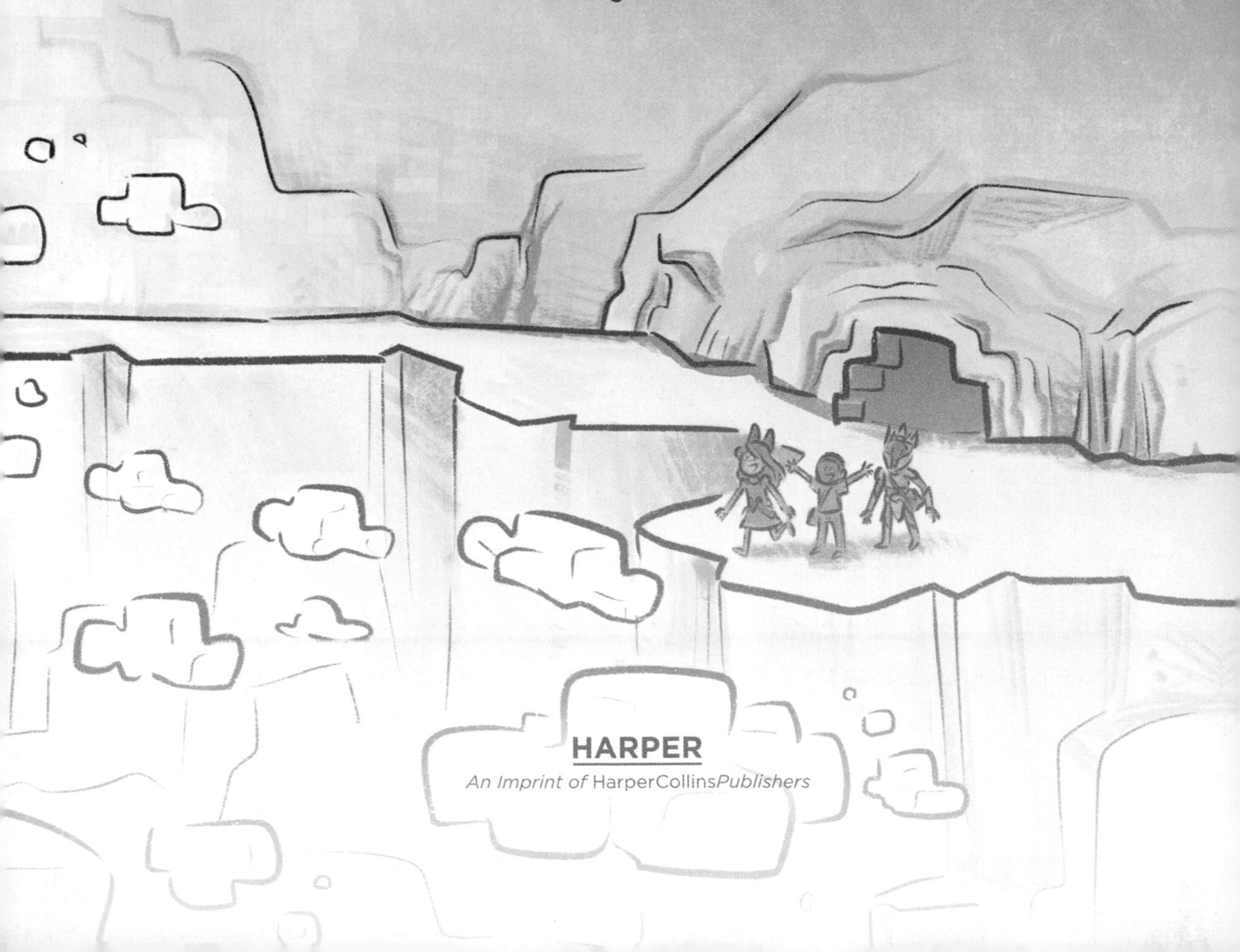

HARPER

An Imprint of Harper Collins*Publishers*

Hey, what's going on, guys!

It's Pat, and welcome to my first book! If you've ever seen my videos, then you know that I love playing games and creating my own characters, from Bomby to Captain Cookie and, best of all, Evil Jen. For the past couple of years, I've been lucky enough to be able to share all the thrilling quests that my characters have embarked on through my YouTube channel, but this graphic novel lets me take our stories to a whole new level.

Now my characters can go on an epic adventure the likes of which I could only ever create in these pages. With a magical unicorn, an army of zombies, and a dangerous underworld, our heroes are trying to escape the hole new world that comes straight out of my imagination.

Wherever your own imagination happens to take you, I hope this book sparks your own creativity.

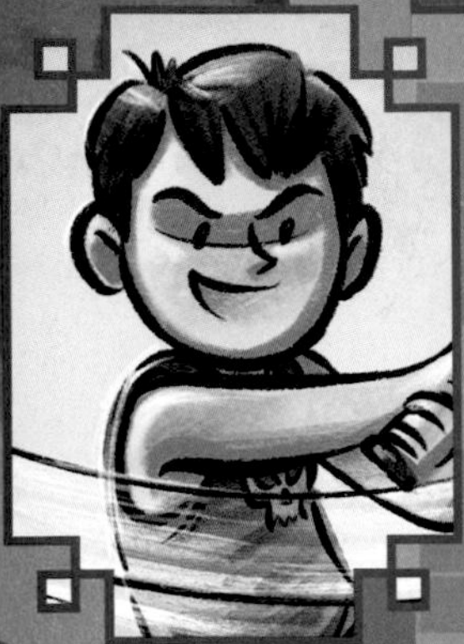

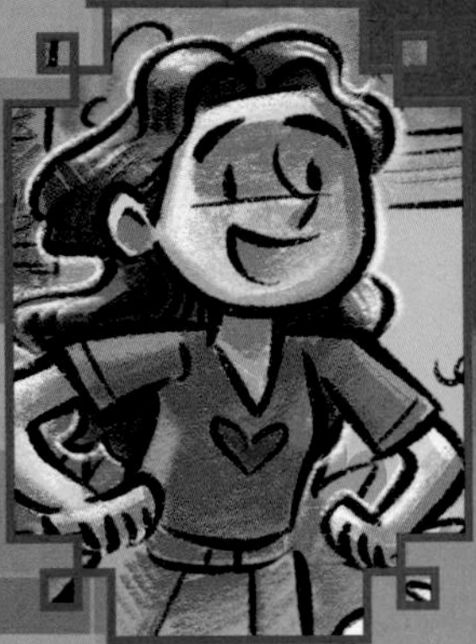

PAT & JEN

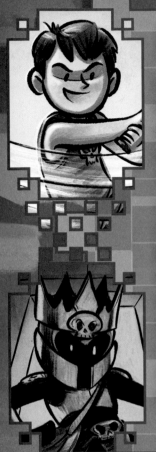

Pat is an awesome dude who's always looking for an epic adventure with his partner, the Super Girly Gamer Jen. Pat loves to have fun with his friends and take control of every situation with his cool weapons and can-do attitude. Jen is the sweetest person in the world and loves to laugh, but don't let her cheeriness fool you—she's also fierce. In fact, she could be an even greater adventurer than Pat . . . if she weren't so clumsy. Together, along with their cat, Cloud, they have a bond that can never be broken.

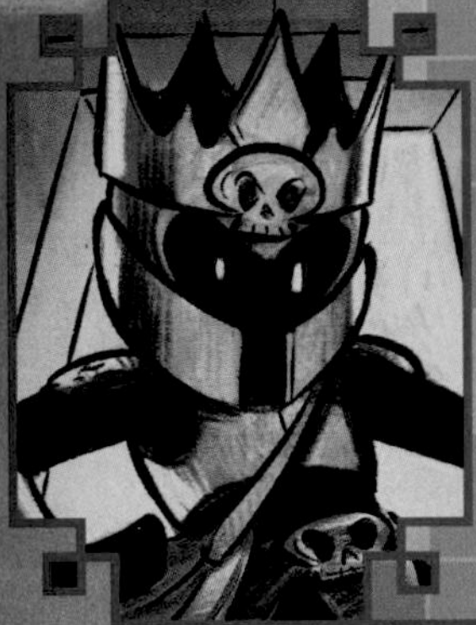

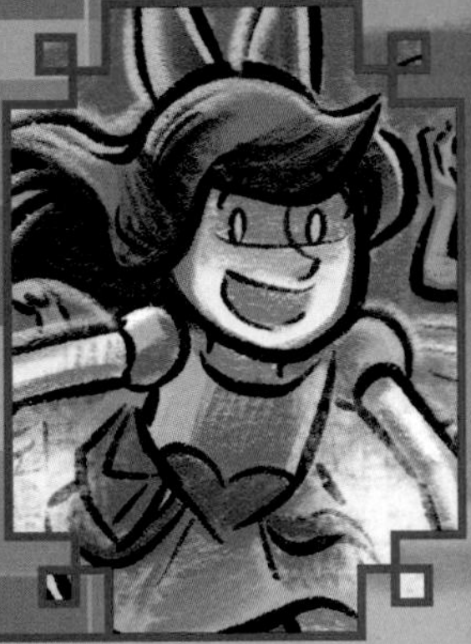

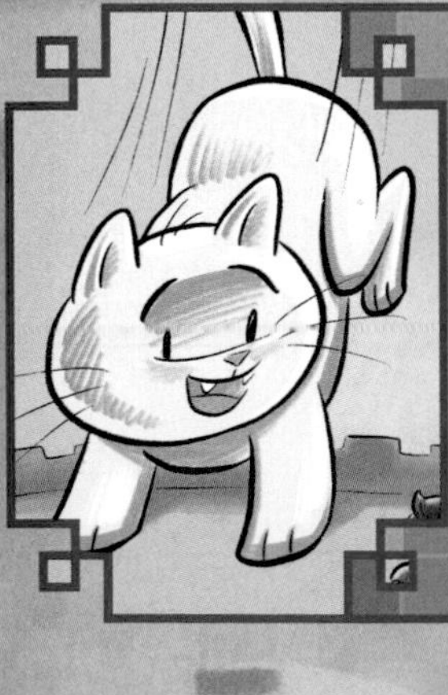

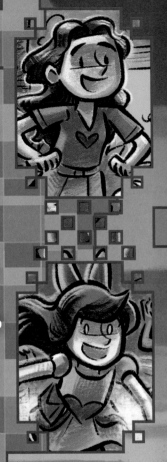

CLOUD

Cloud is Pat and Jen's white Persian cat. He may have a fluffy exterior, but underneath, he's all *savage*.

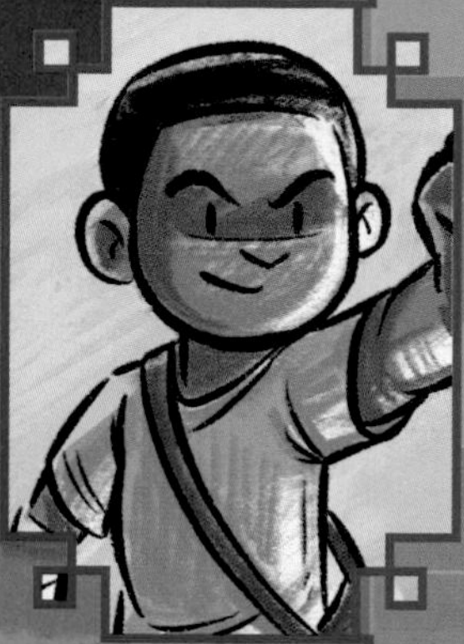

CARTER

Carter is Jen's best friend and biggest fan, but he doesn't seem to like Pat very much at all. Carter is also not very smart and is known for carrying a pickle that he thinks is a green sword! But Carter means well, and if Pat and Jen hope to survive, they're going to have to trust him.

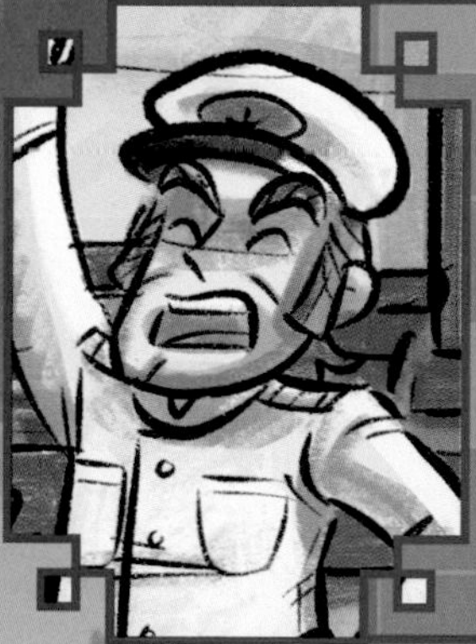

CAPTAIN COOKIE

No one is quite sure if Captain Cookie is a real sea captain or if he just dresses the part. He doesn't seem to be very good at anything, but that doesn't stop him from bragging about how great he is! He's rude to everyone he meets but always in a funny way.

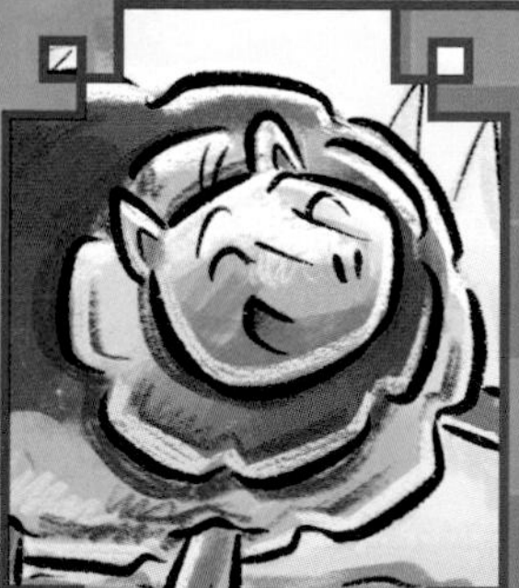

MR. RAINBOW

Mr. Rainbow is a magical sheep whose wool can appear to be any color of the rainbow. He's the leader of the resistance against Evil Jen's tyranny and arms his friends with mystery boxes that contain secret weapons!

GIZMO

Gizmo is a magical unicorn who leaves a trail of rainbows wherever he goes!

HONEY BOO BOO

Honey Boo Boo is a golem of iron on the outside but is all softy on the inside!

BOMBY

Bomby is somewhat of a pet to Pat and Jen but also Pat's best friend. You can usually find him by following the craters left by the TNT that he loves to watch explode. He doesn't talk, but when he goes missing, the adventure that follows speaks volumes for how much he is loved by everyone.

EVIL JEN

Evil Jen's favorite thing is chaos. She lives for wreaking havoc on the world. What makes her truly evil, however, is that she would take someone as sweet as Jen and become an evil version of her. She even looks *exactly* like her (just don't tell Jen we said that!).

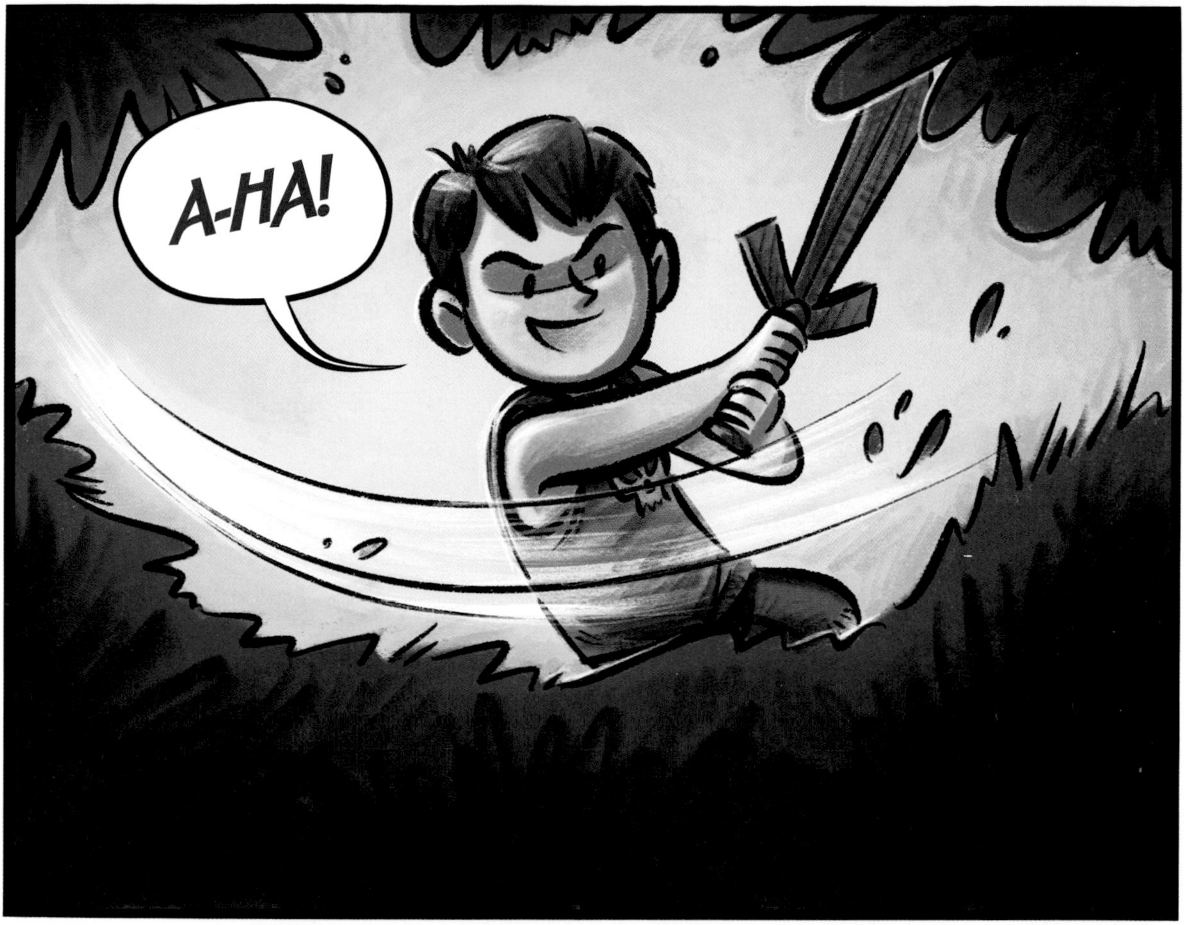
A-HA!

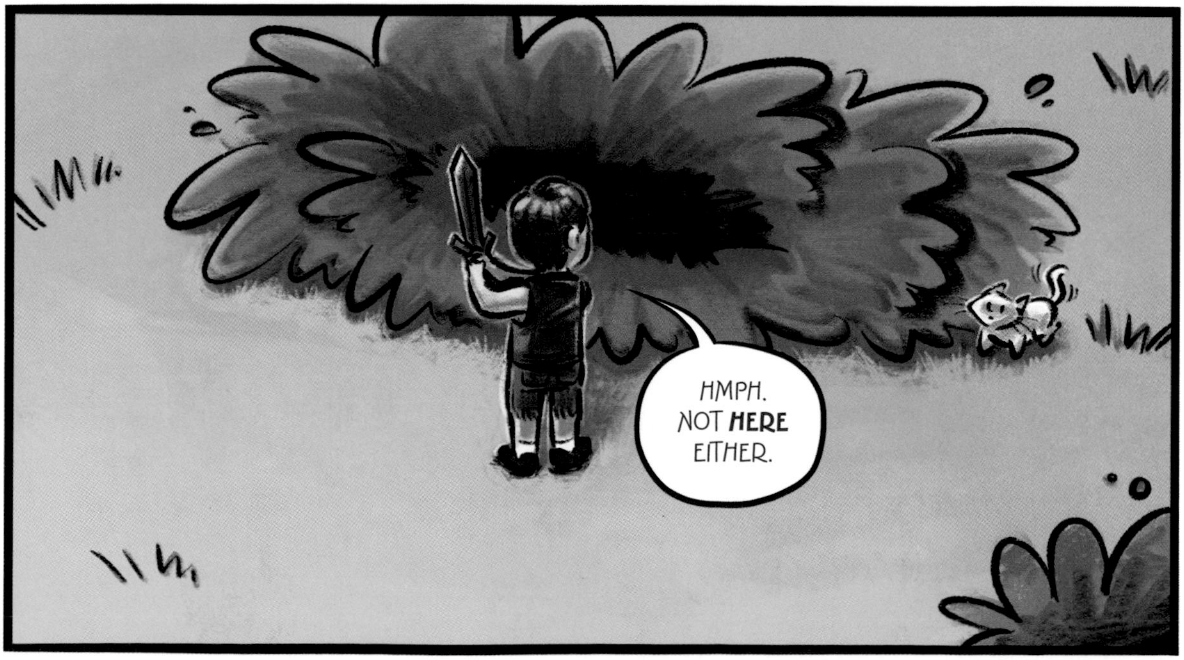
HMPH. NOT **HERE** EITHER.

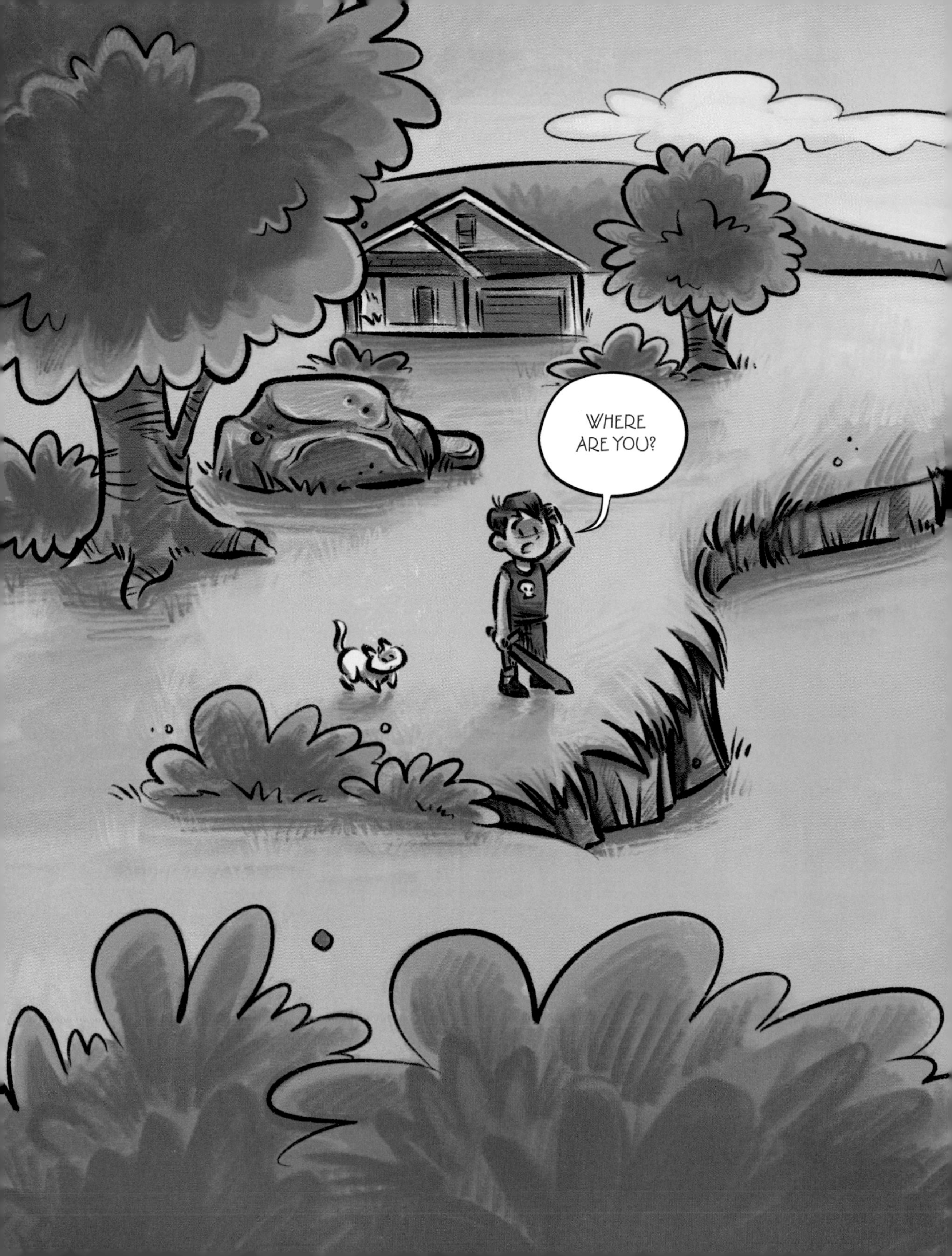
WHERE ARE YOU?

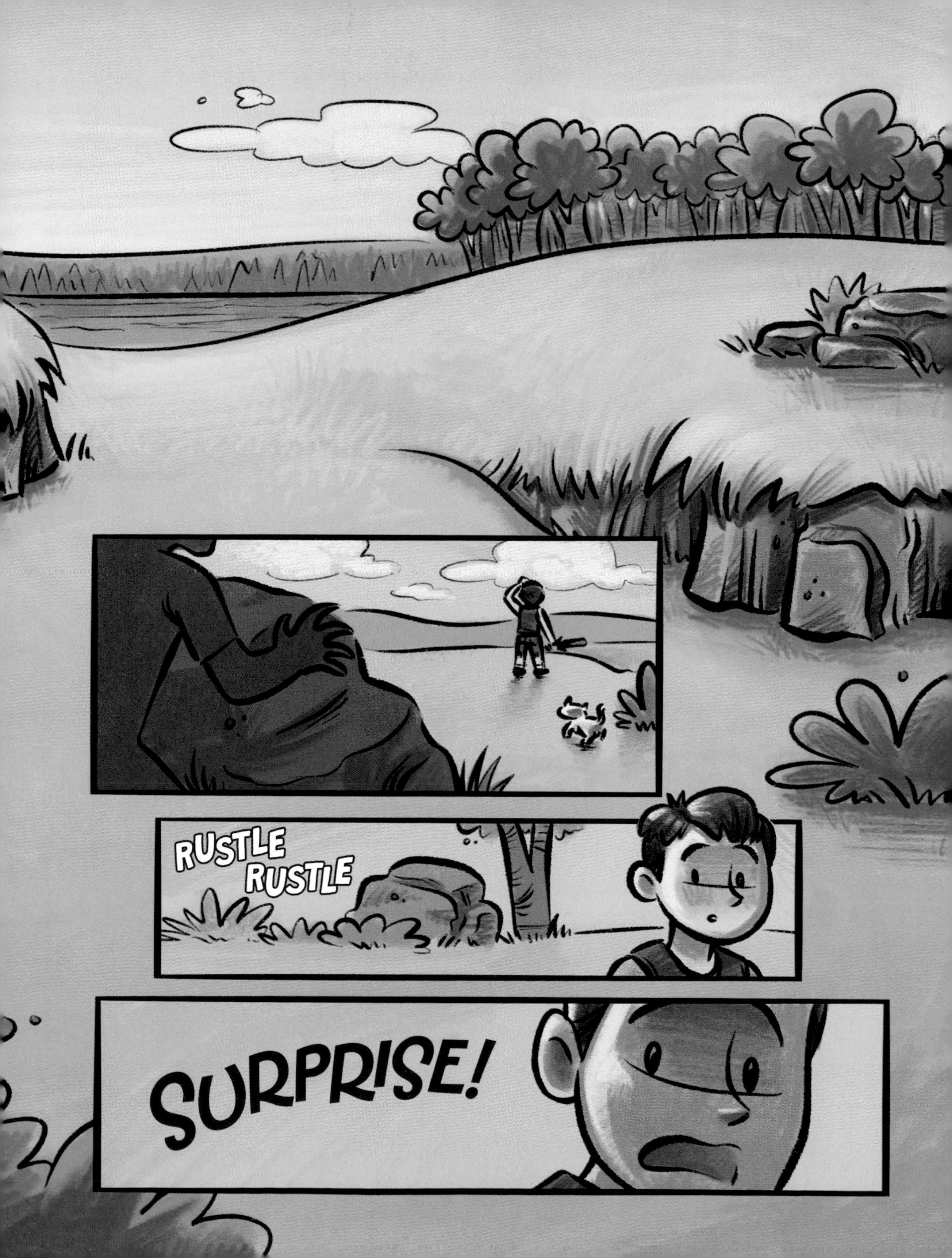
RUSTLE
RUSTLE
SURPRISE!

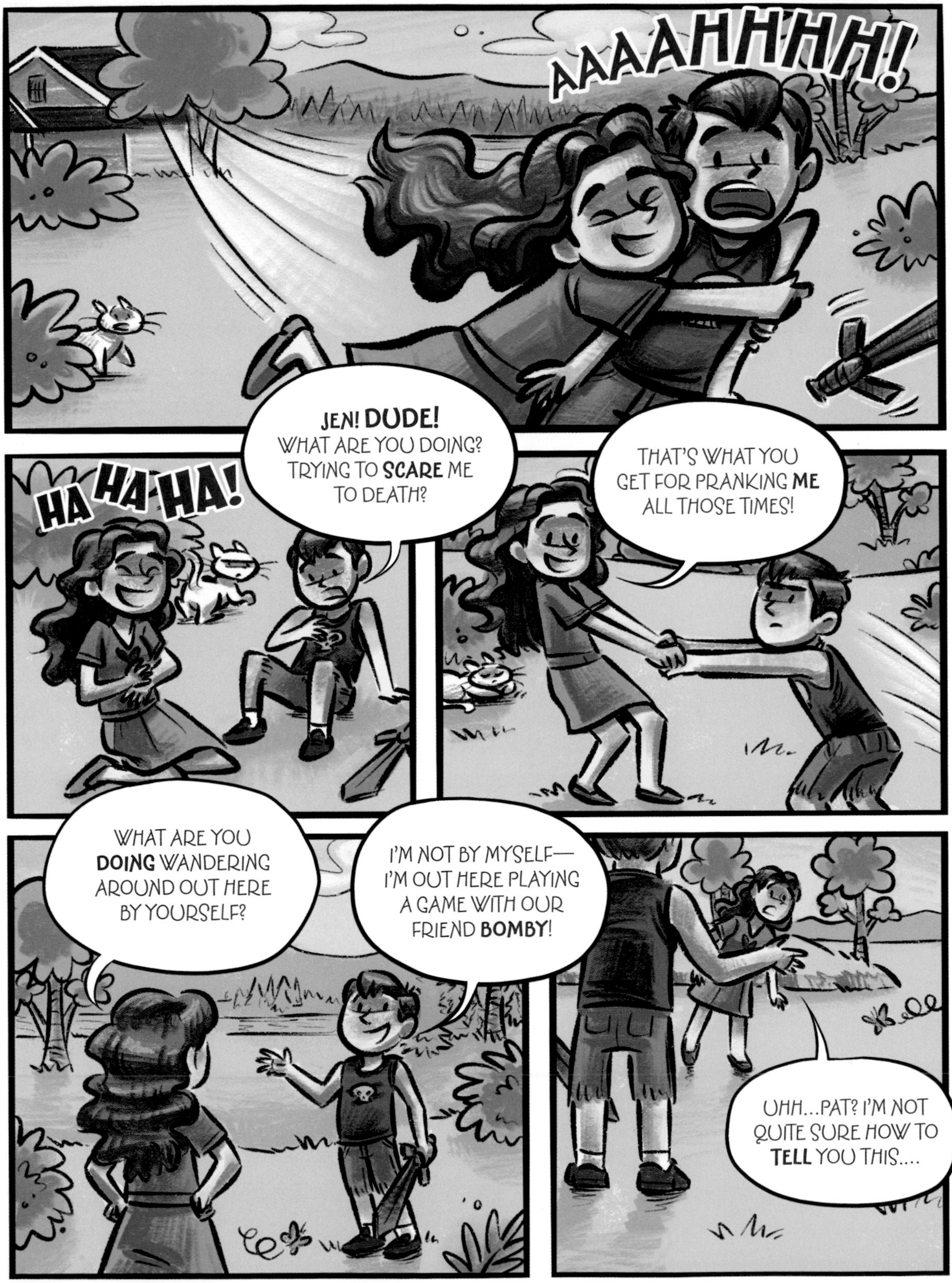
AAAAHHHH!
HA HA HA!
JEN! DUDE! WHAT ARE YOU DOING? TRYING TO SCARE ME TO DEATH?
THAT'S WHAT YOU GET FOR PRANKING ME ALL THOSE TIMES!
WHAT ARE YOU DOING WANDERING AROUND OUT HERE BY YOURSELF?
I'M NOT BY MYSELF— I'M OUT HERE PLAYING A GAME WITH OUR FRIEND BOMBY!
UHH...PAT? I'M NOT QUITE SURE HOW TO TELL YOU THIS....

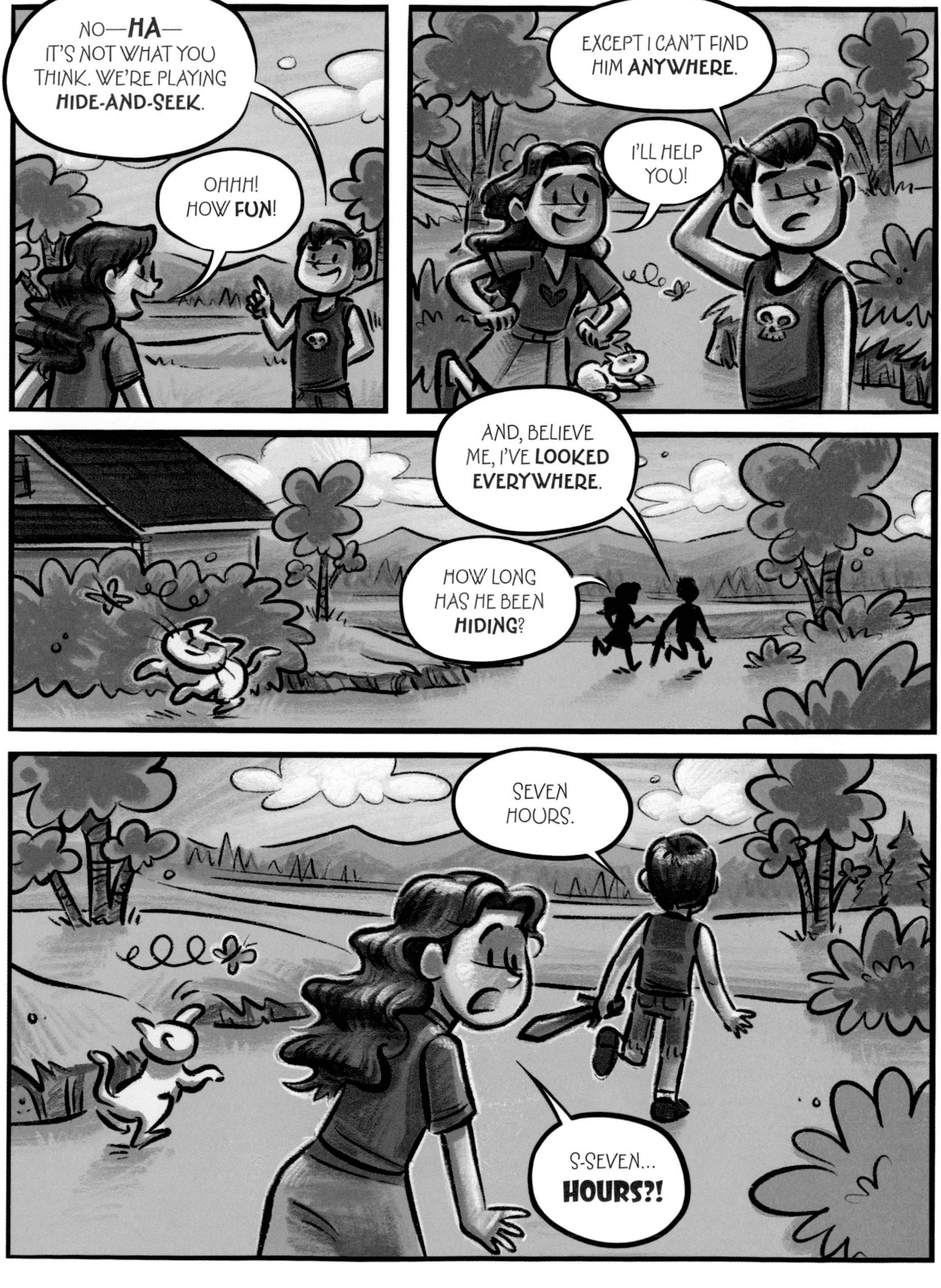
NO—**HA**—
IT'S NOT WHAT YOU THINK. WE'RE PLAYING **HIDE-AND-SEEK**.
OHHH! HOW **FUN**!
EXCEPT I CAN'T FIND HIM **ANYWHERE**.
I'LL HELP YOU!
AND, BELIEVE ME, I'VE **LOOKED EVERYWHERE**.
HOW LONG HAS HE BEEN **HIDING**?
SEVEN HOURS.
S-SEVEN... **HOURS?!**

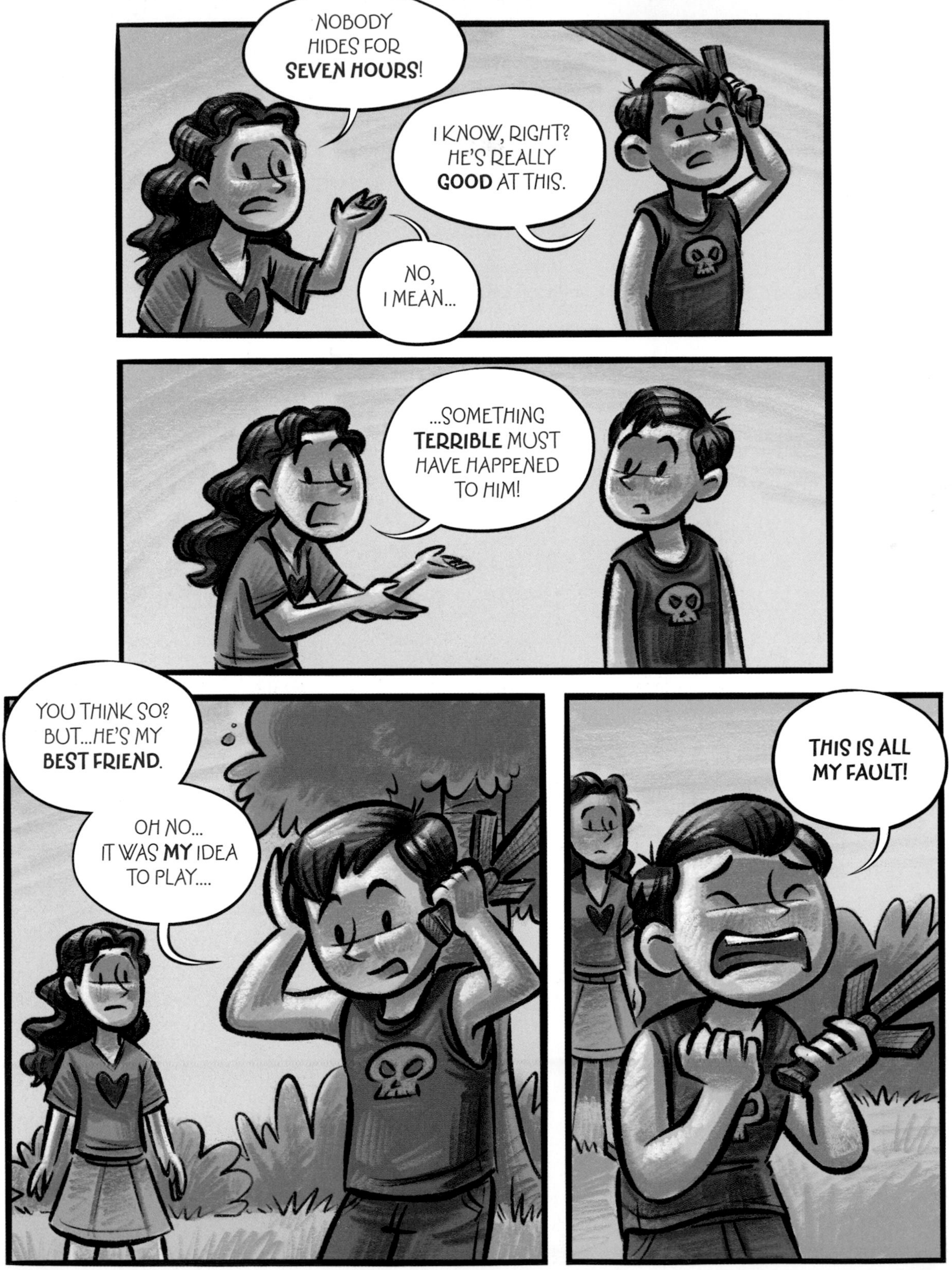
NOBODY HIDES FOR **SEVEN HOURS**!
I KNOW, RIGHT? HE'S REALLY **GOOD** AT THIS.
NO, I MEAN...
...SOMETHING **TERRIBLE** MUST HAVE HAPPENED TO HIM!
YOU THINK SO? BUT...HE'S MY **BEST FRIEND**.
OH NO... IT WAS **MY** IDEA TO PLAY....
THIS IS ALL MY FAULT!

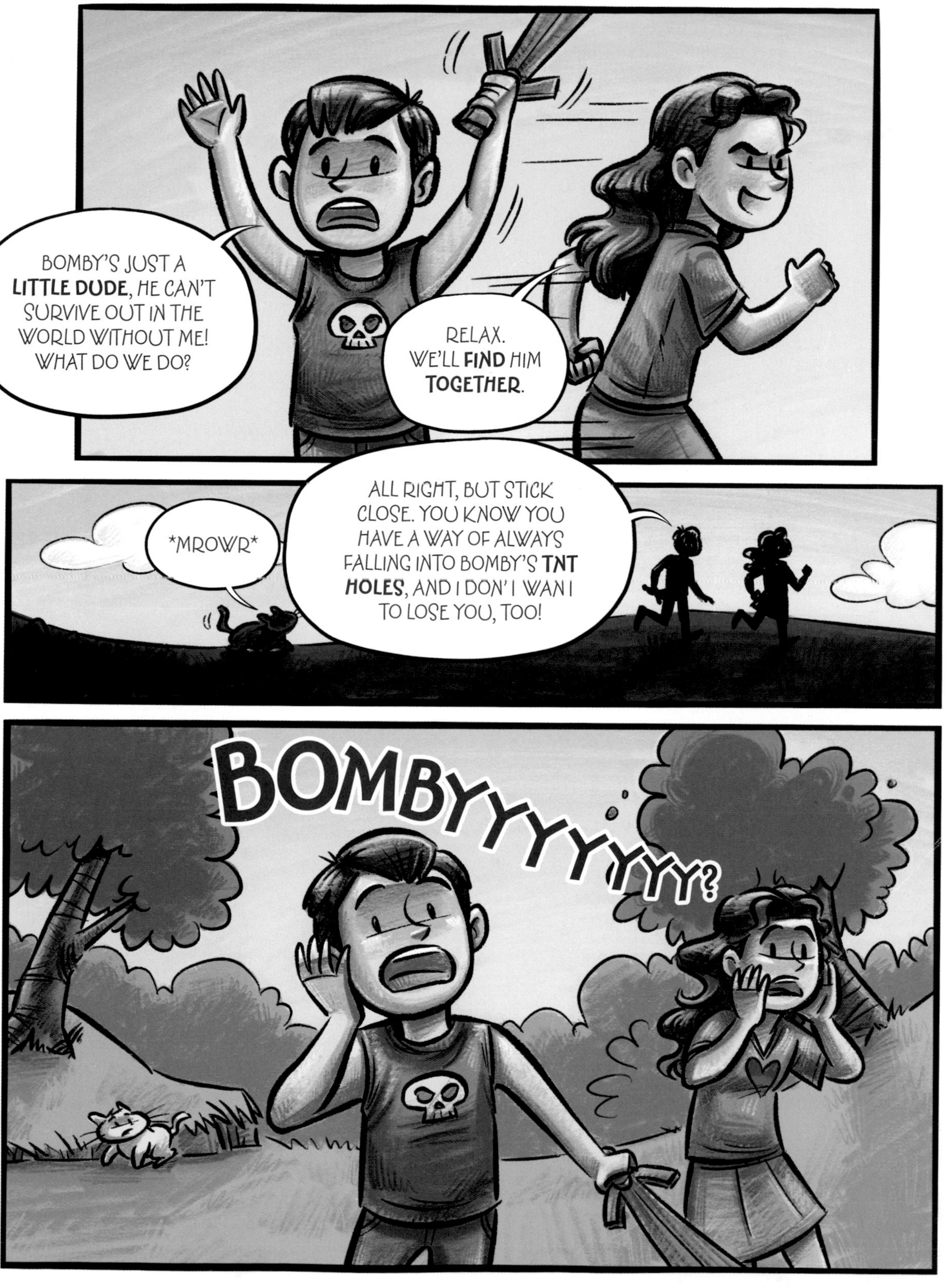
BOMBY'S JUST A LITTLE DUDE, HE CAN'T SURVIVE OUT IN THE WORLD WITHOUT ME! WHAT DO WE DO?
RELAX. WE'LL FIND HIM TOGETHER.
MROWR
ALL RIGHT, BUT STICK CLOSE. YOU KNOW YOU HAVE A WAY OF ALWAYS FALLING INTO BOMBY'S TNT HOLES, AND I DON'T WANT TO LOSE YOU, TOO!
BOMBYYYYYYY?

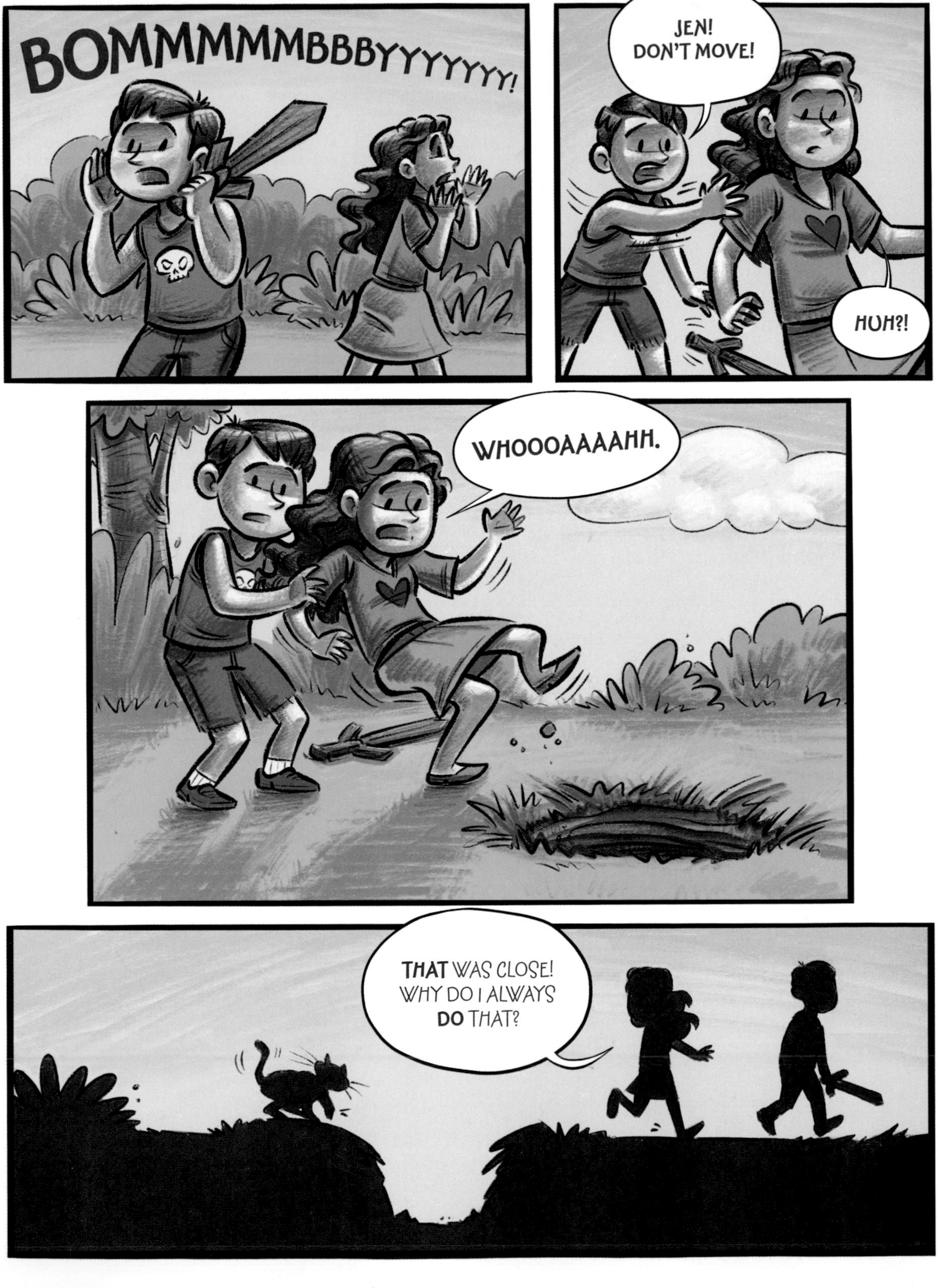
BOMMMMMBBBYYYYYYY!
JEN! DON'T MOVE!
HUH?!
WHOOOAAAAHH.
THAT WAS CLOSE! WHY DO I ALWAYS DO THAT?

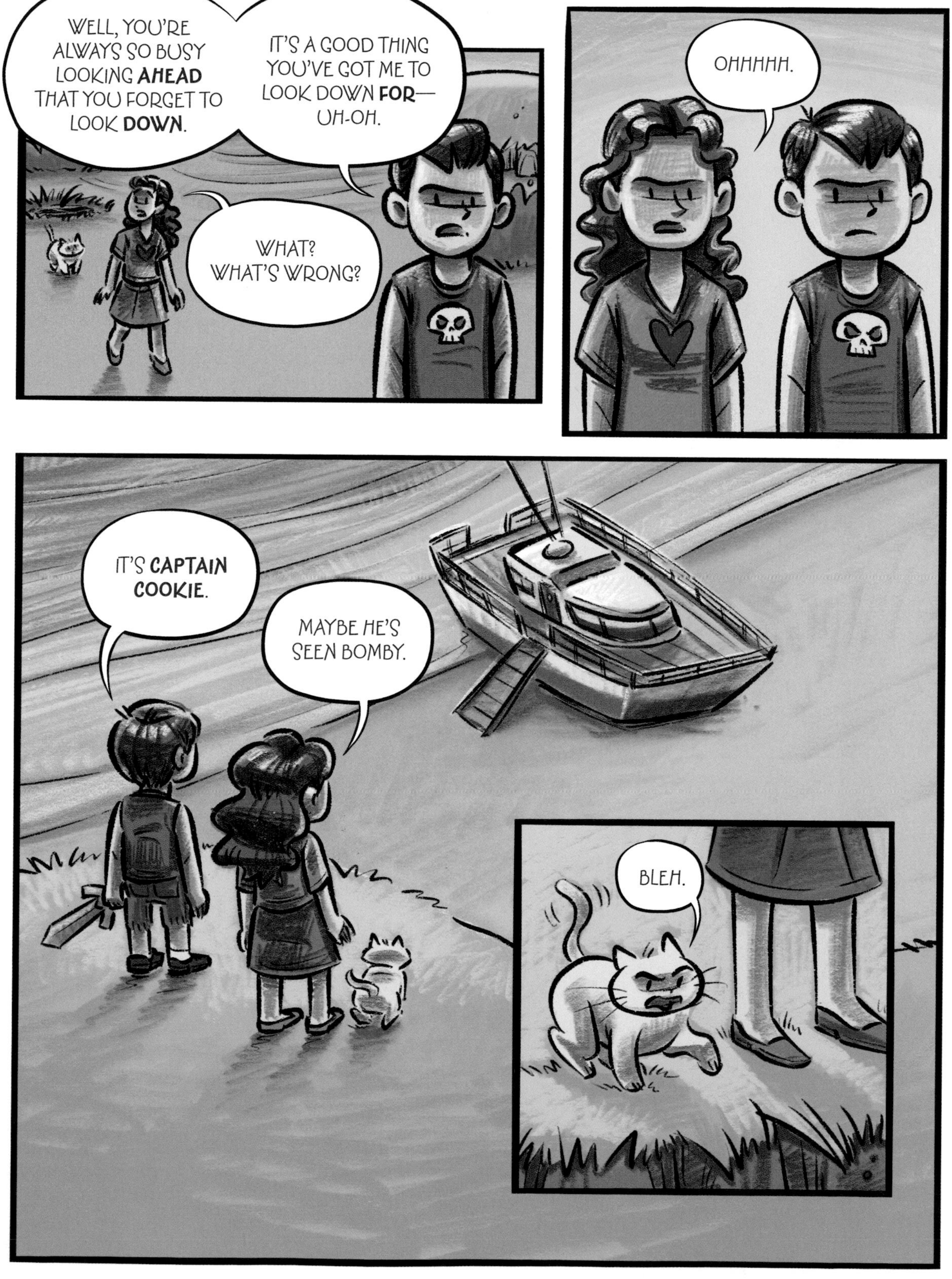
WELL, YOU'RE ALWAYS SO BUSY LOOKING **AHEAD** THAT YOU FORGET TO LOOK **DOWN**.
IT'S A GOOD THING YOU'VE GOT ME TO LOOK DOWN **FOR**— UH-OH.
WHAT? WHAT'S WRONG?
OHHHHH.
IT'S **CAPTAIN COOKIE**.
MAYBE HE'S SEEN BOMBY.
BLEH.

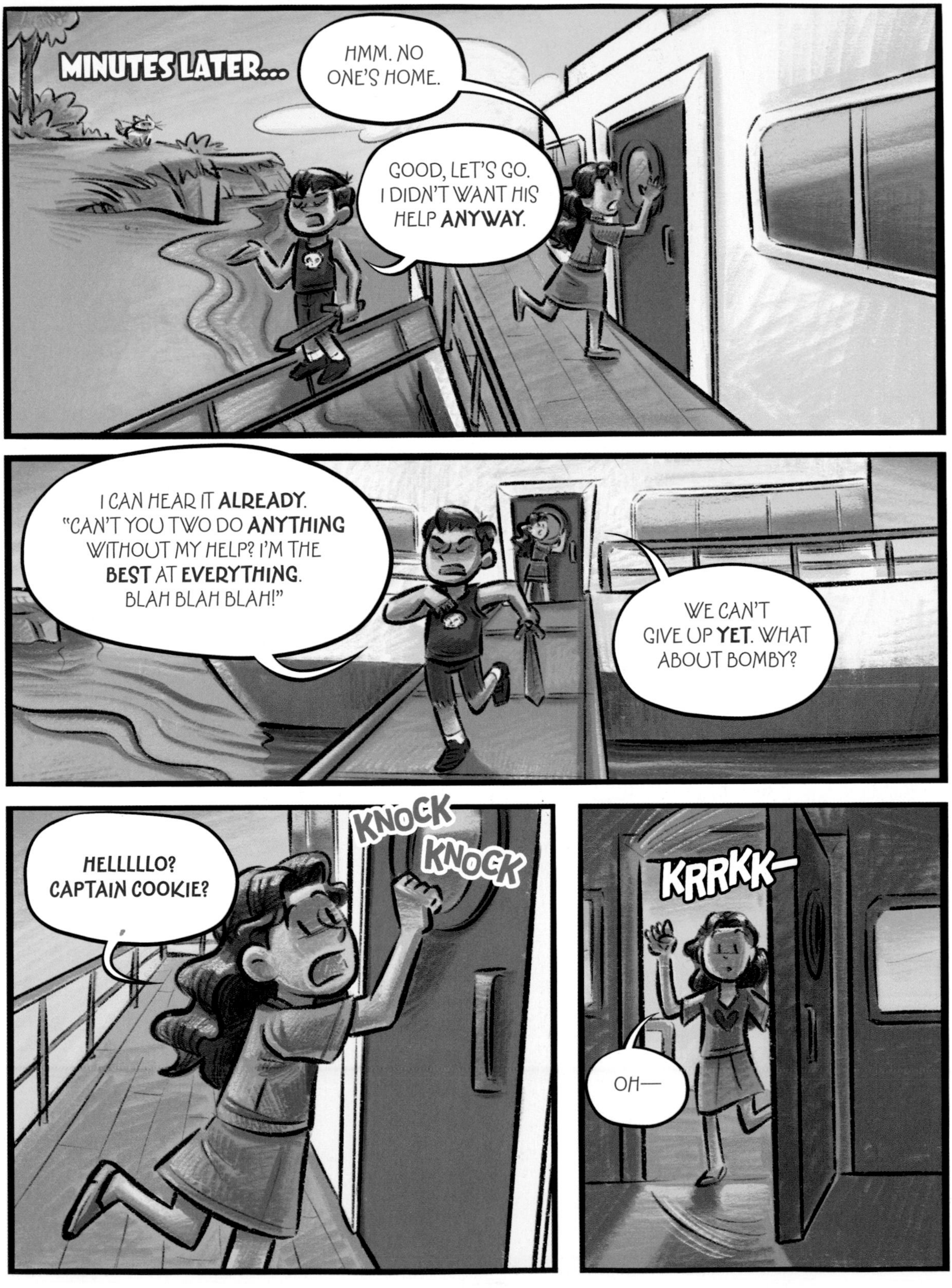
MINUTES LATER...
HMM. NO ONE'S HOME.
GOOD, LET'S GO. I DIDN'T WANT HIS HELP **ANYWAY**.
I CAN HEAR IT **ALREADY**. "CAN'T YOU TWO DO **ANYTHING** WITHOUT MY HELP? I'M THE **BEST** AT **EVERYTHING**. BLAH BLAH BLAH!"
WE CAN'T GIVE UP **YET**. WHAT ABOUT BOMBY?
KNOCK KNOCK
HELLLLLO? CAPTAIN COOKIE?
KRRKK-
OH—

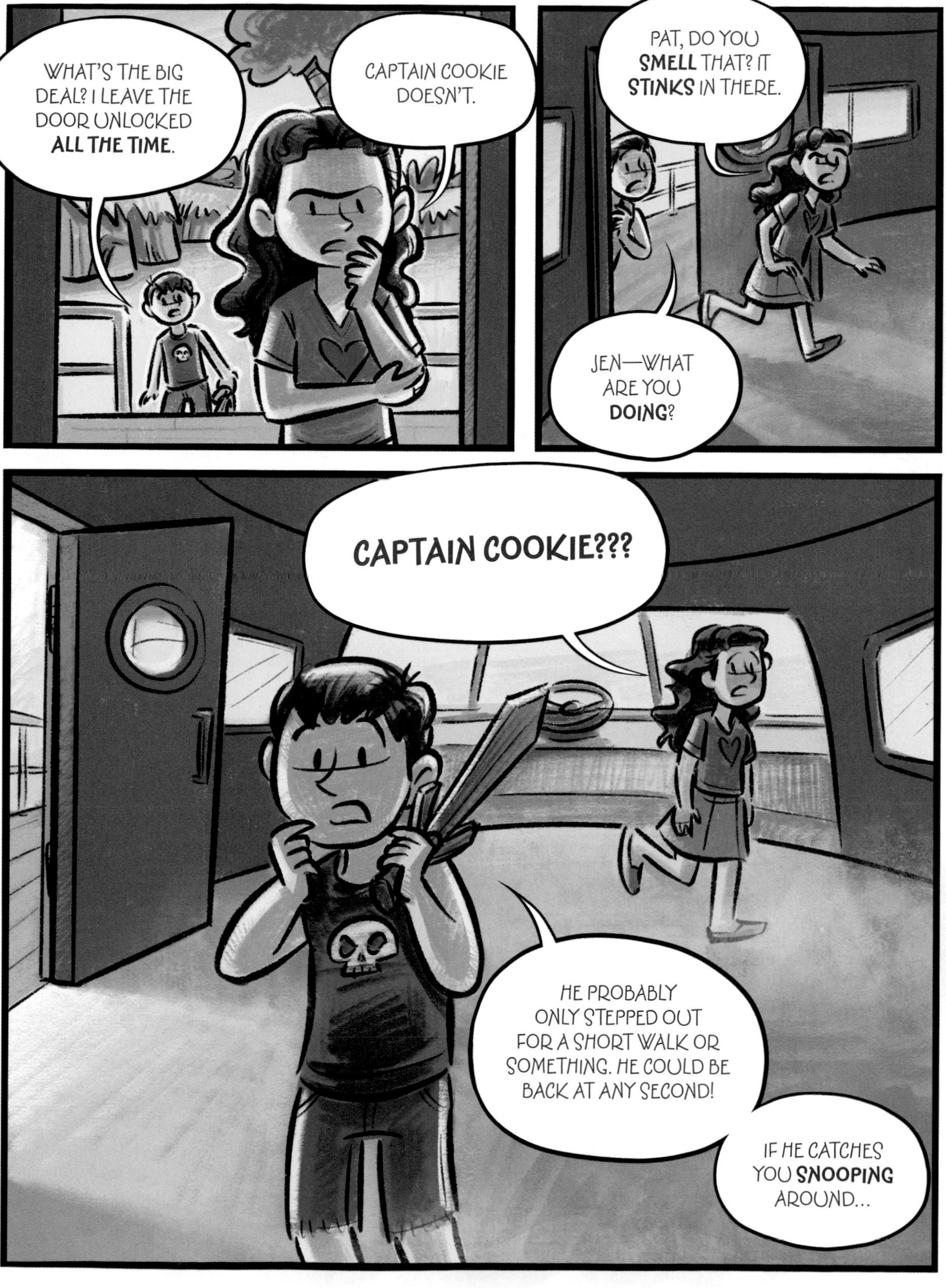
WHAT'S THE BIG DEAL? I LEAVE THE DOOR UNLOCKED **ALL THE TIME**.
CAPTAIN COOKIE DOESN'T.
PAT, DO YOU **SMELL** THAT? IT **STINKS** IN THERE.
JEN—WHAT ARE YOU **DOING**?
CAPTAIN COOKIE???
HE PROBABLY ONLY STEPPED OUT FOR A SHORT WALK OR SOMETHING. HE COULD BE BACK AT ANY SECOND!
IF HE CATCHES YOU **SNOOPING** AROUND...

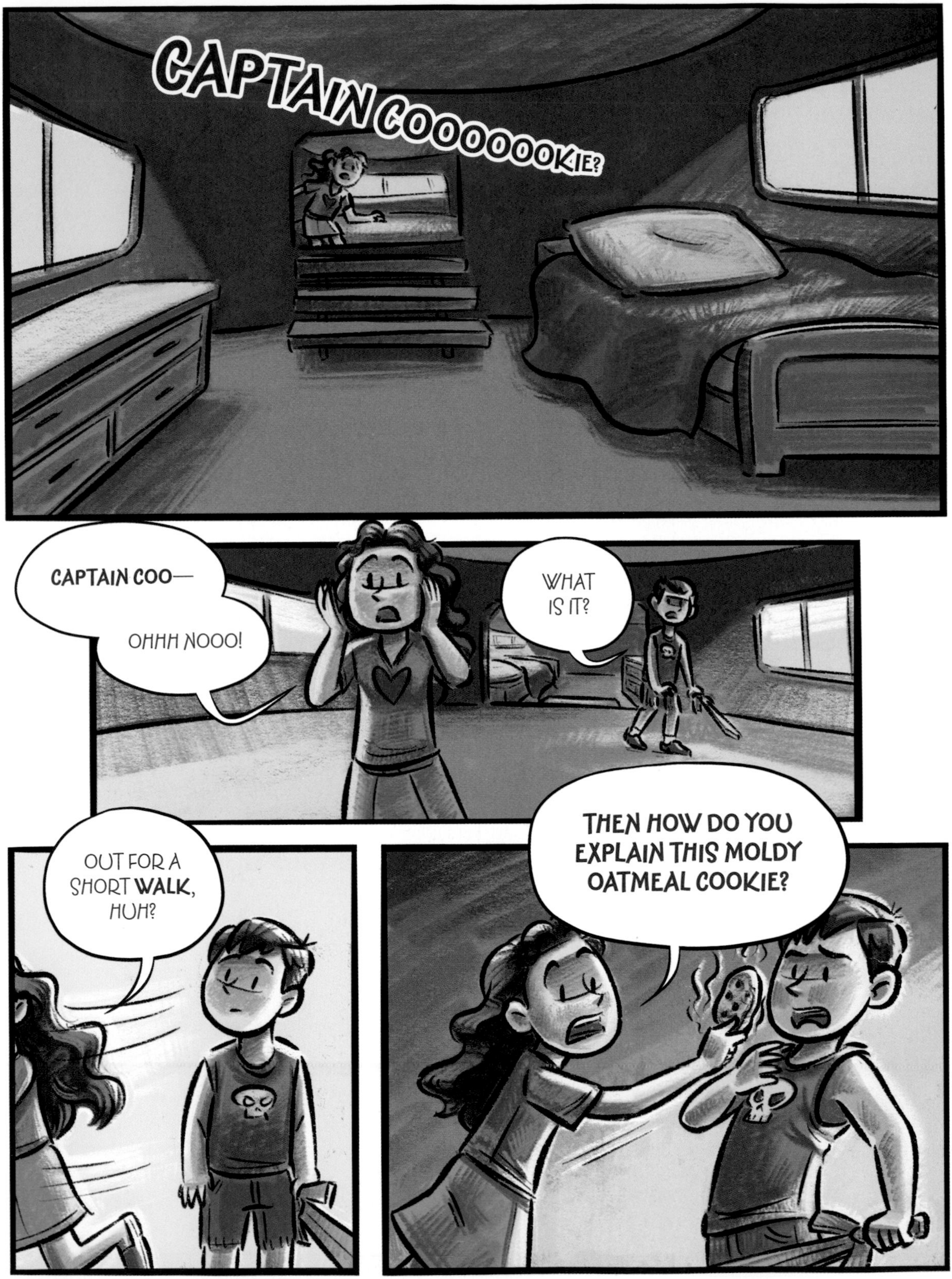
CAPTAIN COOOOOOOKIE?
CAPTAIN COO—
OHHH NOOO!
WHAT IS IT?
OUT FOR A SHORT WALK, HUH?
THEN HOW DO YOU EXPLAIN THIS MOLDY OATMEAL COOKIE?

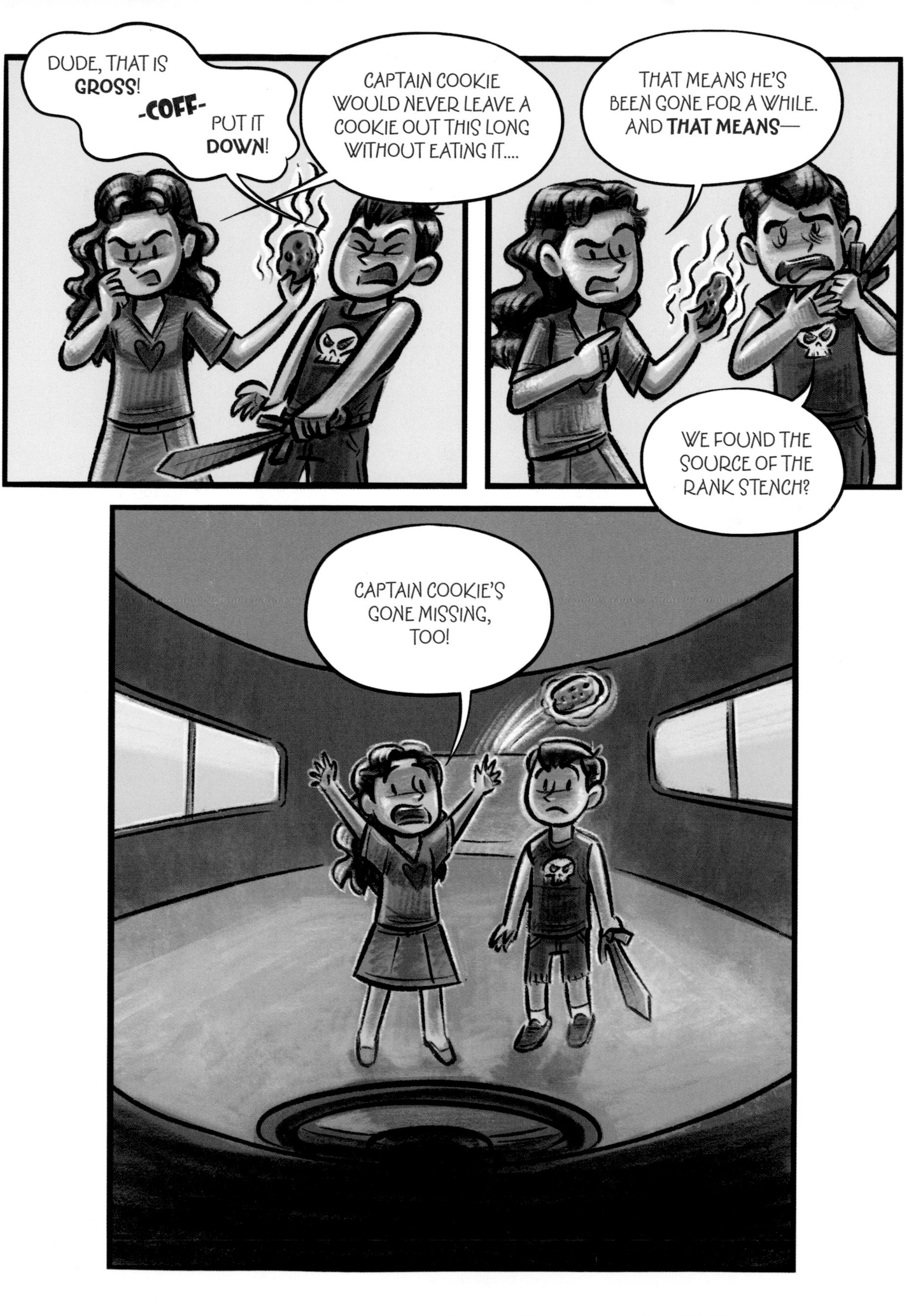

DUDE, THAT IS **GROSS**!
-COFF-
PUT IT **DOWN**!
CAPTAIN COOKIE WOULD NEVER LEAVE A COOKIE OUT THIS LONG WITHOUT EATING IT....
THAT MEANS HE'S BEEN GONE FOR A WHILE. AND **THAT MEANS**—
WE FOUND THE SOURCE OF THE RANK STENCH?
CAPTAIN COOKIE'S GONE MISSING, TOO!

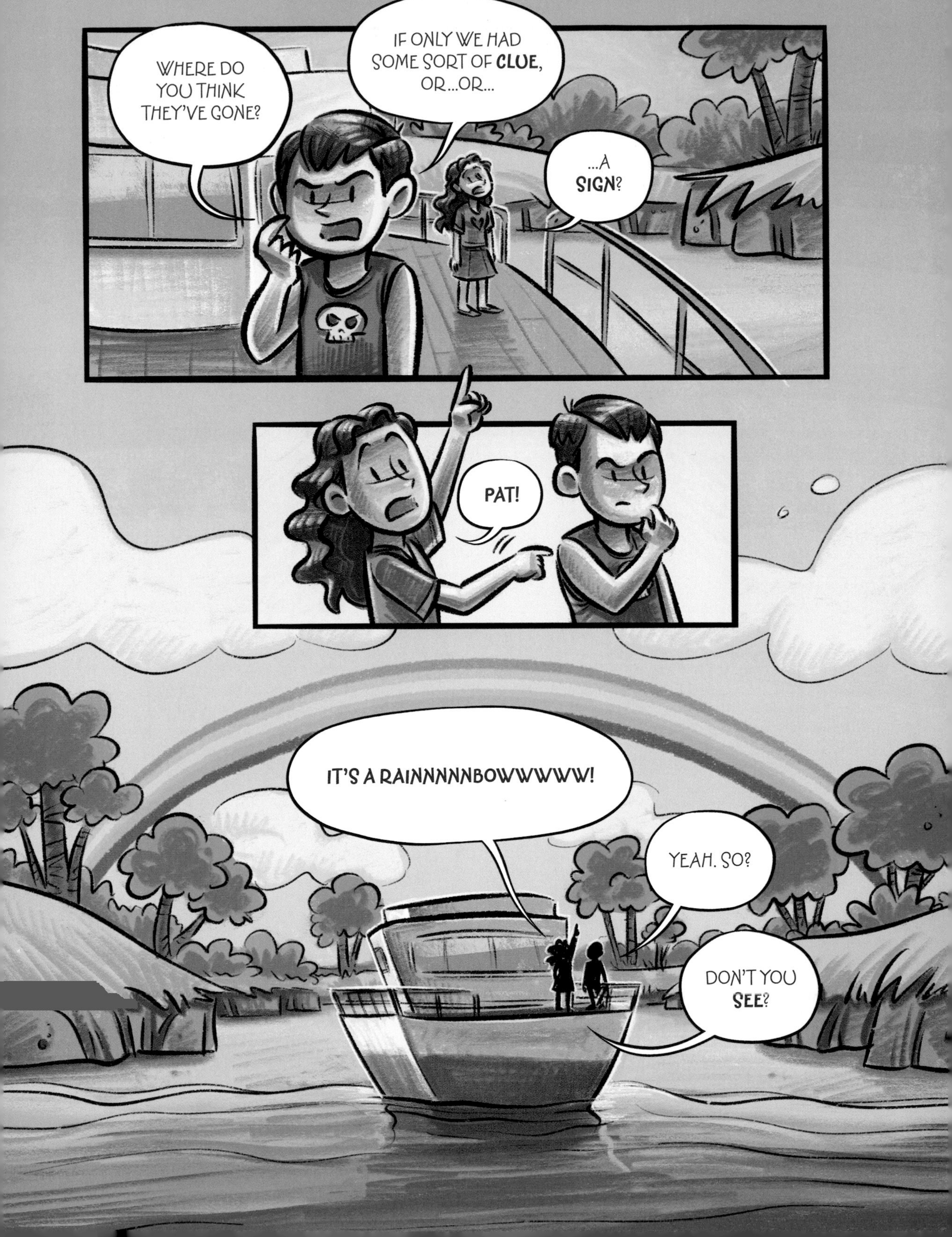
WHERE DO YOU THINK THEY'VE GONE?
IF ONLY WE HAD SOME SORT OF **CLUE**, OR...OR...
...A **SIGN**?
PAT!
IT'S A RAINNNNNBOWWWWW!
YEAH. SO?
DON'T YOU **SEE**?

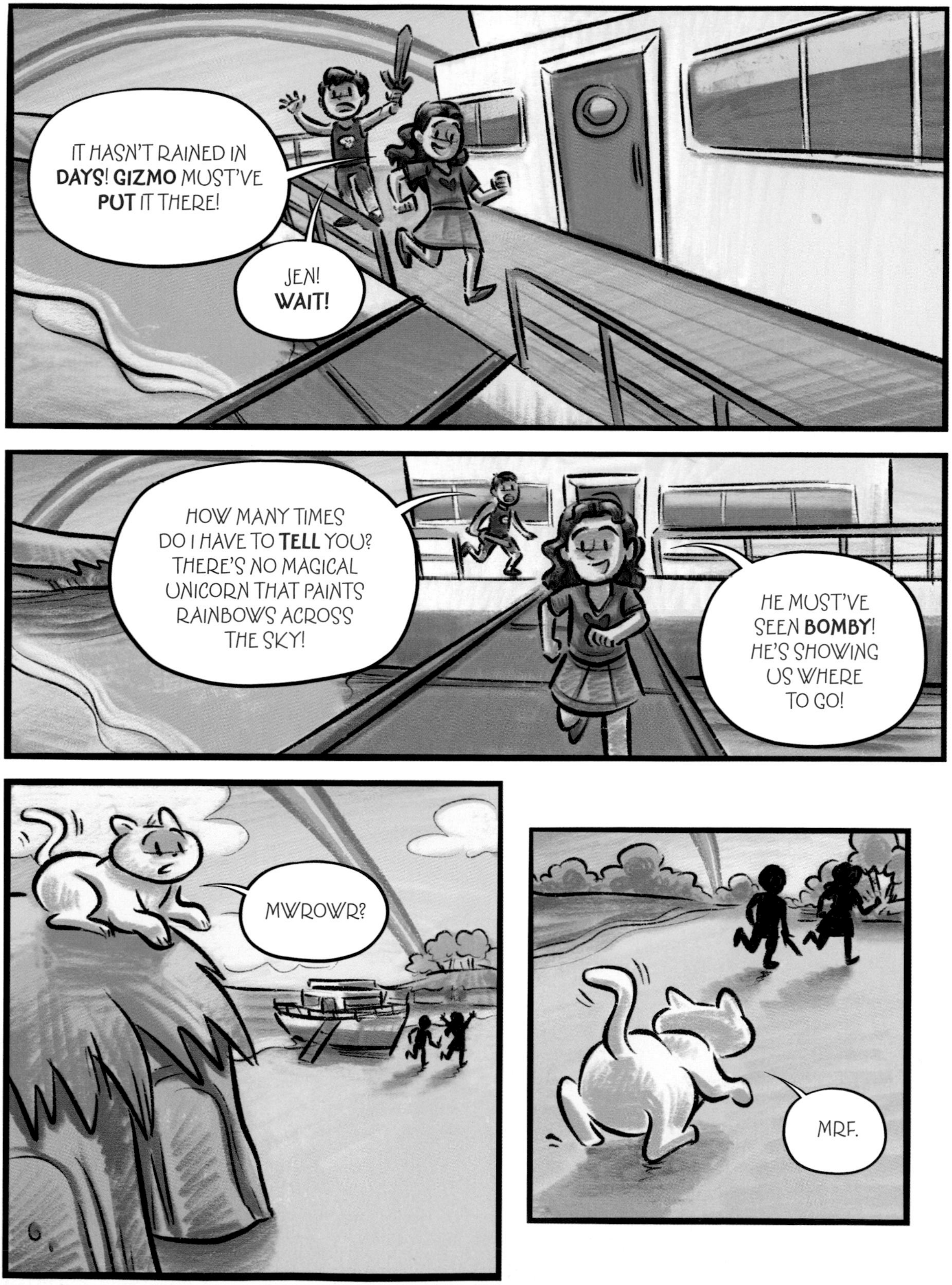
IT HASN'T RAINED IN DAYS! GIZMO MUST'VE PUT IT THERE!
JEN! WAIT!
HOW MANY TIMES DO I HAVE TO TELL YOU? THERE'S NO MAGICAL UNICORN THAT PAINTS RAINBOWS ACROSS THE SKY!
HE MUST'VE SEEN BOMBY! HE'S SHOWING US WHERE TO GO!
MWROWR?
MRF.

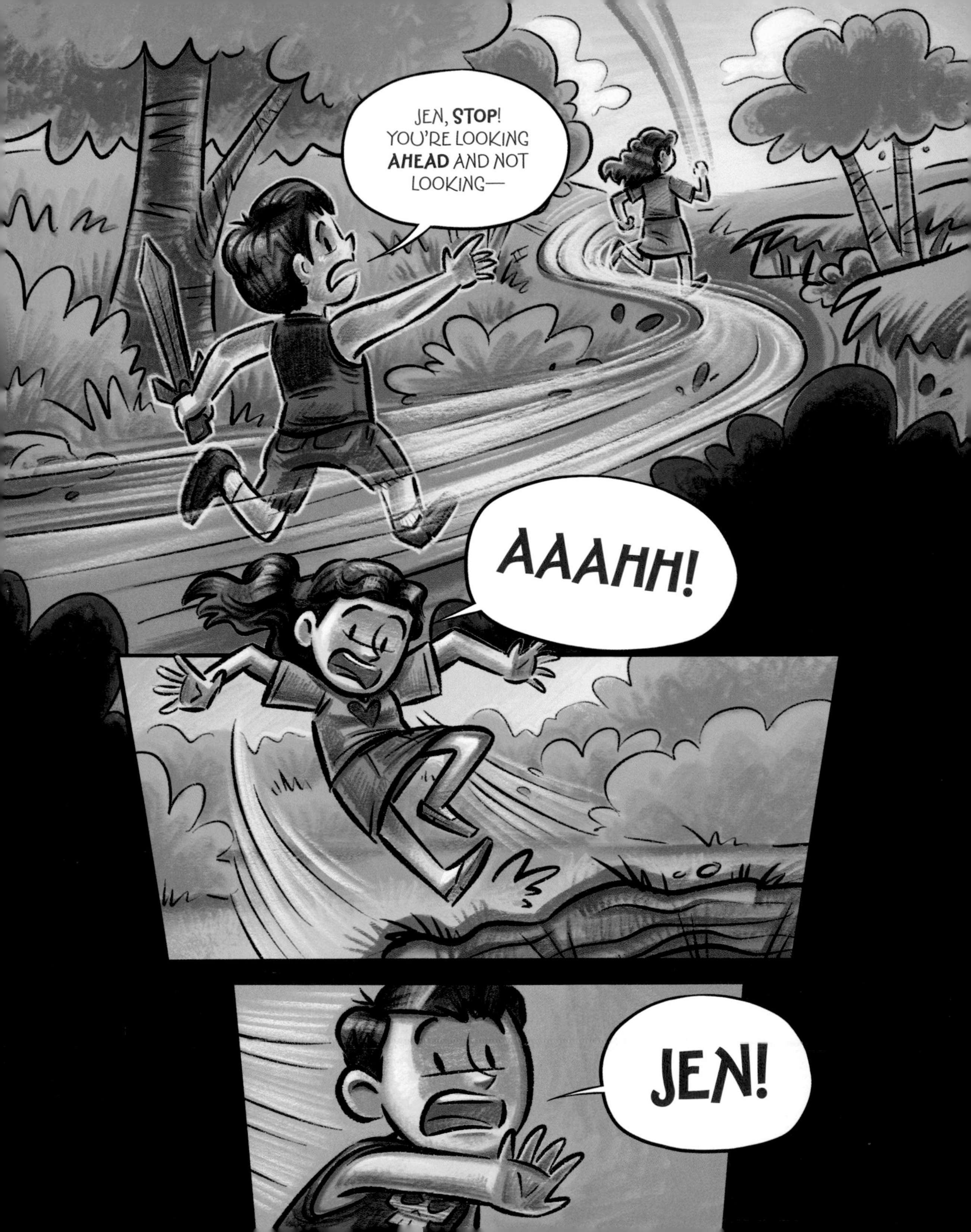
JEN, **STOP**! YOU'RE LOOKING **AHEAD** AND NOT LOOKING—
AAAHH!
JEN!

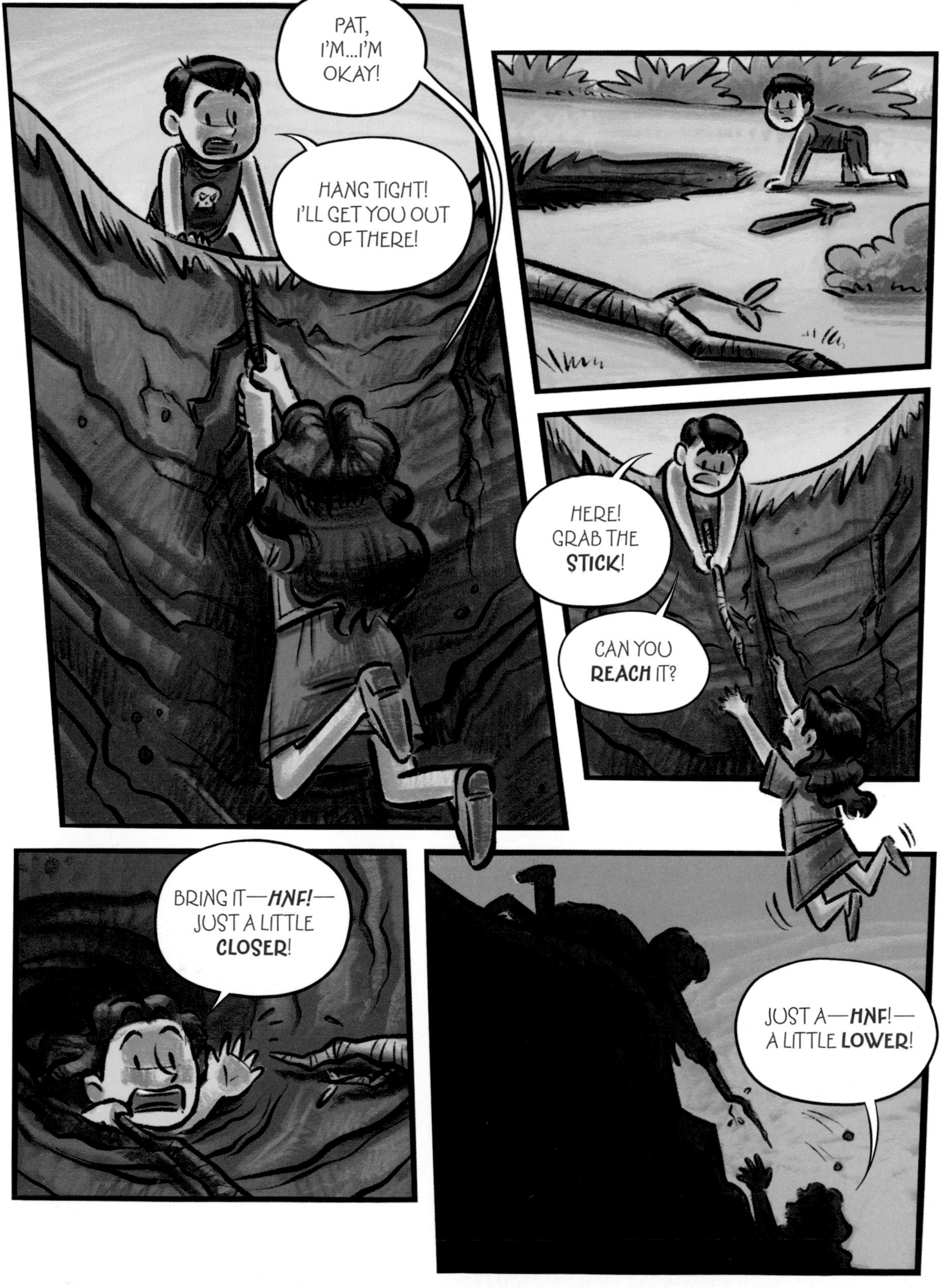
PAT, I'M...I'M OKAY!
HANG TIGHT! I'LL GET YOU OUT OF THERE!
HERE! GRAB THE **STICK**!
CAN YOU **REACH** IT?
BRING IT—***HNF!***—JUST A LITTLE **CLOSER**!
JUST A—**HNF**!—A LITTLE **LOWER**!

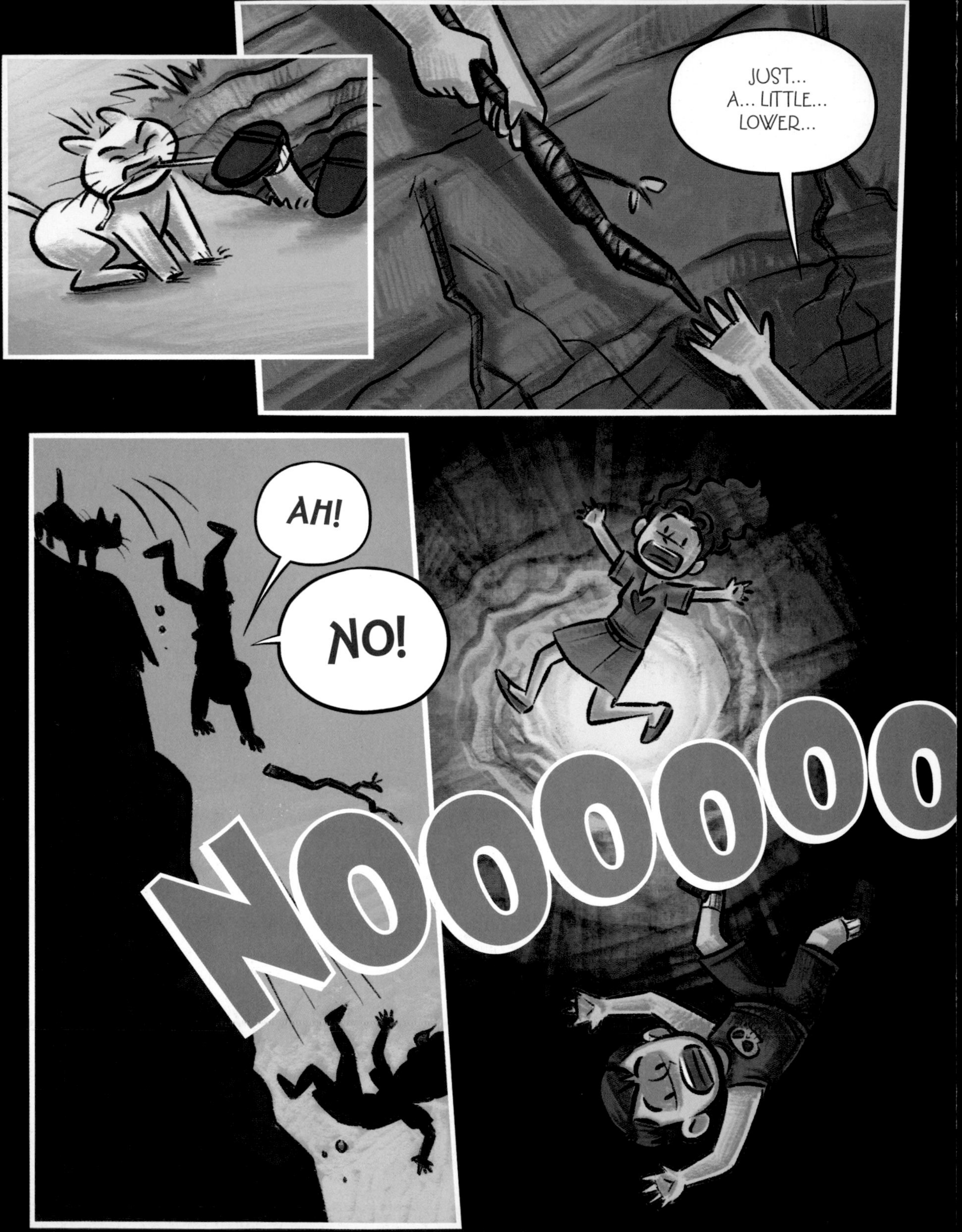
JUST... A... LITTLE... LOWER...
AH!
NO!
NOOOOOOO

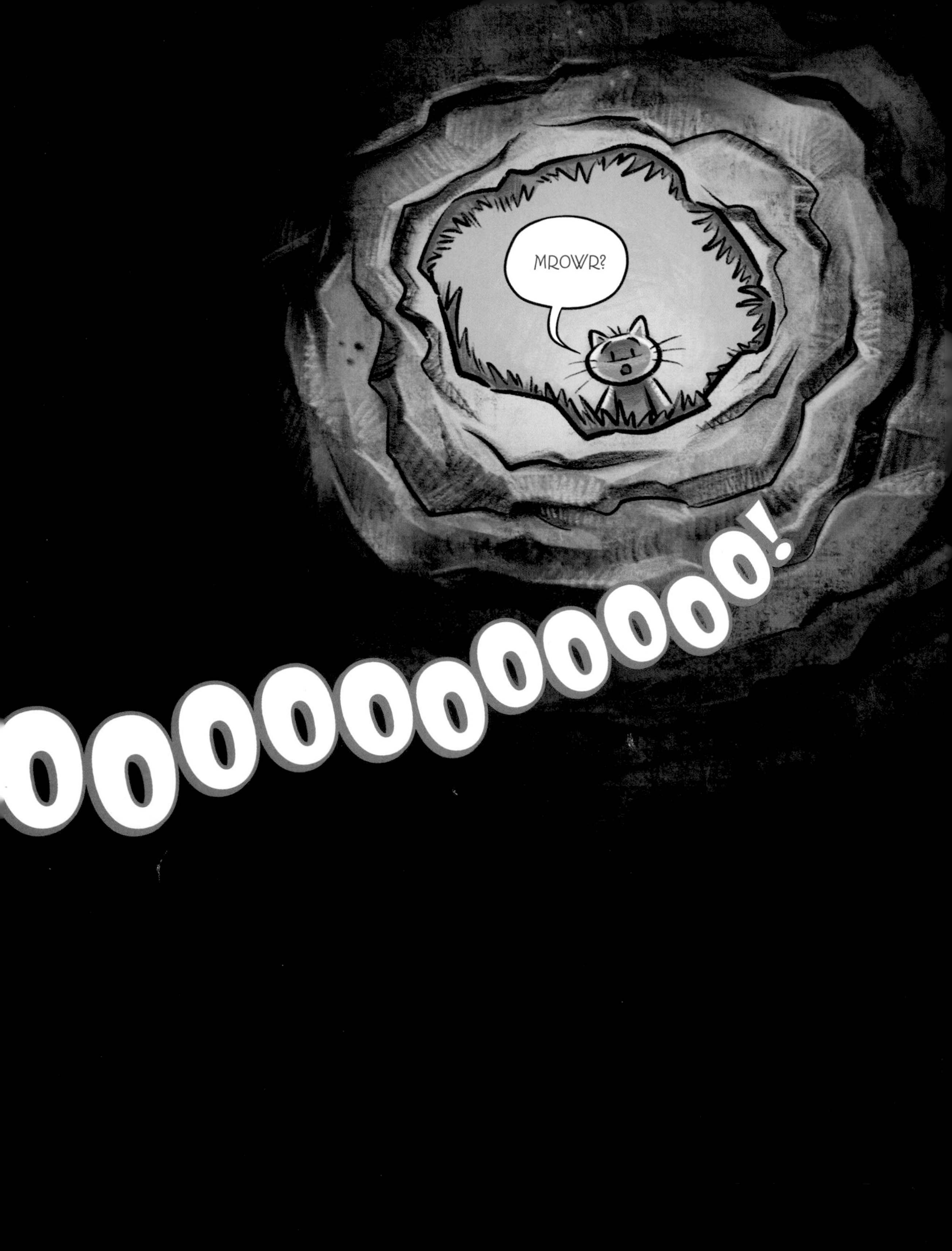
MROWR?
OOOOOOOOOOO!

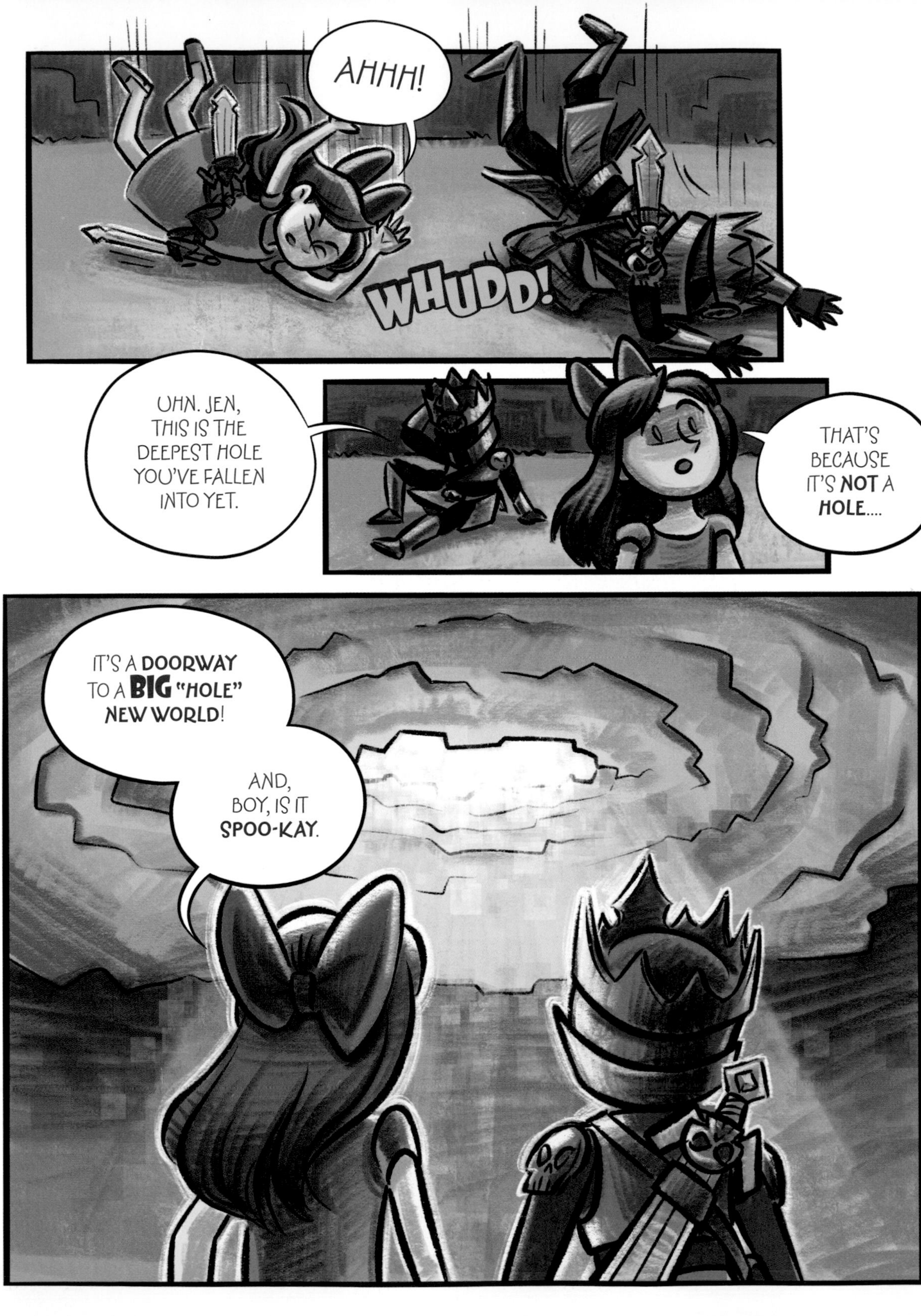
AHHH!
WHUDD!
UHN. JEN, THIS IS THE DEEPEST HOLE YOU'VE FALLEN INTO YET.
THAT'S BECAUSE IT'S **NOT** A **HOLE**....
IT'S A **DOORWAY** TO A **BIG "HOLE" NEW WORLD**!
AND, BOY, IS IT **SPOO-KAY**.

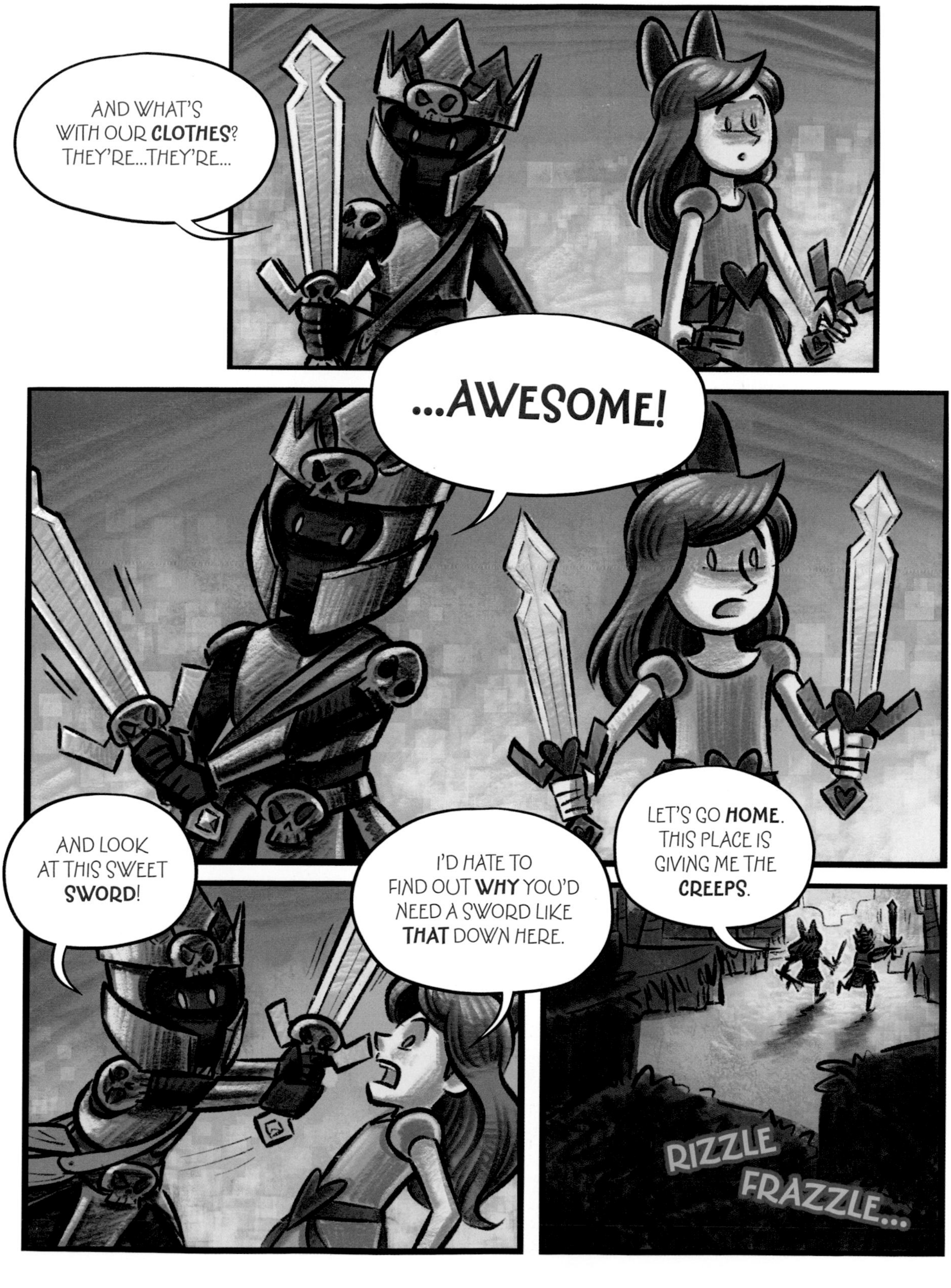
AND WHAT'S WITH OUR **CLOTHES**? THEY'RE...THEY'RE...
...AWESOME!
AND LOOK AT THIS SWEET **SWORD**!
I'D HATE TO FIND OUT **WHY** YOU'D NEED A SWORD LIKE **THAT** DOWN HERE.
LET'S GO **HOME**. THIS PLACE IS GIVING ME THE **CREEPS**.
RIZZLE
FRAZZLE...

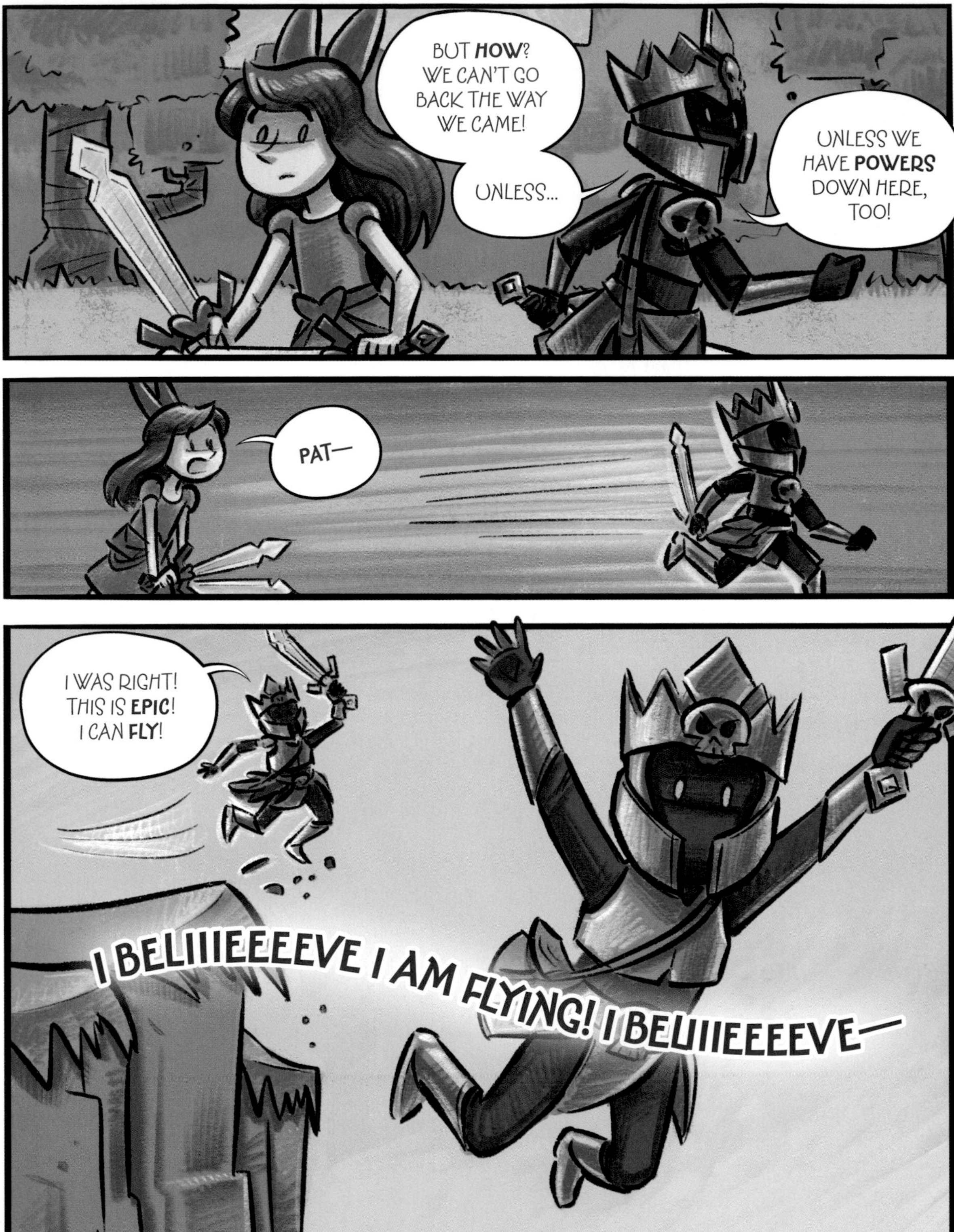
BUT **HOW**? WE CAN'T GO BACK THE WAY WE CAME!
UNLESS...
UNLESS WE HAVE **POWERS** DOWN HERE, TOO!
PAT—
I WAS RIGHT! THIS IS **EPIC**! I CAN **FLY**!
I BELIIIEEEEVE I AM FLYING! I BELIIIEEEEVE—

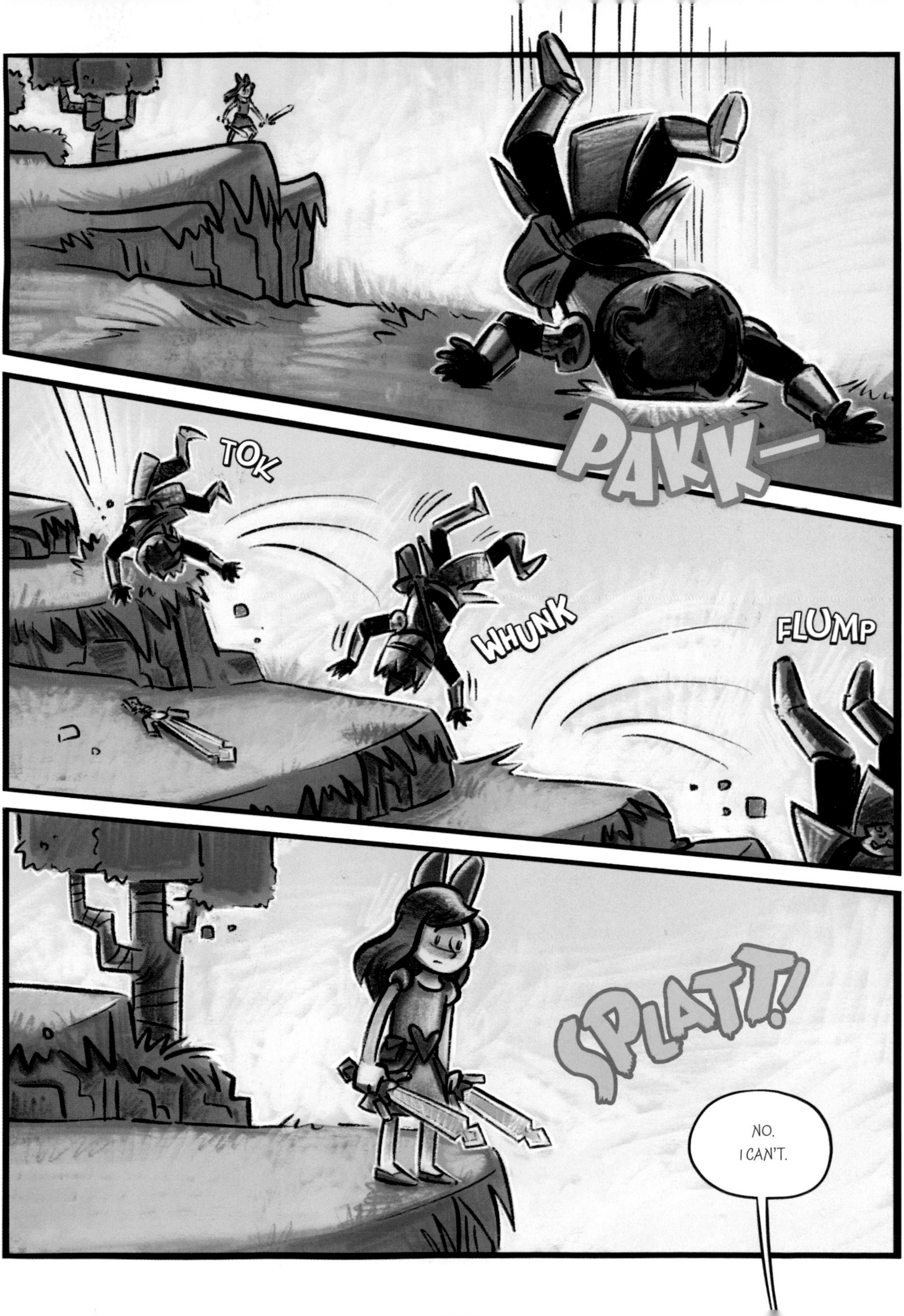
PAKK—
TOK
WHUNK
FLUMP
SPLATT!
NO. I CAN'T.

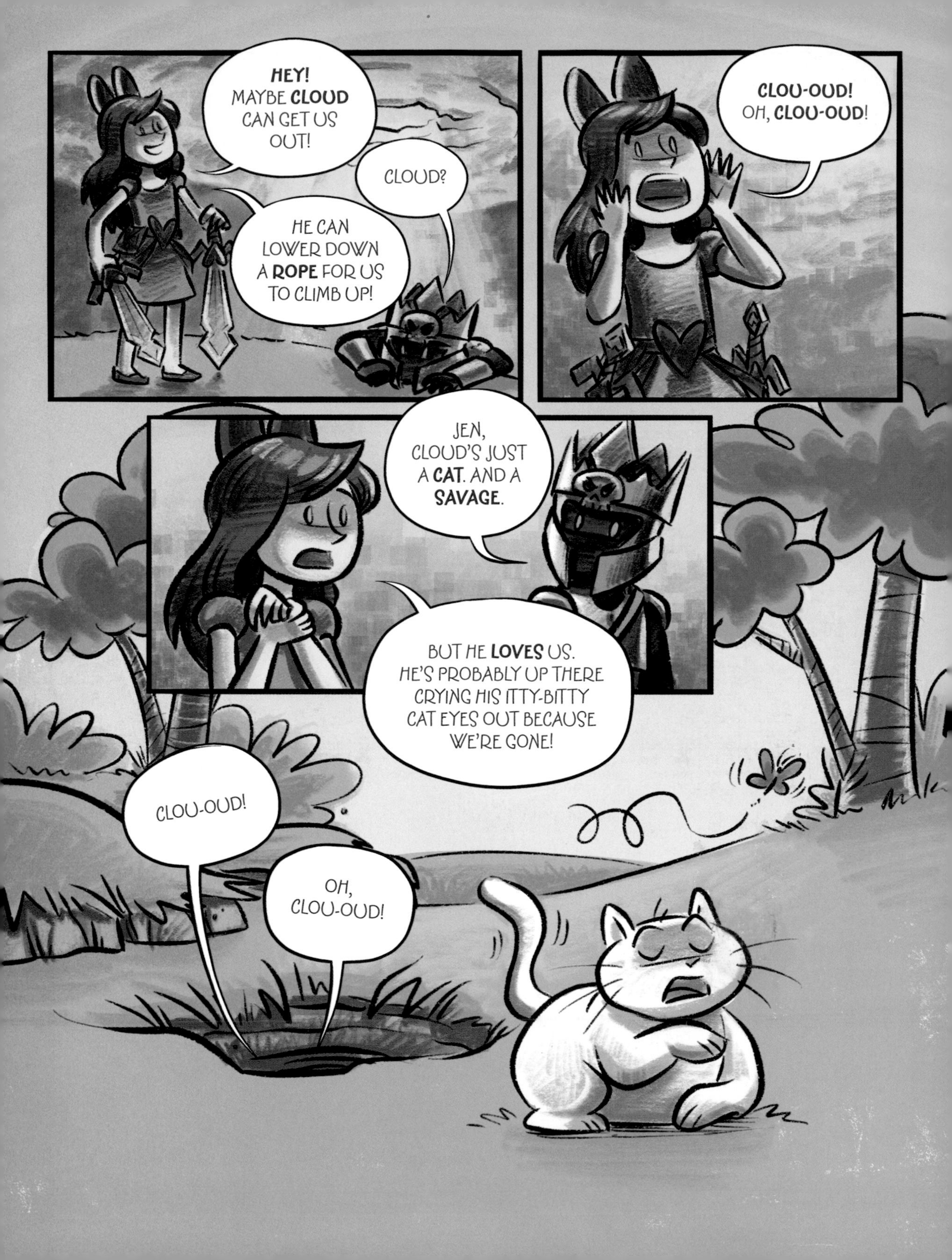
HEY! MAYBE CLOUD CAN GET US OUT!
CLOUD?
HE CAN LOWER DOWN A ROPE FOR US TO CLIMB UP!
CLOU-OUD! OH, CLOU-OUD!
JEN, CLOUD'S JUST A CAT. AND A SAVAGE.
BUT HE LOVES US. HE'S PROBABLY UP THERE CRYING HIS ITTY-BITTY CAT EYES OUT BECAUSE WE'RE GONE!
CLOU-OUD!
OH, CLOU-OUD!

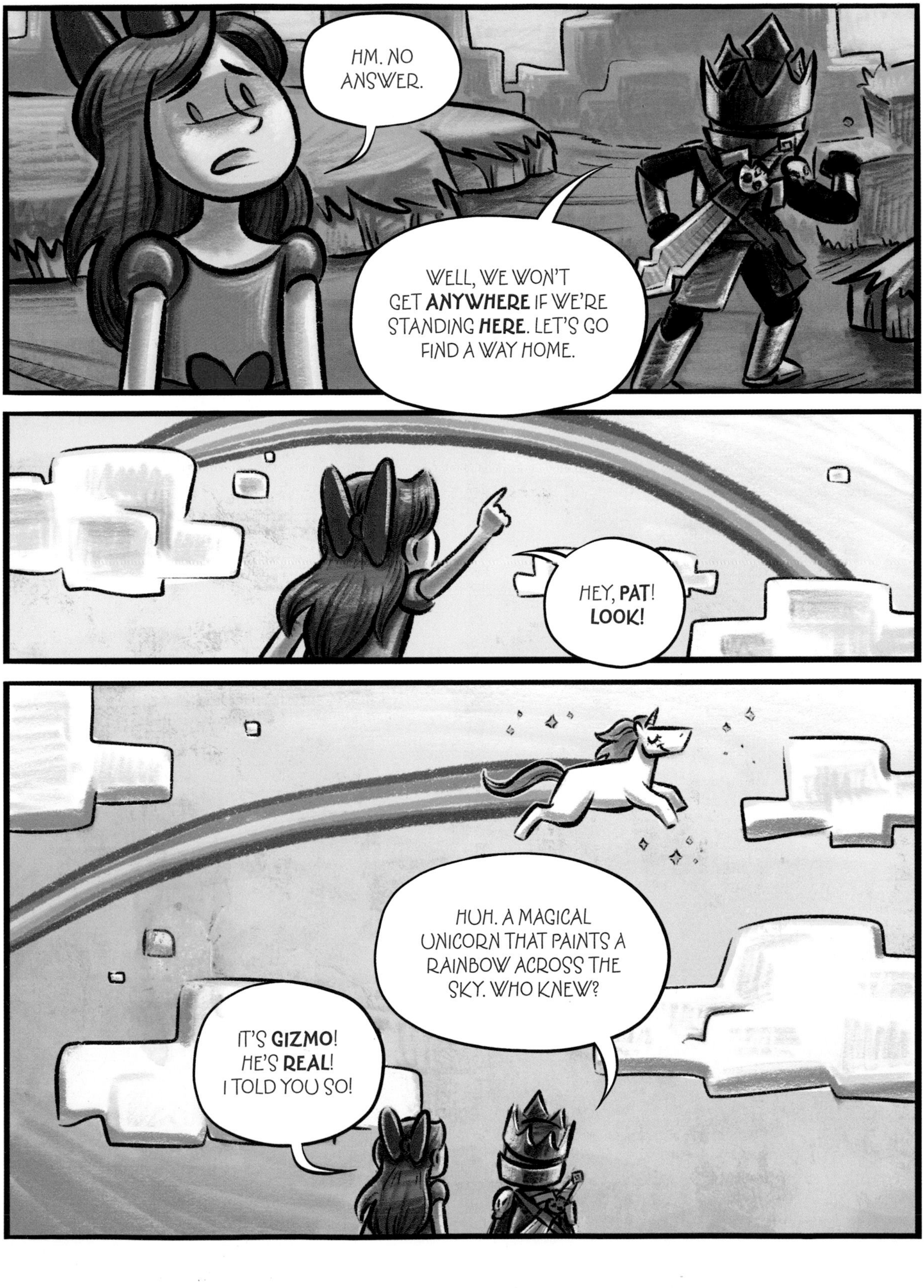
HM. NO ANSWER.
WELL, WE WON'T GET **ANYWHERE** IF WE'RE STANDING **HERE**. LET'S GO FIND A WAY HOME.
HEY, **PAT**! **LOOK!**
HUH. A MAGICAL UNICORN THAT PAINTS A RAINBOW ACROSS THE SKY. WHO KNEW?
IT'S **GIZMO**! HE'S **REAL**! I TOLD YOU SO!

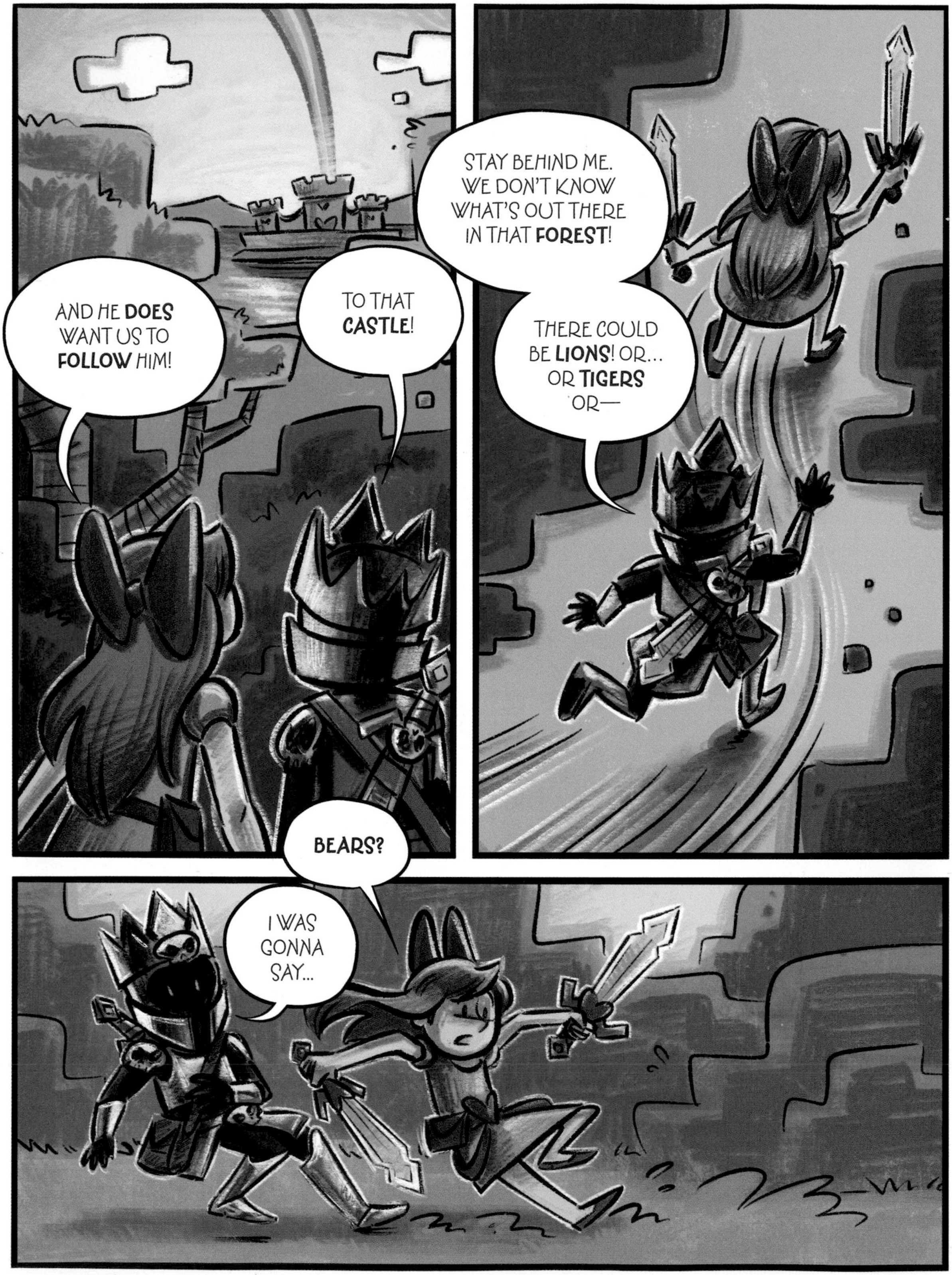

AND HE DOES WANT US TO FOLLOW HIM!
TO THAT CASTLE!
STAY BEHIND ME. WE DON'T KNOW WHAT'S OUT THERE IN THAT FOREST!
THERE COULD BE LIONS! OR... OR TIGERS OR—
BEARS?
I WAS GONNA SAY...

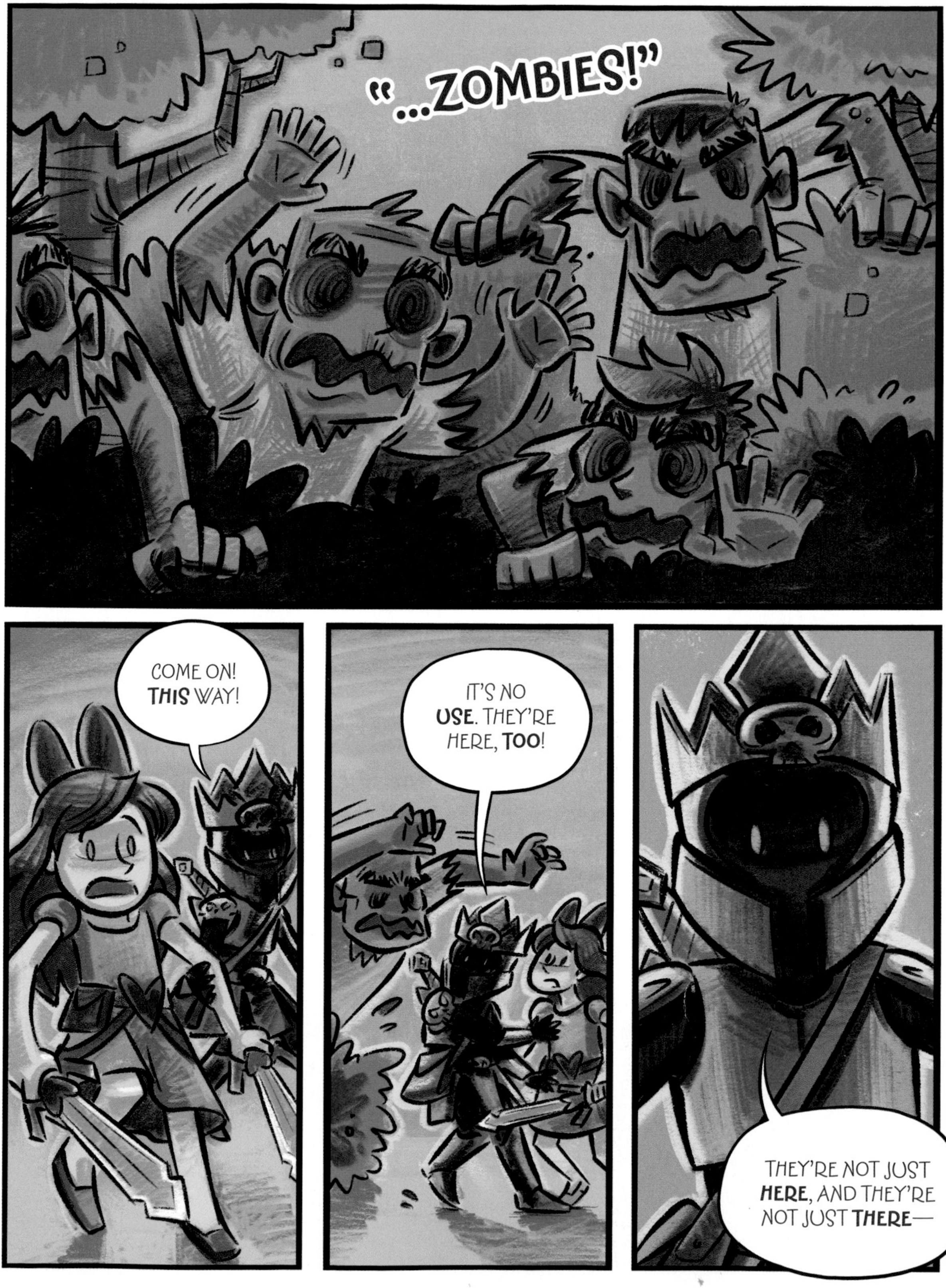
"...ZOMBIES!"
COME ON! THIS WAY!
IT'S NO USE. THEY'RE HERE, TOO!
THEY'RE NOT JUST HERE, AND THEY'RE NOT JUST THERE—

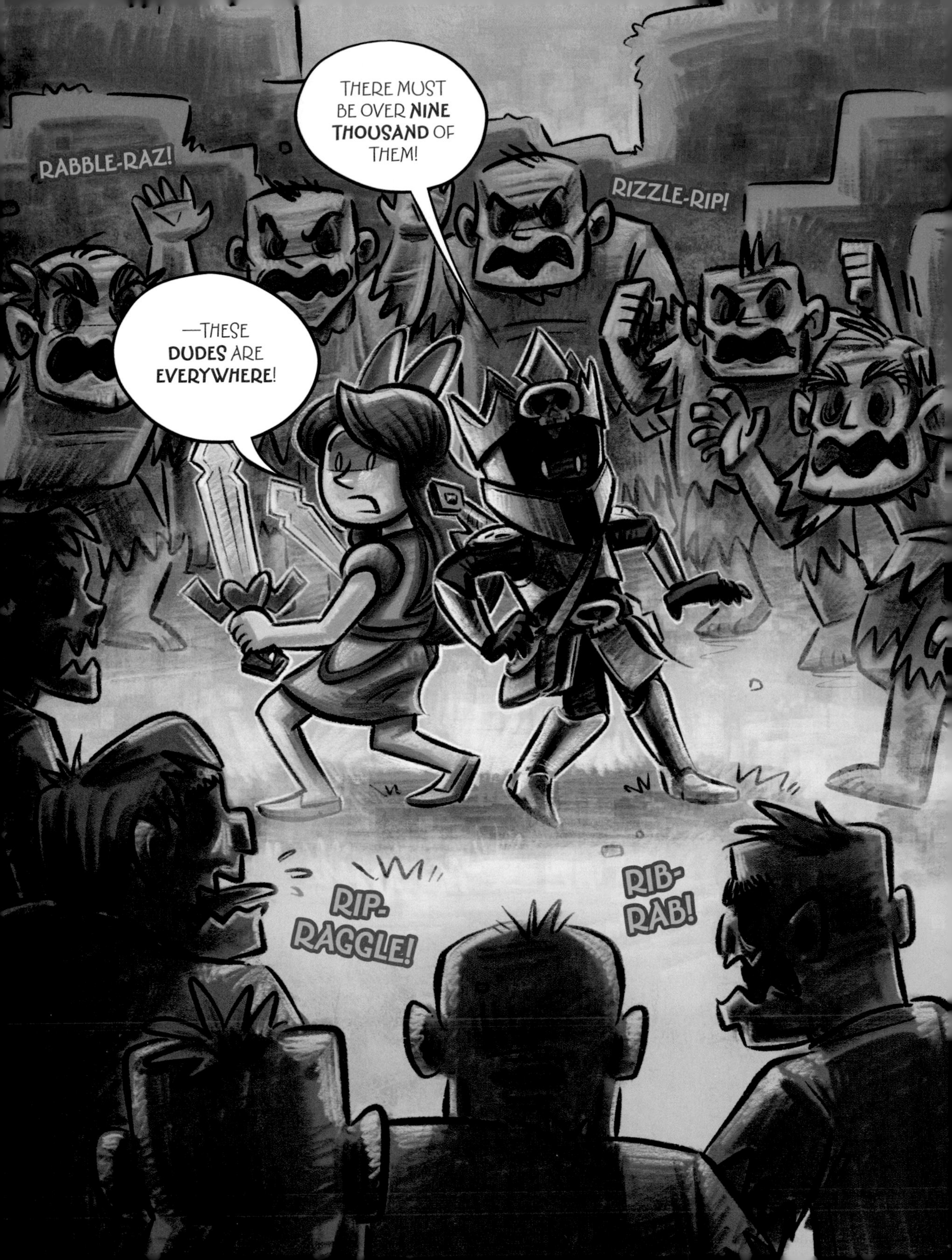
THERE MUST BE OVER NINE THOUSAND OF THEM!
RABBLE-RAZ!
RIZZLE-RIP!
—THESE DUDES ARE EVERYWHERE!
RIP-RAGGLE!
RIB-RAB!

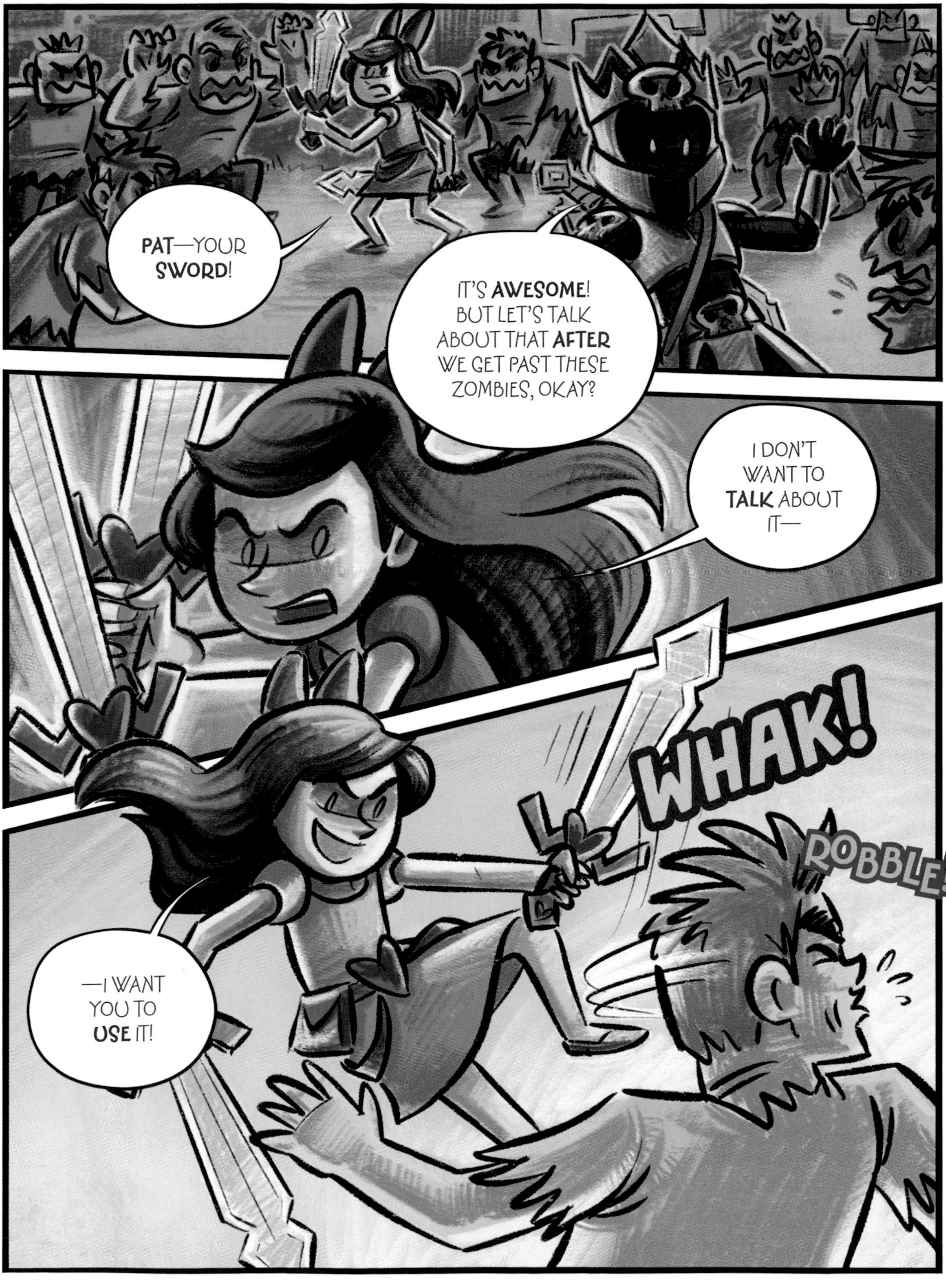
PAT—YOUR SWORD!
IT'S AWESOME! BUT LET'S TALK ABOUT THAT AFTER WE GET PAST THESE ZOMBIES, OKAY?
I DON'T WANT TO TALK ABOUT IT—
WHAK!
ROBBLE!
—I WANT YOU TO USE IT!

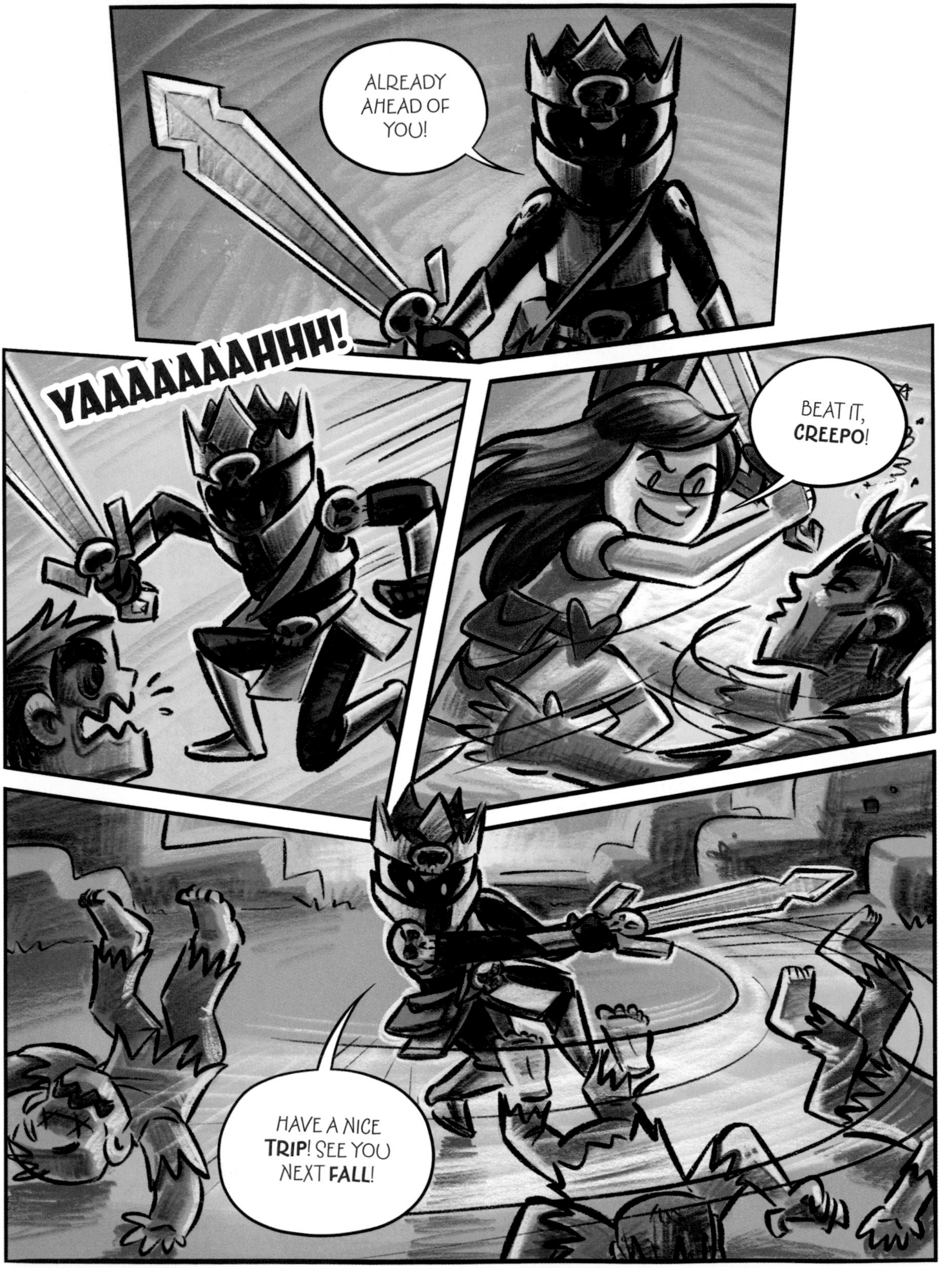
ALREADY AHEAD OF YOU!
YAAAAAAAHHH!
BEAT IT, **CREEPO**!
HAVE A NICE **TRIP**! SEE YOU NEXT **FALL**!

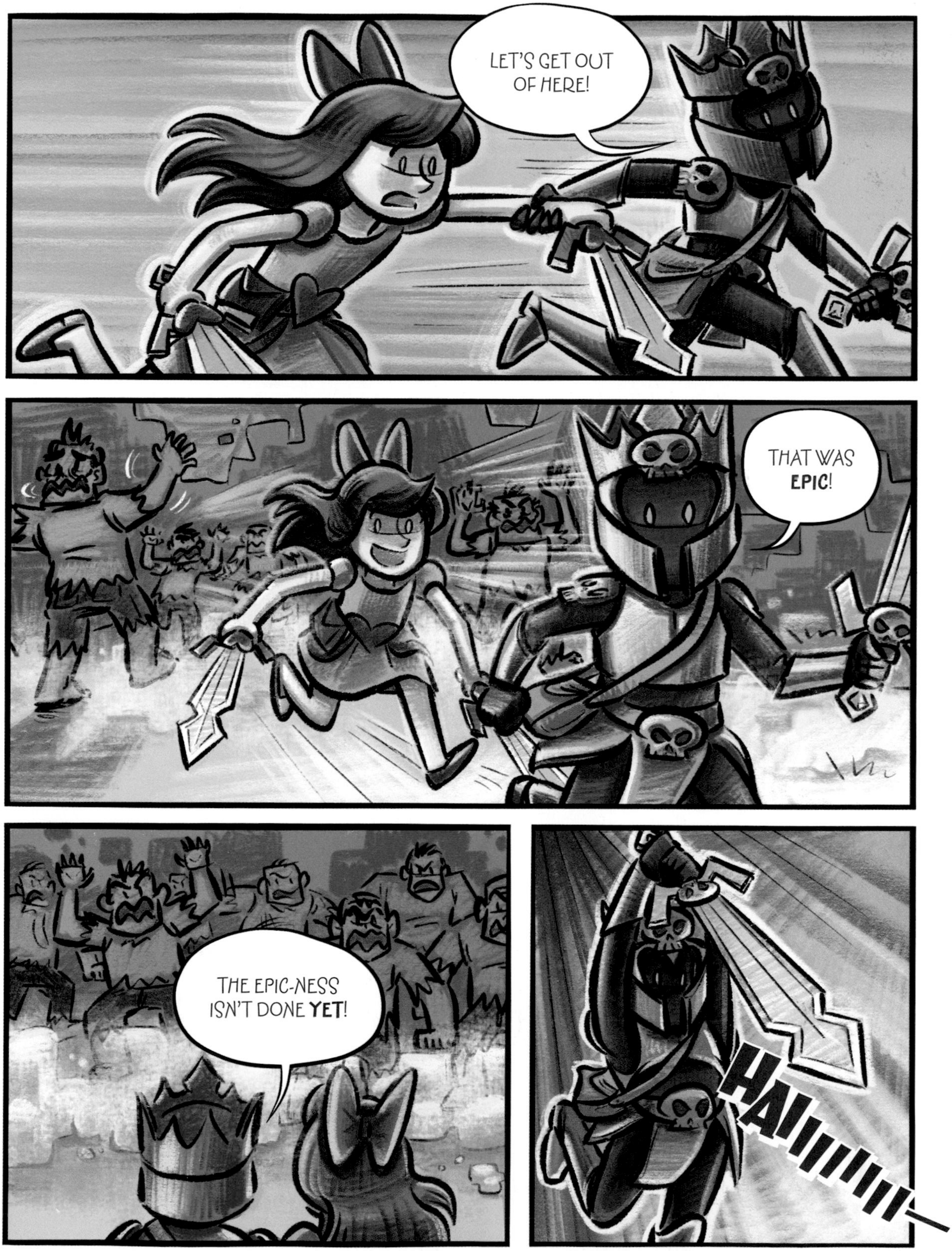
LET'S GET OUT OF HERE!
THAT WAS EPIC!
THE EPIC-NESS ISN'T DONE YET!
HAI!!!!!!!!—

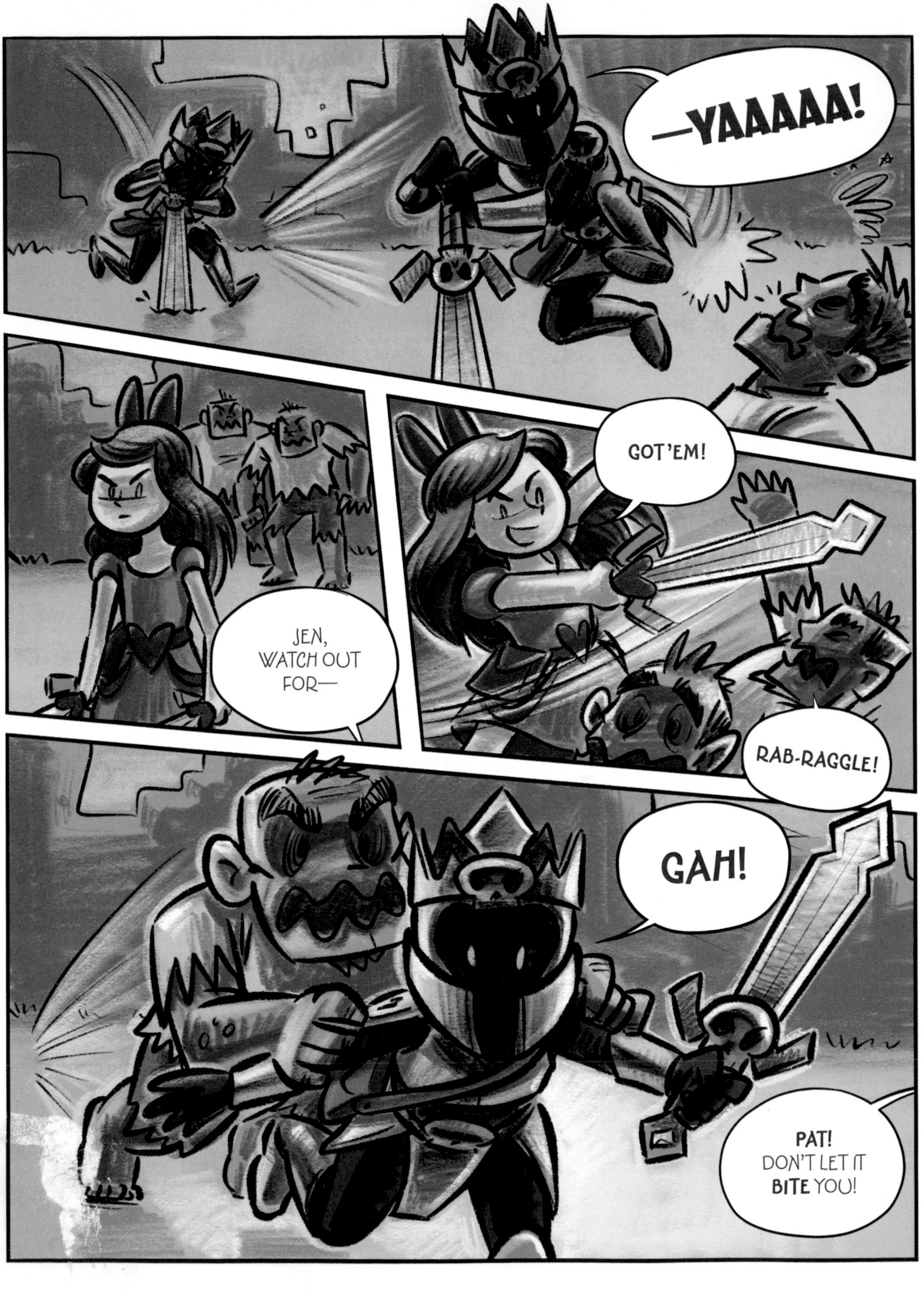
—YAAAAA!
JEN, WATCH OUT FOR—
GOT'EM!
RAB-RAGGLE!
GAH!
PAT! DON'T LET IT BITE YOU!

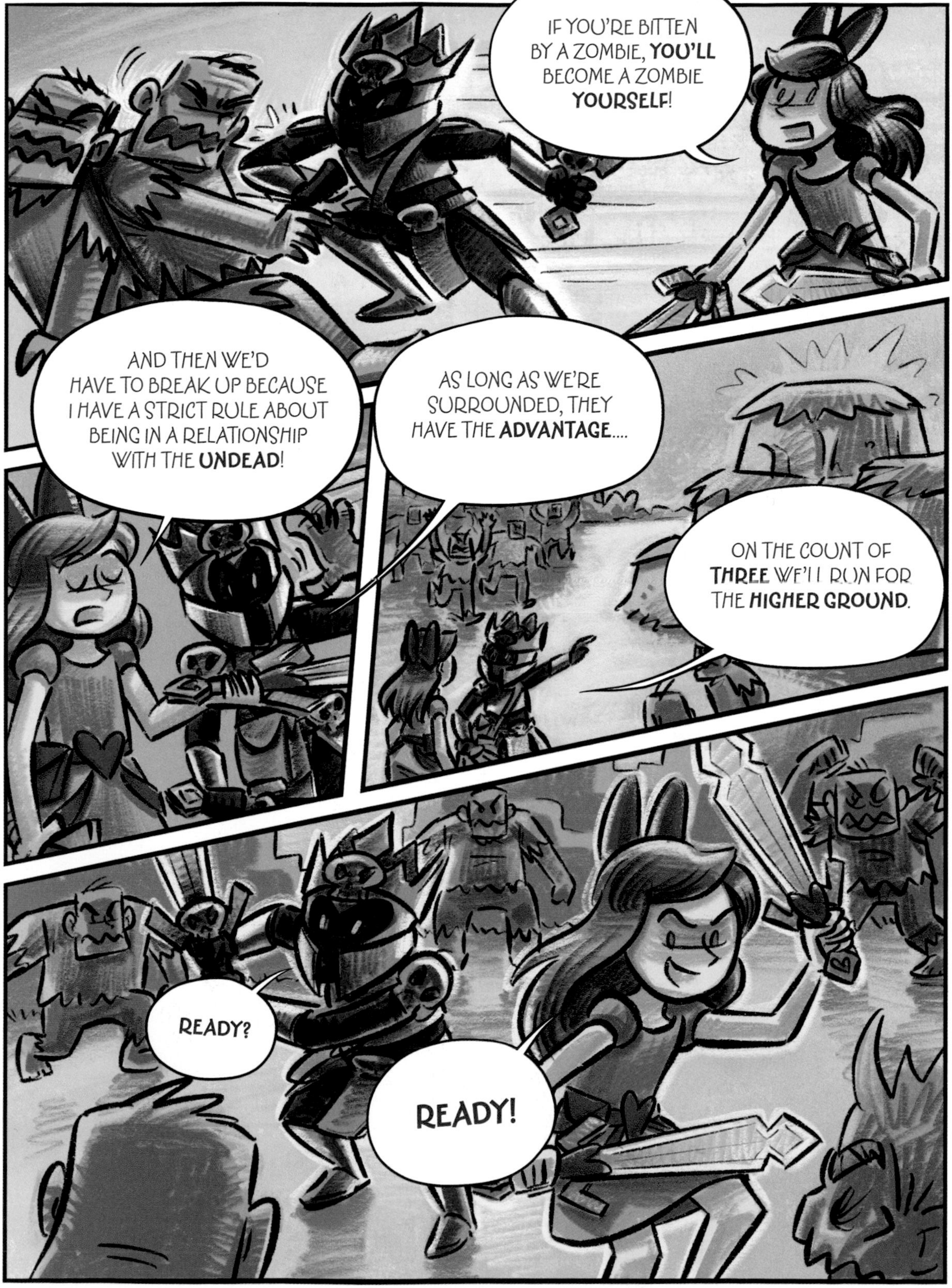
IF YOU'RE BITTEN BY A ZOMBIE, **YOU'LL** BECOME A ZOMBIE **YOURSELF**!
AND THEN WE'D HAVE TO BREAK UP BECAUSE I HAVE A STRICT RULE ABOUT BEING IN A RELATIONSHIP WITH THE **UNDEAD**!
AS LONG AS WE'RE SURROUNDED, THEY HAVE THE **ADVANTAGE**....
ON THE COUNT OF **THREE** WE'LL RUN FOR THE **HIGHER GROUND**.
READY?
READY!

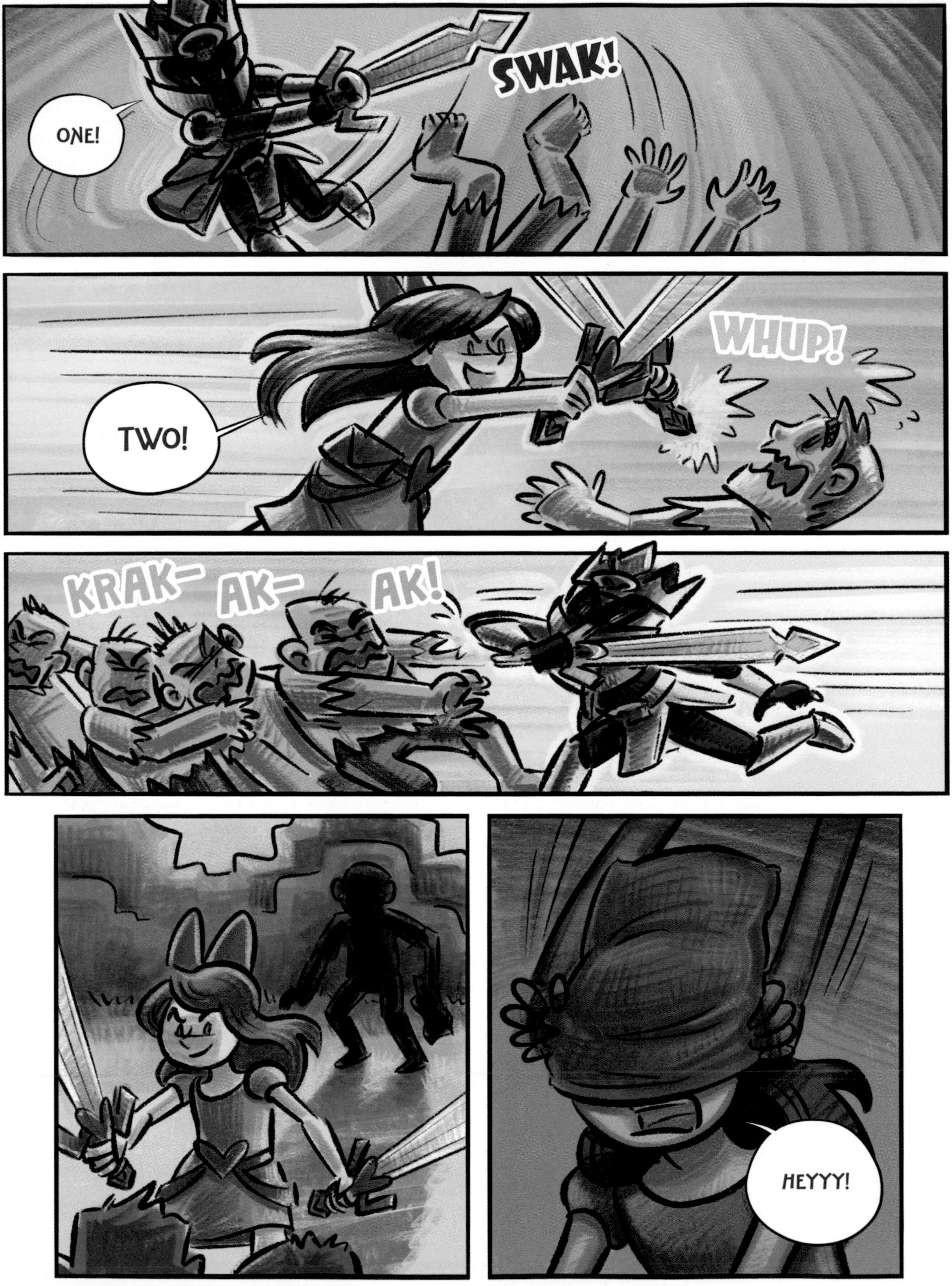
ONE!
SWAK!
TWO!
WHUP!
KRAK- AK- AK!
HEYYY!

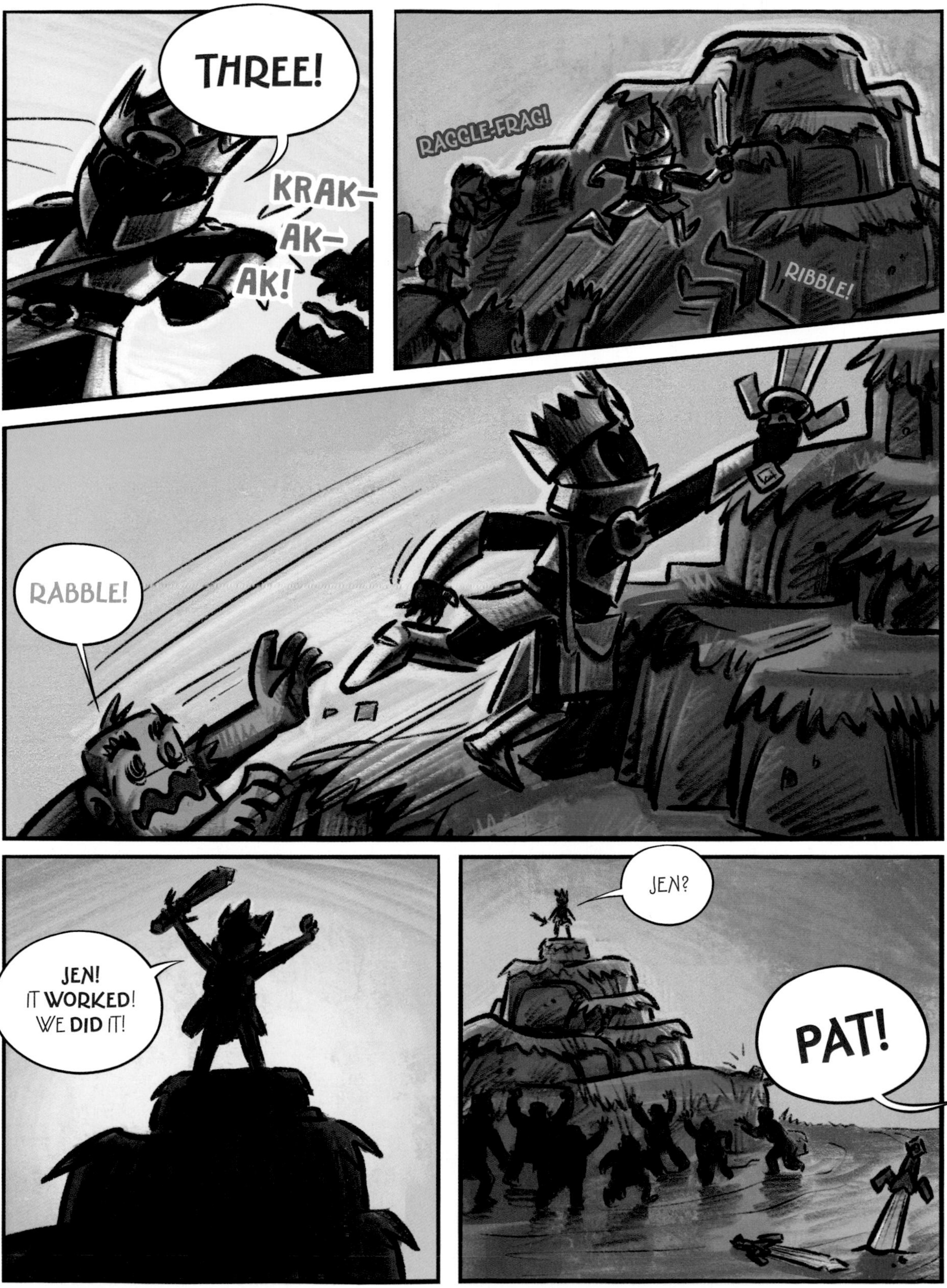
THREE!
KRAK-
AK-
AK!
RAGGLE-FRAG!
RIBBLE!
RABBLE!
JEN!
IT WORKED!
WE DID IT!
JEN?
PAT!

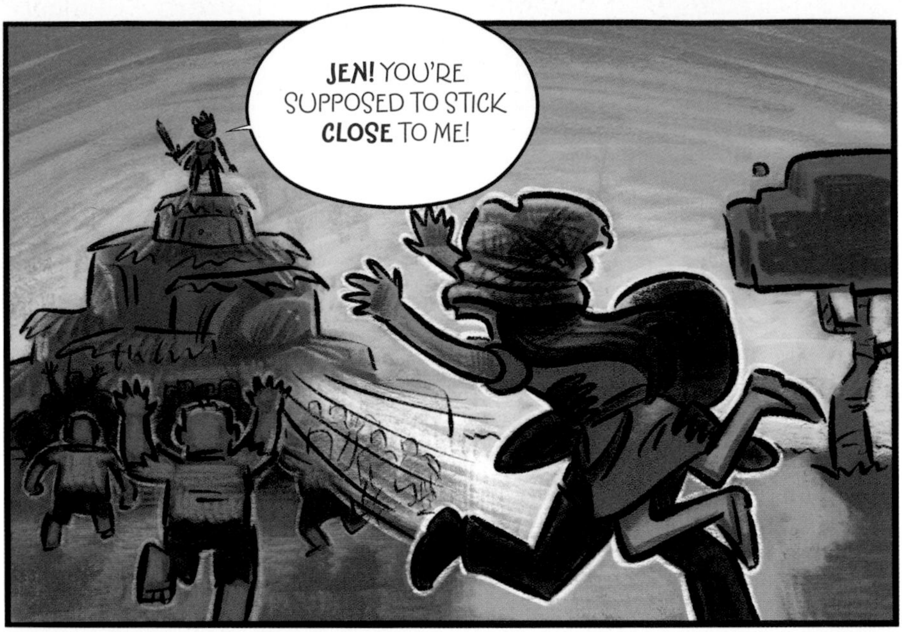
JEN! YOU'RE SUPPOSED TO STICK **CLOSE** TO ME!

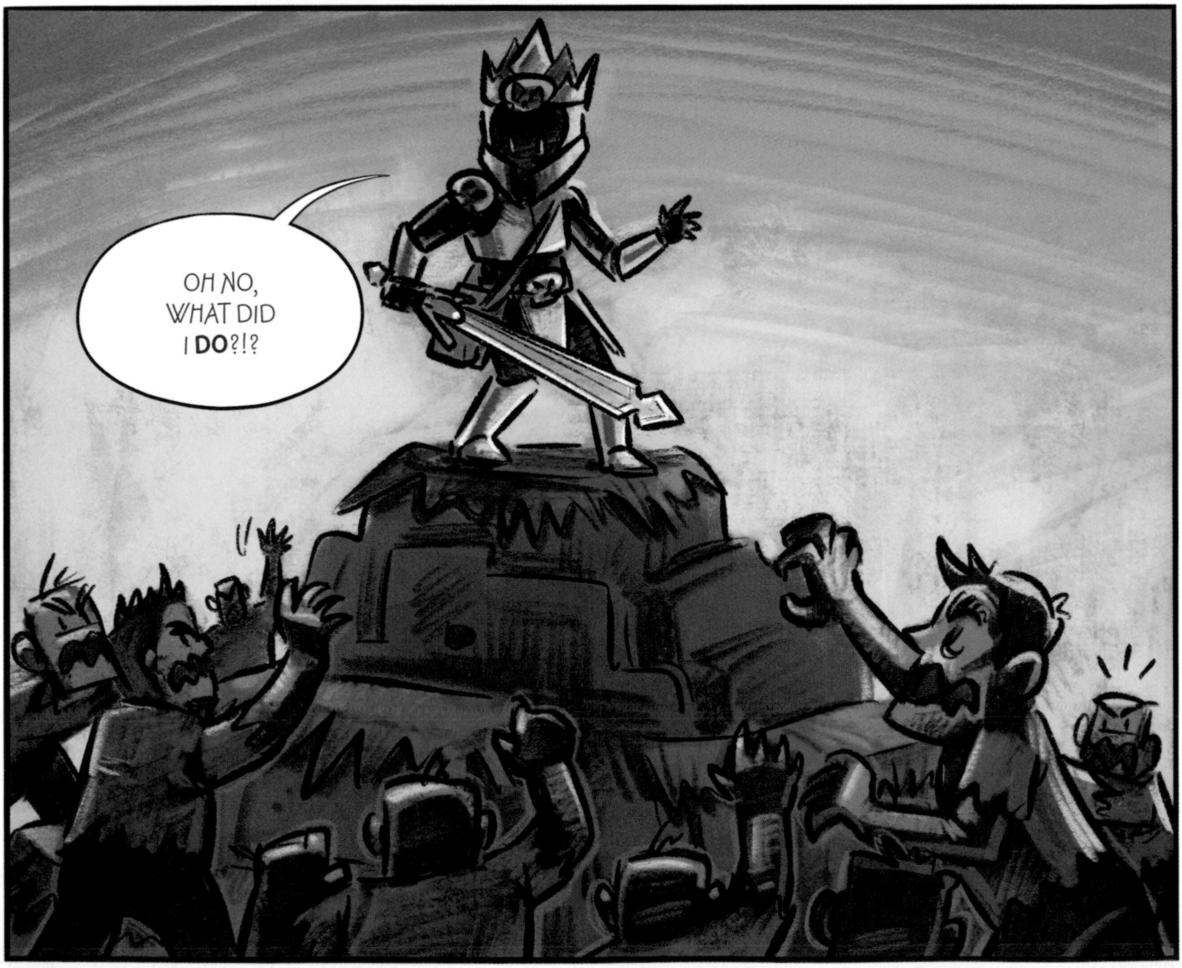
OH NO, WHAT DID I **DO**?!?

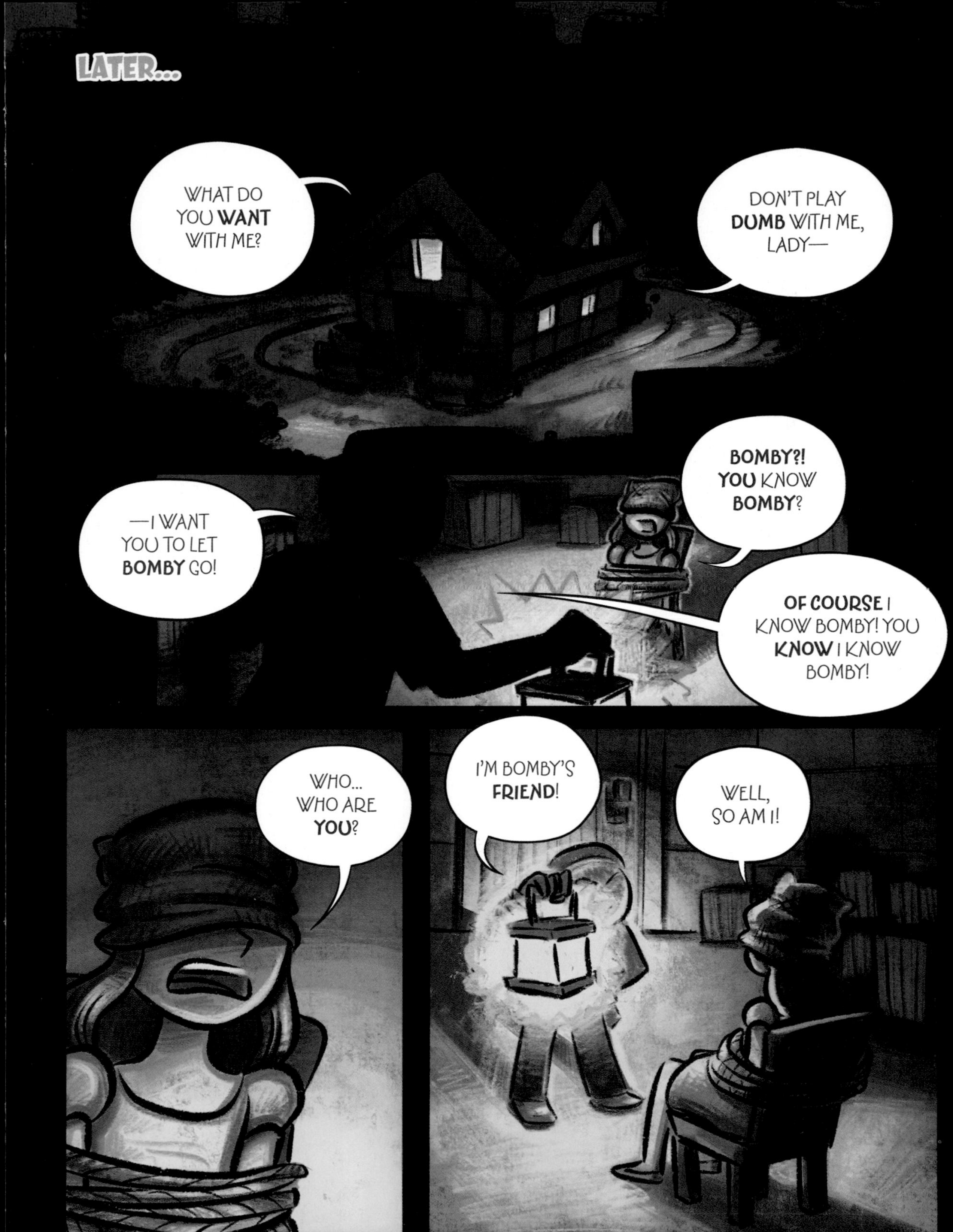
LATER...
WHAT DO YOU WANT WITH ME?
DON'T PLAY DUMB WITH ME, LADY—
—I WANT YOU TO LET BOMBY GO!
BOMBY?! YOU KNOW BOMBY?
OF COURSE I KNOW BOMBY! YOU KNOW I KNOW BOMBY!
WHO... WHO ARE YOU?
I'M BOMBY'S FRIEND!
WELL, SO AM I!

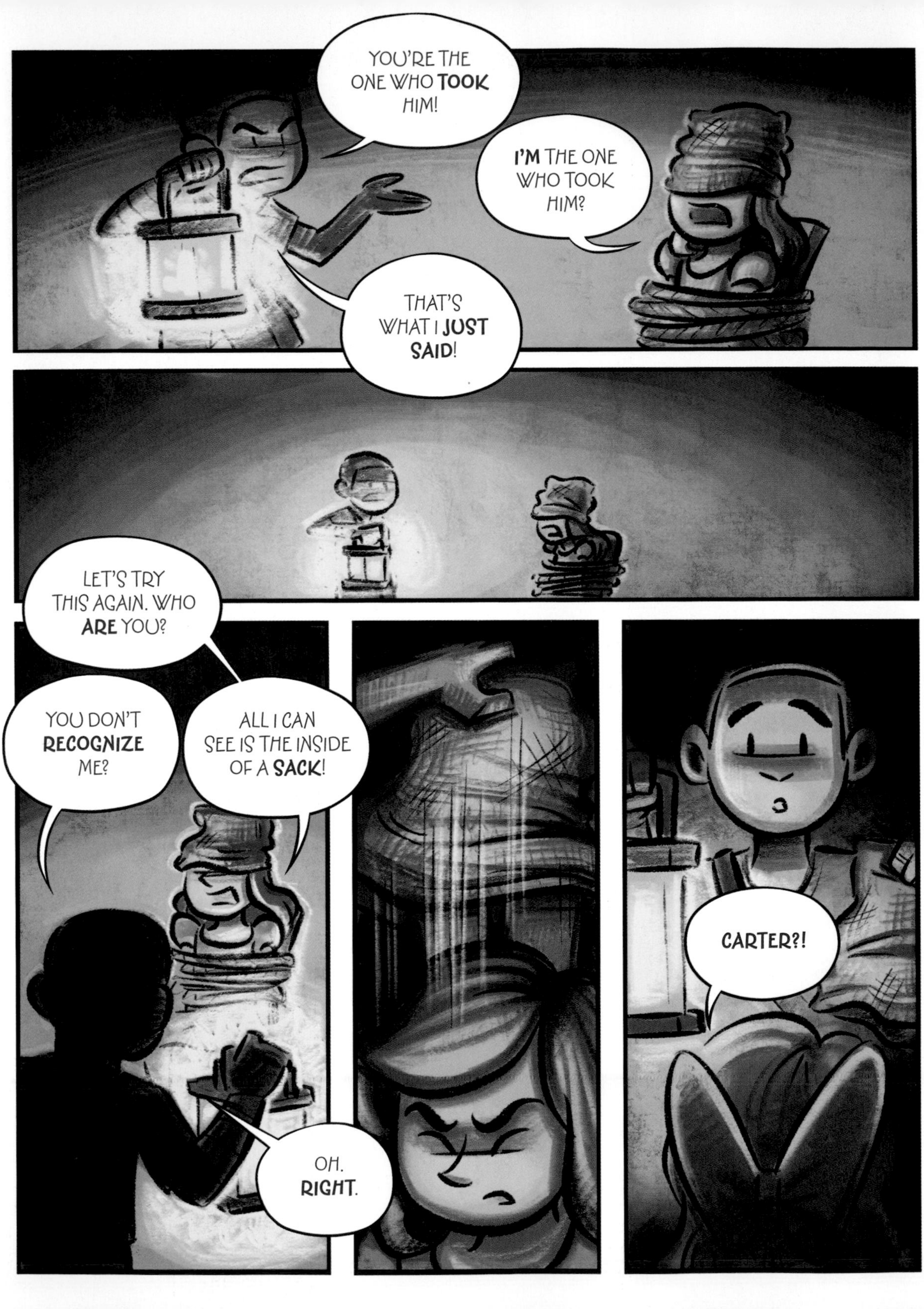

YOU'RE THE ONE WHO **TOOK** HIM!
I'M THE ONE WHO TOOK HIM?
THAT'S WHAT I **JUST SAID**!
LET'S TRY THIS AGAIN. WHO **ARE** YOU?
ALL I CAN SEE IS THE INSIDE OF A **SACK**!
YOU DON'T **RECOGNIZE** ME?
OH. **RIGHT**.
CARTER?!

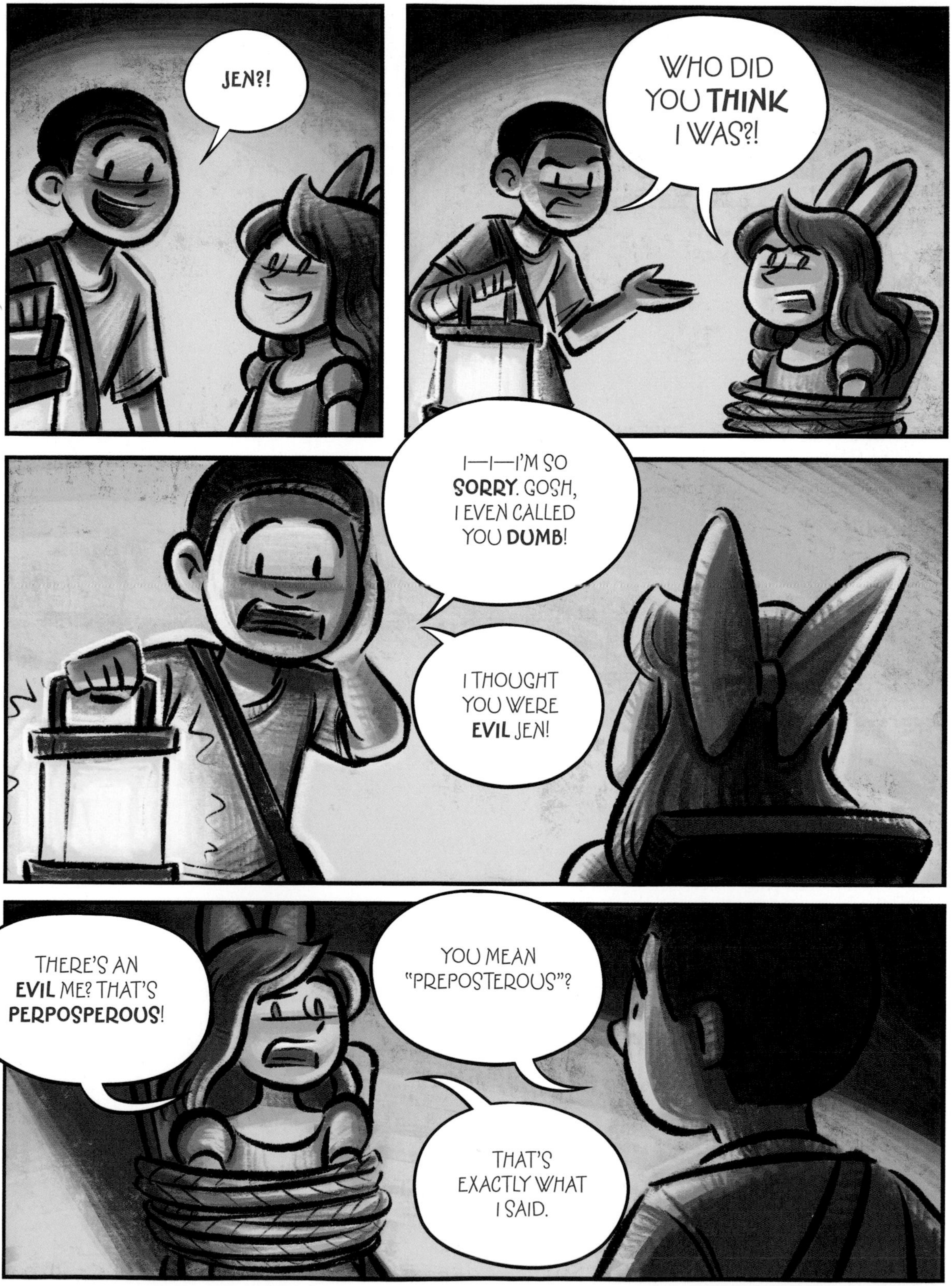
JEN?!
WHO DID YOU **THINK** I WAS?!
I—I—I'M SO **SORRY**. GOSH, I EVEN CALLED YOU **DUMB**!
I THOUGHT YOU WERE **EVIL** JEN!
THERE'S AN **EVIL** ME? THAT'S **PERPOSPEROUS**!
YOU MEAN "PREPOSTEROUS"?
THAT'S EXACTLY WHAT I SAID.

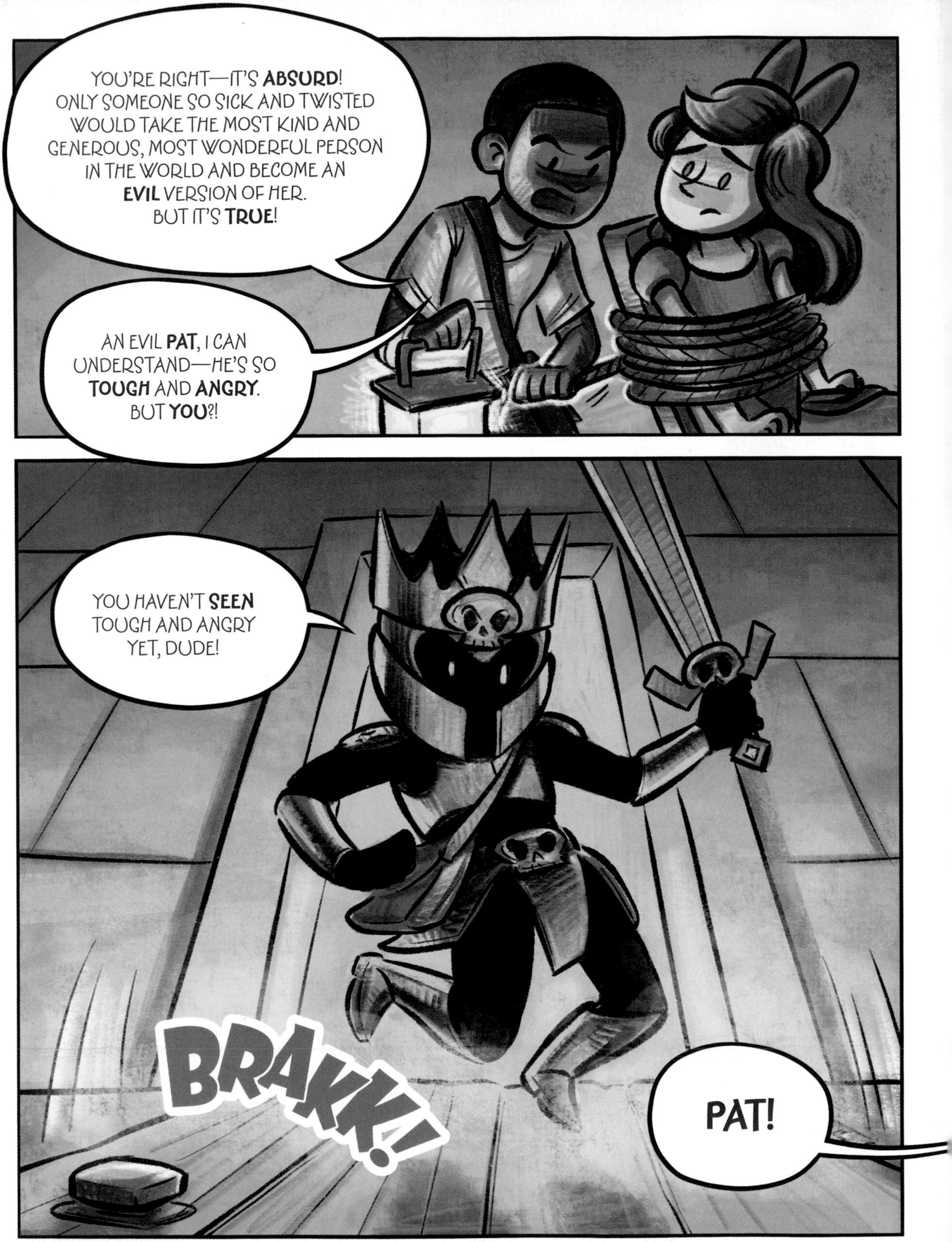
YOU'RE RIGHT—IT'S **ABSURD**! ONLY SOMEONE SO SICK AND TWISTED WOULD TAKE THE MOST KIND AND GENEROUS, MOST WONDERFUL PERSON IN THE WORLD AND BECOME AN **EVIL** VERSION OF HER. BUT IT'S **TRUE**!
AN EVIL **PAT**, I CAN UNDERSTAND—HE'S SO **TOUGH** AND **ANGRY**. BUT **YOU**?!
YOU HAVEN'T **SEEN** TOUGH AND ANGRY YET, DUDE!
BRAKK!
PAT!

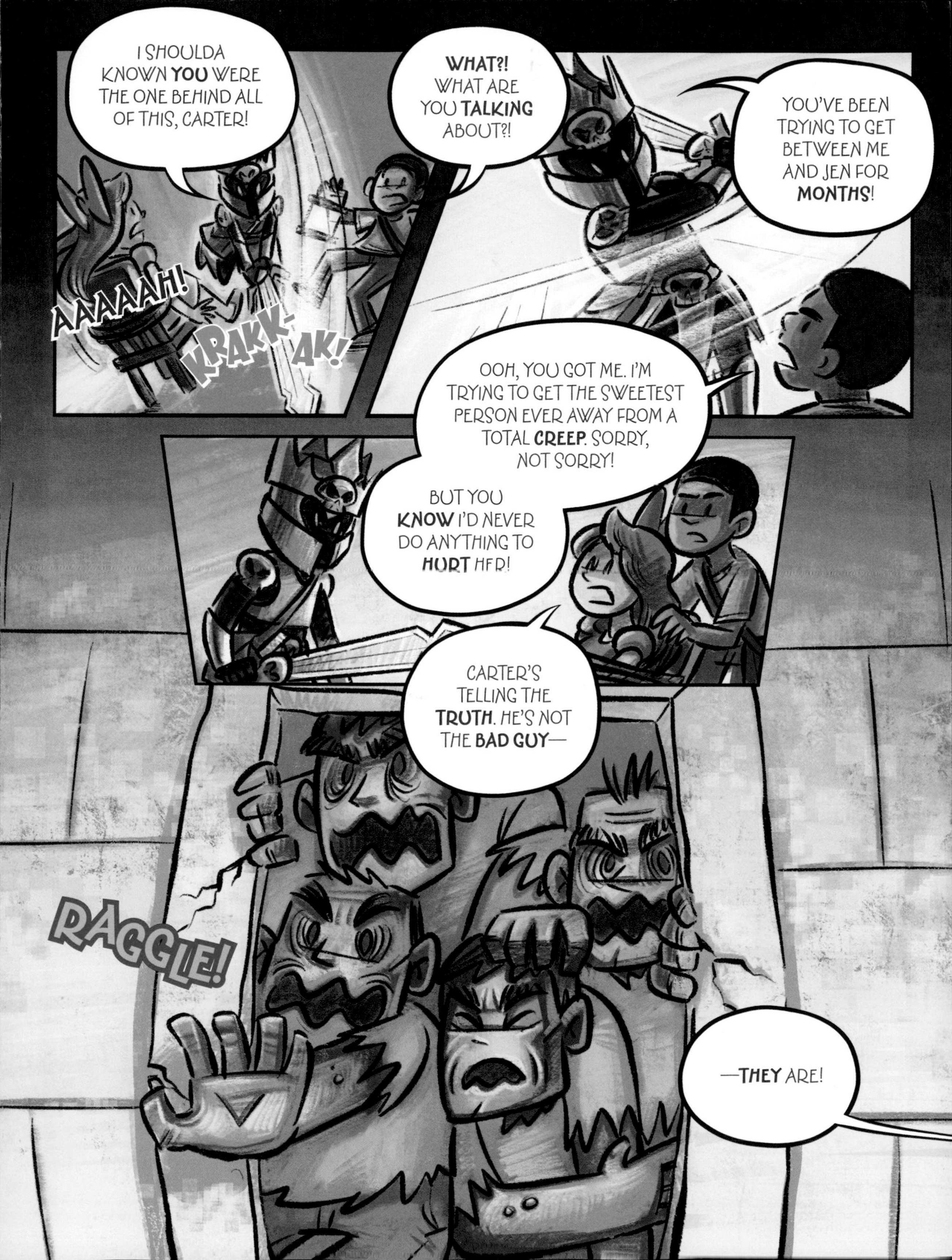

I SHOULDA KNOWN YOU WERE THE ONE BEHIND ALL OF THIS, CARTER!
AAAAAH!
KRAKK-AK!
WHAT?! WHAT ARE YOU TALKING ABOUT?!
YOU'VE BEEN TRYING TO GET BETWEEN ME AND JEN FOR MONTHS!
OOH, YOU GOT ME. I'M TRYING TO GET THE SWEETEST PERSON EVER AWAY FROM A TOTAL CREEP. SORRY, NOT SORRY!
BUT YOU KNOW I'D NEVER DO ANYTHING TO HURT HER!
CARTER'S TELLING THE TRUTH. HE'S NOT THE BAD GUY—
RAGGLE!
—THEY ARE!

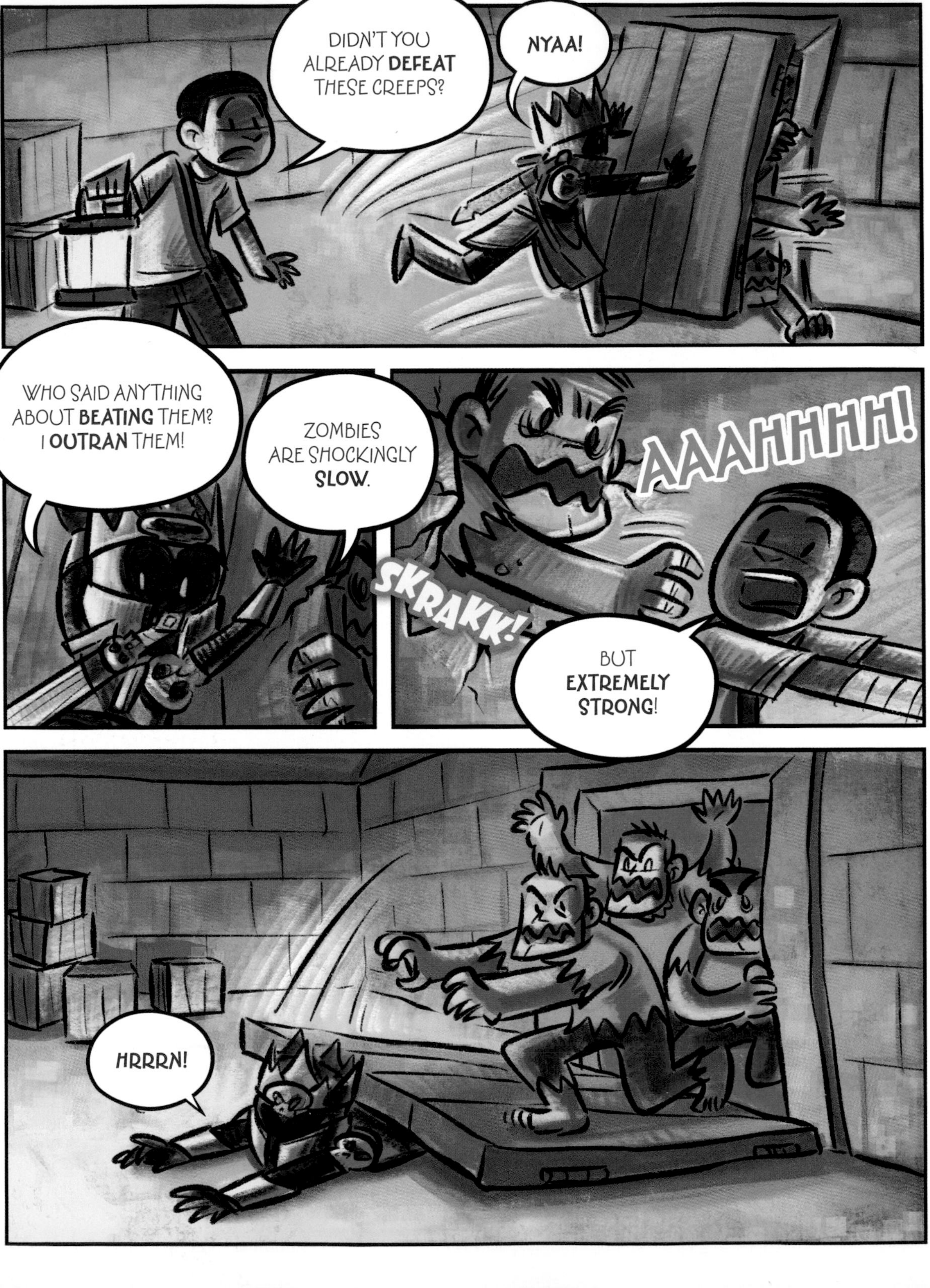
DIDN'T YOU ALREADY **DEFEAT** THESE CREEPS?
NYAA!
WHO SAID ANYTHING ABOUT **BEATING** THEM? I **OUTRAN** THEM!
ZOMBIES ARE SHOCKINGLY **SLOW**.
SKRAKK!
AAAHHHH!
BUT **EXTREMELY STRONG**!
HRRRN!

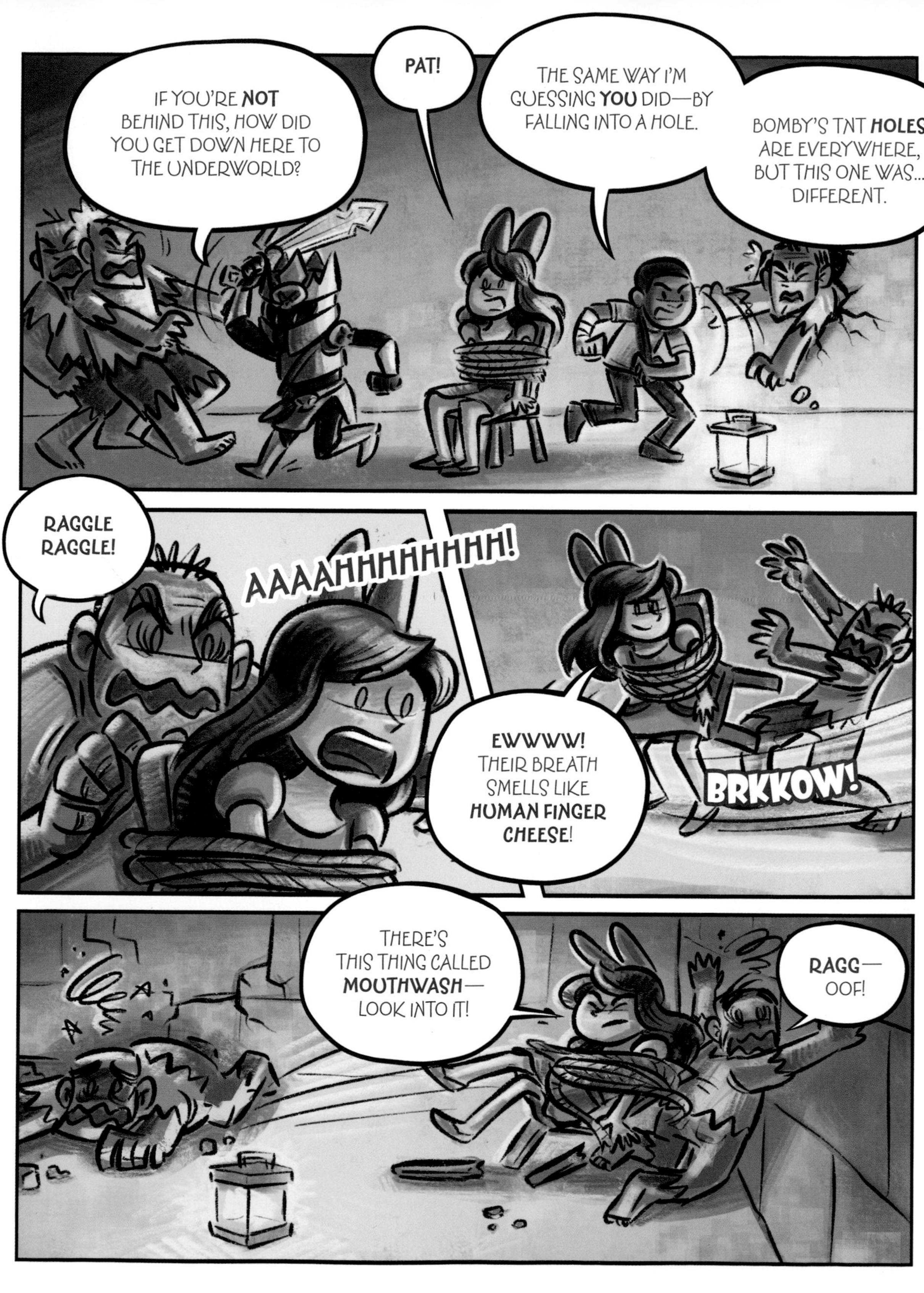
IF YOU'RE **NOT** BEHIND THIS, HOW DID YOU GET DOWN HERE TO THE UNDERWORLD?
PAT!
THE SAME WAY I'M GUESSING **YOU** DID—BY FALLING INTO A HOLE.
BOMBY'S TNT **HOLES** ARE EVERYWHERE, BUT THIS ONE WAS... DIFFERENT.
RAGGLE RAGGLE!
AAAAHHHHHHHH!
EWWWW! THEIR BREATH SMELLS LIKE **HUMAN FINGER CHEESE**!
BRKKOW!
THERE'S THIS THING CALLED **MOUTHWASH**—LOOK INTO IT!
RAGG—OOF!

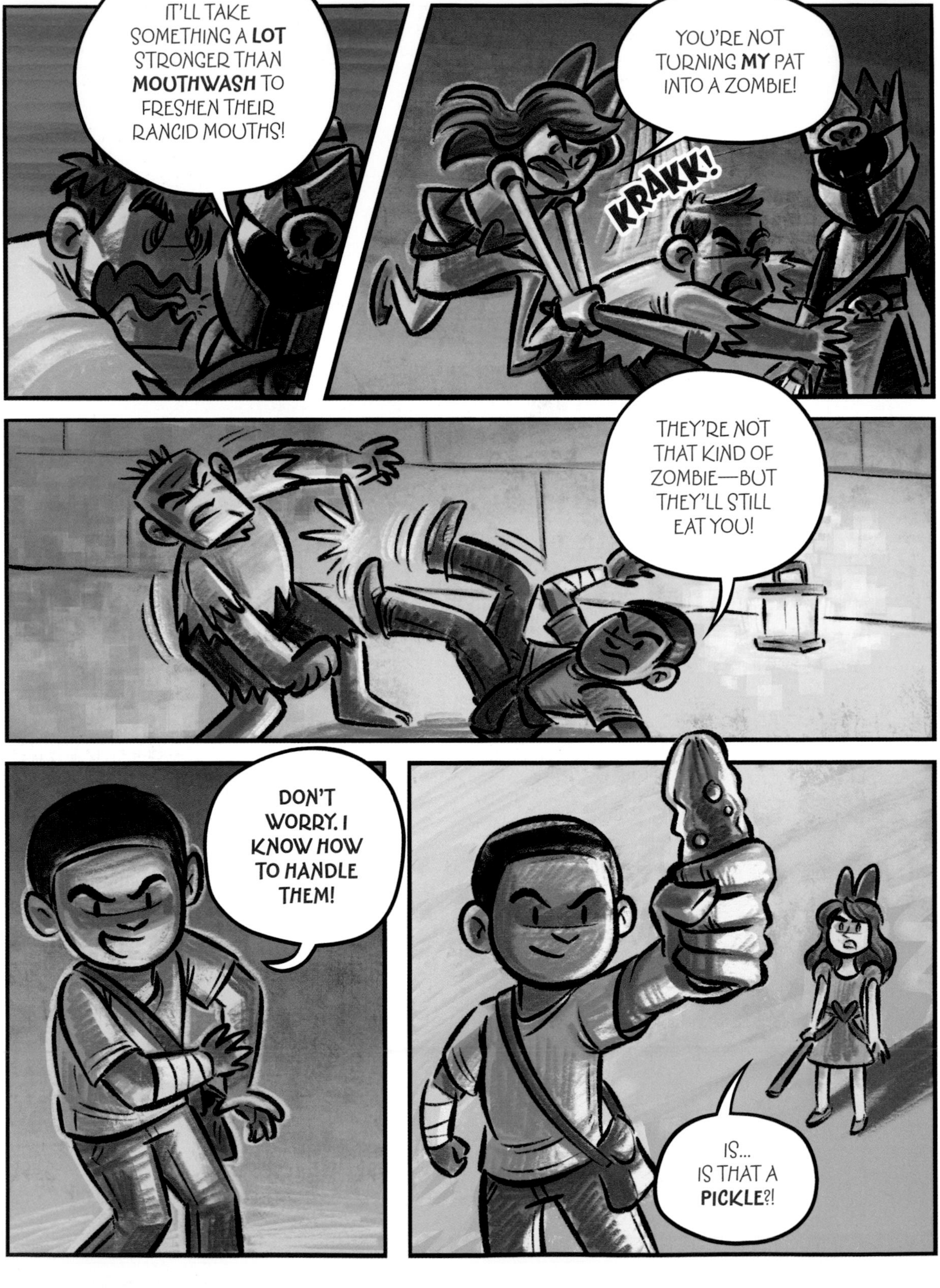
IT'LL TAKE SOMETHING A **LOT** STRONGER THAN **MOUTHWASH** TO FRESHEN THEIR RANCID MOUTHS!
YOU'RE NOT TURNING **MY** PAT INTO A ZOMBIE!
KRAKK!
THEY'RE NOT THAT KIND OF ZOMBIE—BUT THEY'LL STILL EAT YOU!
DON'T WORRY. I KNOW HOW TO HANDLE THEM!
IS... IS THAT A **PICKLE**?!

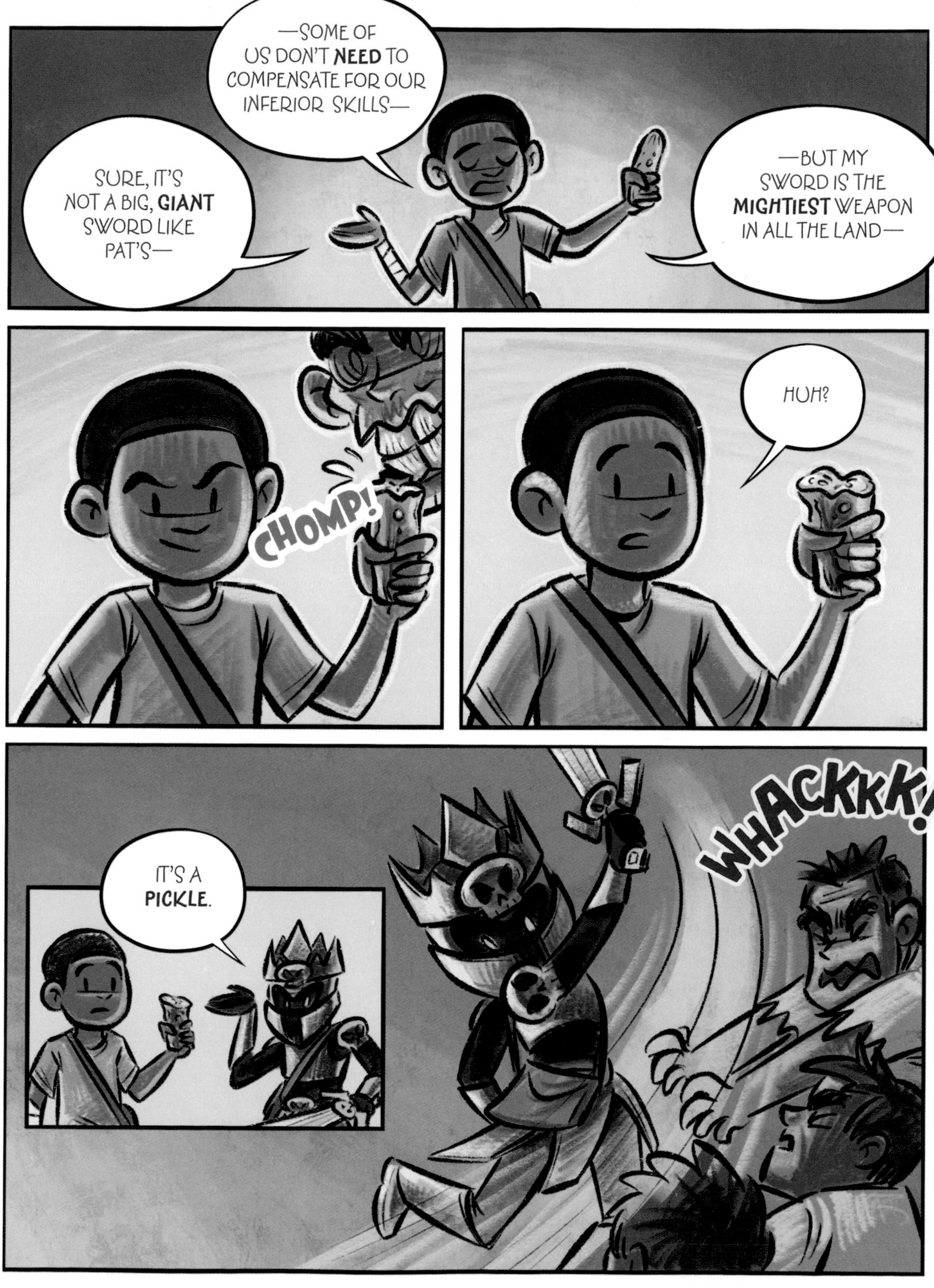
—SOME OF US DON'T **NEED** TO COMPENSATE FOR OUR INFERIOR SKILLS—
SURE, IT'S NOT A BIG, **GIANT** SWORD LIKE PAT'S—
—BUT MY SWORD IS THE **MIGHTIEST** WEAPON IN ALL THE LAND—
CHOMP!
HUH?
IT'S A **PICKLE**.
WHACKKK!

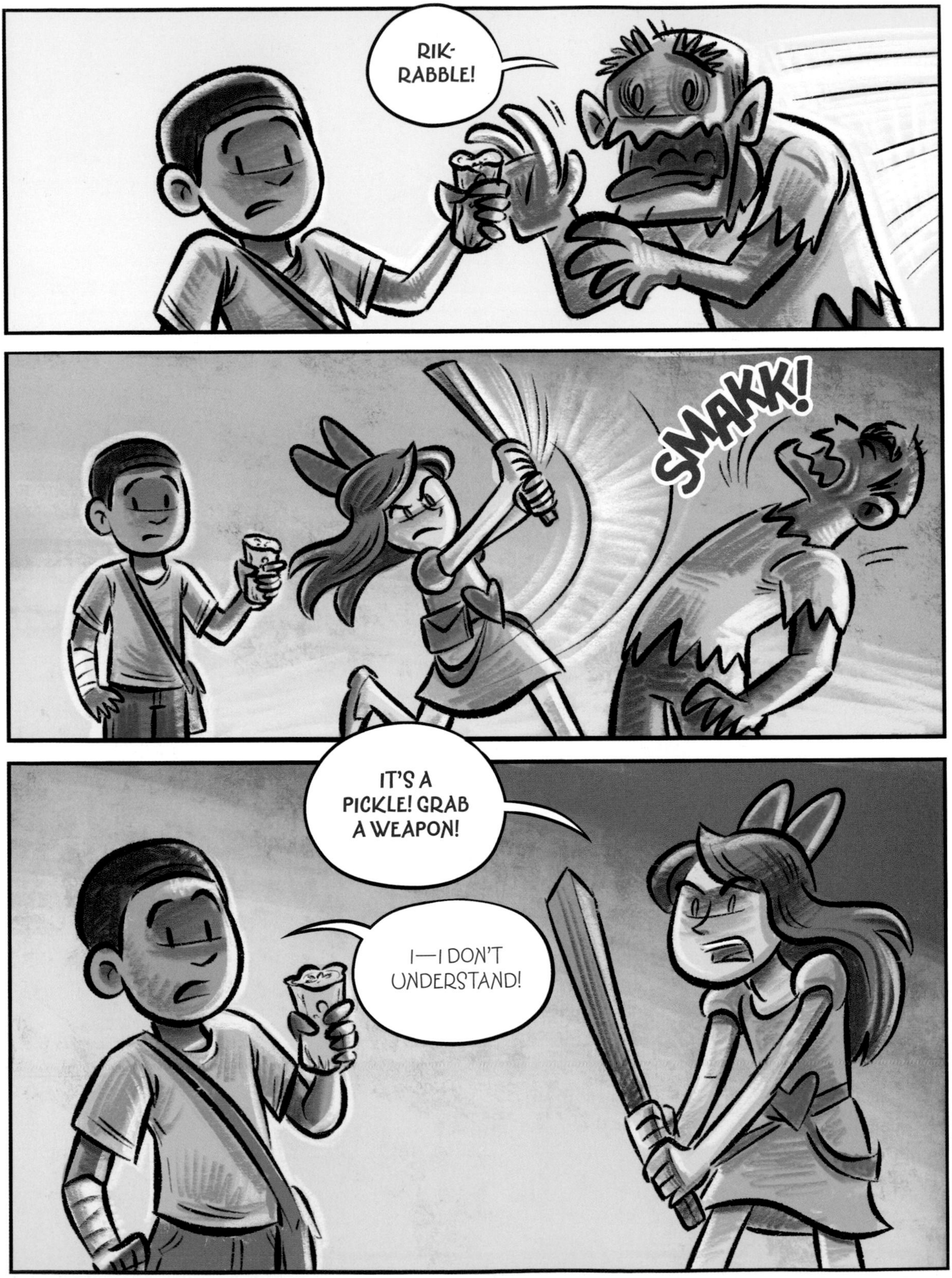
RIK-
RABBLE!
SMAKK!
IT'S A
PICKLE! GRAB
A WEAPON!
I—I DON'T
UNDERSTAND!

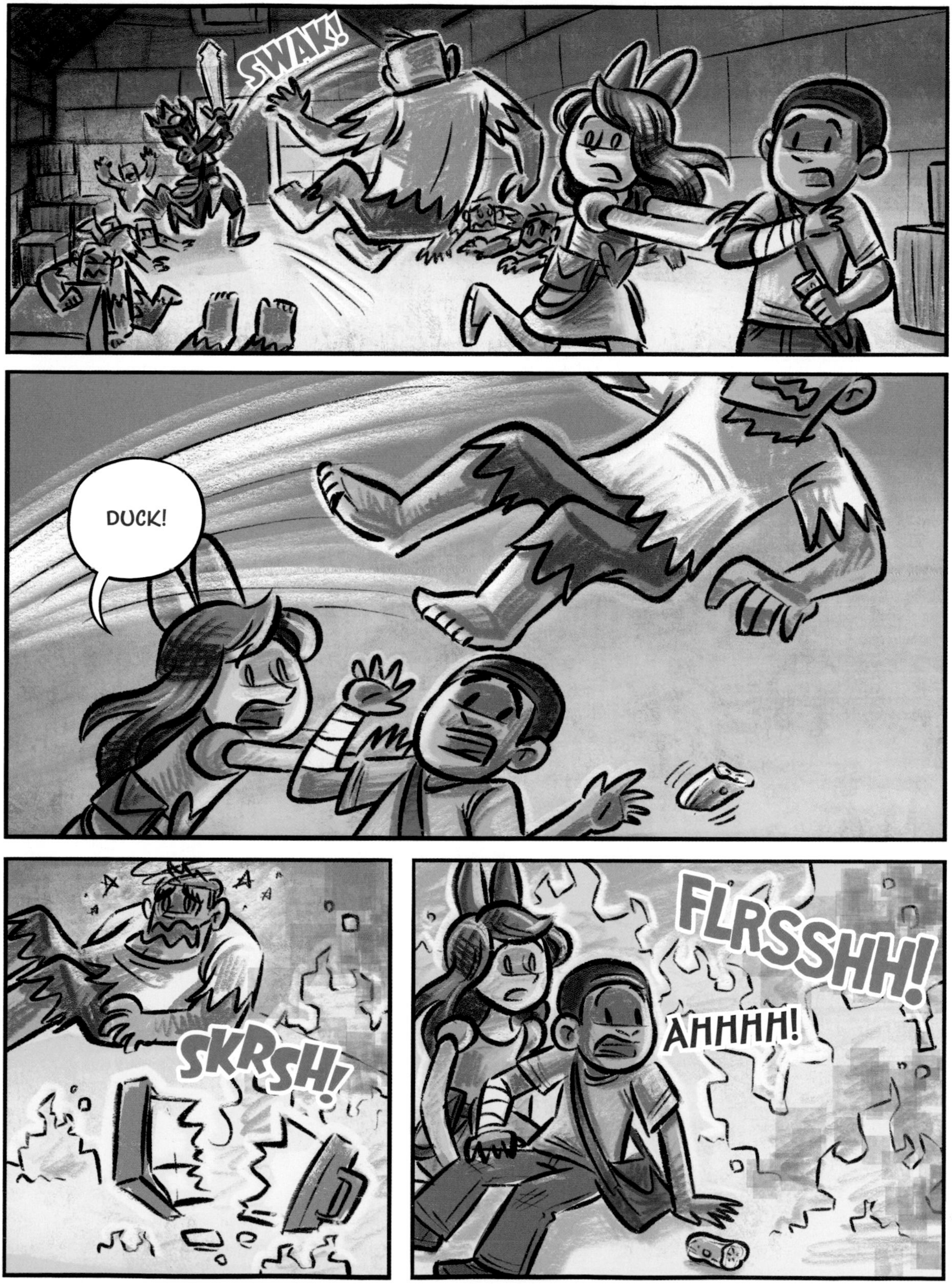
SWAK!
DUCK!
SKRSH!
FLRSSHH!
AHHHH!

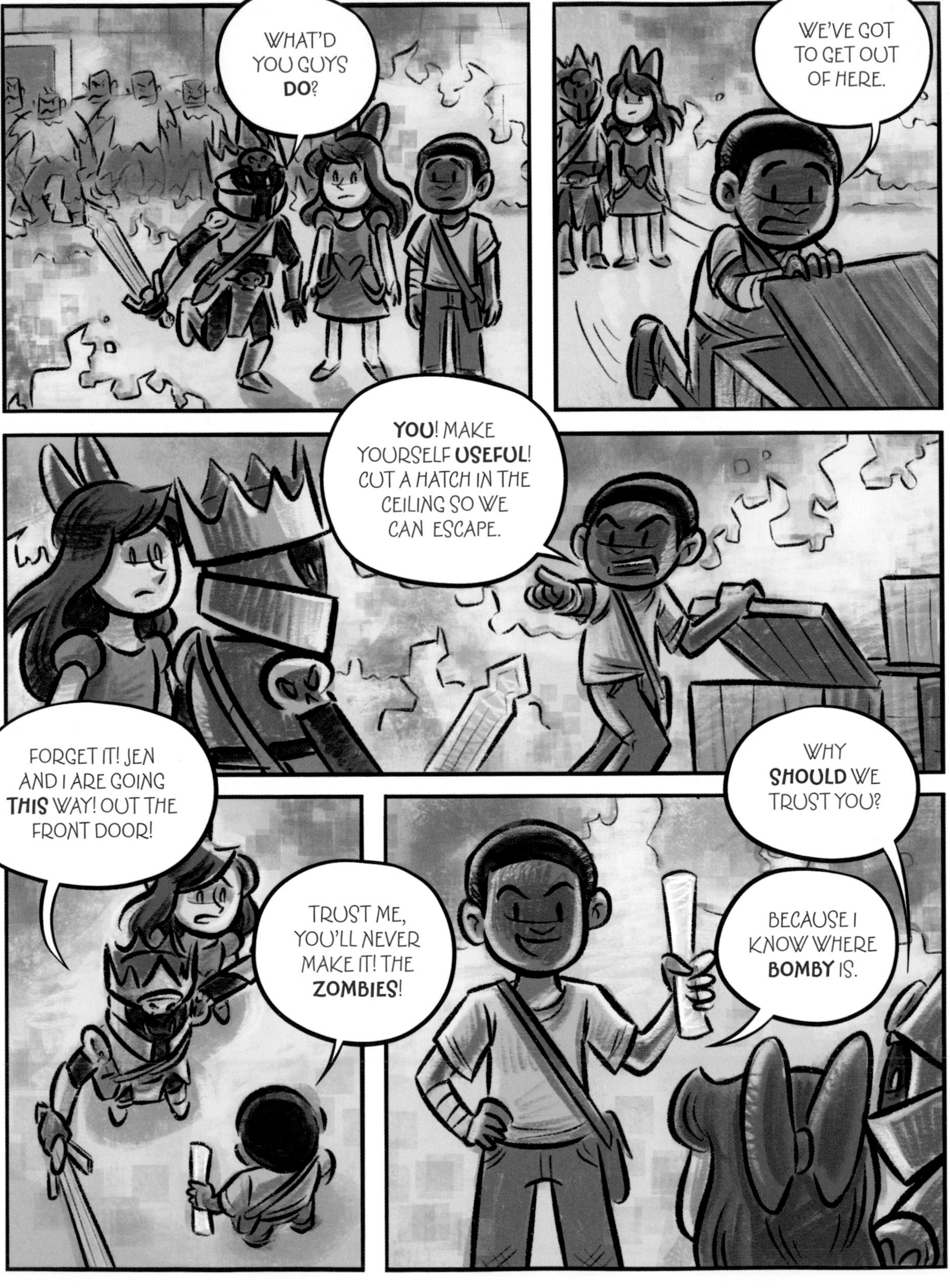
WHAT'D YOU GUYS DO?
WE'VE GOT TO GET OUT OF HERE.
YOU! MAKE YOURSELF USEFUL! CUT A HATCH IN THE CEILING SO WE CAN ESCAPE.
FORGET IT! JEN AND I ARE GOING THIS WAY! OUT THE FRONT DOOR!
TRUST ME, YOU'LL NEVER MAKE IT! THE ZOMBIES!
WHY SHOULD WE TRUST YOU?
BECAUSE I KNOW WHERE BOMBY IS.

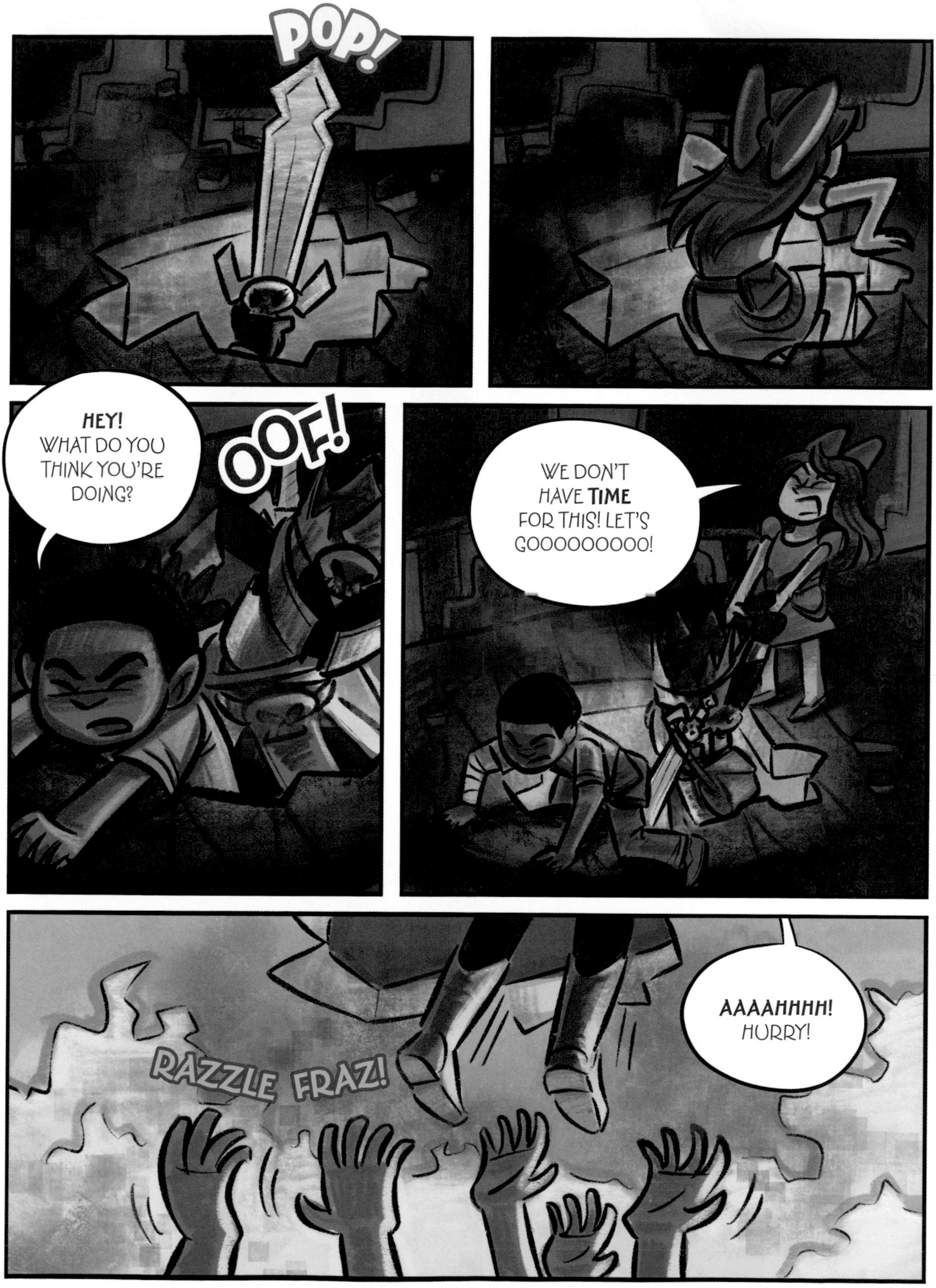
POP!
HEY! WHAT DO YOU THINK YOU'RE DOING?
OOF!
WE DON'T HAVE TIME FOR THIS! LET'S GOOOOOOOOO!
RAZZLE FRAZ!
AAAAHHHH! HURRY!

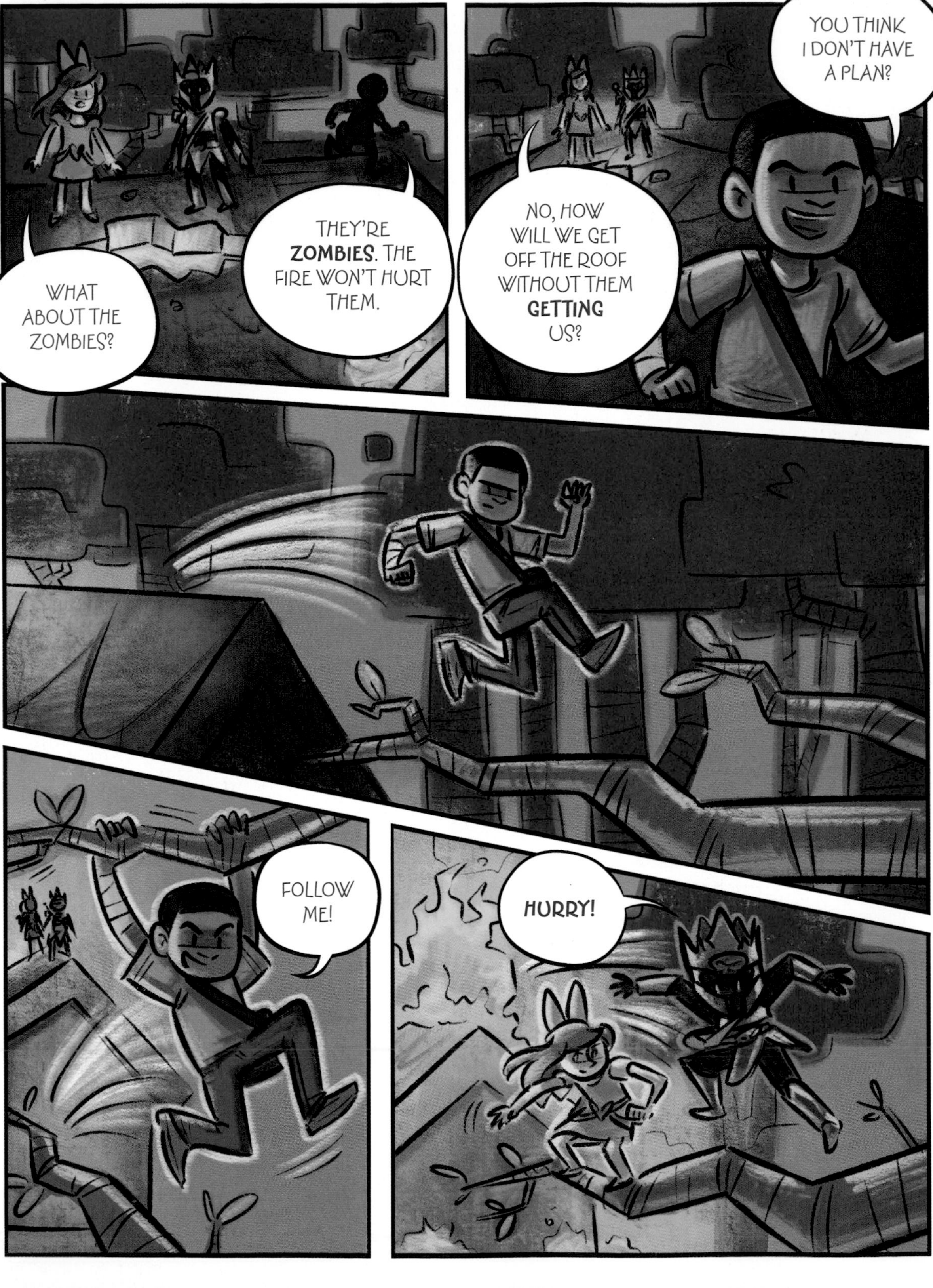
WHAT ABOUT THE ZOMBIES?
THEY'RE **ZOMBIES**. THE FIRE WON'T HURT THEM.
NO, HOW WILL WE GET OFF THE ROOF WITHOUT THEM **GETTING** US?
YOU THINK I DON'T HAVE A PLAN?
FOLLOW ME!
HURRY!

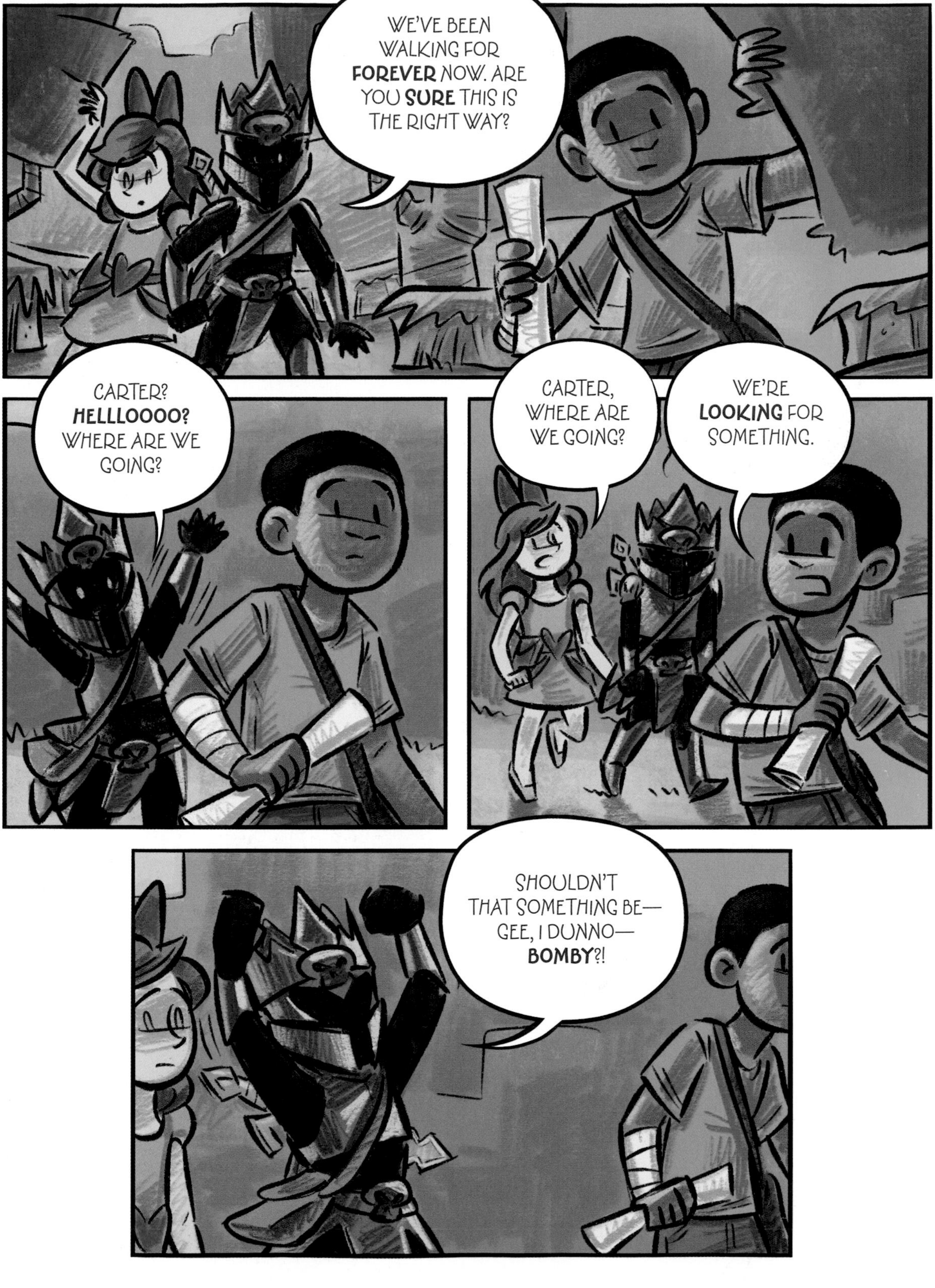
WE'VE BEEN WALKING FOR **FOREVER** NOW. ARE YOU **SURE** THIS IS THE RIGHT WAY?
CARTER? **HELLLOOOO?** WHERE ARE WE GOING?
CARTER, WHERE ARE WE GOING?
WE'RE **LOOKING** FOR SOMETHING.
SHOULDN'T THAT SOMETHING BE— GEE, I DUNNO— **BOMBY**?!

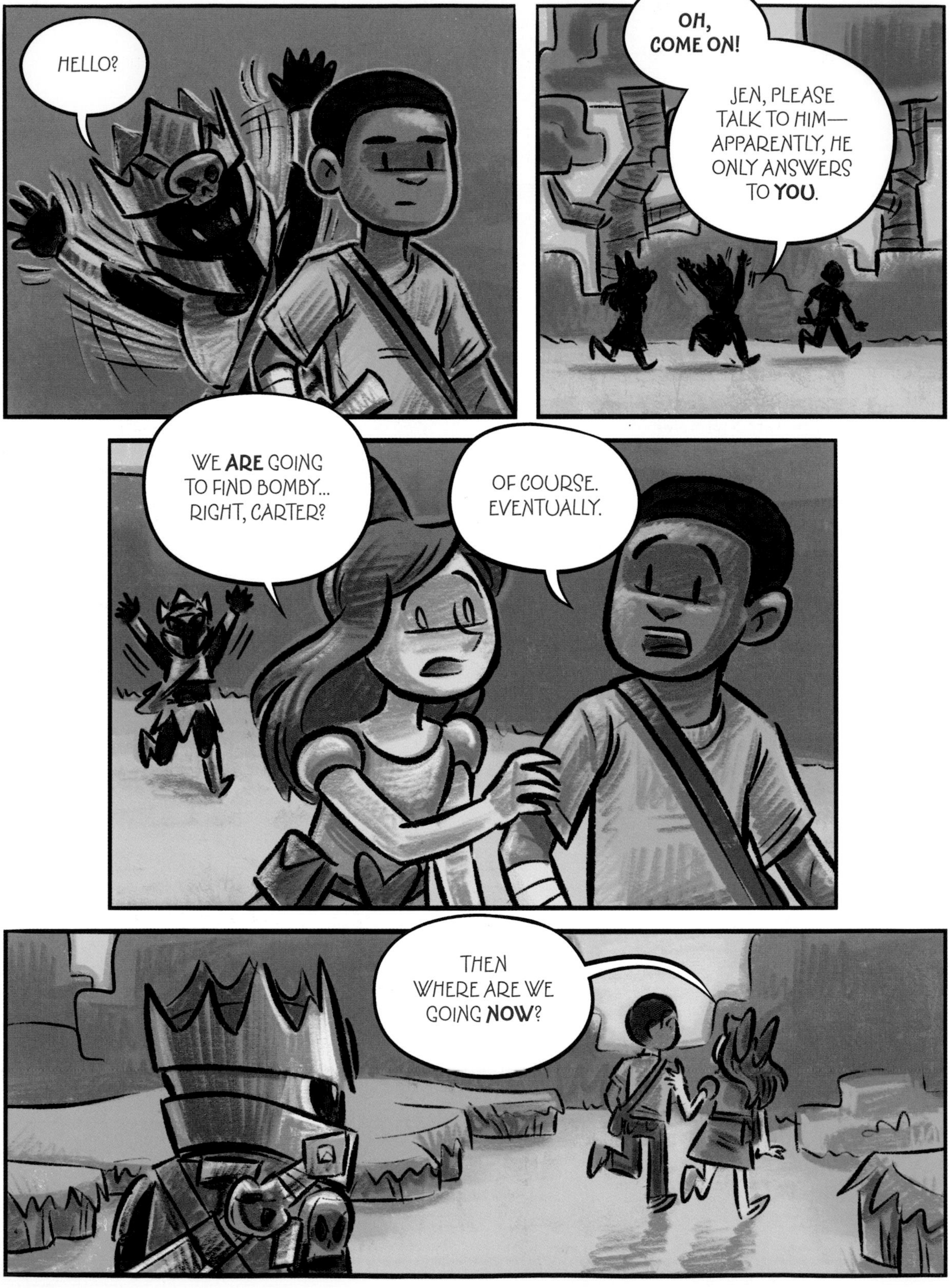
HELLO?
OH, COME ON!
JEN, PLEASE TALK TO HIM—APPARENTLY, HE ONLY ANSWERS TO **YOU**.
WE **ARE** GOING TO FIND BOMBY... RIGHT, CARTER?
OF COURSE. EVENTUALLY.
THEN WHERE ARE WE GOING **NOW**?

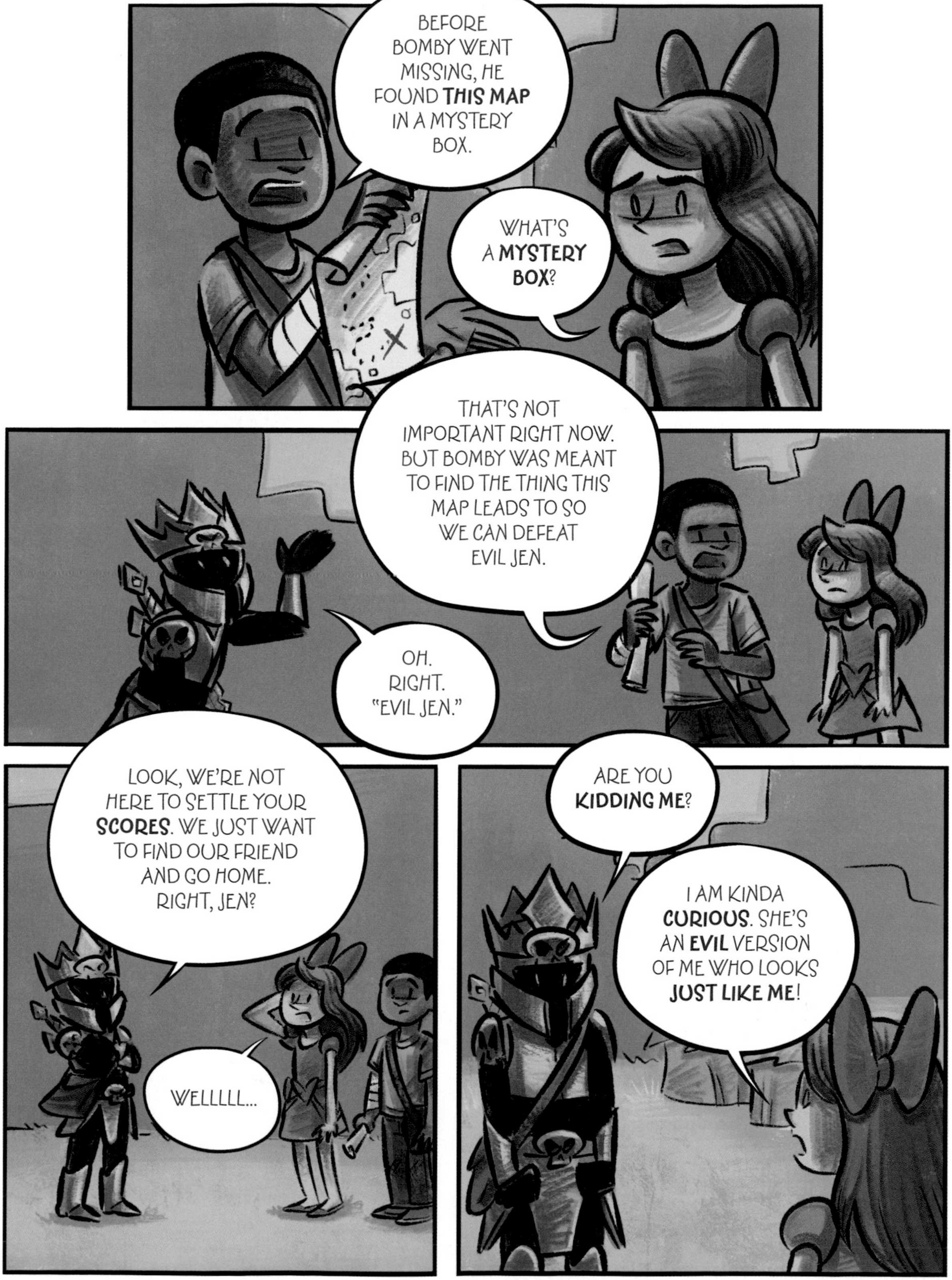
BEFORE BOMBY WENT MISSING, HE FOUND **THIS MAP** IN A MYSTERY BOX.
WHAT'S A **MYSTERY BOX**?
THAT'S NOT IMPORTANT RIGHT NOW. BUT BOMBY WAS MEANT TO FIND THE THING THIS MAP LEADS TO SO WE CAN DEFEAT EVIL JEN.
OH. RIGHT. "EVIL JEN."
LOOK, WE'RE NOT HERE TO SETTLE YOUR **SCORES**. WE JUST WANT TO FIND OUR FRIEND AND GO HOME. RIGHT, JEN?
WELLLLL...
ARE YOU **KIDDING ME**?
I AM KINDA **CURIOUS**. SHE'S AN **EVIL** VERSION OF ME WHO LOOKS **JUST LIKE ME**!

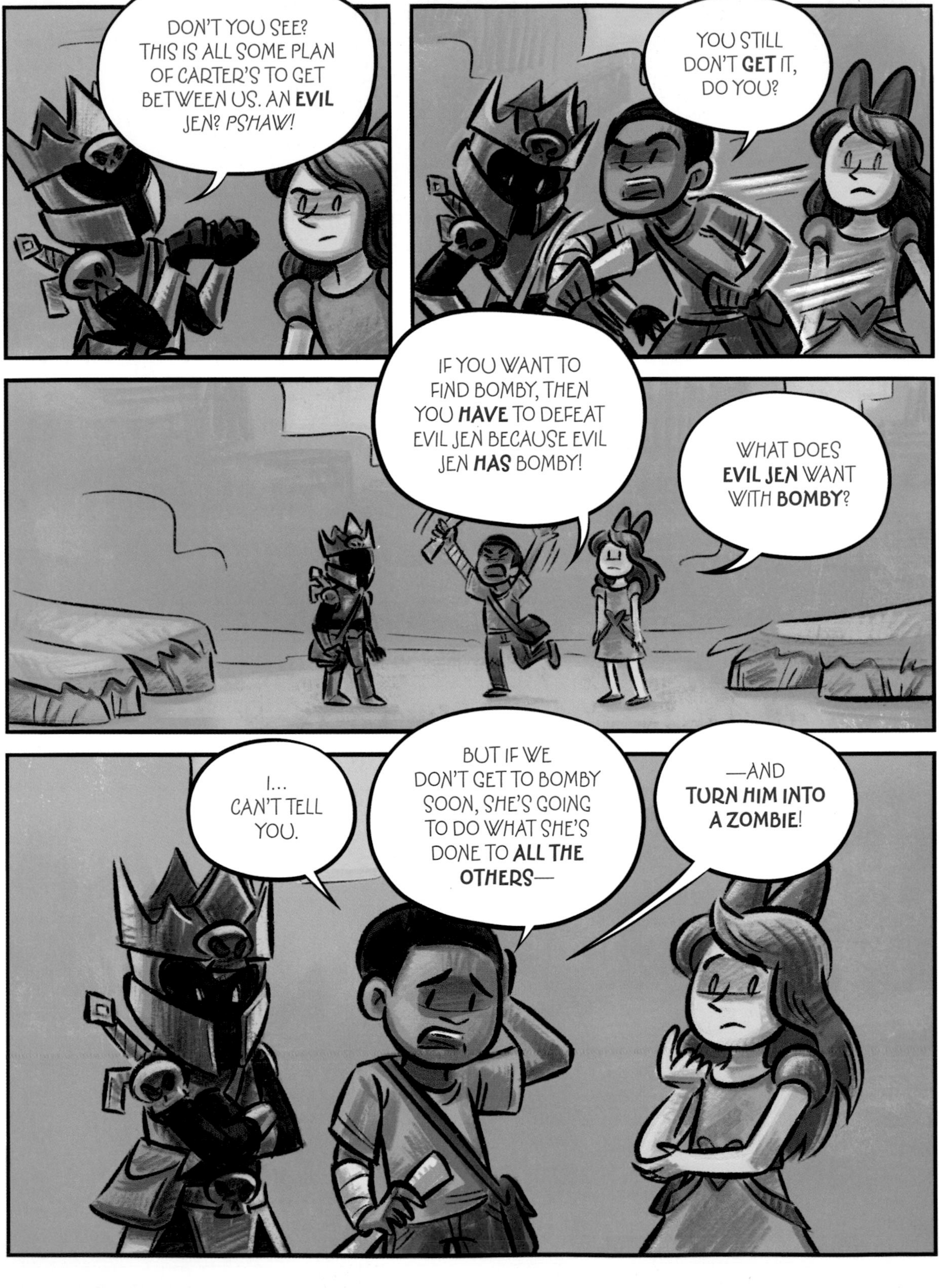
DON'T YOU SEE? THIS IS ALL SOME PLAN OF CARTER'S TO GET BETWEEN US. AN **EVIL** JEN? *PSHAW!*
YOU STILL DON'T **GET** IT, DO YOU?
IF YOU WANT TO FIND BOMBY, THEN YOU **HAVE** TO DEFEAT EVIL JEN BECAUSE EVIL JEN **HAS** BOMBY!
WHAT DOES **EVIL JEN** WANT WITH **BOMBY**?
I... CAN'T TELL YOU.
BUT IF WE DON'T GET TO BOMBY SOON, SHE'S GOING TO DO WHAT SHE'S DONE TO **ALL THE OTHERS**—
—AND **TURN HIM INTO A ZOMBIE**!

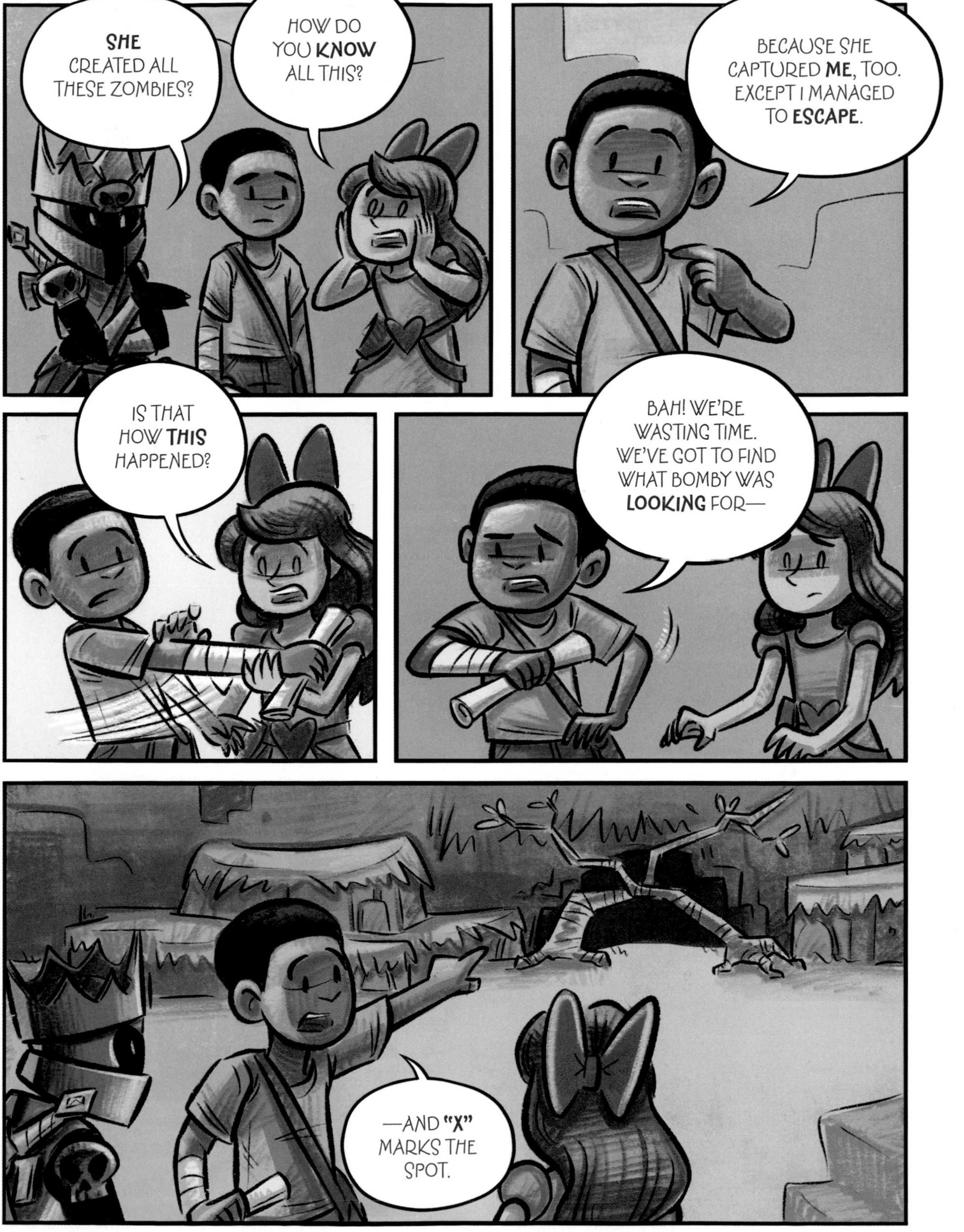
SHE CREATED ALL THESE ZOMBIES?
HOW DO YOU KNOW ALL THIS?
BECAUSE SHE CAPTURED ME, TOO. EXCEPT I MANAGED TO ESCAPE.
IS THAT HOW THIS HAPPENED?
BAH! WE'RE WASTING TIME. WE'VE GOT TO FIND WHAT BOMBY WAS LOOKING FOR—
—AND "X" MARKS THE SPOT.

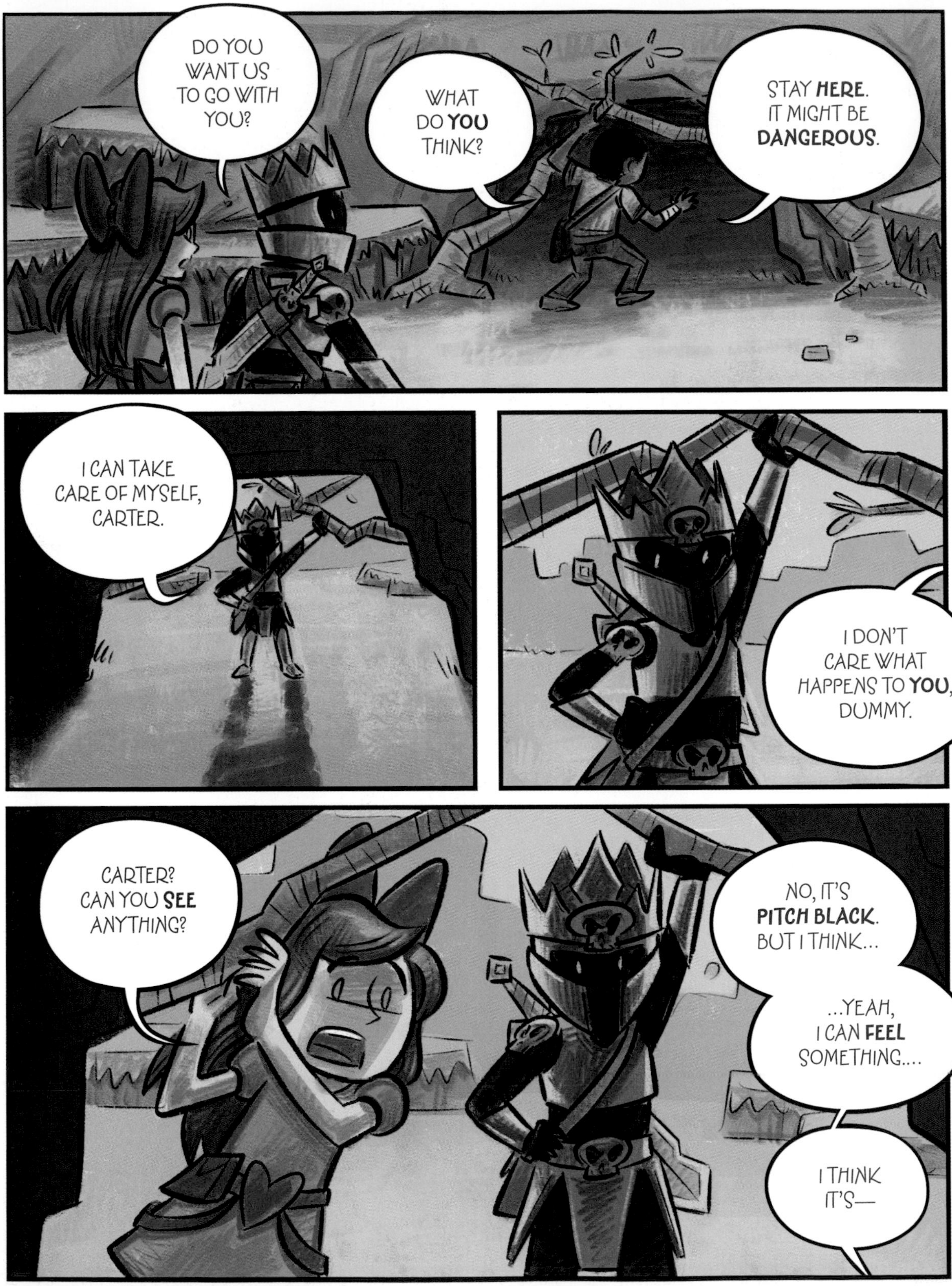
DO YOU WANT US TO GO WITH YOU?
WHAT DO **YOU** THINK?
STAY **HERE**. IT MIGHT BE **DANGEROUS**.
I CAN TAKE CARE OF MYSELF, CARTER.
I DON'T CARE WHAT HAPPENS TO **YOU**, DUMMY.
CARTER? CAN YOU **SEE** ANYTHING?
NO, IT'S **PITCH BLACK**. BUT I THINK...
...YEAH, I CAN **FEEL** SOMETHING....
I THINK IT'S—

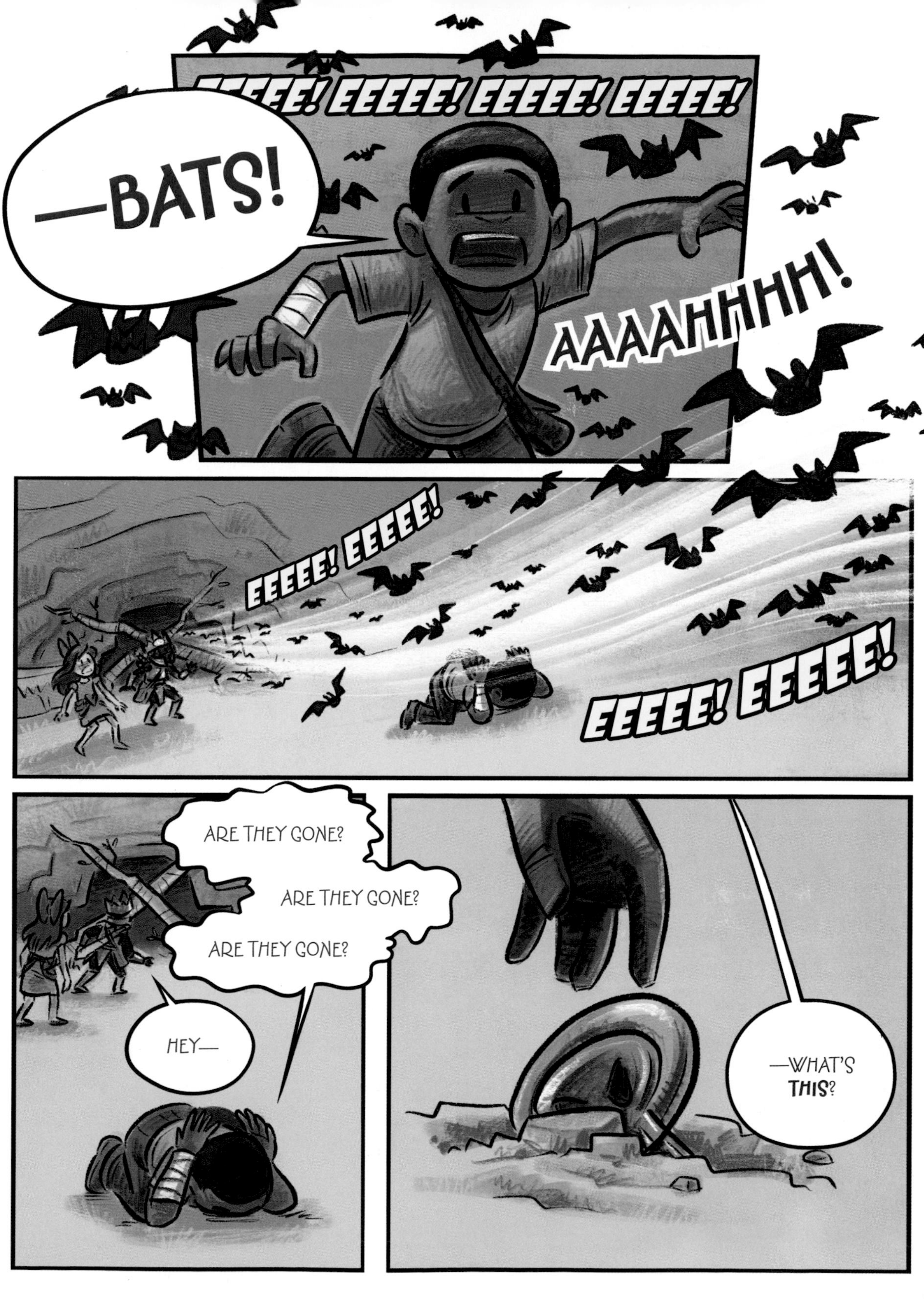
EEEEE! EEEEE! EEEEE! EEEEE!
—BATS!
AAAAHHHH!
EEEEE! EEEEE!
EEEEE! EEEEE!
ARE THEY GONE?
ARE THEY GONE?
ARE THEY GONE?
HEY—
—WHAT'S THIS?

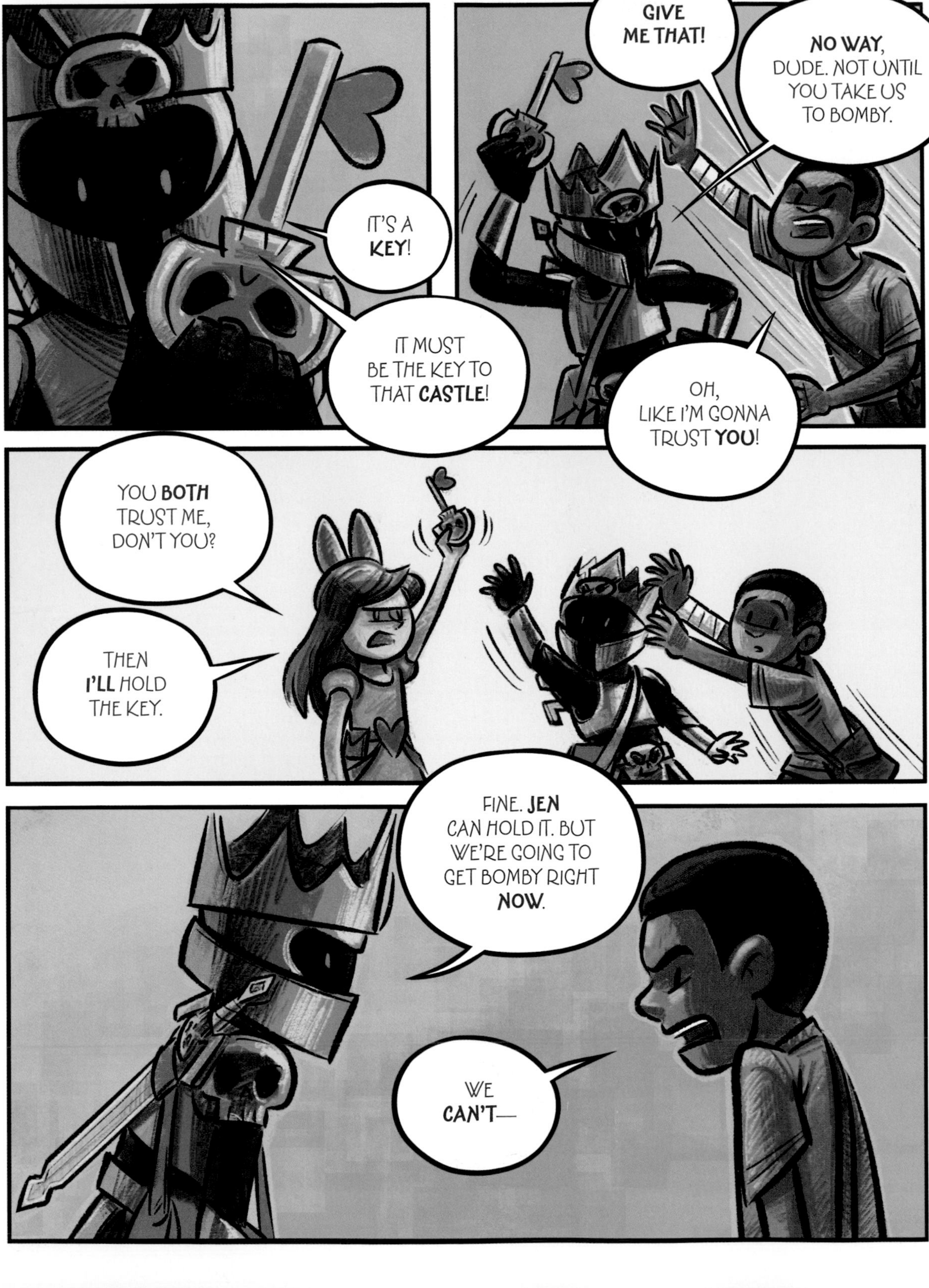
IT'S A **KEY**!
IT MUST BE THE KEY TO THAT **CASTLE**!
GIVE ME THAT!
NO WAY, DUDE. NOT UNTIL YOU TAKE US TO BOMBY.
OH, LIKE I'M GONNA TRUST **YOU**!
YOU **BOTH** TRUST ME, DON'T YOU?
THEN **I'LL** HOLD THE KEY.
FINE. **JEN** CAN HOLD IT. BUT WE'RE GOING TO GET BOMBY RIGHT **NOW**.
WE **CAN'T**—

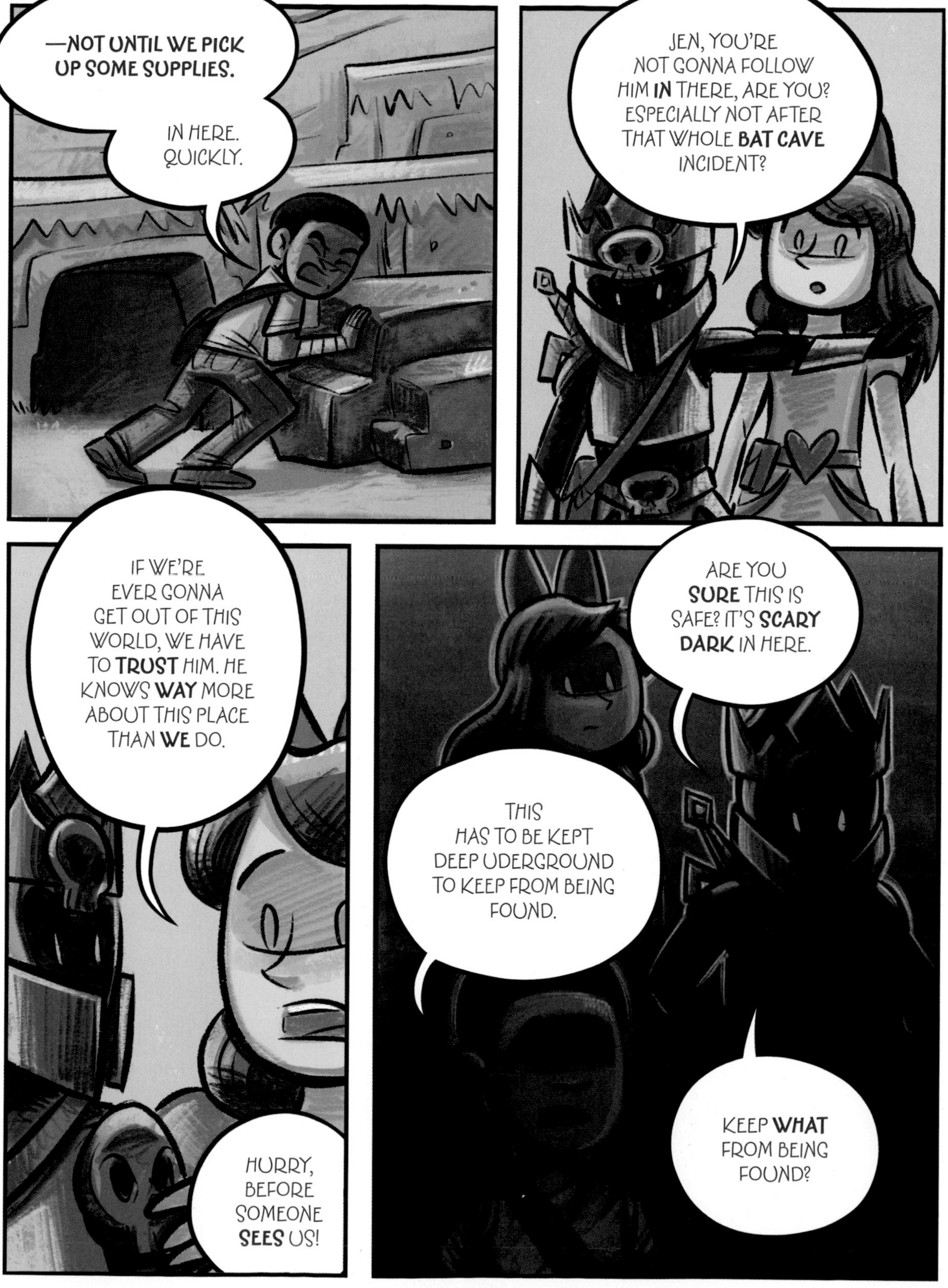
—NOT UNTIL WE PICK UP SOME SUPPLIES.
IN HERE. QUICKLY.
JEN, YOU'RE NOT GONNA FOLLOW HIM IN THERE, ARE YOU? ESPECIALLY NOT AFTER THAT WHOLE BAT CAVE INCIDENT?
IF WE'RE EVER GONNA GET OUT OF THIS WORLD, WE HAVE TO TRUST HIM. HE KNOWS WAY MORE ABOUT THIS PLACE THAN WE DO.
HURRY, BEFORE SOMEONE SEES US!
ARE YOU SURE THIS IS SAFE? IT'S SCARY DARK IN HERE.
THIS HAS TO BE KEPT DEEP UDERGROUND TO KEEP FROM BEING FOUND.
KEEP WHAT FROM BEING FOUND?

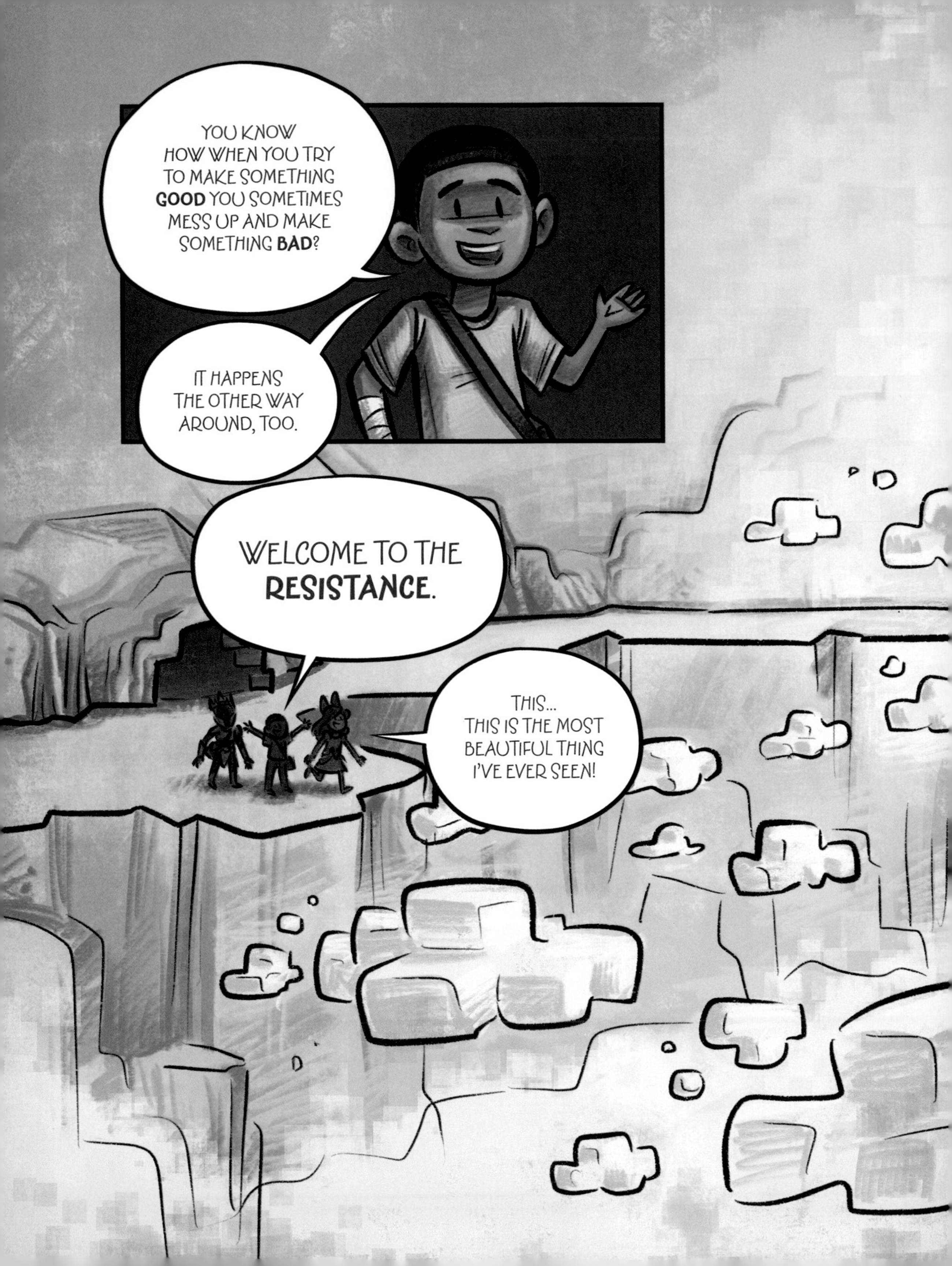
YOU KNOW HOW WHEN YOU TRY TO MAKE SOMETHING **GOOD** YOU SOMETIMES MESS UP AND MAKE SOMETHING **BAD**?
IT HAPPENS THE OTHER WAY AROUND, TOO.
WELCOME TO THE **RESISTANCE**.
THIS... THIS IS THE MOST BEAUTIFUL THING I'VE EVER SEEN!

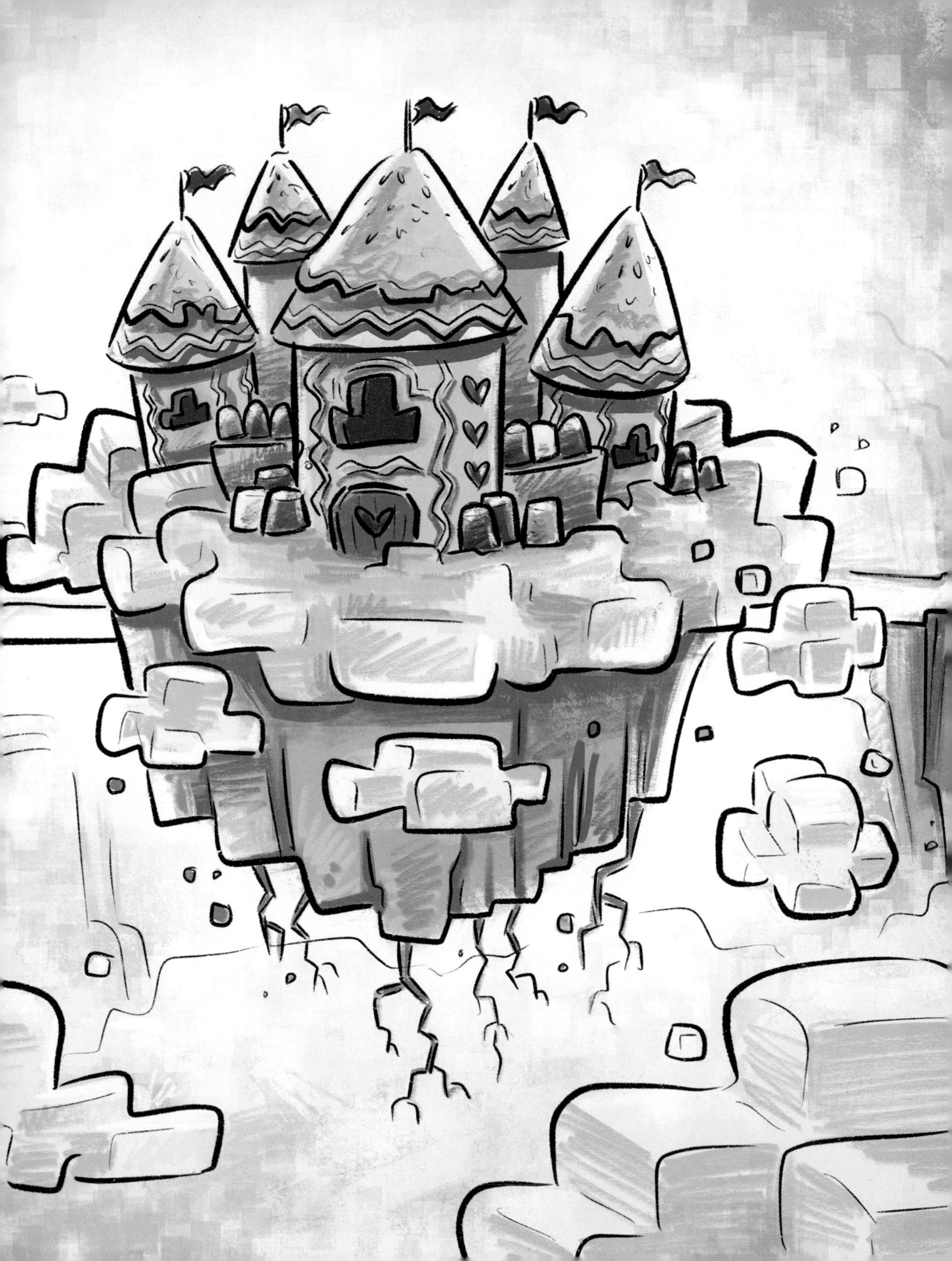

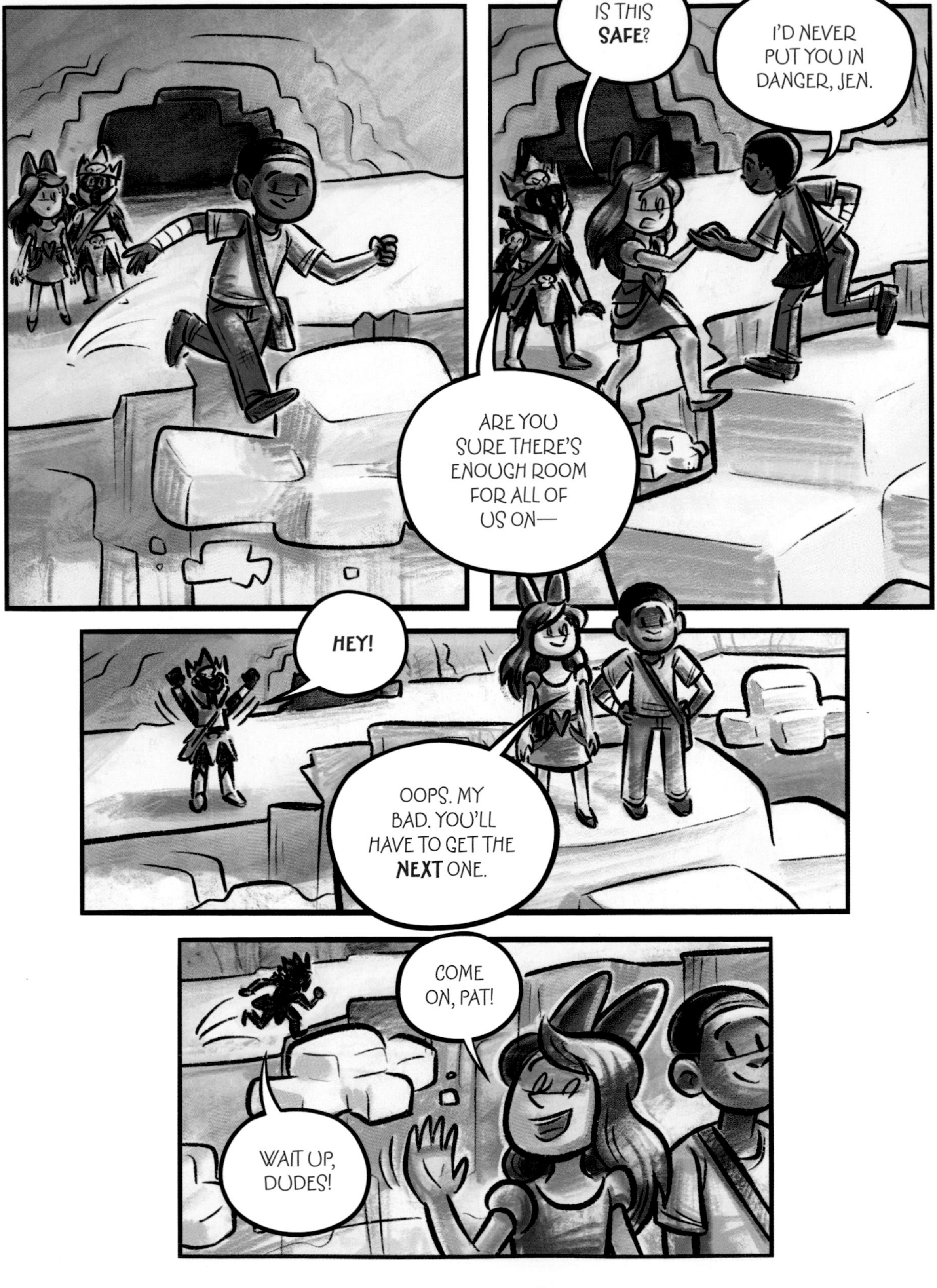
IS THIS **SAFE**?
I'D NEVER PUT YOU IN DANGER, JEN.
ARE YOU SURE THERE'S ENOUGH ROOM FOR ALL OF US ON—
HEY!
OOPS. MY BAD. YOU'LL HAVE TO GET THE **NEXT** ONE.
COME ON, PAT!
WAIT UP, DUDES!

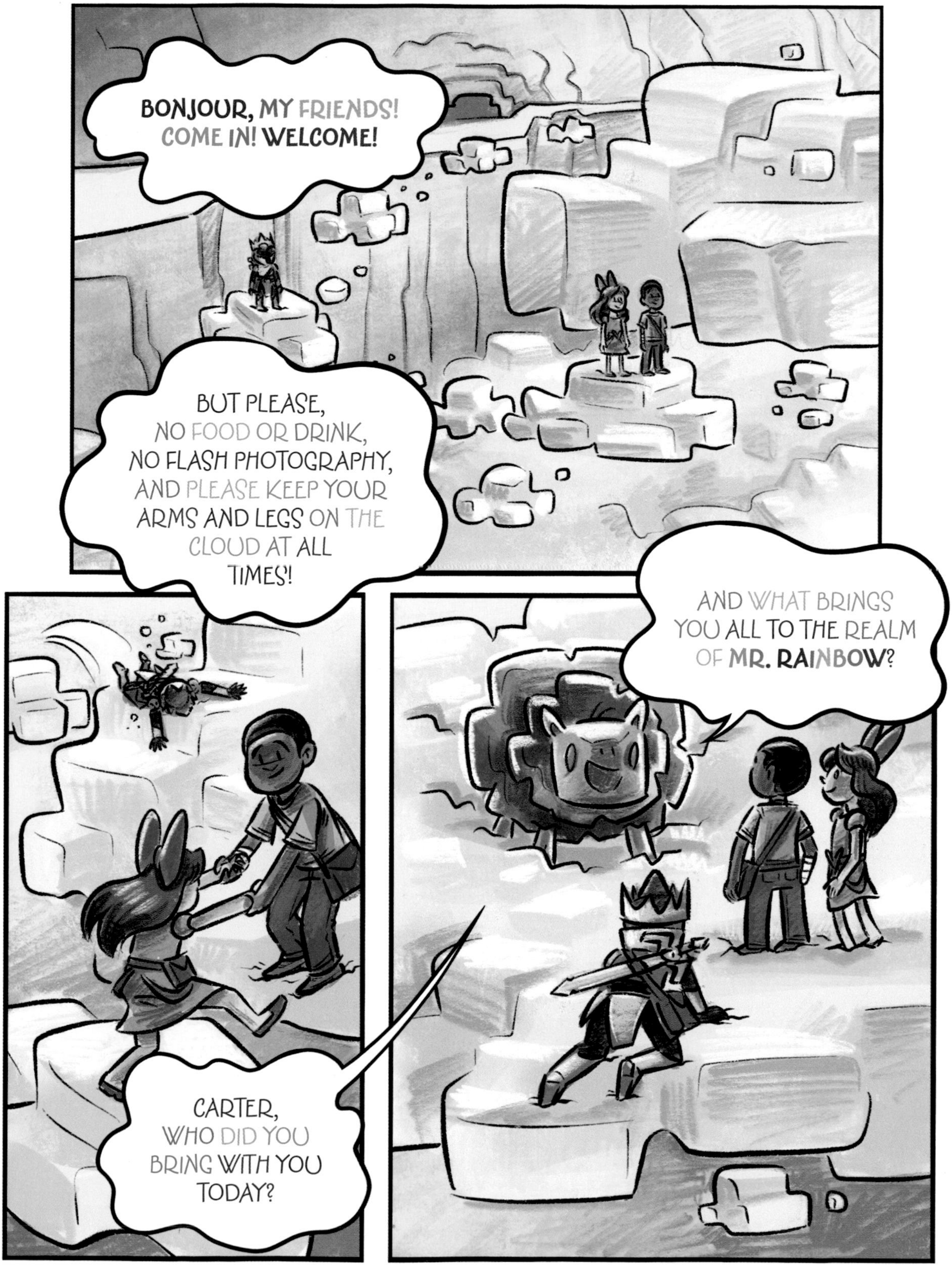
BONJOUR, MY FRIENDS! COME IN! WELCOME!
BUT PLEASE, NO FOOD OR DRINK, NO FLASH PHOTOGRAPHY, AND PLEASE KEEP YOUR ARMS AND LEGS ON THE CLOUD AT ALL TIMES!
CARTER, WHO DID YOU BRING WITH YOU TODAY?
AND WHAT BRINGS YOU ALL TO THE REALM OF MR. RAINBOW?

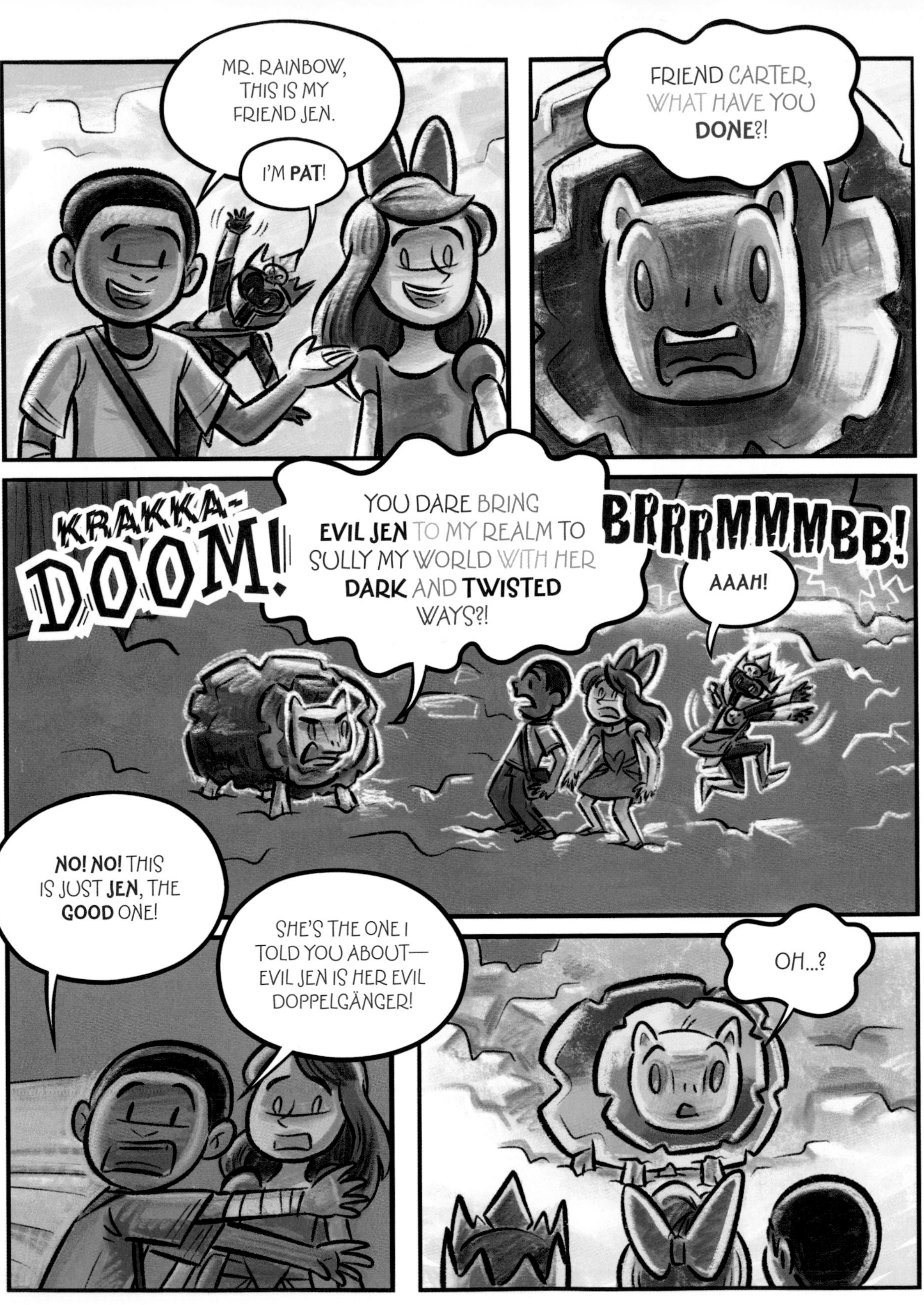
MR. RAINBOW, THIS IS MY FRIEND JEN.
I'M **PAT**!
FRIEND CARTER, WHAT HAVE YOU **DONE**?!
KRAKKA-DOOM!
YOU DARE BRING **EVIL JEN** TO MY REALM TO SULLY MY WORLD WITH HER **DARK** AND **TWISTED** WAYS?!
BRRRMMMBB!
AAAH!
NO! NO! THIS IS JUST **JEN**, THE **GOOD** ONE!
SHE'S THE ONE I TOLD YOU ABOUT— EVIL JEN IS HER EVIL DOPPELGÄNGER!
OH...?

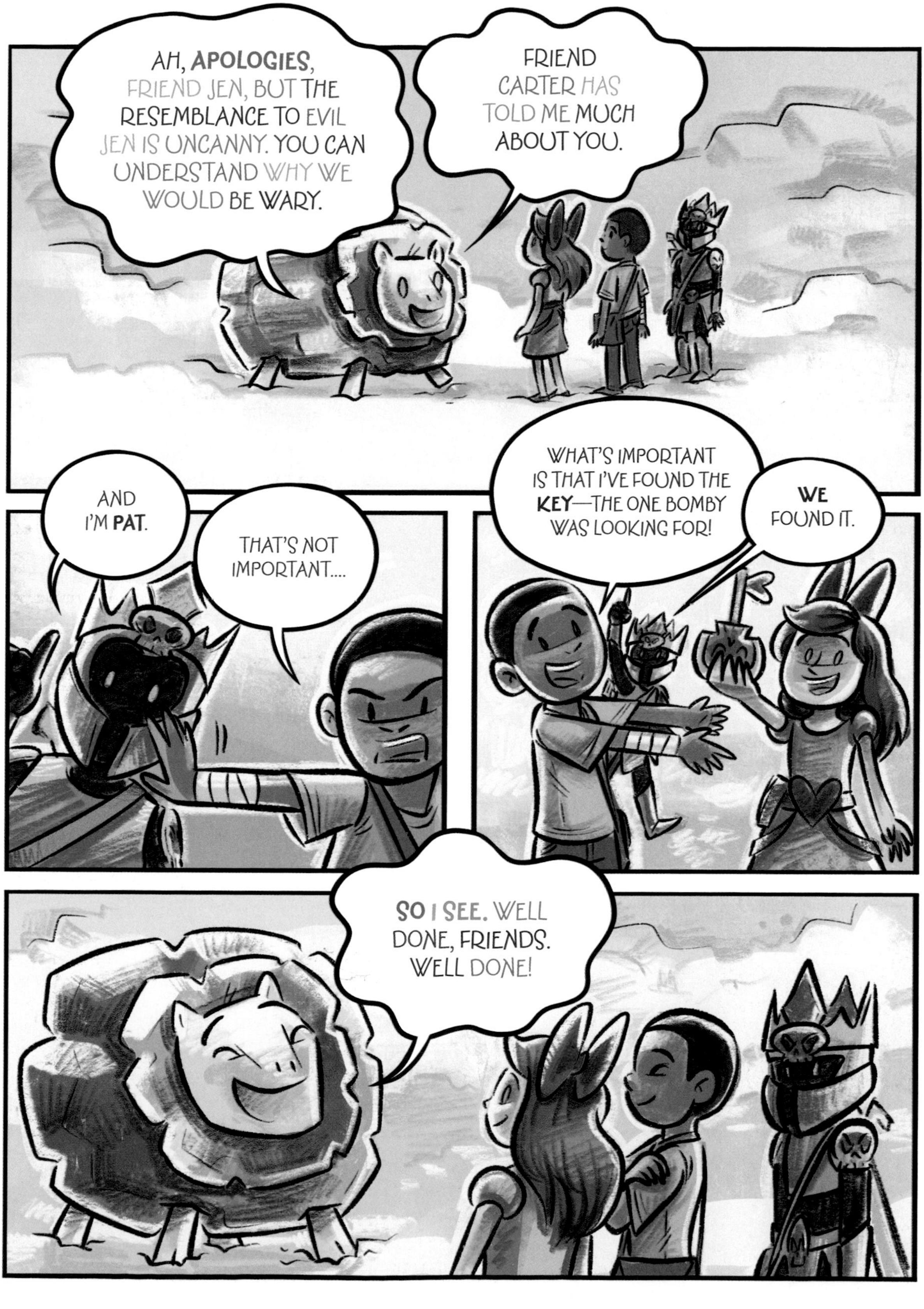

AH, APOLOGIES, FRIEND JEN, BUT THE RESEMBLANCE TO EVIL JEN IS UNCANNY. YOU CAN UNDERSTAND WHY WE WOULD BE WARY.
FRIEND CARTER HAS TOLD ME MUCH ABOUT YOU.
AND I'M PAT.
THAT'S NOT IMPORTANT....
WHAT'S IMPORTANT IS THAT I'VE FOUND THE KEY—THE ONE BOMBY WAS LOOKING FOR!
WE FOUND IT.
SO I SEE. WELL DONE, FRIENDS. WELL DONE!

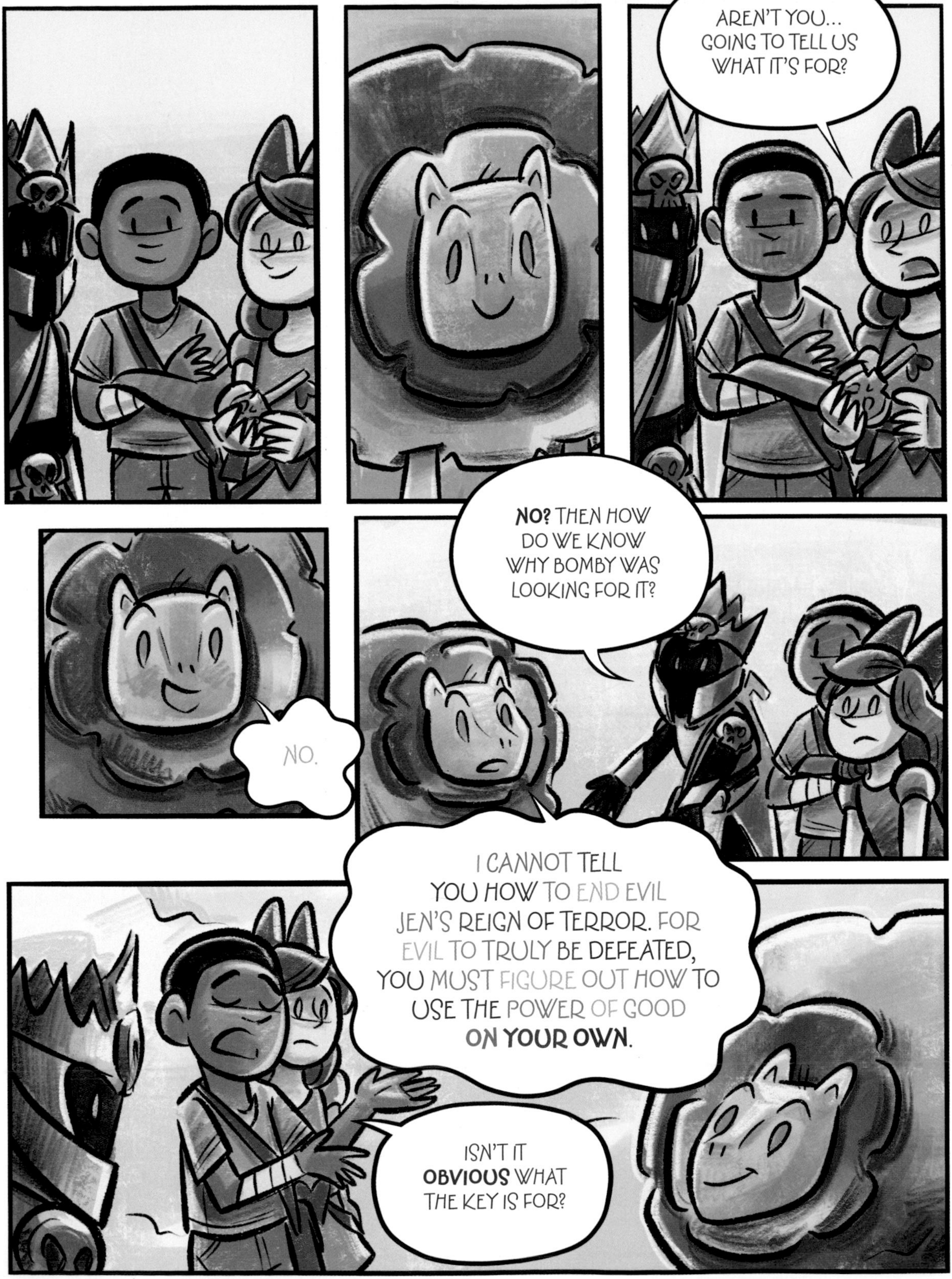
AREN'T YOU... GOING TO TELL US WHAT IT'S FOR?
NO.
NO? THEN HOW DO WE KNOW WHY BOMBY WAS LOOKING FOR IT?
I CANNOT TELL YOU HOW TO END EVIL JEN'S REIGN OF TERROR. FOR EVIL TO TRULY BE DEFEATED, YOU MUST FIGURE OUT HOW TO USE THE POWER OF GOOD **ON YOUR OWN**.
ISN'T IT **OBVIOUS** WHAT THE KEY IS FOR?

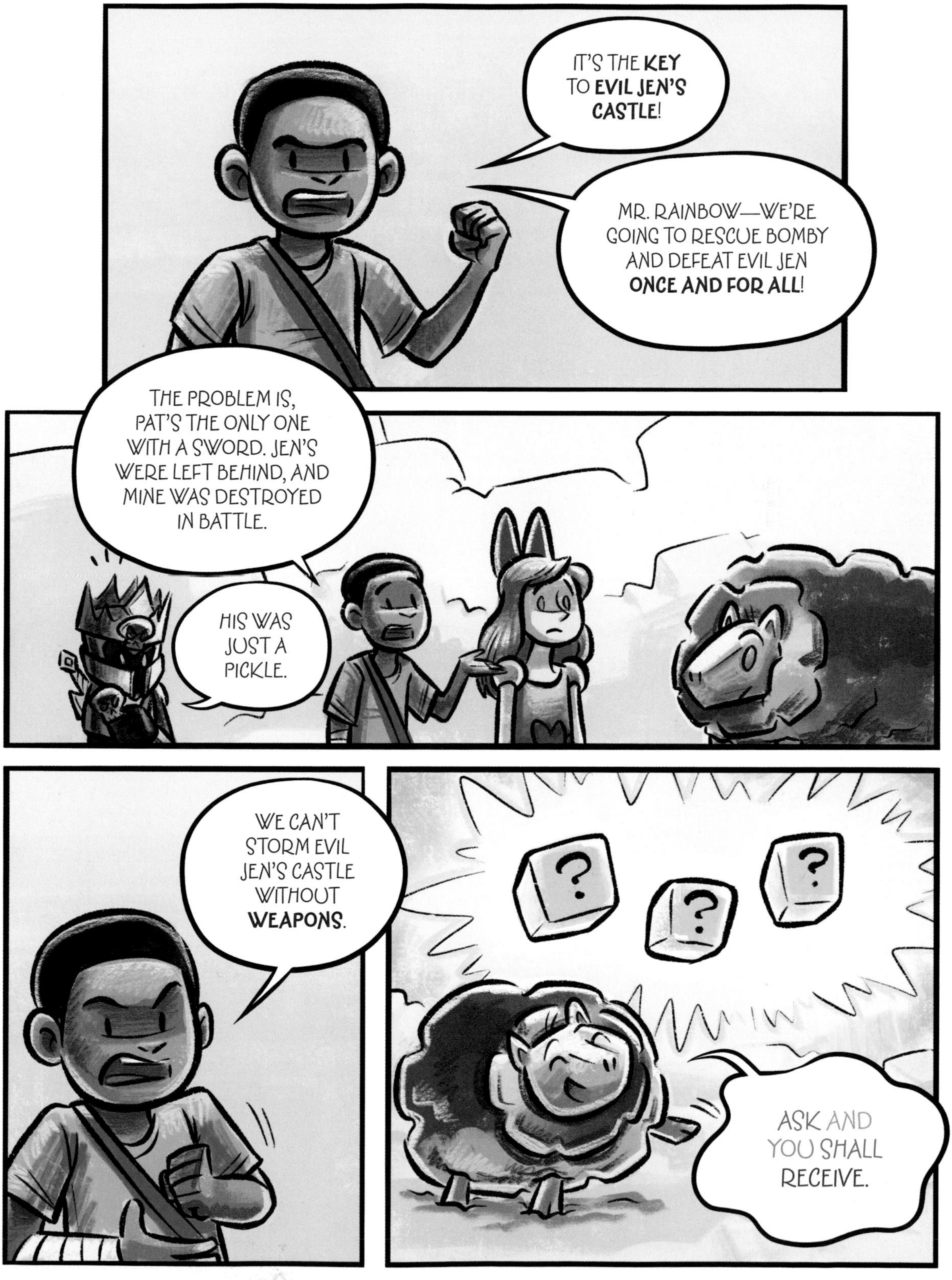
IT'S THE **KEY** TO **EVIL JEN'S CASTLE**!
MR. RAINBOW—WE'RE GOING TO RESCUE BOMBY AND DEFEAT EVIL JEN **ONCE AND FOR ALL**!
THE PROBLEM IS, PAT'S THE ONLY ONE WITH A SWORD. JEN'S WERE LEFT BEHIND, AND MINE WAS DESTROYED IN BATTLE.
HIS WAS JUST A PICKLE.
WE CAN'T STORM EVIL JEN'S CASTLE WITHOUT **WEAPONS**.
?
?
?
ASK AND YOU SHALL RECEIVE.

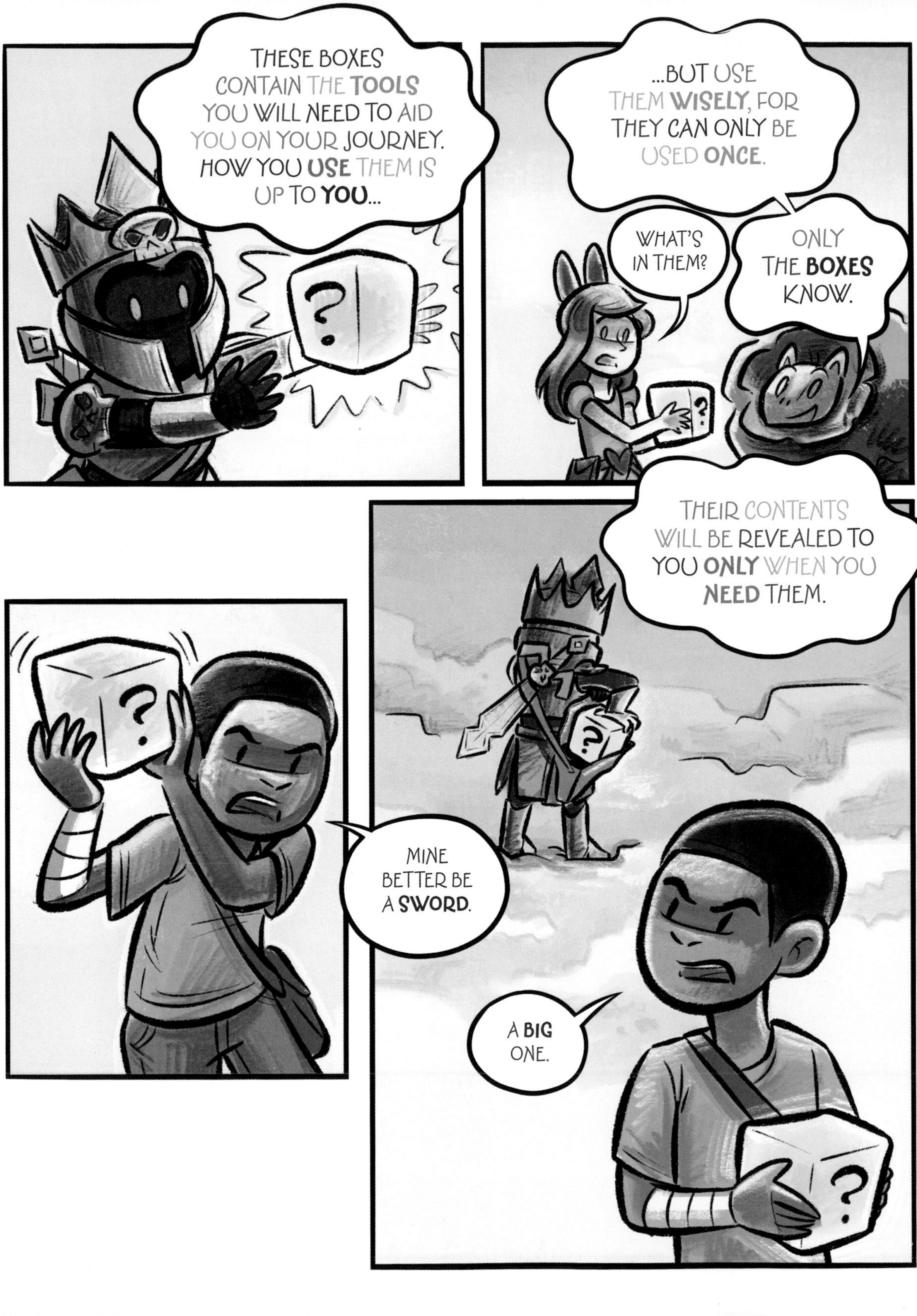
THESE BOXES CONTAIN THE TOOLS YOU WILL NEED TO AID YOU ON YOUR JOURNEY. HOW YOU USE THEM IS UP TO YOU...
...BUT USE THEM WISELY, FOR THEY CAN ONLY BE USED ONCE.
WHAT'S IN THEM?
ONLY THE BOXES KNOW.
THEIR CONTENTS WILL BE REVEALED TO YOU ONLY WHEN YOU NEED THEM.
MINE BETTER BE A SWORD.
A BIG ONE.

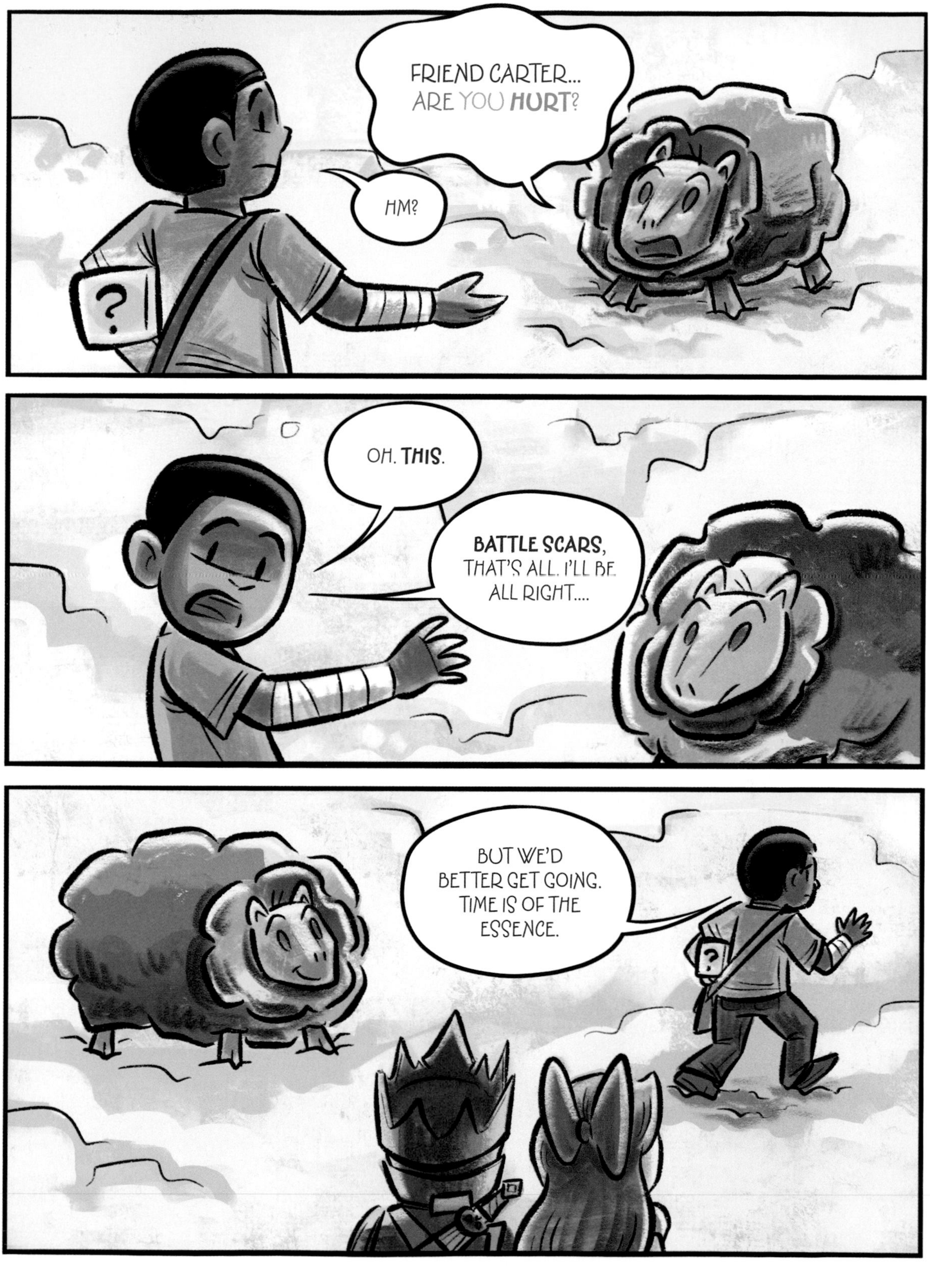
FRIEND CARTER... ARE YOU HURT?
HM?
OH. THIS.
BATTLE SCARS, THAT'S ALL. I'LL BE ALL RIGHT....
BUT WE'D BETTER GET GOING. TIME IS OF THE ESSENCE.

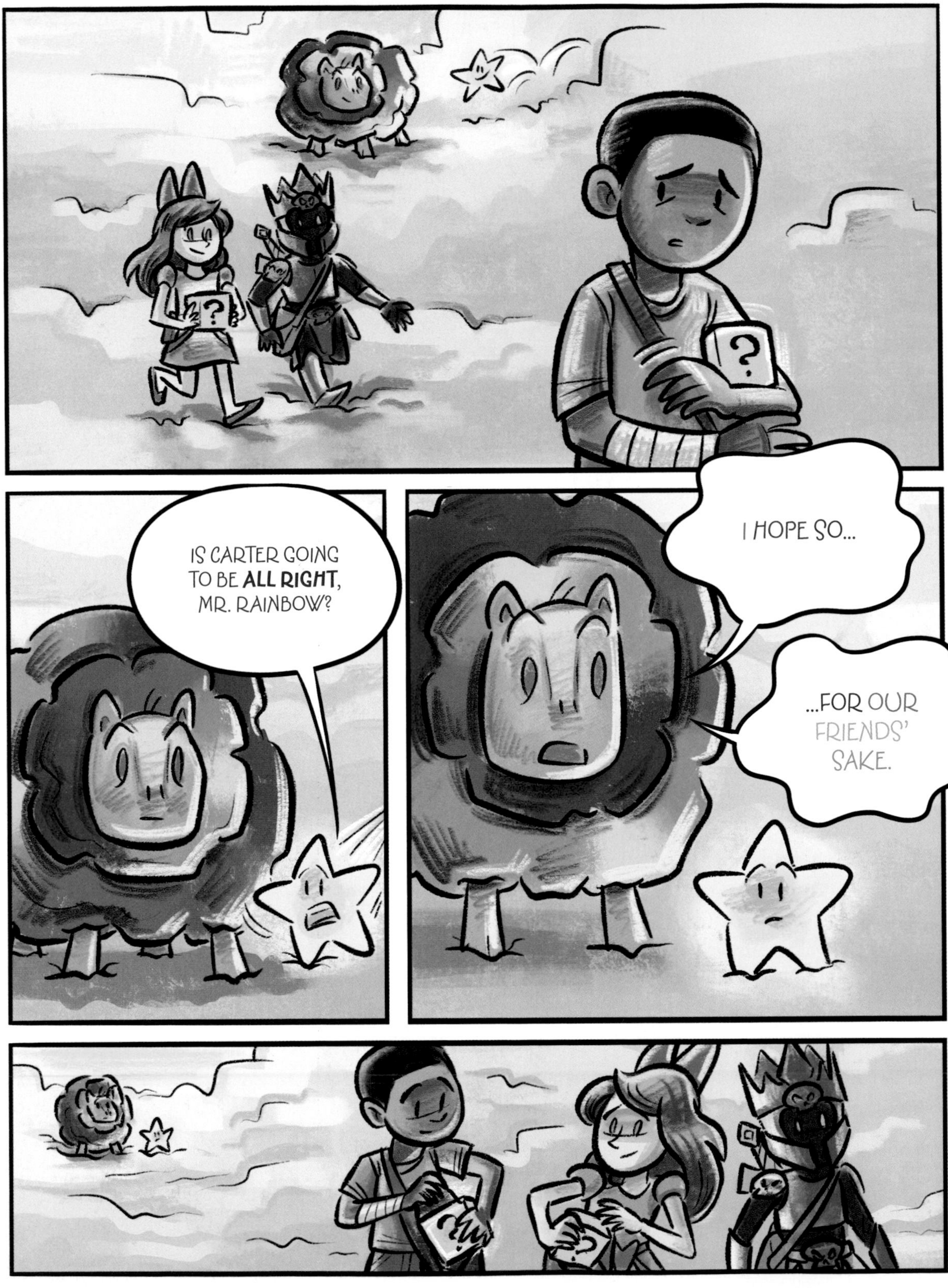
IS CARTER GOING TO BE ALL RIGHT, MR. RAINBOW?
I HOPE SO...
...FOR OUR FRIENDS' SAKE.

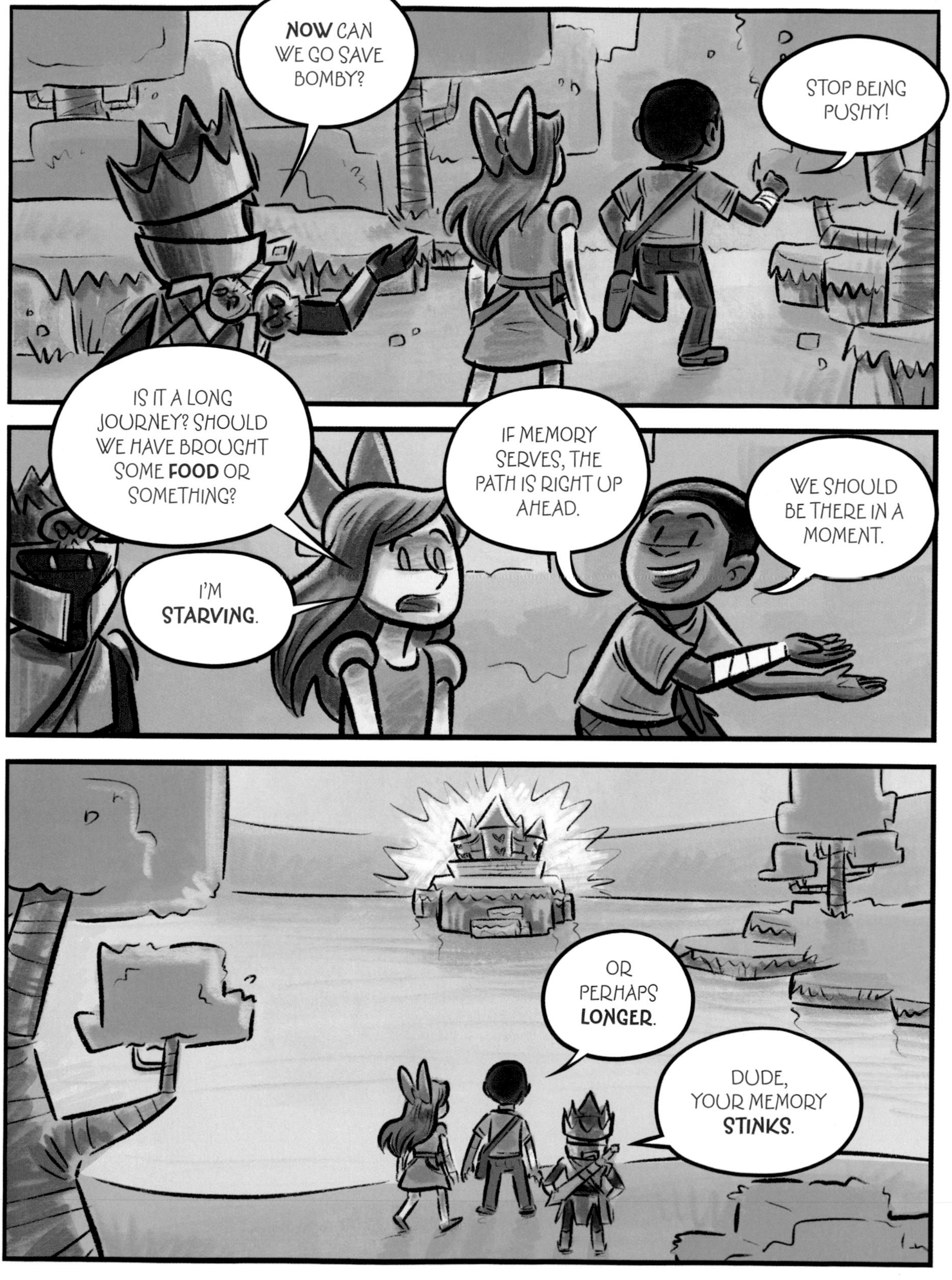
NOW CAN WE GO SAVE BOMBY?
STOP BEING PUSHY!
IS IT A LONG JOURNEY? SHOULD WE HAVE BROUGHT SOME FOOD OR SOMETHING?
I'M STARVING.
IF MEMORY SERVES, THE PATH IS RIGHT UP AHEAD.
WE SHOULD BE THERE IN A MOMENT.
OR PERHAPS LONGER.
DUDE, YOUR MEMORY STINKS.

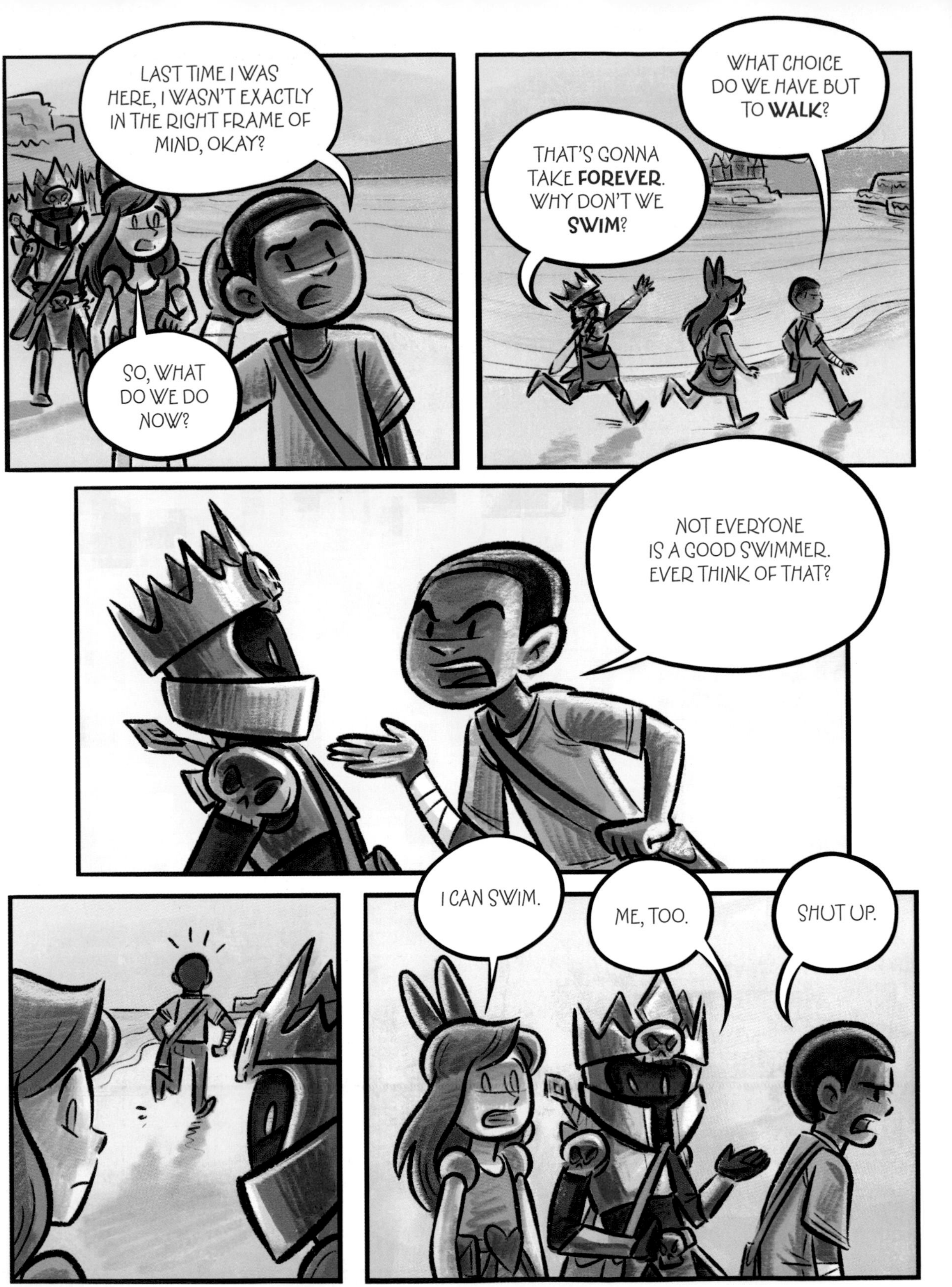
LAST TIME I WAS HERE, I WASN'T EXACTLY IN THE RIGHT FRAME OF MIND, OKAY?
SO, WHAT DO WE DO NOW?
THAT'S GONNA TAKE **FOREVER**. WHY DON'T WE **SWIM**?
WHAT CHOICE DO WE HAVE BUT TO **WALK**?
NOT EVERYONE IS A GOOD SWIMMER. EVER THINK OF THAT?
I CAN SWIM.
ME, TOO.
SHUT UP.

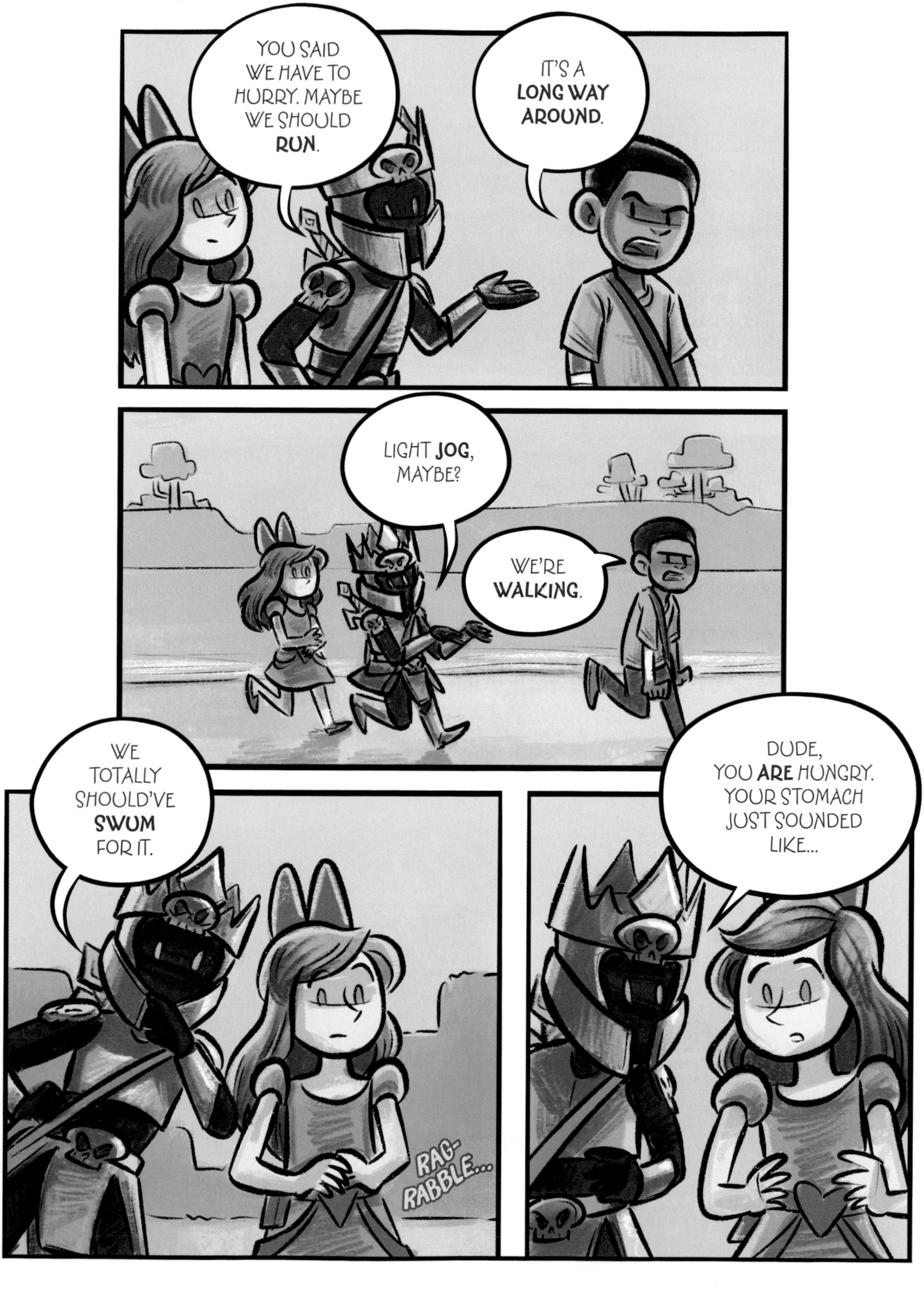
YOU SAID WE HAVE TO HURRY. MAYBE WE SHOULD **RUN**.
IT'S A **LONG WAY AROUND**.
LIGHT **JOG**, MAYBE?
WE'RE **WALKING**.
WE TOTALLY SHOULD'VE **SWUM** FOR IT.
RAG-RABBLE...
DUDE, YOU **ARE** HUNGRY. YOUR STOMACH JUST SOUNDED LIKE...

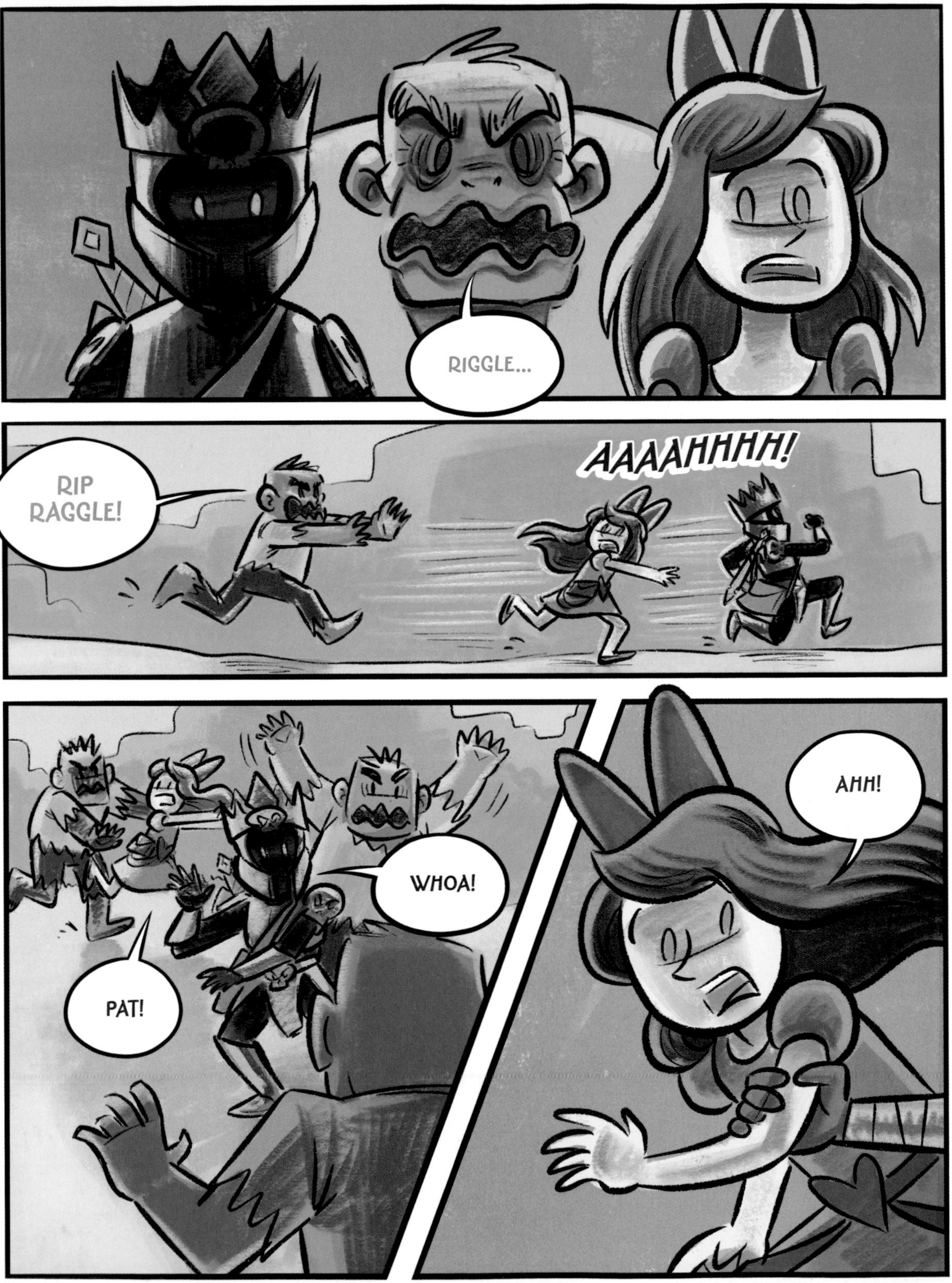
RIGGLE...
RIP RAGGLE!
AAAAHHHH!
WHOA!
PAT!
AHH!

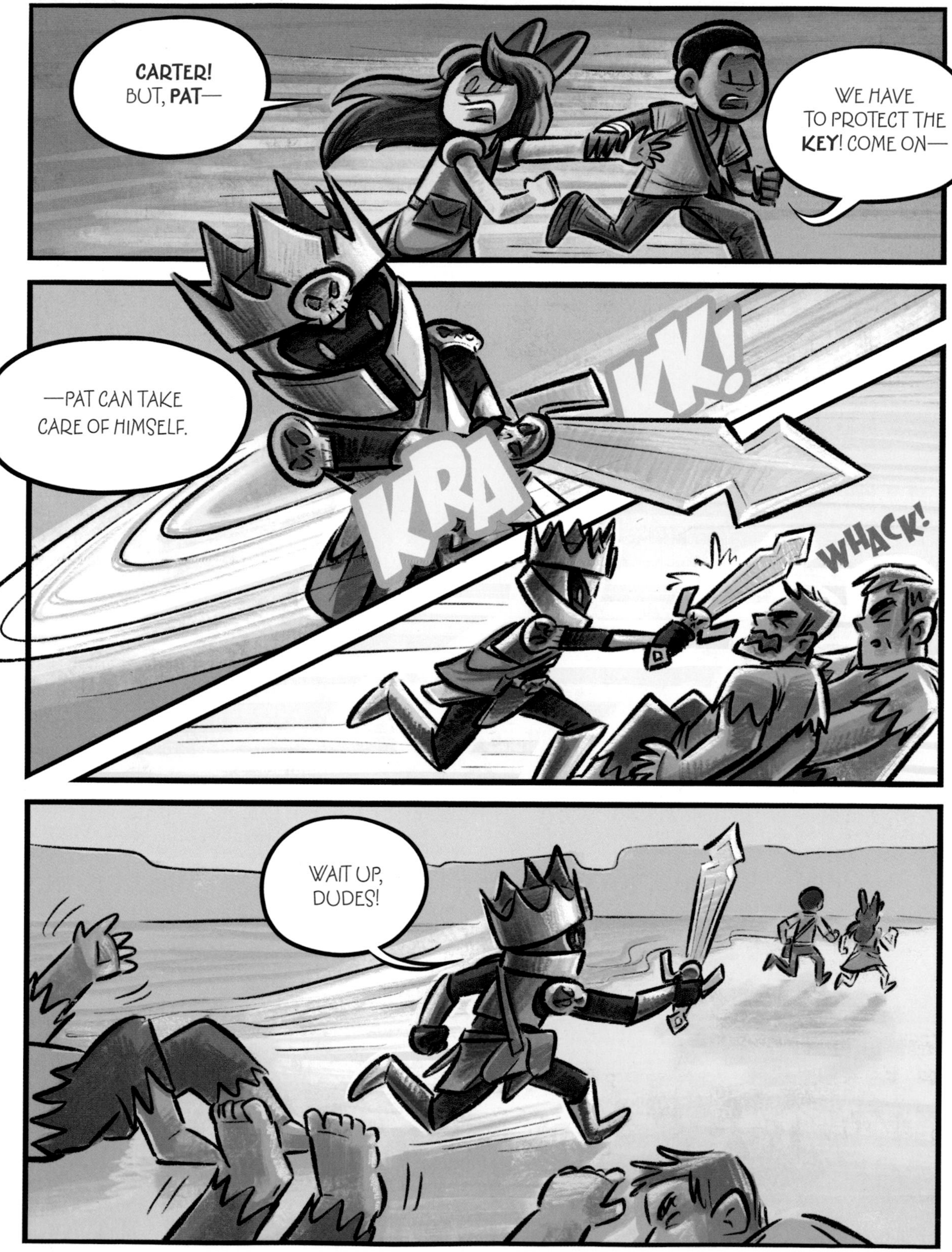
CARTER! BUT, PAT—
WE HAVE TO PROTECT THE KEY! COME ON—
—PAT CAN TAKE CARE OF HIMSELF.
KRAKK!
WHACK!
WAIT UP, DUDES!

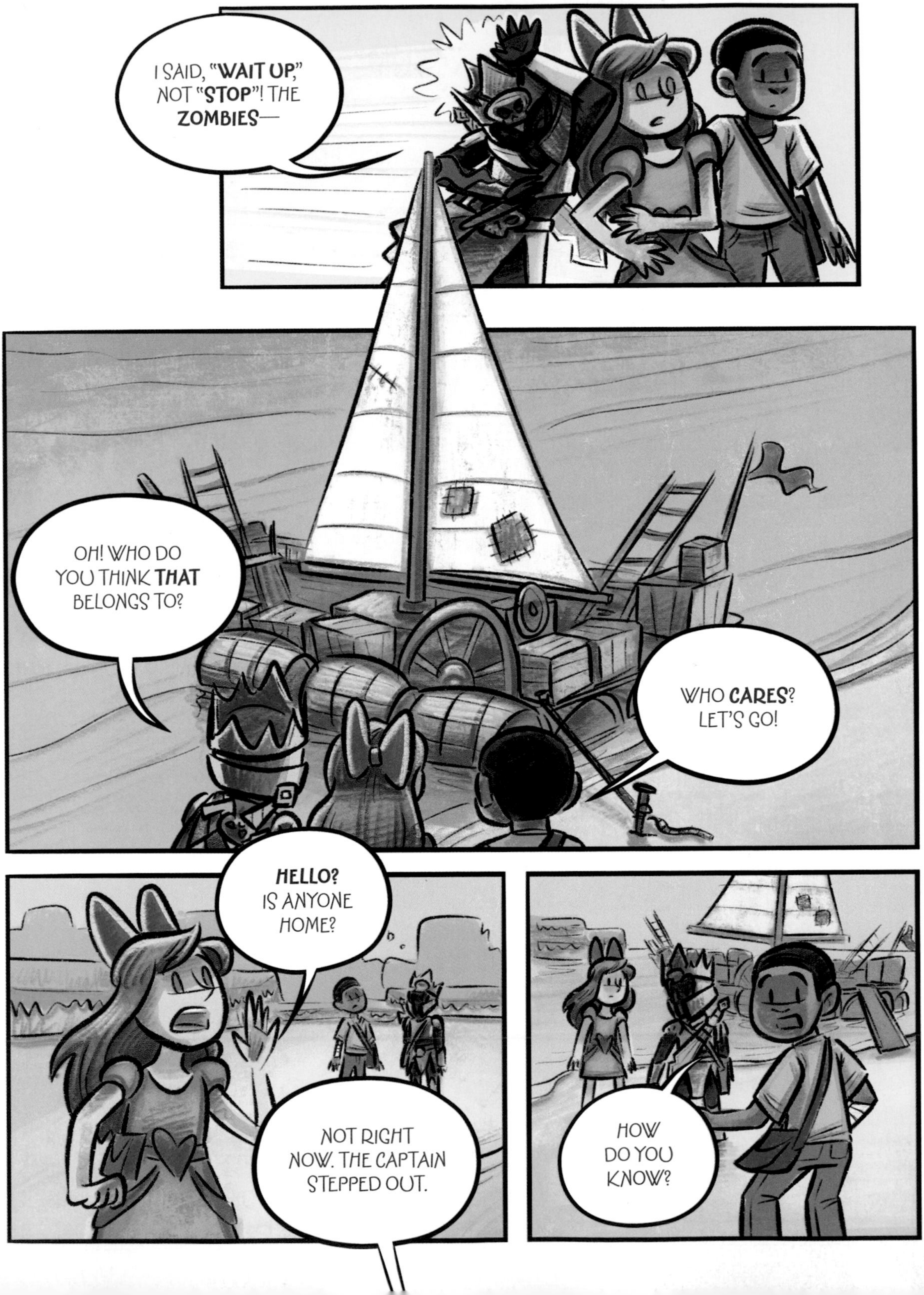
I SAID, "WAIT UP," NOT "STOP"! THE ZOMBIES—
OH! WHO DO YOU THINK THAT BELONGS TO?
WHO CARES? LET'S GO!
HELLO? IS ANYONE HOME?
NOT RIGHT NOW. THE CAPTAIN STEPPED OUT.
HOW DO YOU KNOW?

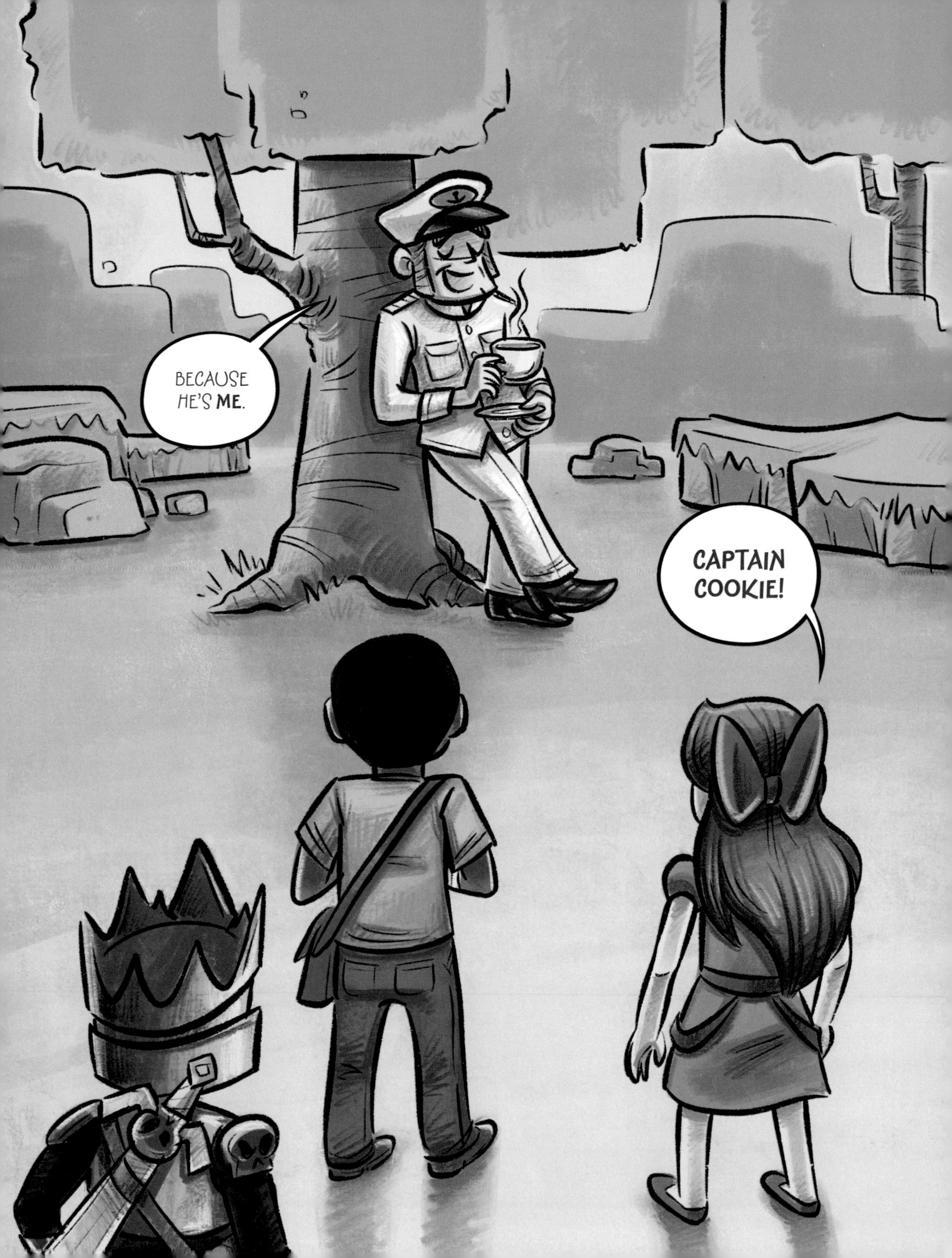
BECAUSE HE'S **ME**.
CAPTAIN COOKIE!

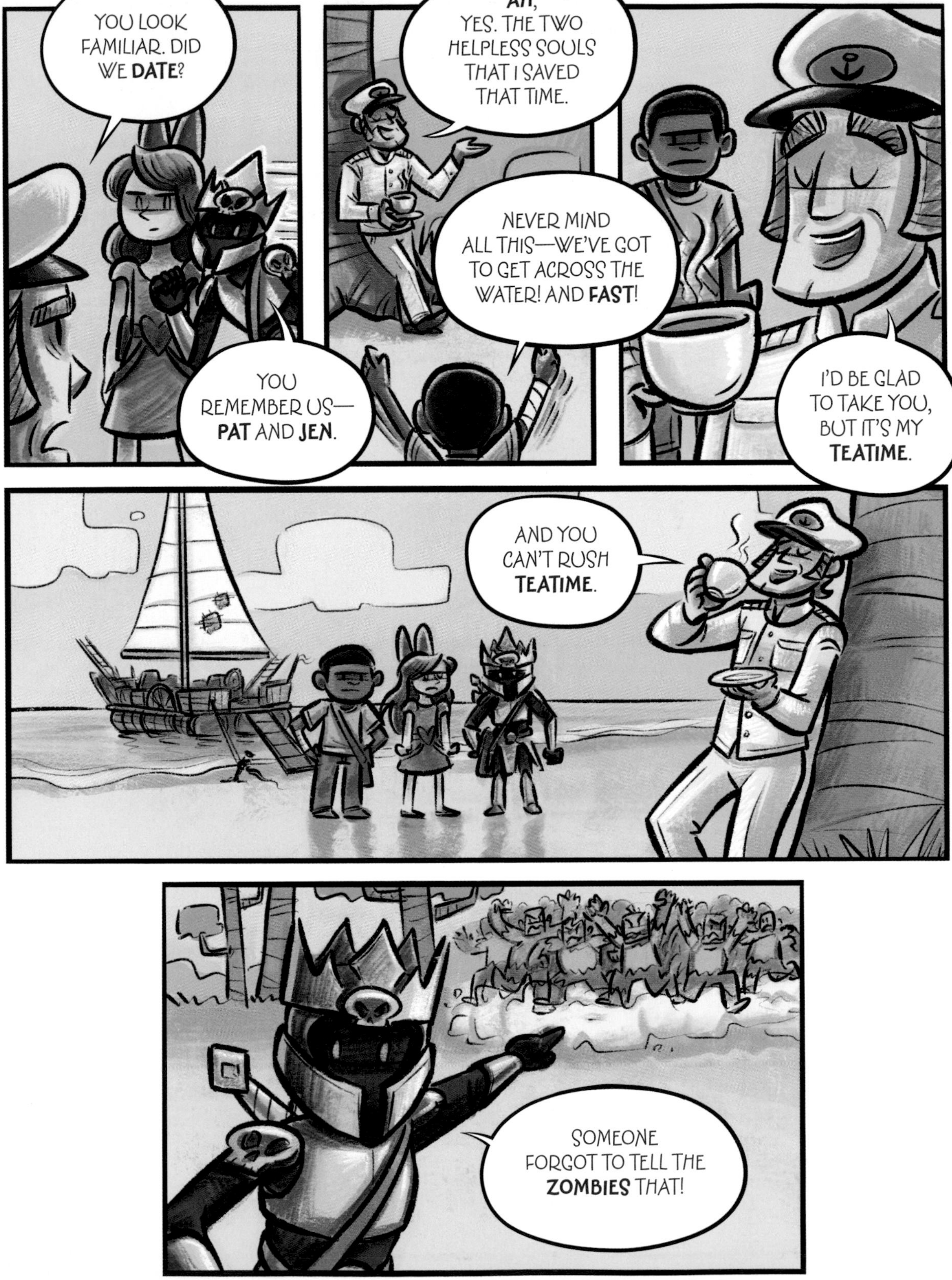
YOU LOOK FAMILIAR. DID WE **DATE**?
AH, YES. THE TWO HELPLESS SOULS THAT I SAVED THAT TIME.
YOU REMEMBER US—**PAT** AND **JEN**.
NEVER MIND ALL THIS—WE'VE GOT TO GET ACROSS THE WATER! AND **FAST**!
I'D BE GLAD TO TAKE YOU, BUT IT'S MY **TEATIME**.
AND YOU CAN'T RUSH **TEATIME**.
SOMEONE FORGOT TO TELL THE **ZOMBIES** THAT!

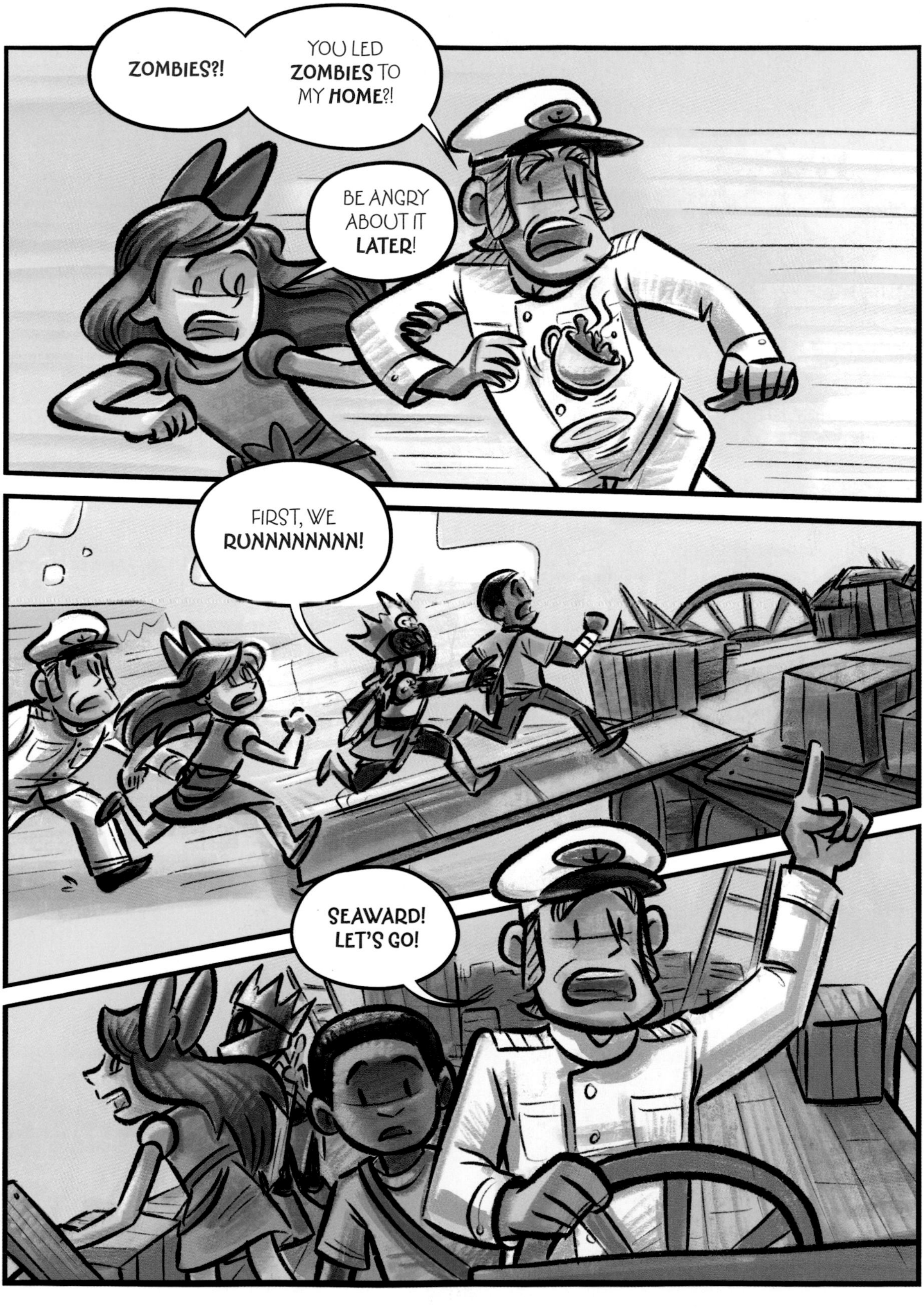
ZOMBIES?!
YOU LED ZOMBIES TO MY HOME?!
BE ANGRY ABOUT IT LATER!
FIRST, WE RUNNNNNNNN!
SEAWARD! LET'S GO!

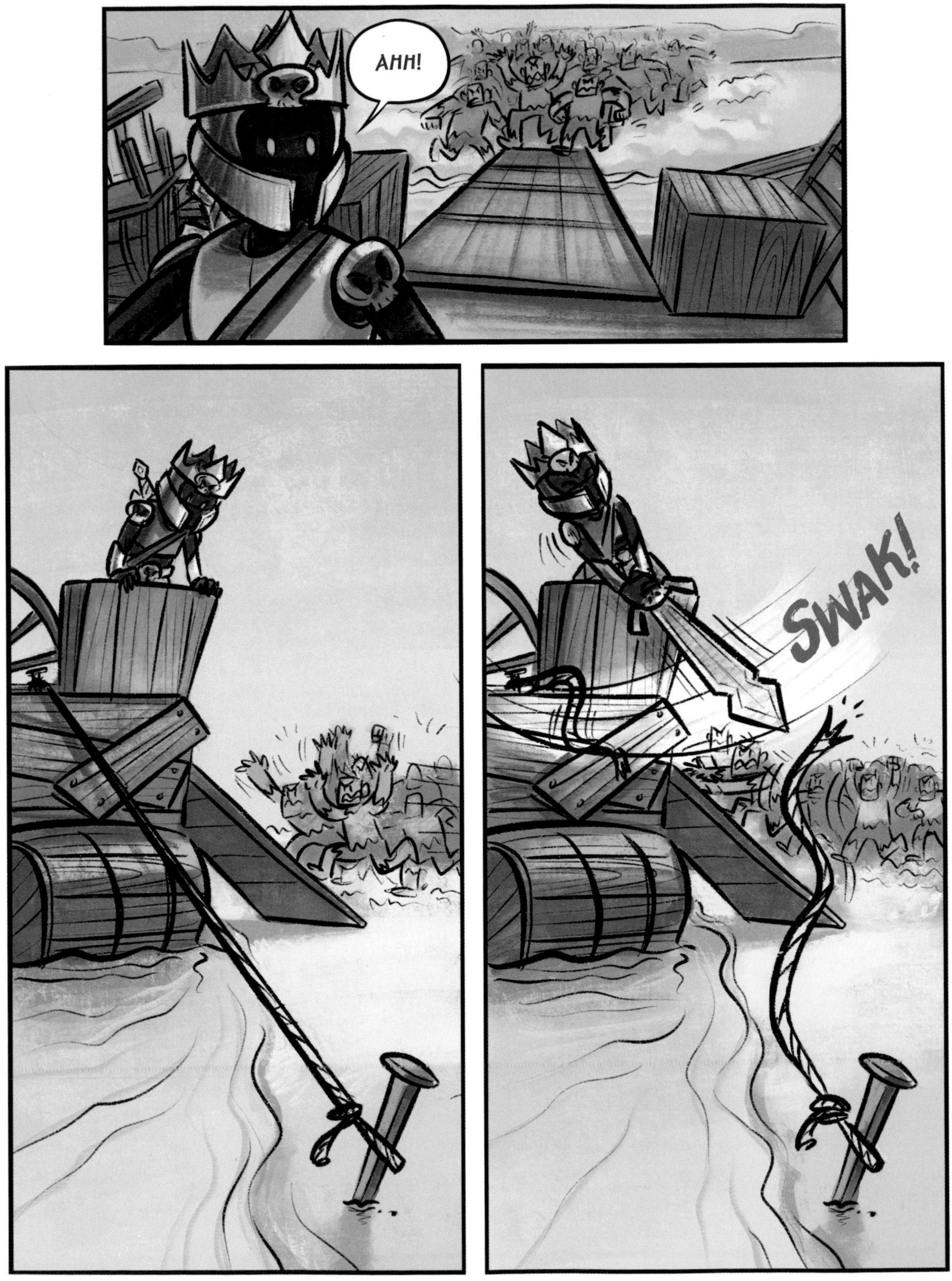
AHH!
SWAK!

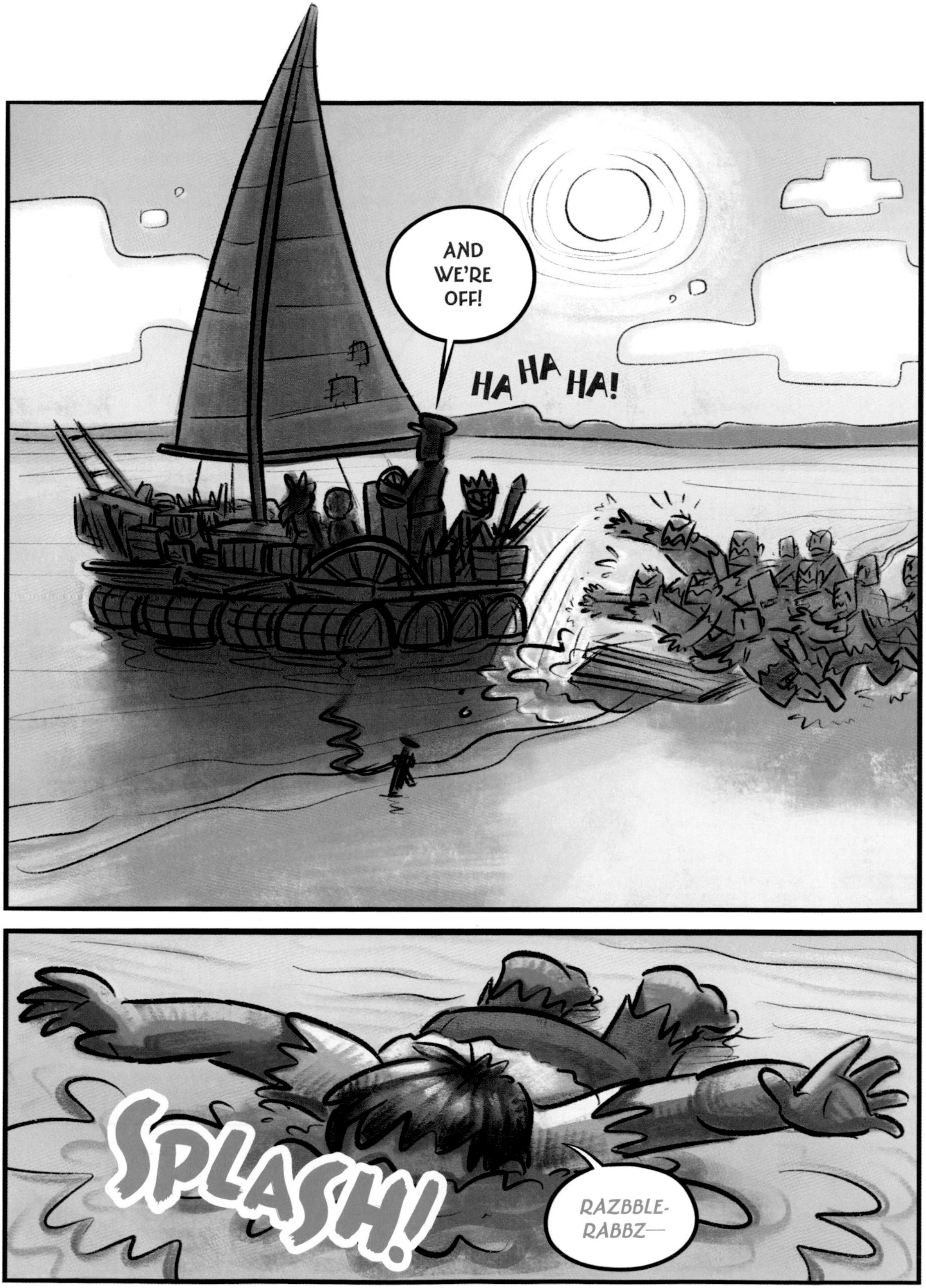
AND WE'RE OFF!
HA HA HA!
SPLASH!
RAZBBLE-RABBZ—

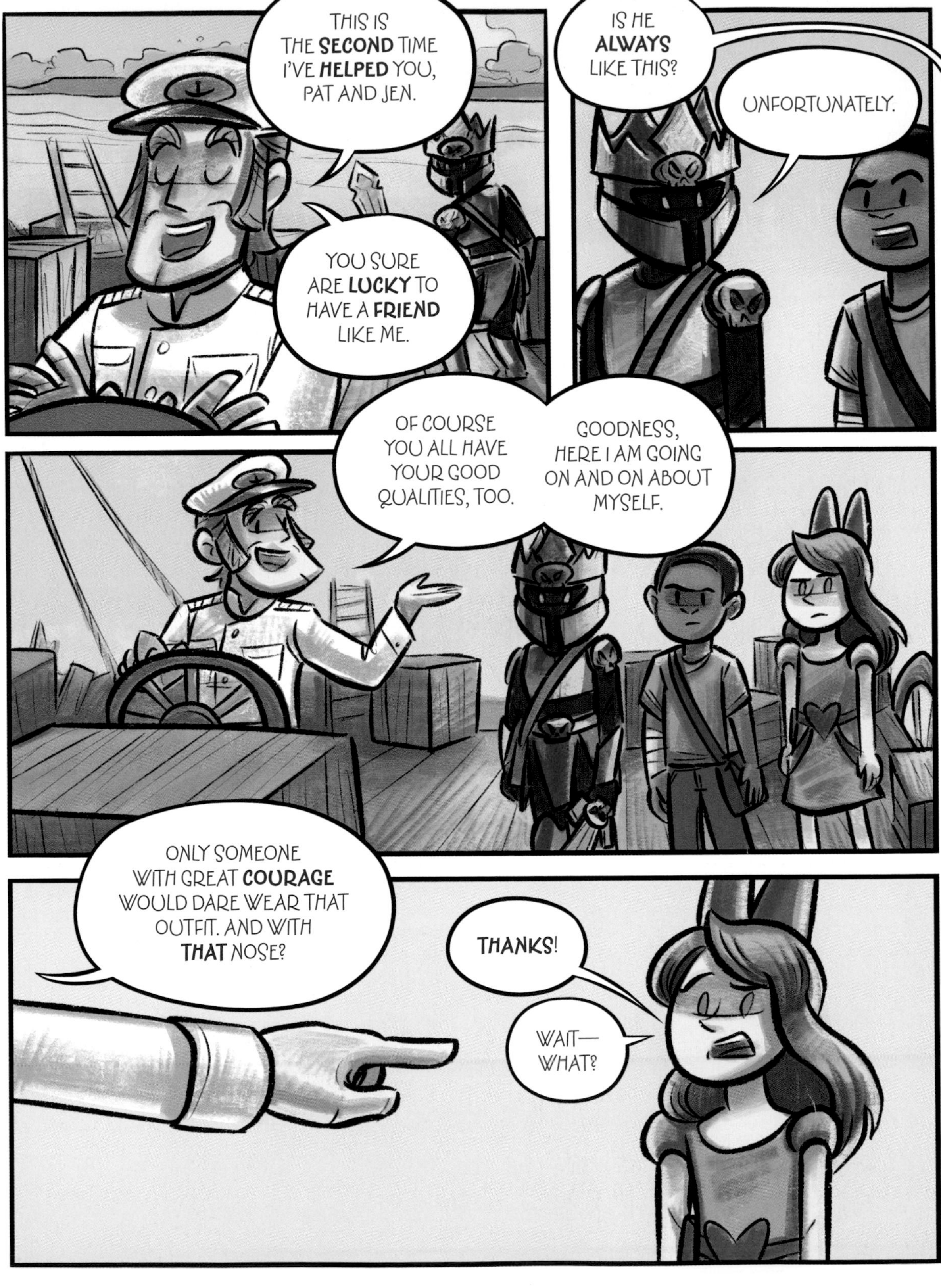
THIS IS THE **SECOND** TIME I'VE **HELPED** YOU, PAT AND JEN.
YOU SURE ARE **LUCKY** TO HAVE A **FRIEND** LIKE ME.
IS HE **ALWAYS** LIKE THIS?
UNFORTUNATELY.
OF COURSE YOU ALL HAVE YOUR GOOD QUALITIES, TOO.
GOODNESS, HERE I AM GOING ON AND ON ABOUT MYSELF.
ONLY SOMEONE WITH GREAT **COURAGE** WOULD DARE WEAR THAT OUTFIT. AND WITH **THAT** NOSE?
THANKS!
WAIT— WHAT?

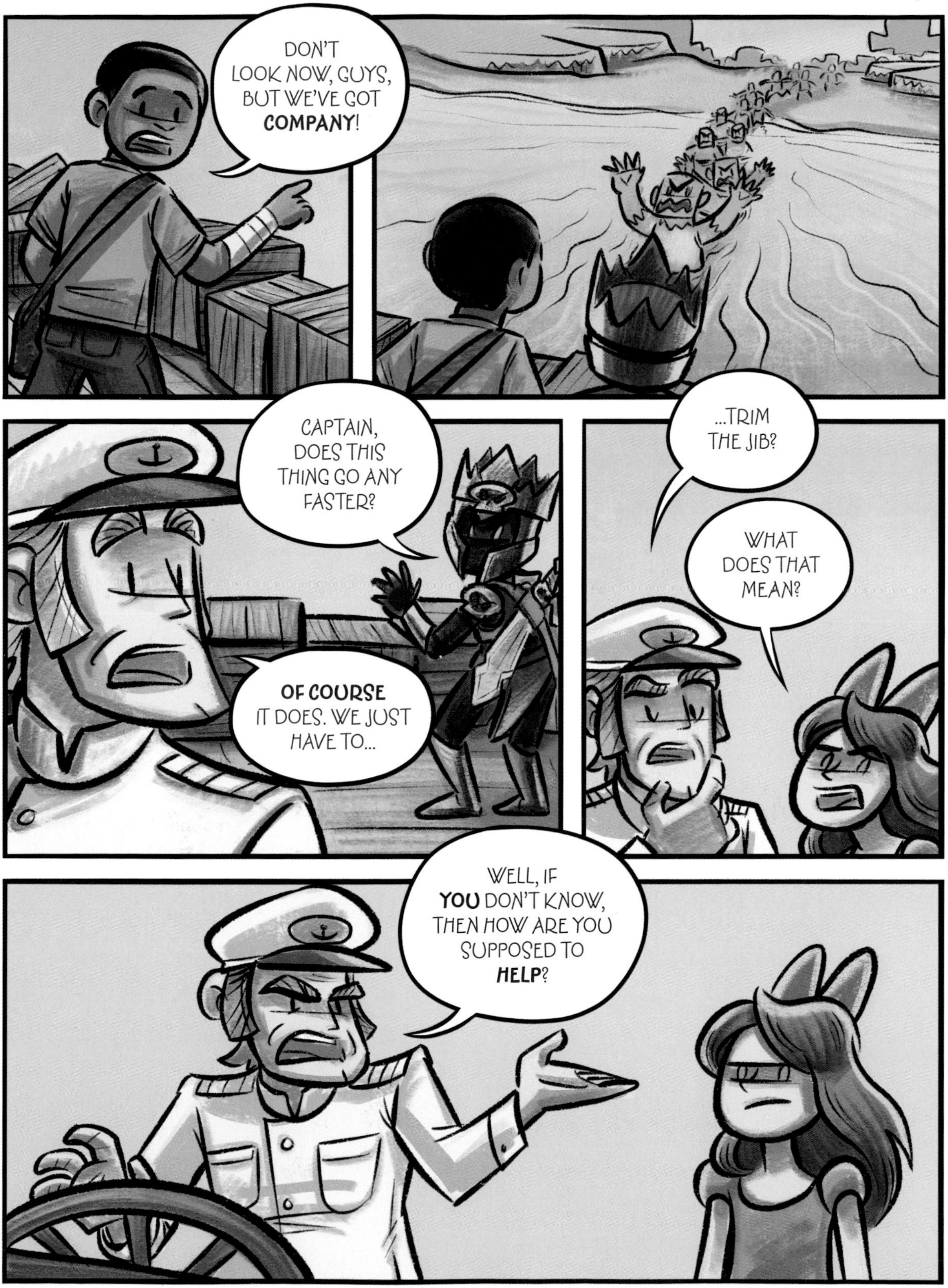
DON'T LOOK NOW, GUYS, BUT WE'VE GOT **COMPANY**!
CAPTAIN, DOES THIS THING GO ANY FASTER?
OF COURSE IT DOES. WE JUST HAVE TO...
...TRIM THE JIB?
WHAT DOES THAT MEAN?
WELL, IF **YOU** DON'T KNOW, THEN HOW ARE YOU SUPPOSED TO **HELP**?

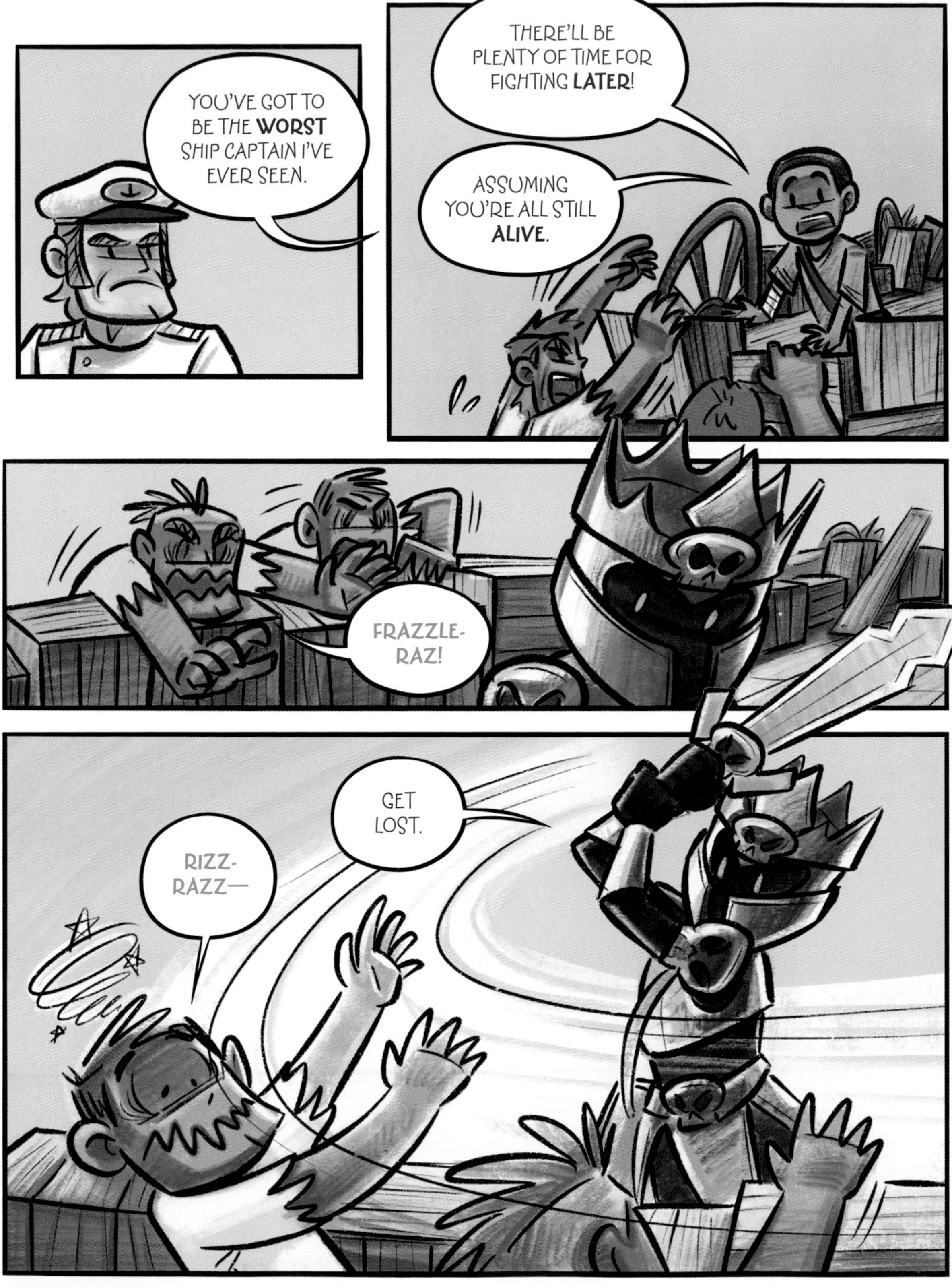
YOU'VE GOT TO BE THE **WORST** SHIP CAPTAIN I'VE EVER SEEN.
THERE'LL BE PLENTY OF TIME FOR FIGHTING **LATER**!
ASSUMING YOU'RE ALL STILL **ALIVE**.
FRAZZLE-RAZ!
GET LOST.
RIZZ-RAZZ—

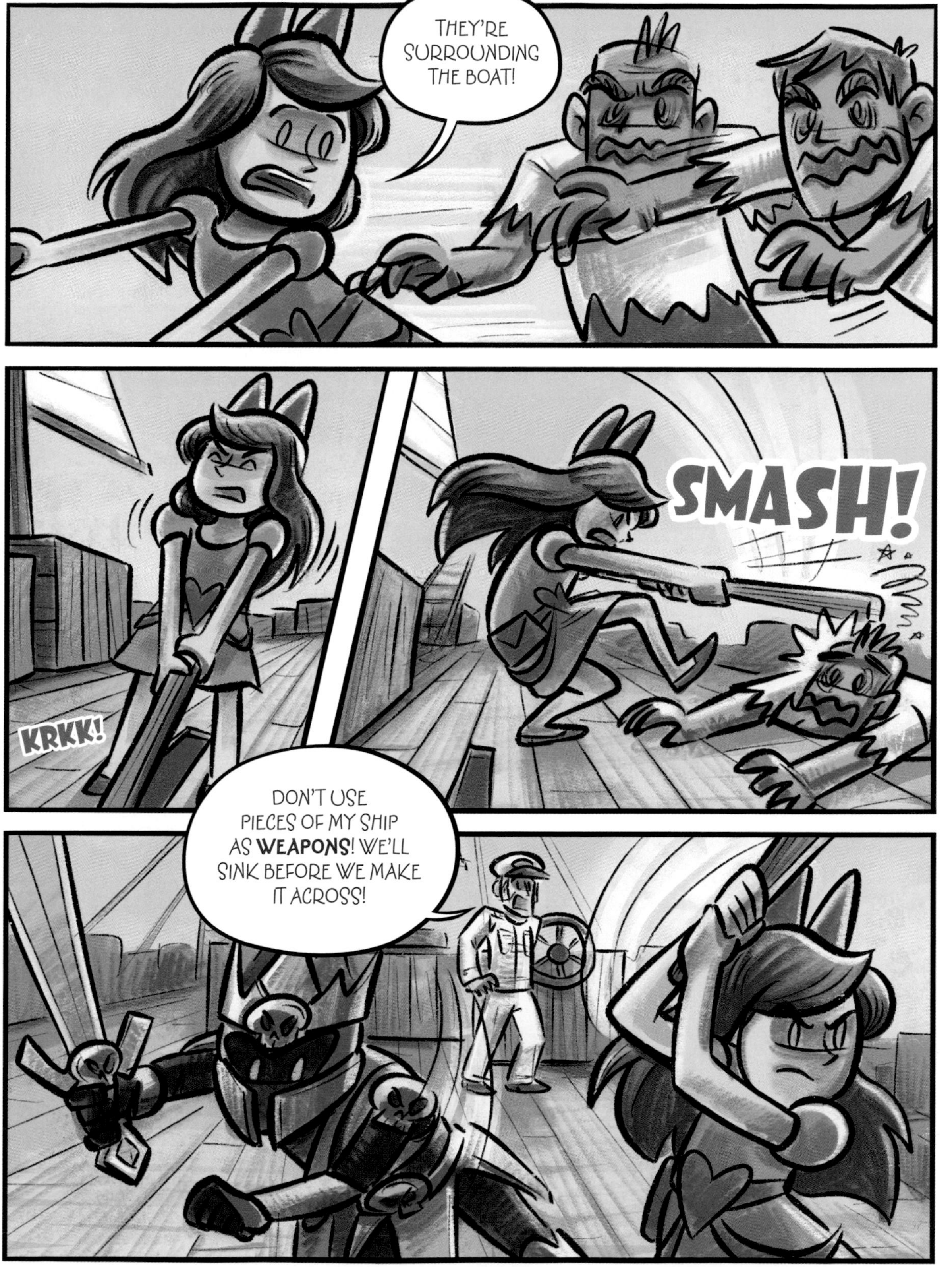
THEY'RE SURROUNDING THE BOAT!
KRKK!
SMASH!
DON'T USE PIECES OF MY SHIP AS **WEAPONS**! WE'LL SINK BEFORE WE MAKE IT ACROSS!

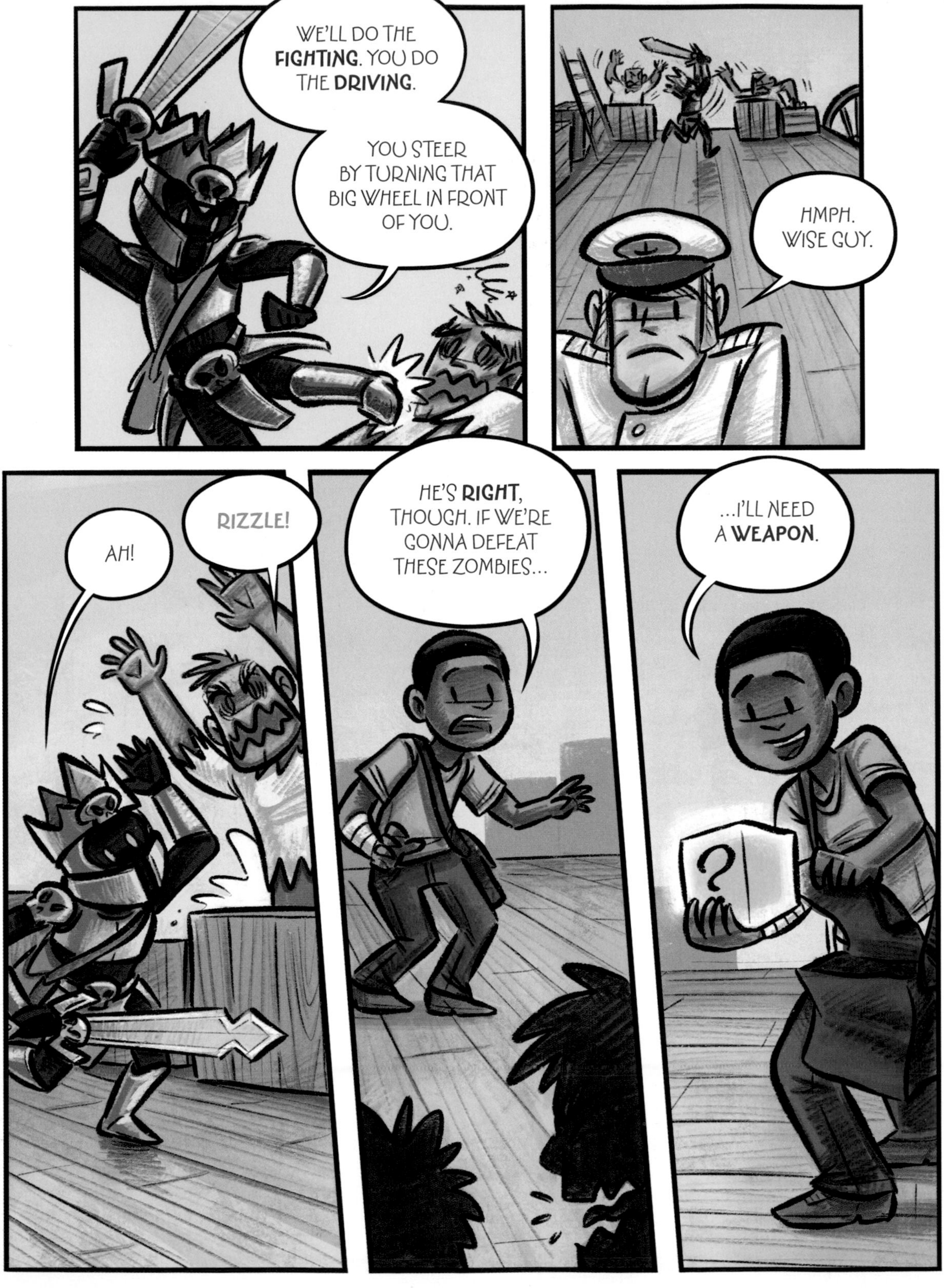

WE'LL DO THE **FIGHTING**. YOU DO THE **DRIVING**.
YOU STEER BY TURNING THAT BIG WHEEL IN FRONT OF YOU.
HMPH. WISE GUY.
AH!
RIZZLE!
HE'S **RIGHT**, THOUGH. IF WE'RE GONNA DEFEAT THESE ZOMBIES...
...I'LL NEED A **WEAPON**.

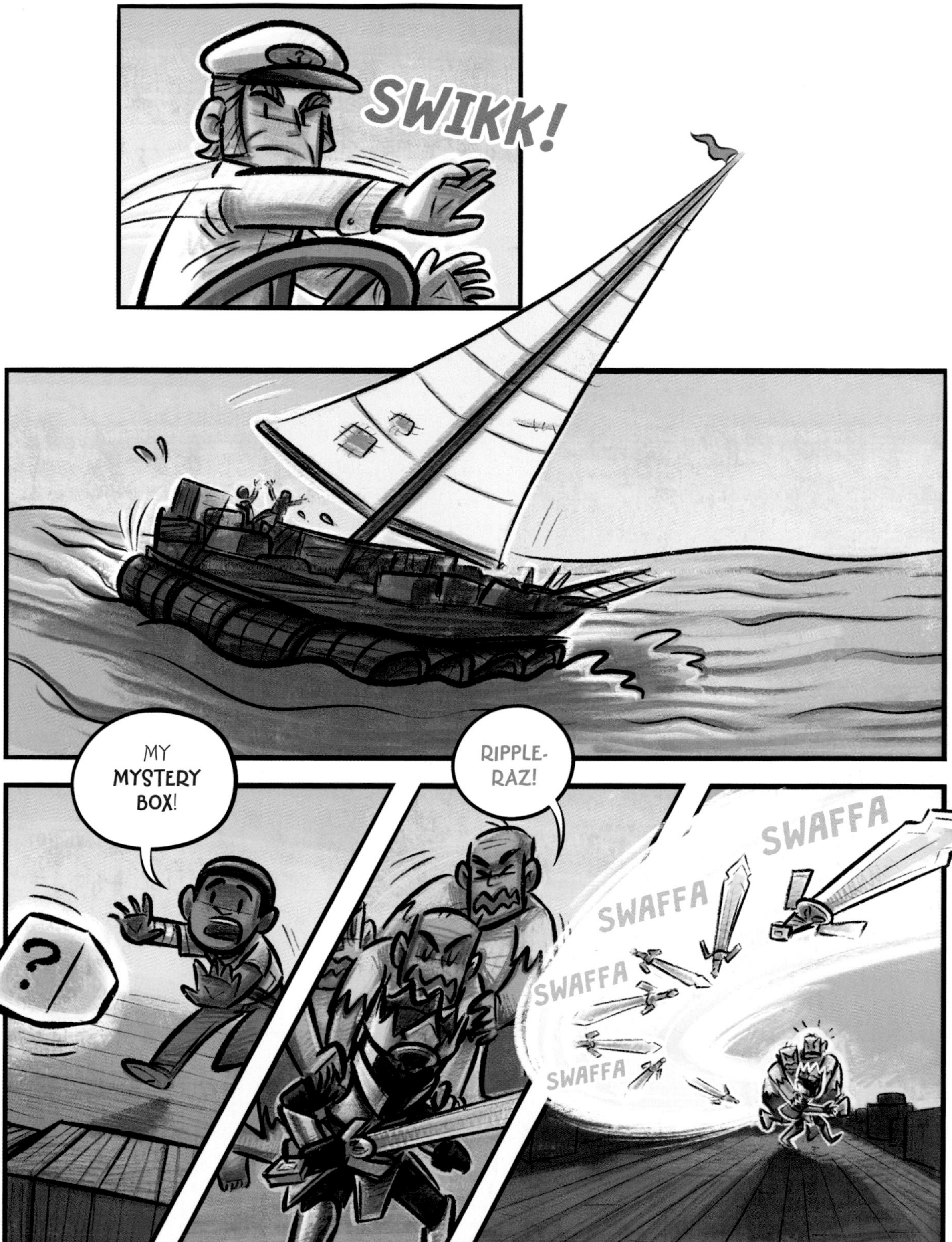
SWIKK!
MY MYSTERY BOX!
?
RIPPLE-RAZ!
SWAFFA
SWAFFA
SWAFFA
SWAFFA

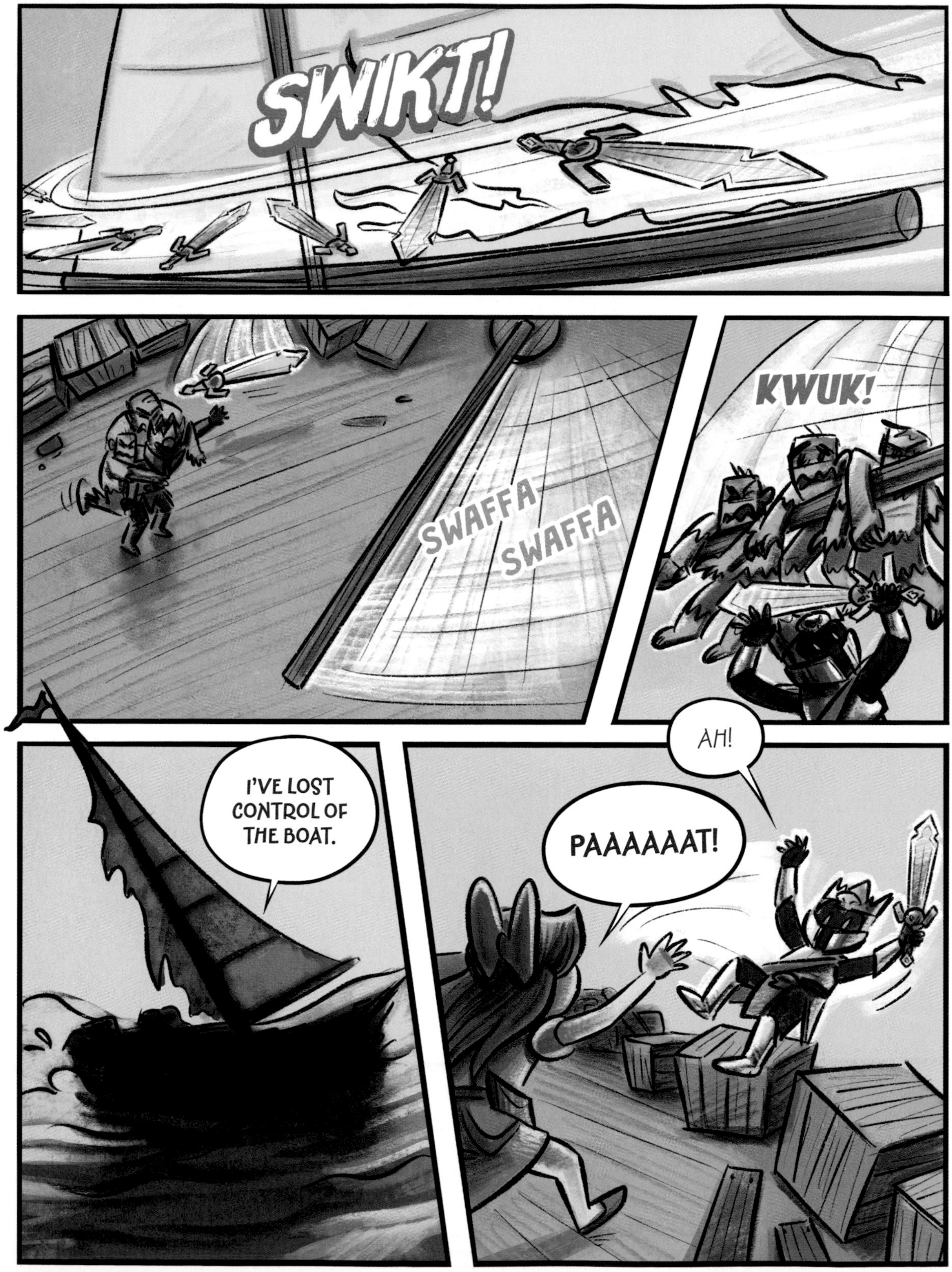
SWIKT!
SWAFFA
SWAFFA
KWUK!
I'VE LOST CONTROL OF THE BOAT.
AH!
PAAAAAAT!

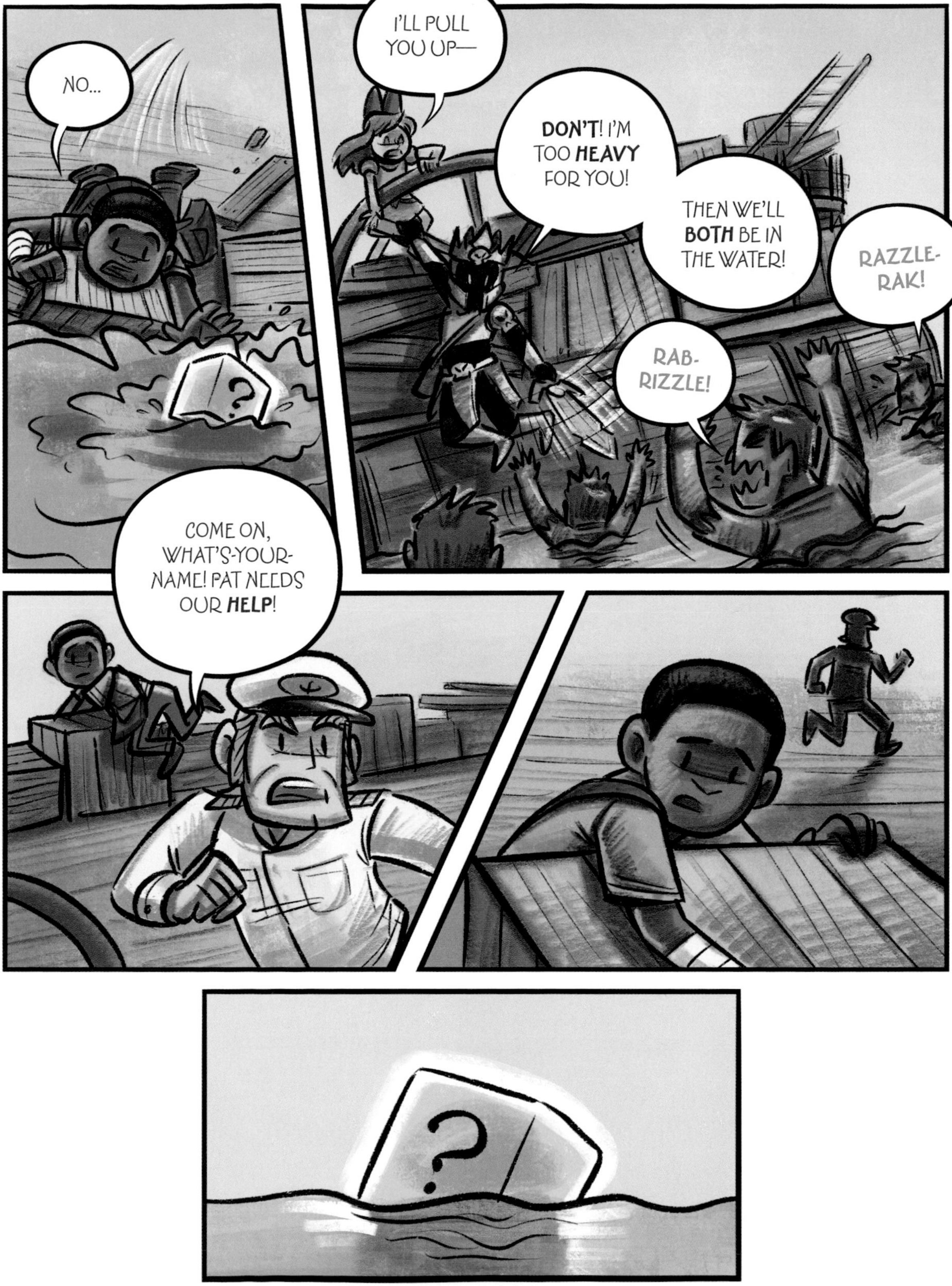
NO...
I'LL PULL YOU UP—
DON'T! I'M TOO HEAVY FOR YOU!
THEN WE'LL BOTH BE IN THE WATER!
RAZZLE-RAK!
RAB-RIZZLE!
COME ON, WHAT'S-YOUR-NAME! PAT NEEDS OUR HELP!

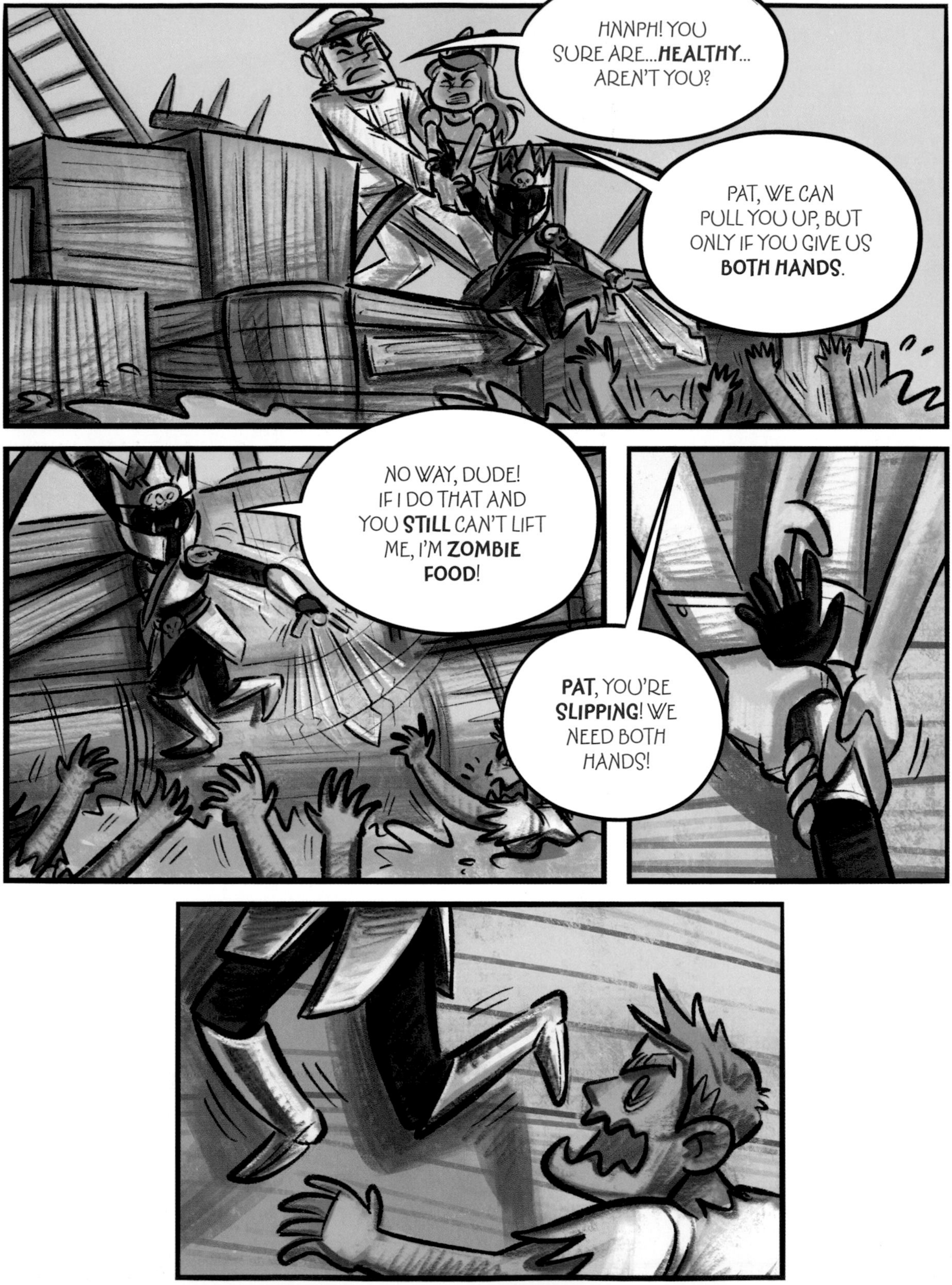
HNNPH! YOU SURE ARE...**HEALTHY**... AREN'T YOU?
PAT, WE CAN PULL YOU UP, BUT ONLY IF YOU GIVE US **BOTH HANDS**.
NO WAY, DUDE! IF I DO THAT AND YOU **STILL** CAN'T LIFT ME, I'M **ZOMBIE FOOD**!
PAT, YOU'RE **SLIPPING**! WE NEED BOTH HANDS!

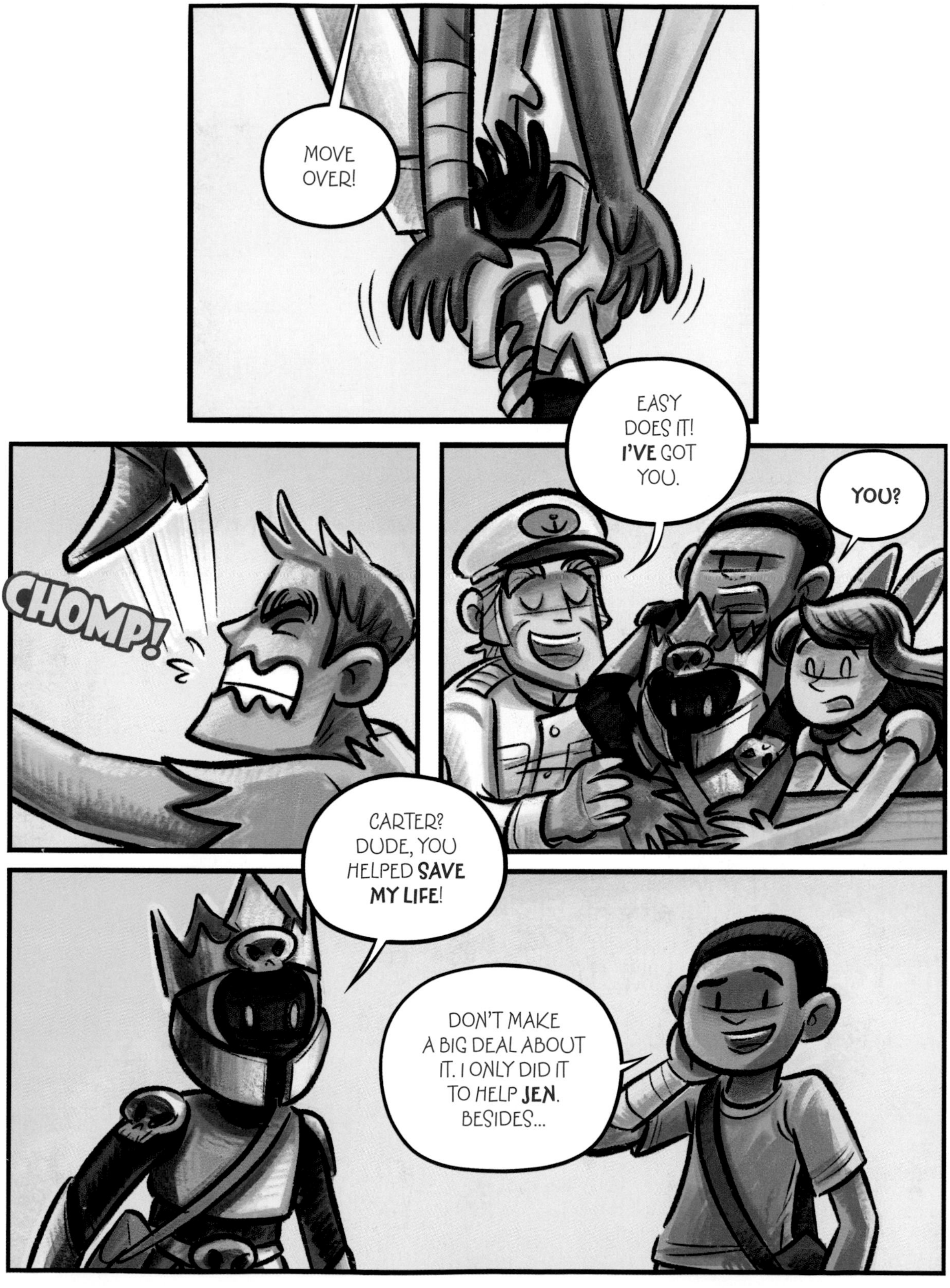
MOVE OVER!
CHOMP!
EASY DOES IT! **I'VE** GOT YOU.
YOU?
CARTER? DUDE, YOU HELPED **SAVE MY LIFE**!
DON'T MAKE A BIG DEAL ABOUT IT. I ONLY DID IT TO HELP **JEN**. BESIDES...

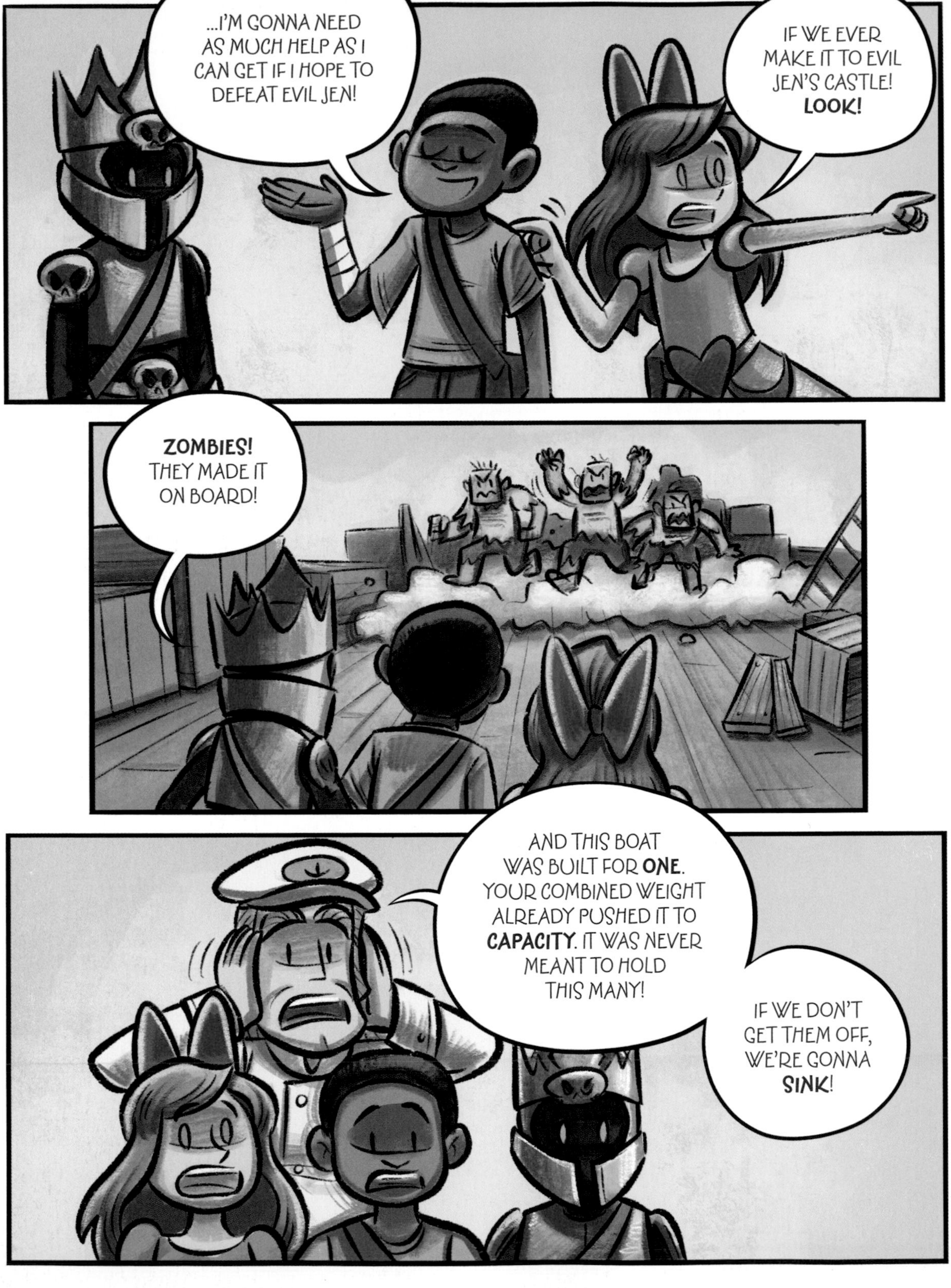

...I'M GONNA NEED AS MUCH HELP AS I CAN GET IF I HOPE TO DEFEAT EVIL JEN!
IF WE EVER MAKE IT TO EVIL JEN'S CASTLE! **LOOK!**
ZOMBIES! THEY MADE IT ON BOARD!
AND THIS BOAT WAS BUILT FOR **ONE**. YOUR COMBINED WEIGHT ALREADY PUSHED IT TO **CAPACITY**. IT WAS NEVER MEANT TO HOLD THIS MANY!
IF WE DON'T GET THEM OFF, WE'RE GONNA **SINK**!

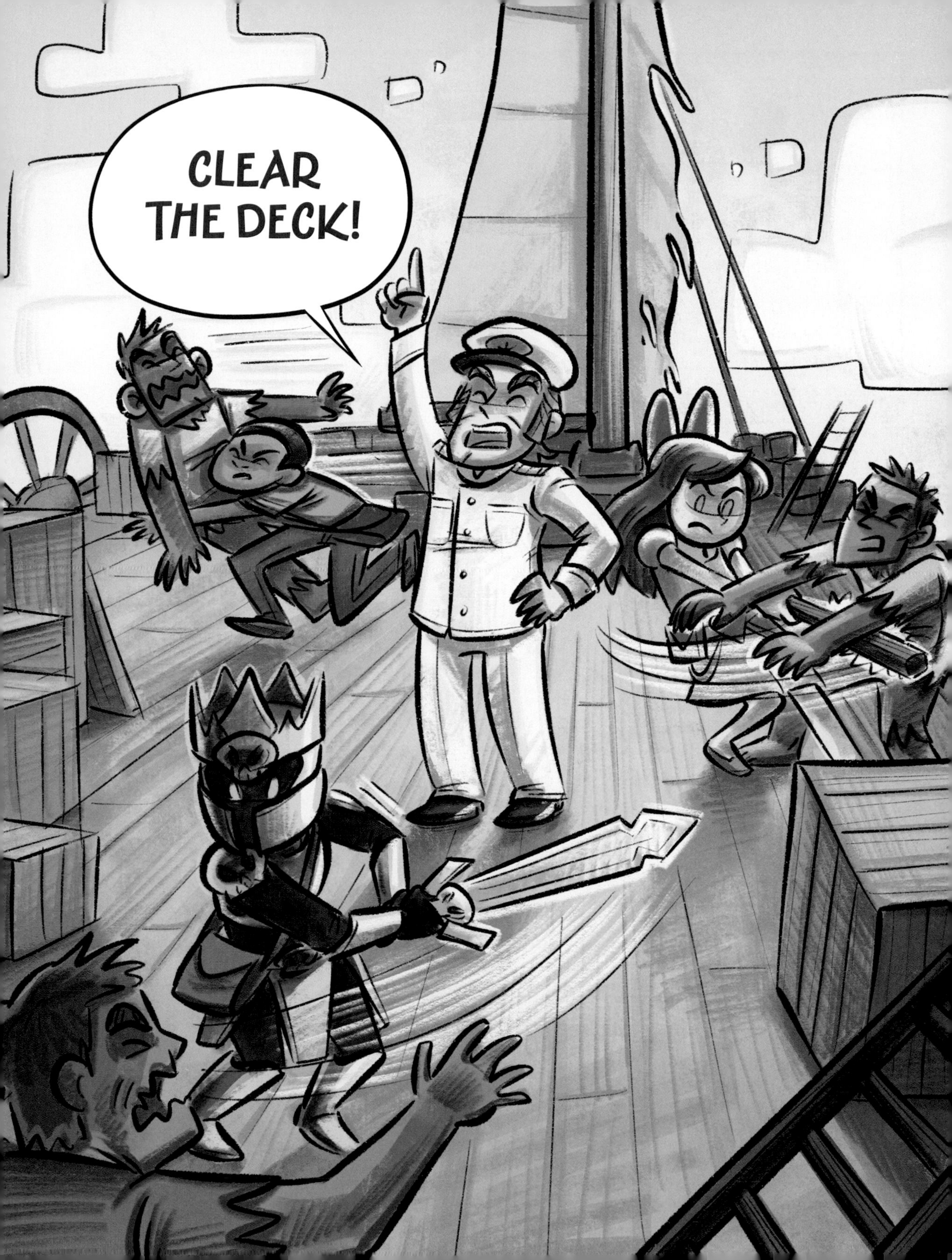
CLEAR THE DECK!

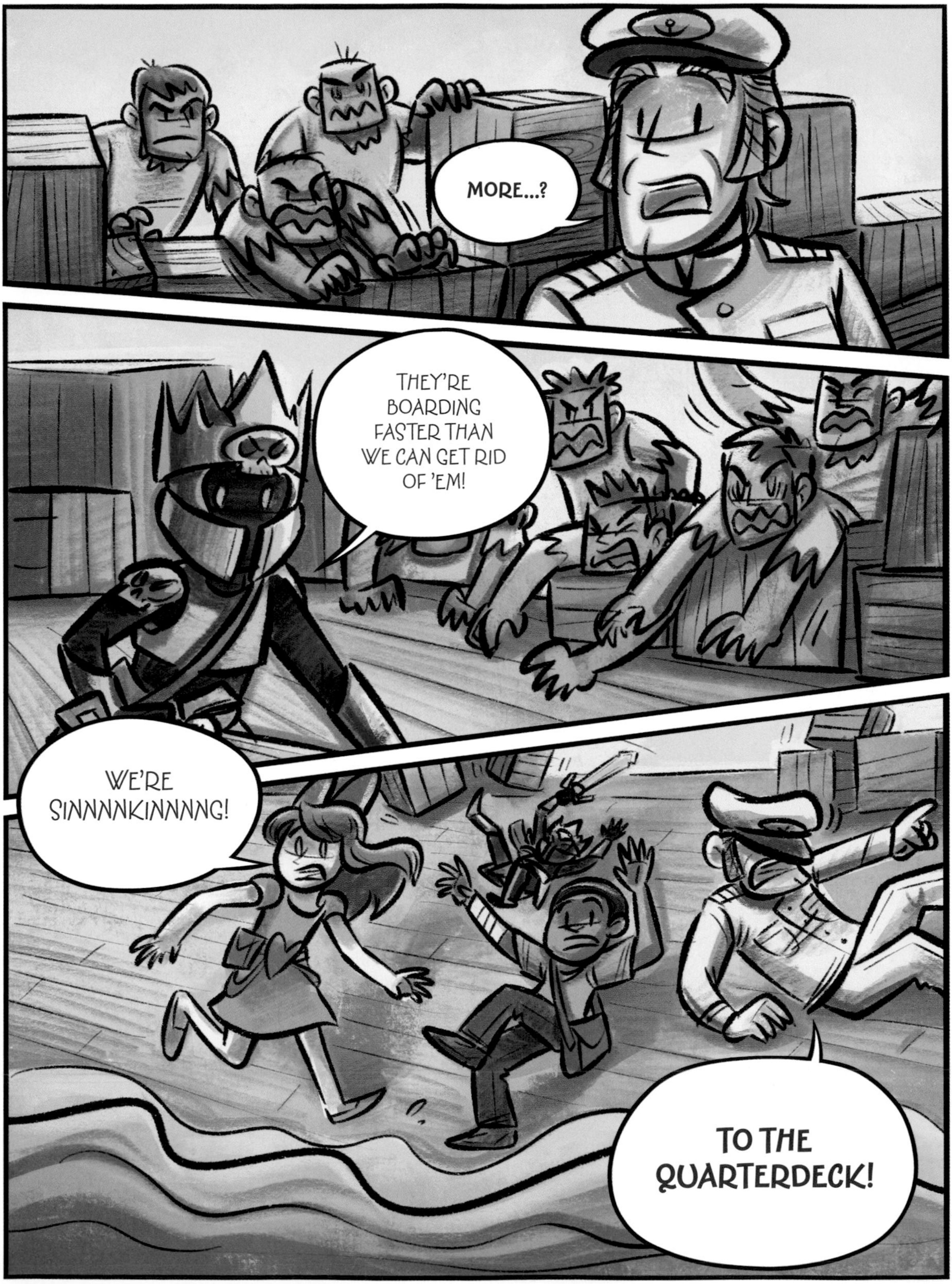
MORE...?
THEY'RE BOARDING FASTER THAN WE CAN GET RID OF 'EM!
WE'RE SINNNNKINNNNG!
TO THE QUARTERDECK!

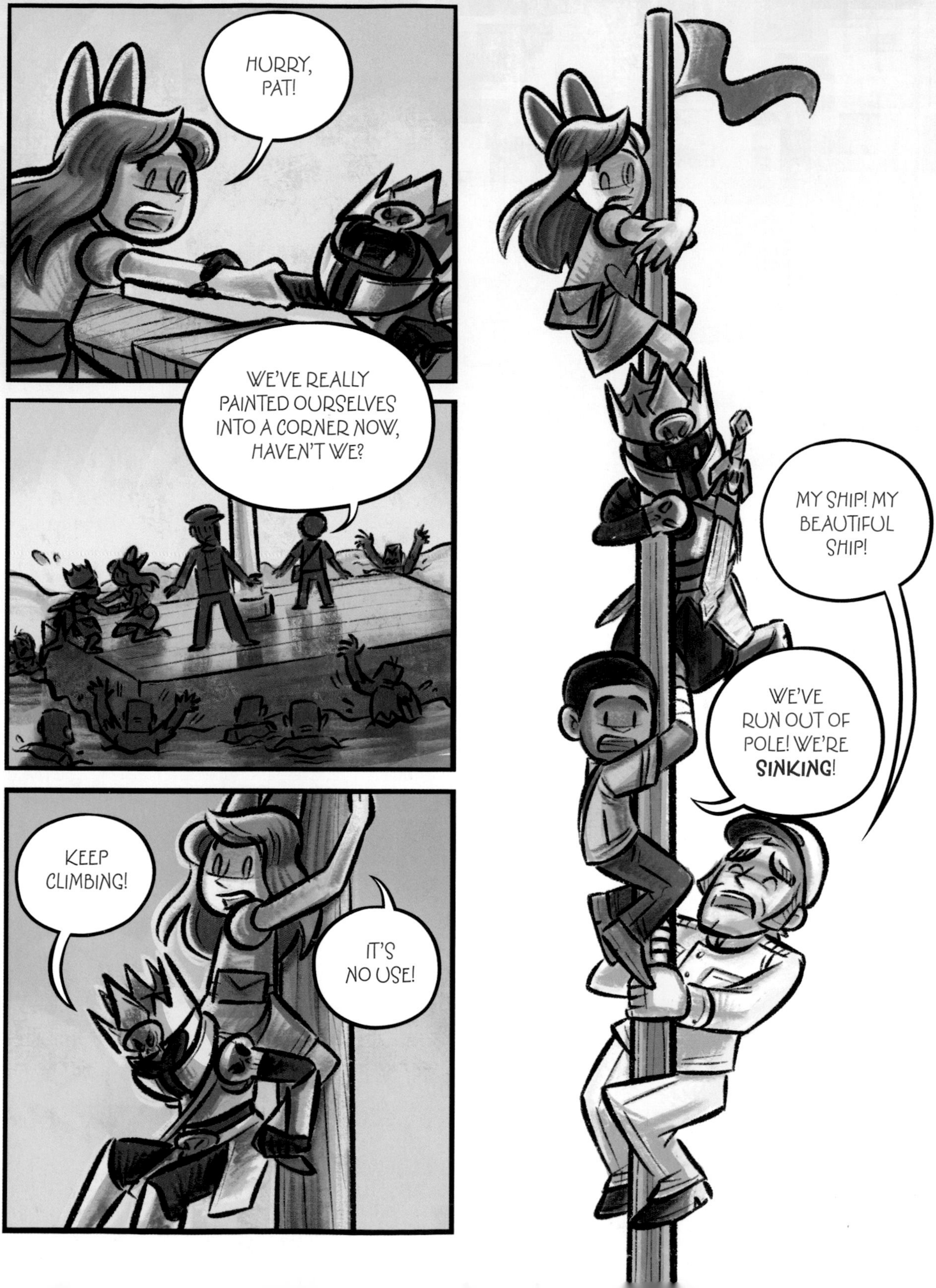
HURRY, PAT!
WE'VE REALLY PAINTED OURSELVES INTO A CORNER NOW, HAVEN'T WE?
KEEP CLIMBING!
IT'S NO USE!
MY SHIP! MY BEAUTIFUL SHIP!
WE'VE RUN OUT OF POLE! WE'RE **SINKING**!

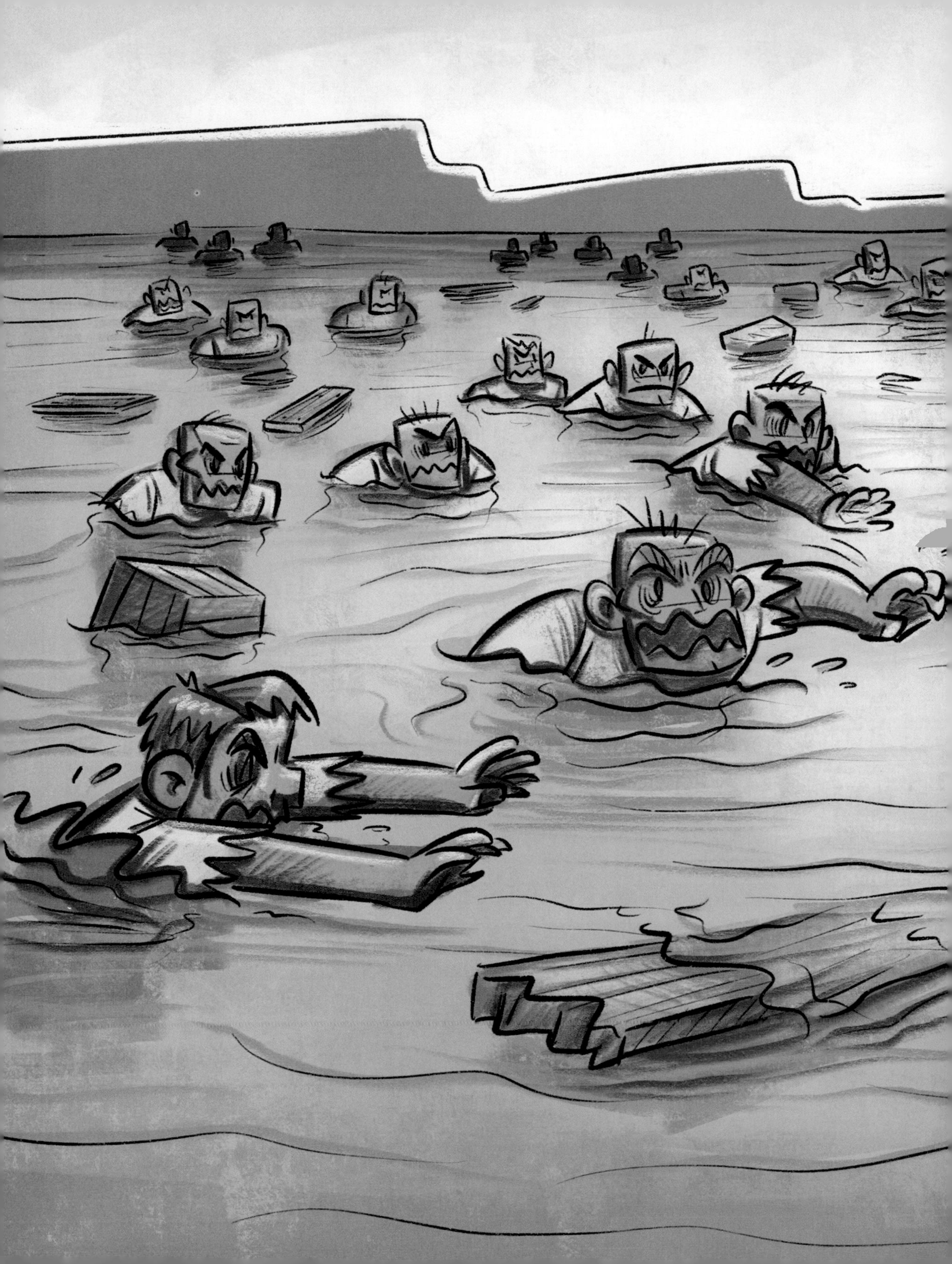

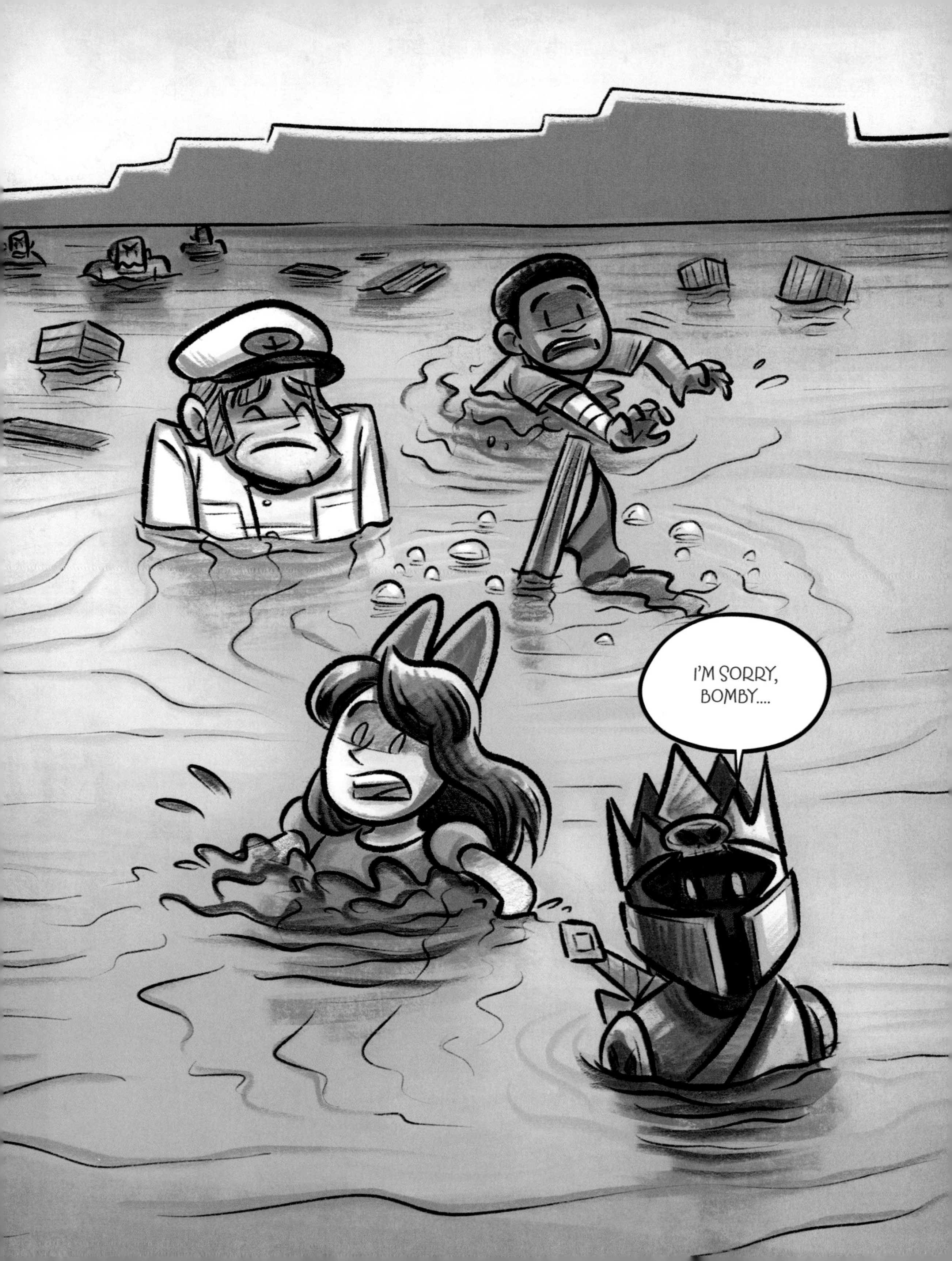
I'M SORRY, BOMBY....

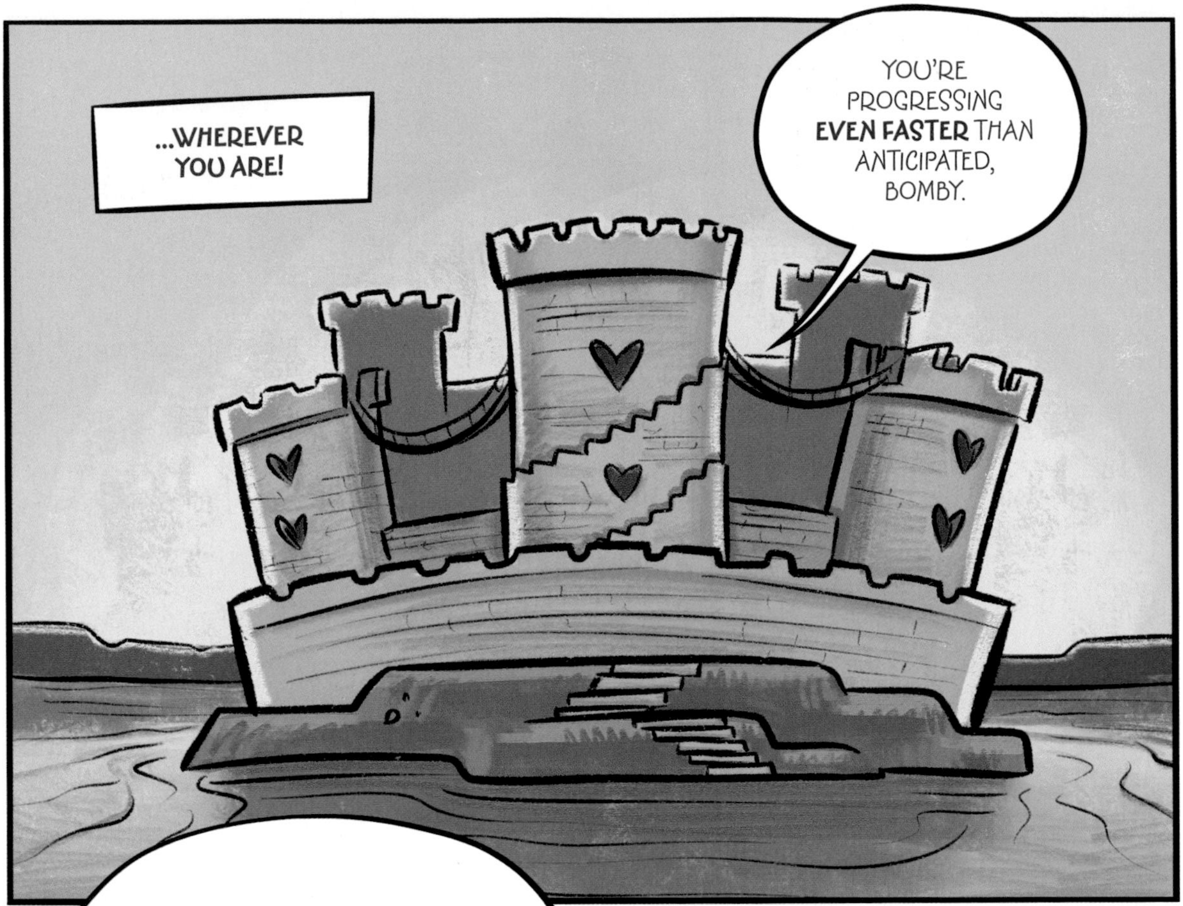
...WHEREVER YOU ARE!
YOU'RE PROGRESSING **EVEN FASTER** THAN ANTICIPATED, BOMBY.

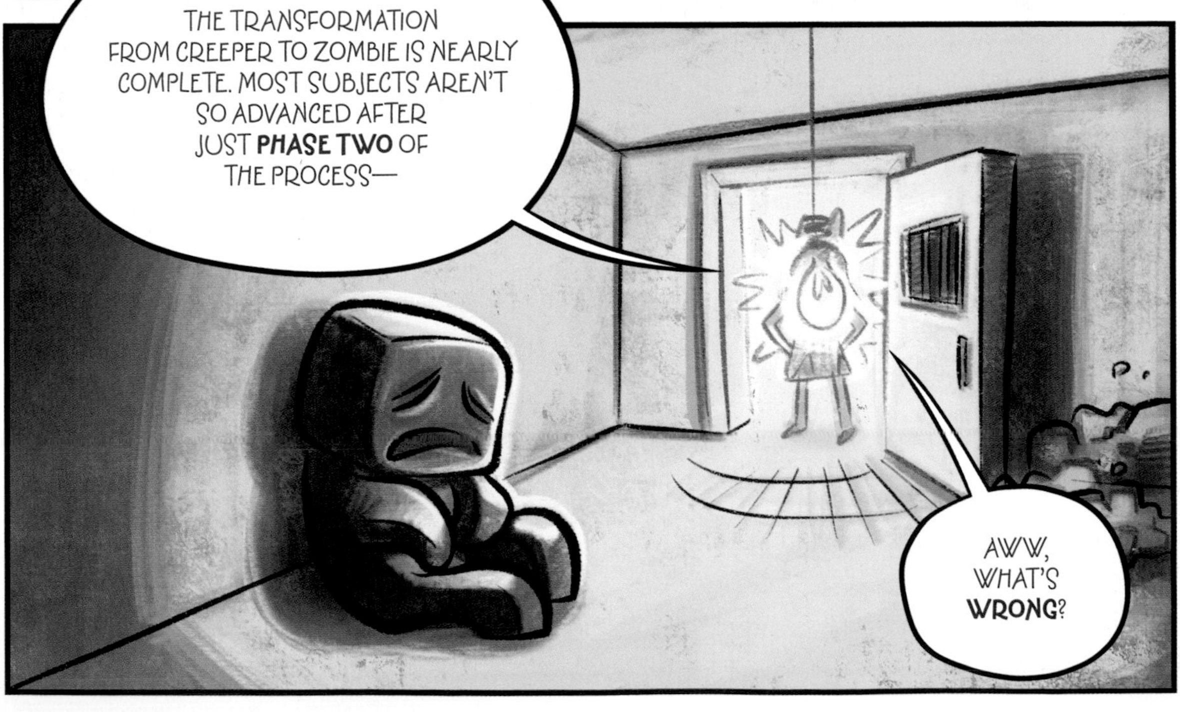
THE TRANSFORMATION FROM CREEPER TO ZOMBIE IS NEARLY COMPLETE. MOST SUBJECTS AREN'T SO ADVANCED AFTER JUST **PHASE TWO** OF THE PROCESS—
AWW, WHAT'S **WRONG**?

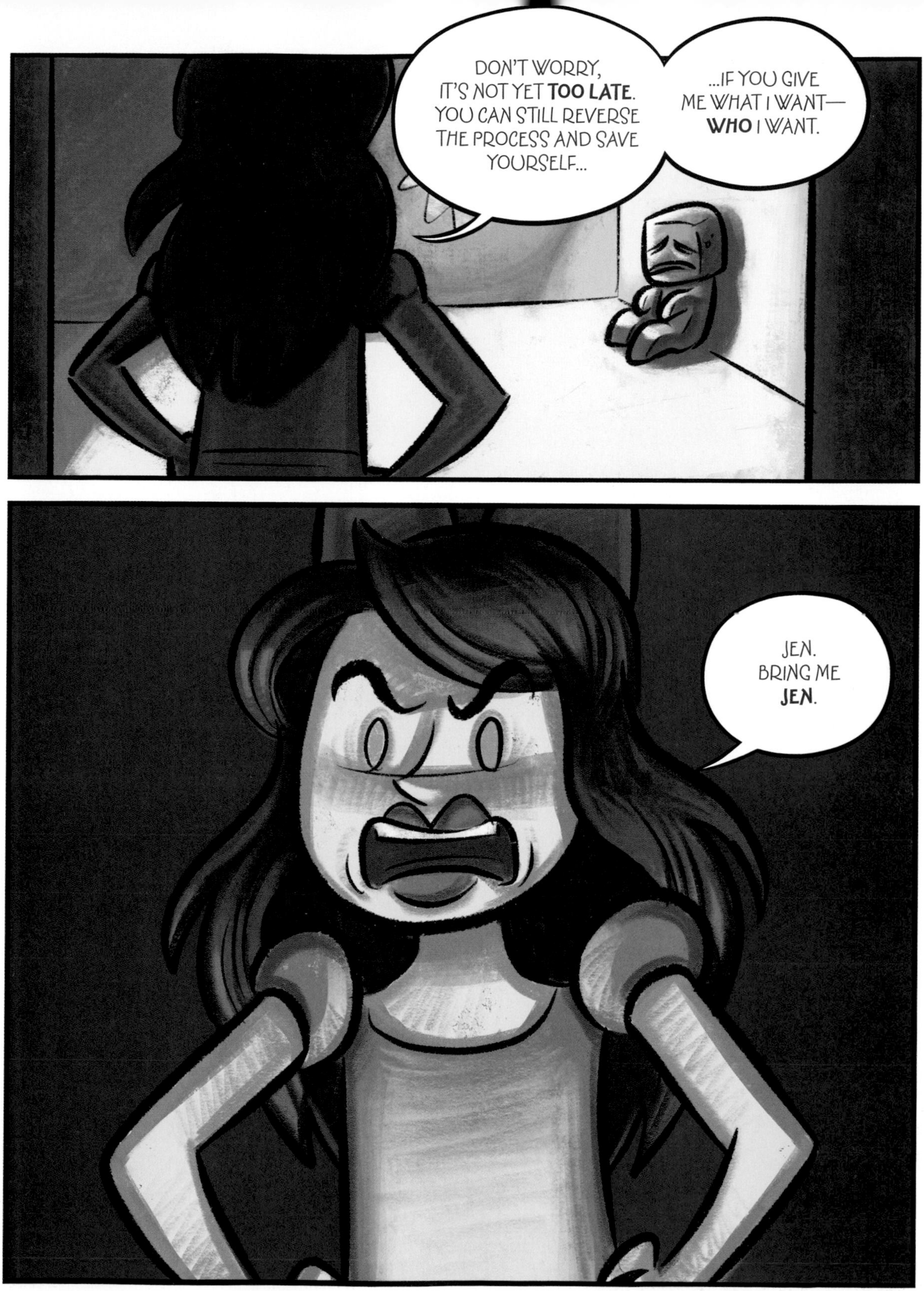
DON'T WORRY, IT'S NOT YET **TOO LATE**. YOU CAN STILL REVERSE THE PROCESS AND SAVE YOURSELF...
...IF YOU GIVE ME WHAT I WANT— **WHO** I WANT.
JEN. BRING ME **JEN**.

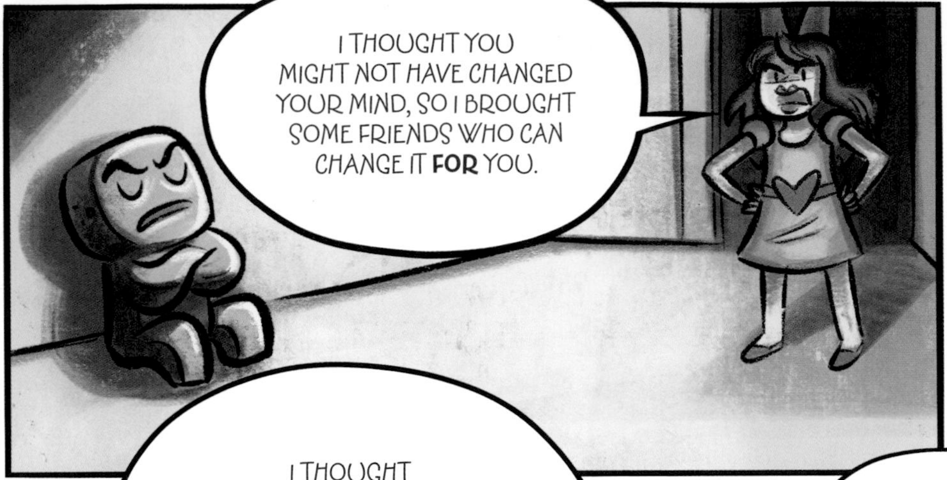
I THOUGHT YOU MIGHT NOT HAVE CHANGED YOUR MIND, SO I BROUGHT SOME FRIENDS WHO CAN CHANGE IT **FOR** YOU.

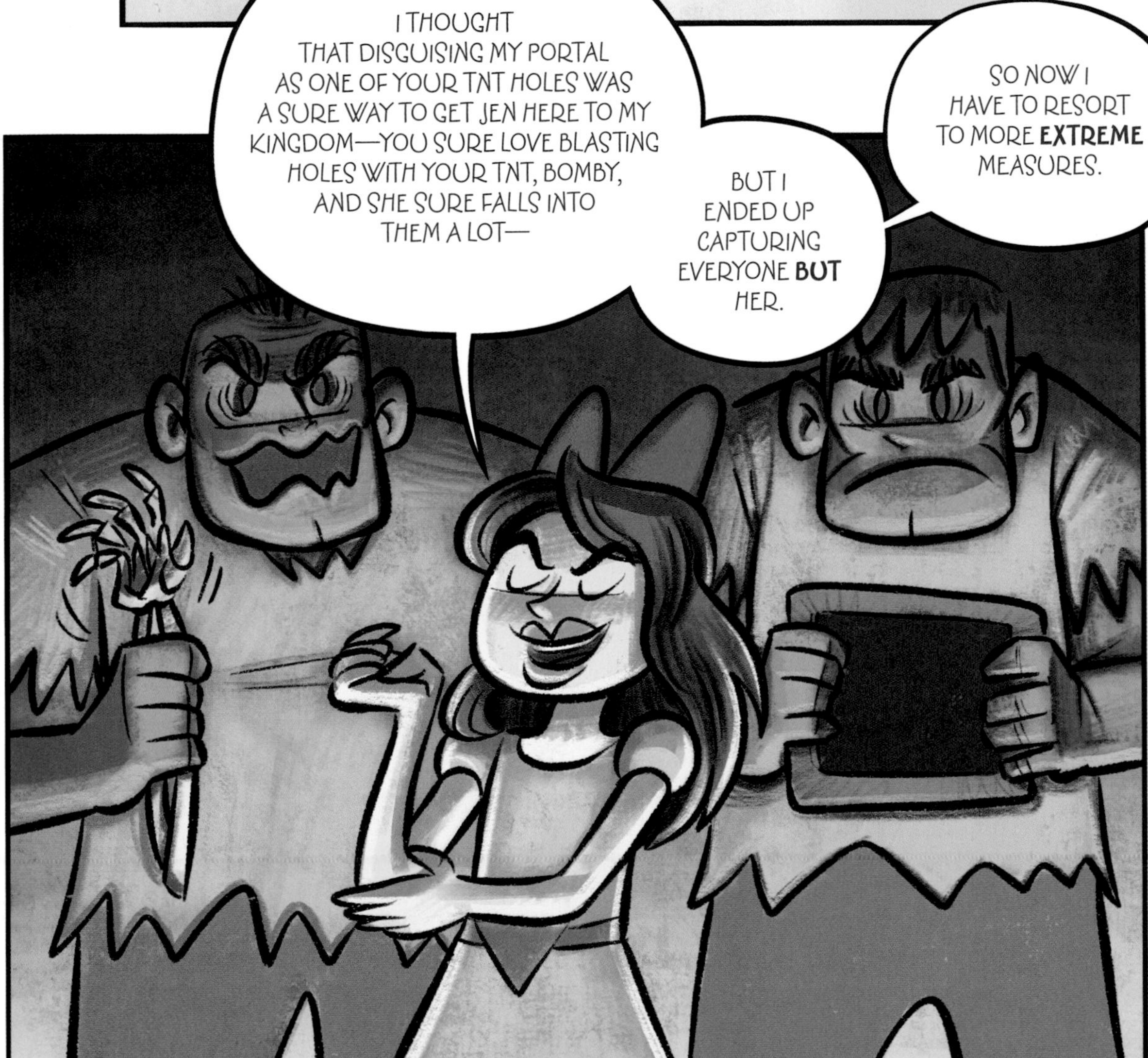
I THOUGHT THAT DISGUISING MY PORTAL AS ONE OF YOUR TNT HOLES WAS A SURE WAY TO GET JEN HERE TO MY KINGDOM—YOU SURE LOVE BLASTING HOLES WITH YOUR TNT, BOMBY, AND SHE SURE FALLS INTO THEM A LOT—
BUT I ENDED UP CAPTURING EVERYONE **BUT** HER.
SO NOW I HAVE TO RESORT TO MORE **EXTREME** MEASURES.

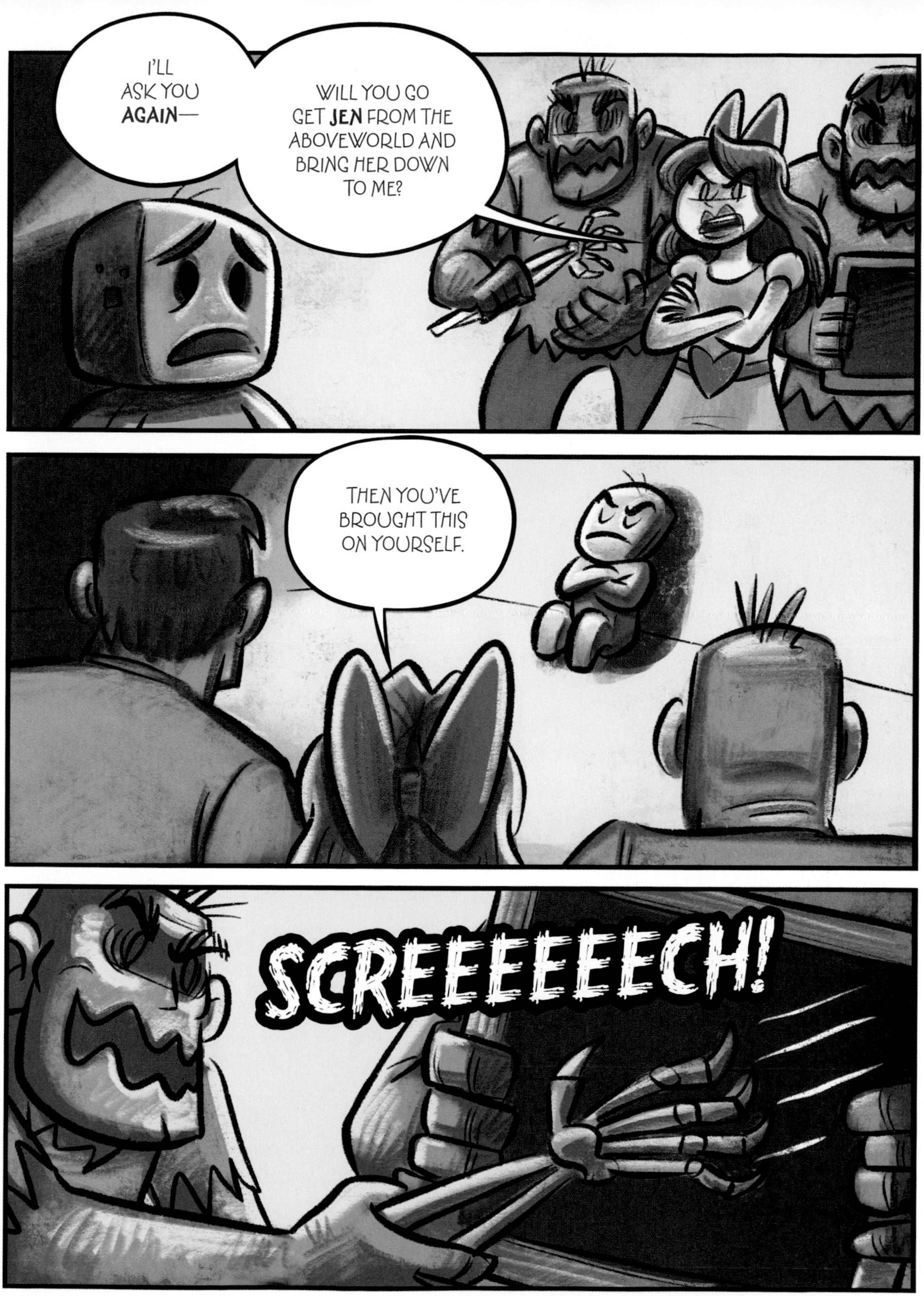

I'LL ASK YOU **AGAIN**—
WILL YOU GO GET **JEN** FROM THE ABOVEWORLD AND BRING HER DOWN TO ME?
THEN YOU'VE BROUGHT THIS ON YOURSELF.
SCREEEEEEECH!

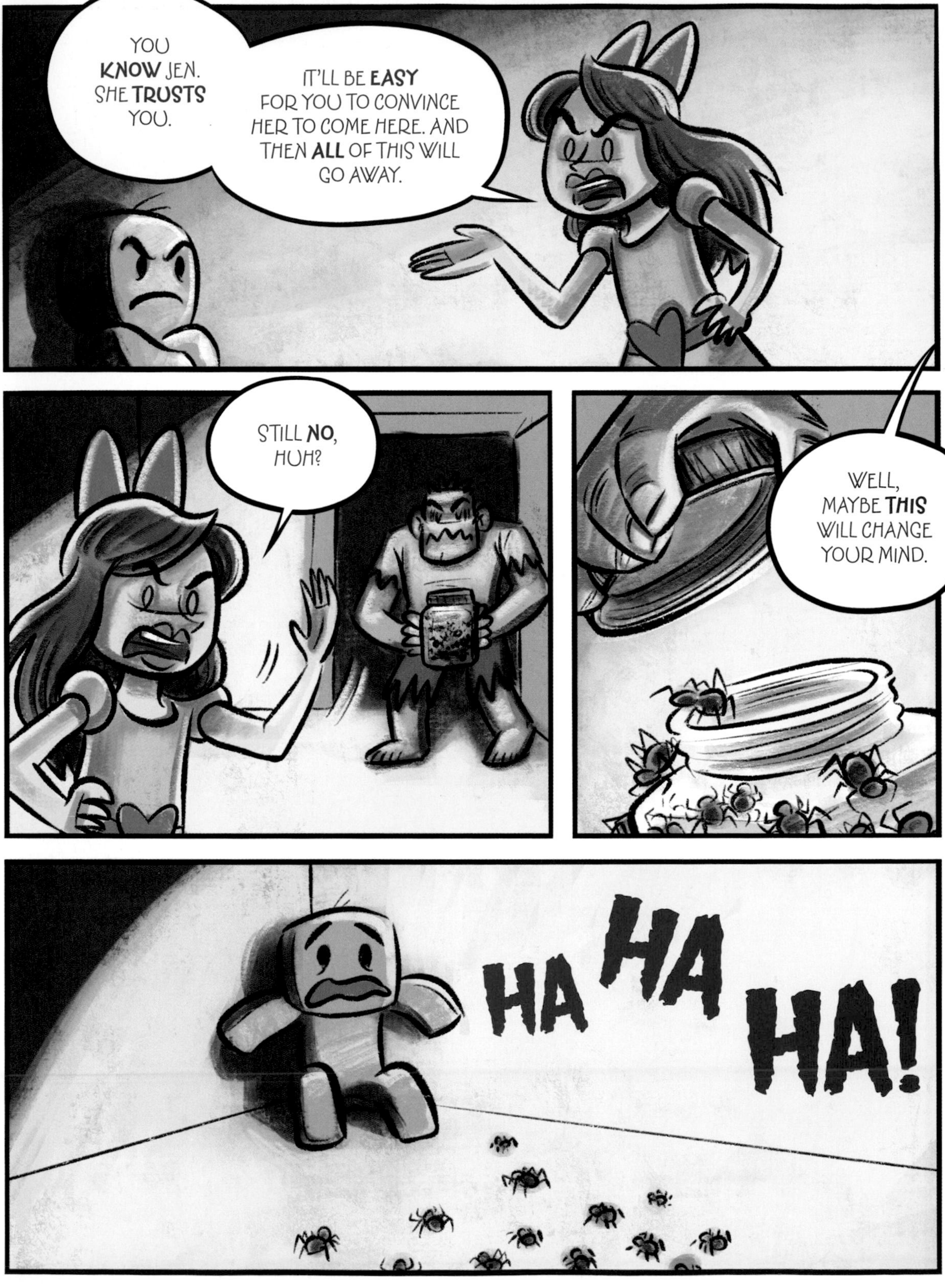
YOU KNOW JEN. SHE TRUSTS YOU.
IT'LL BE EASY FOR YOU TO CONVINCE HER TO COME HERE. AND THEN ALL OF THIS WILL GO AWAY.
STILL NO, HUH?
WELL, MAYBE THIS WILL CHANGE YOUR MIND.
HA HA HA HA!

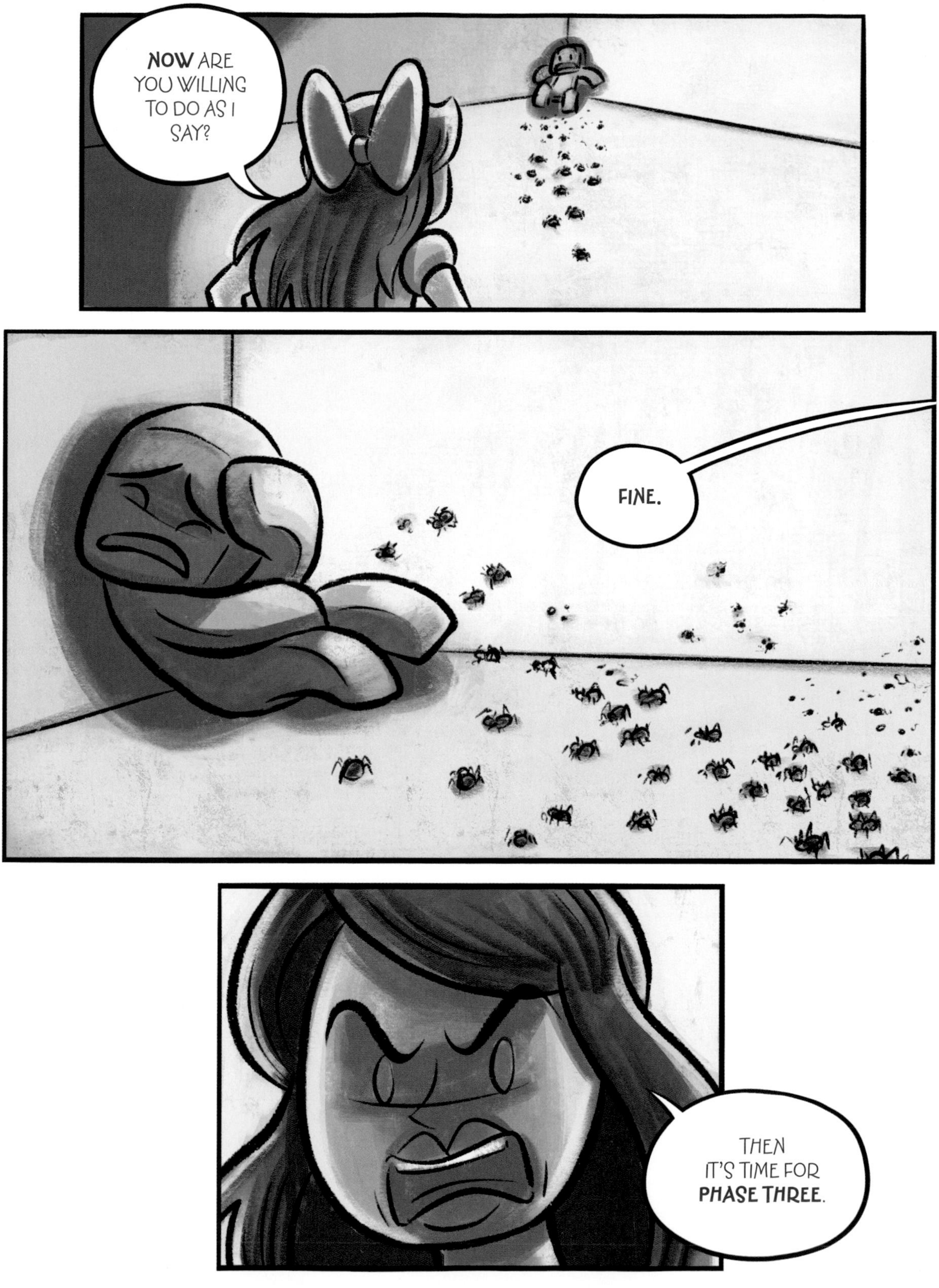
NOW ARE YOU WILLING TO DO AS I SAY?
FINE.
THEN IT'S TIME FOR PHASE THREE.

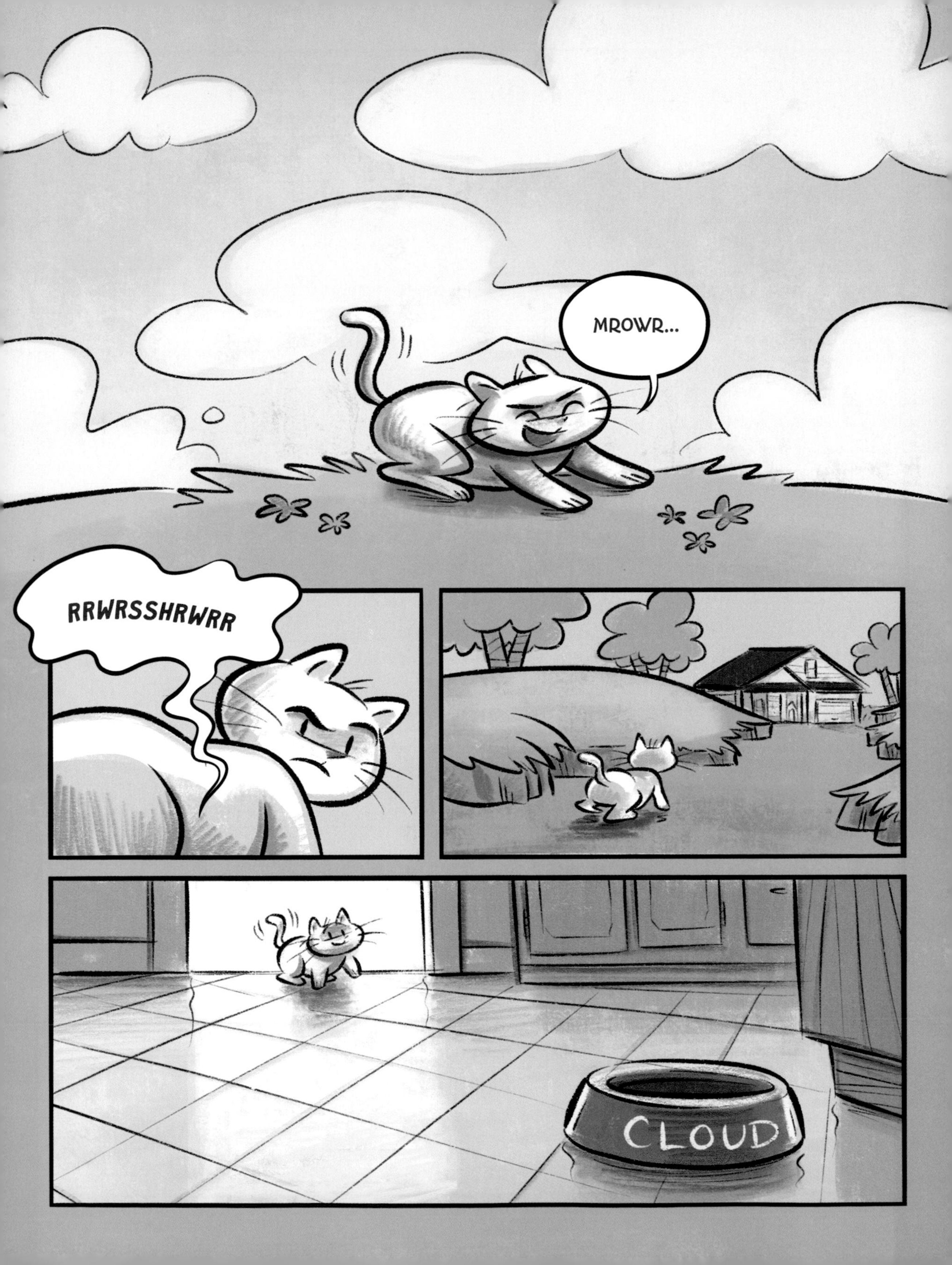
MROWR...
RRWRSSHRWRR
CLOUD

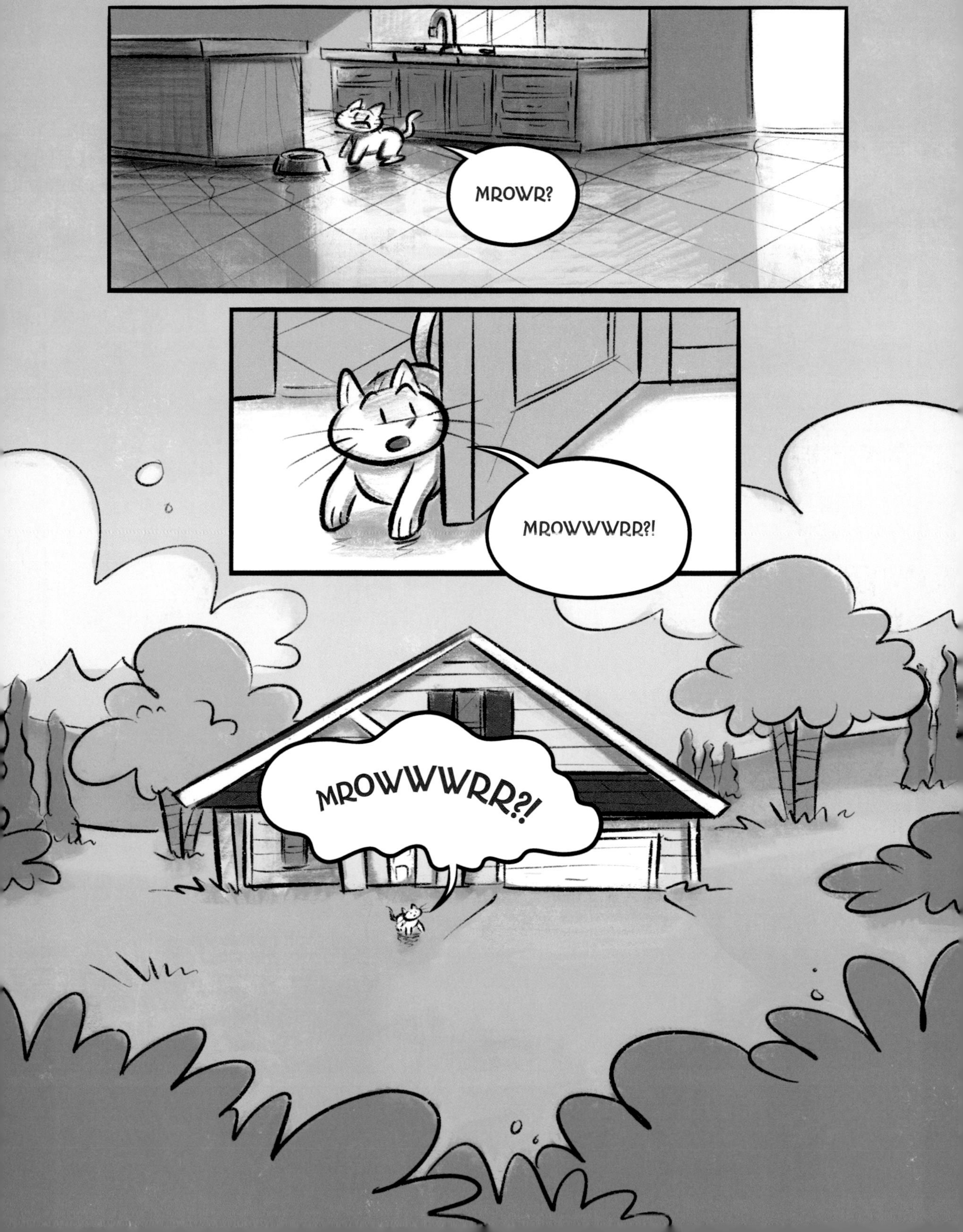
MROWR?
MROWWWRR?!
MROWWWRR?!

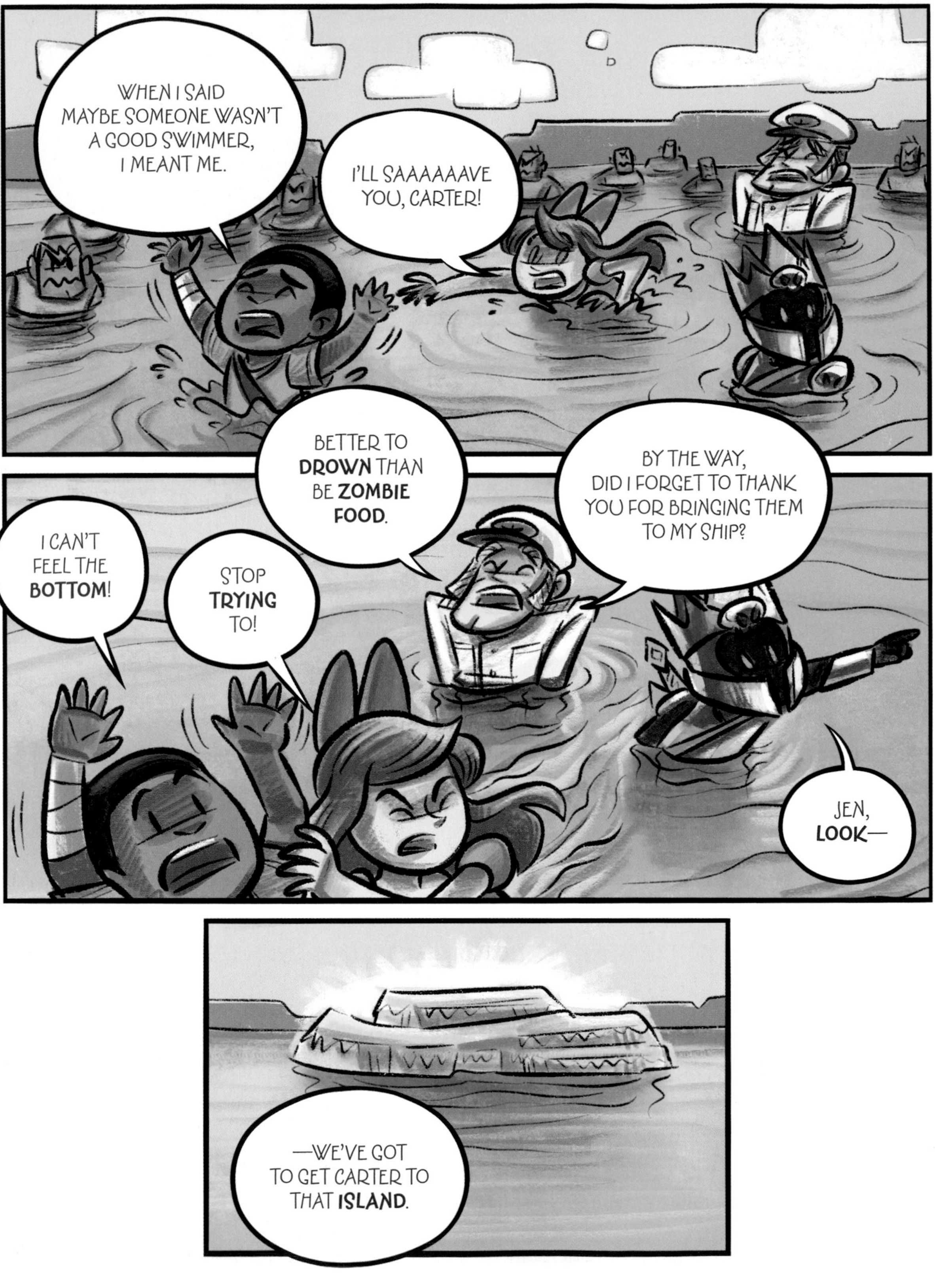

WHEN I SAID MAYBE SOMEONE WASN'T A GOOD SWIMMER, I MEANT ME.
I'LL SAAAAAAVE YOU, CARTER!
BETTER TO **DROWN** THAN BE **ZOMBIE FOOD**.
BY THE WAY, DID I FORGET TO THANK YOU FOR BRINGING THEM TO MY SHIP?
I CAN'T FEEL THE **BOTTOM**!
STOP **TRYING** TO!
JEN, **LOOK**—
—WE'VE GOT TO GET CARTER TO THAT **ISLAND**.

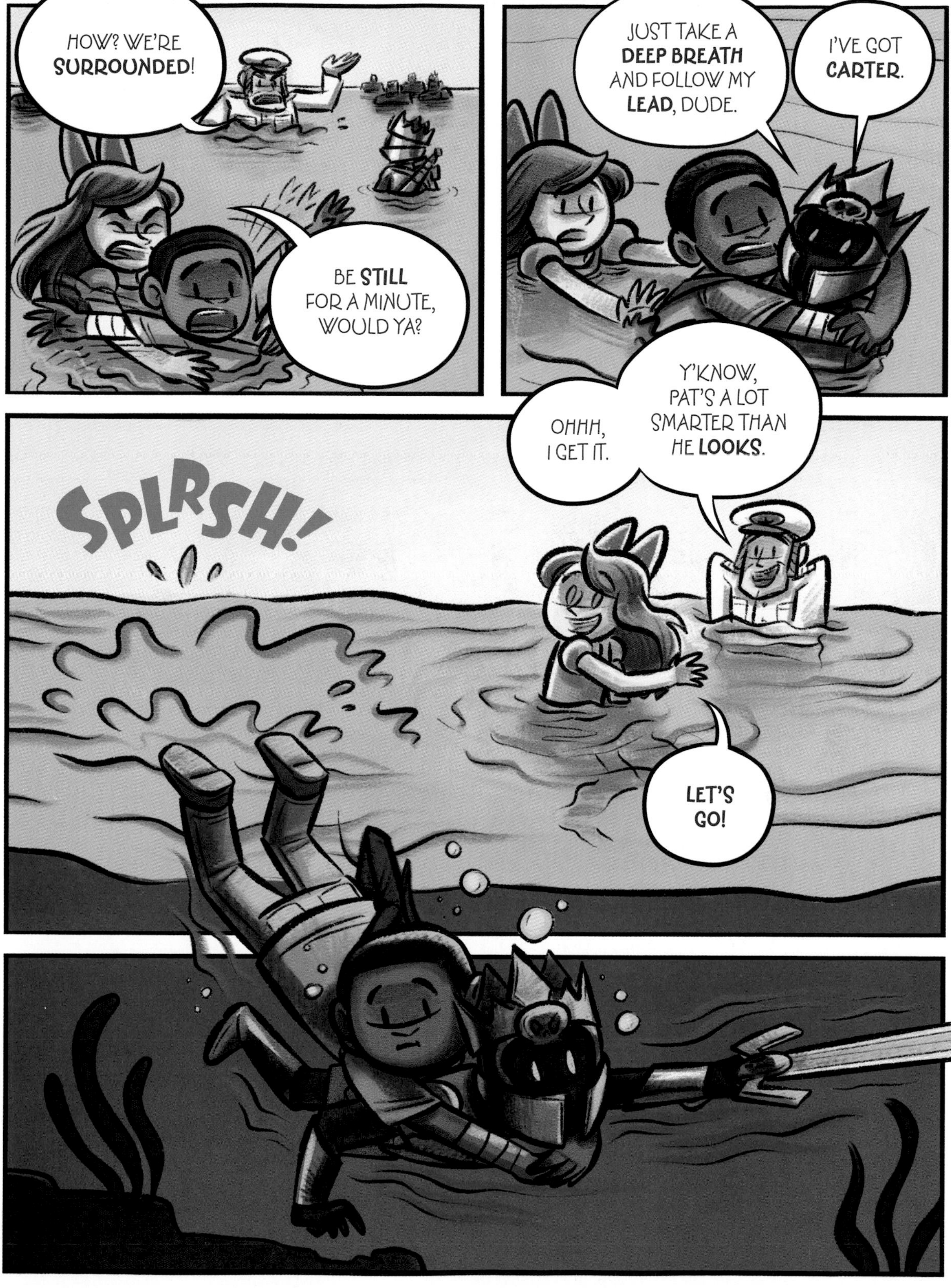
HOW? WE'RE **SURROUNDED**!
BE **STILL** FOR A MINUTE, WOULD YA?
JUST TAKE A **DEEP BREATH** AND FOLLOW MY **LEAD**, DUDE.
I'VE GOT **CARTER**.
OHHH, I GET IT.
Y'KNOW, PAT'S A LOT SMARTER THAN HE **LOOKS**.
SPLRSH!
LET'S GO!

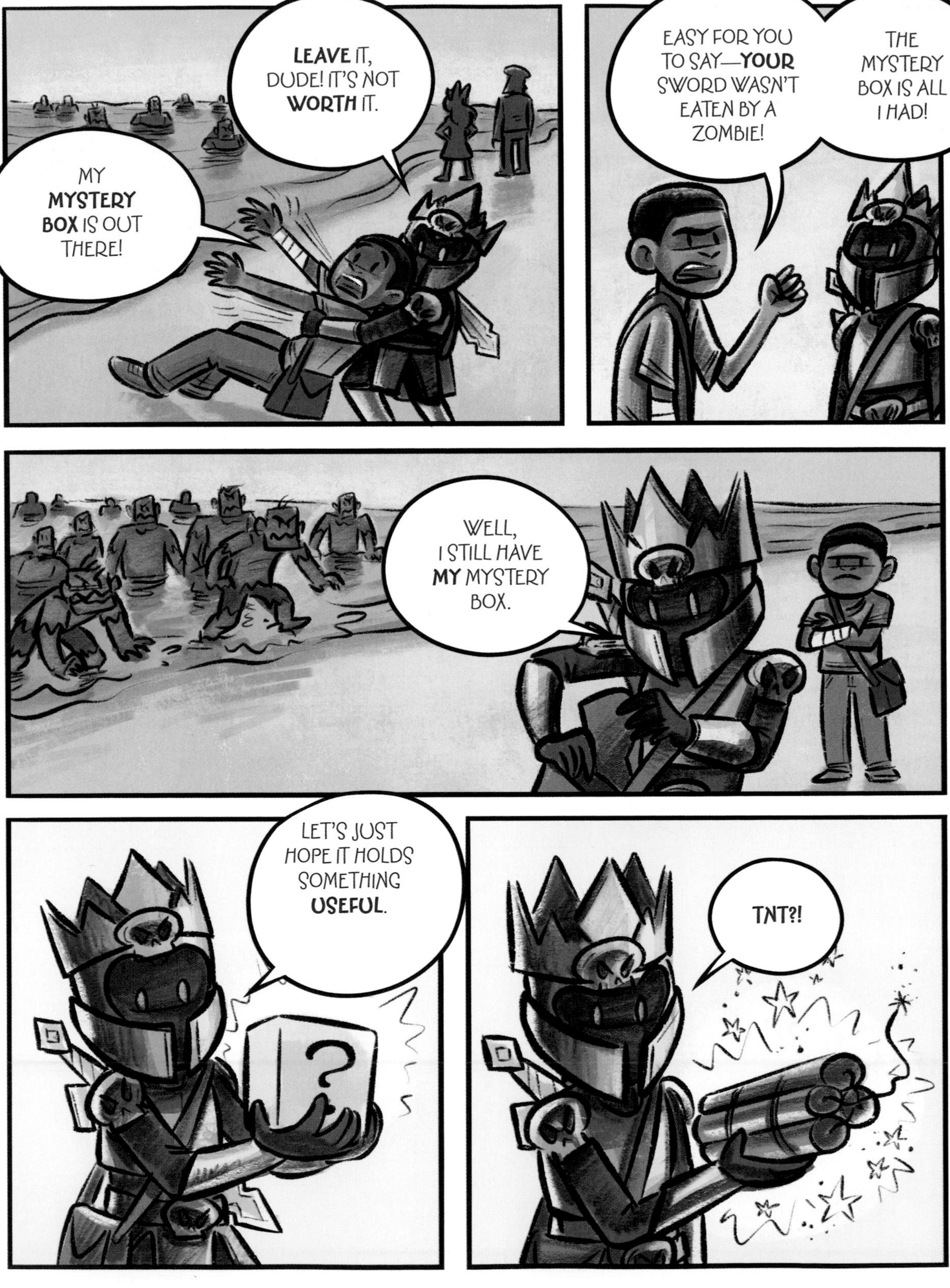

LEAVE IT, DUDE! IT'S NOT WORTH IT.
MY MYSTERY BOX IS OUT THERE!
EASY FOR YOU TO SAY—YOUR SWORD WASN'T EATEN BY A ZOMBIE!
THE MYSTERY BOX IS ALL I HAD!
WELL, I STILL HAVE MY MYSTERY BOX.
LET'S JUST HOPE IT HOLDS SOMETHING USEFUL.
TNT?!

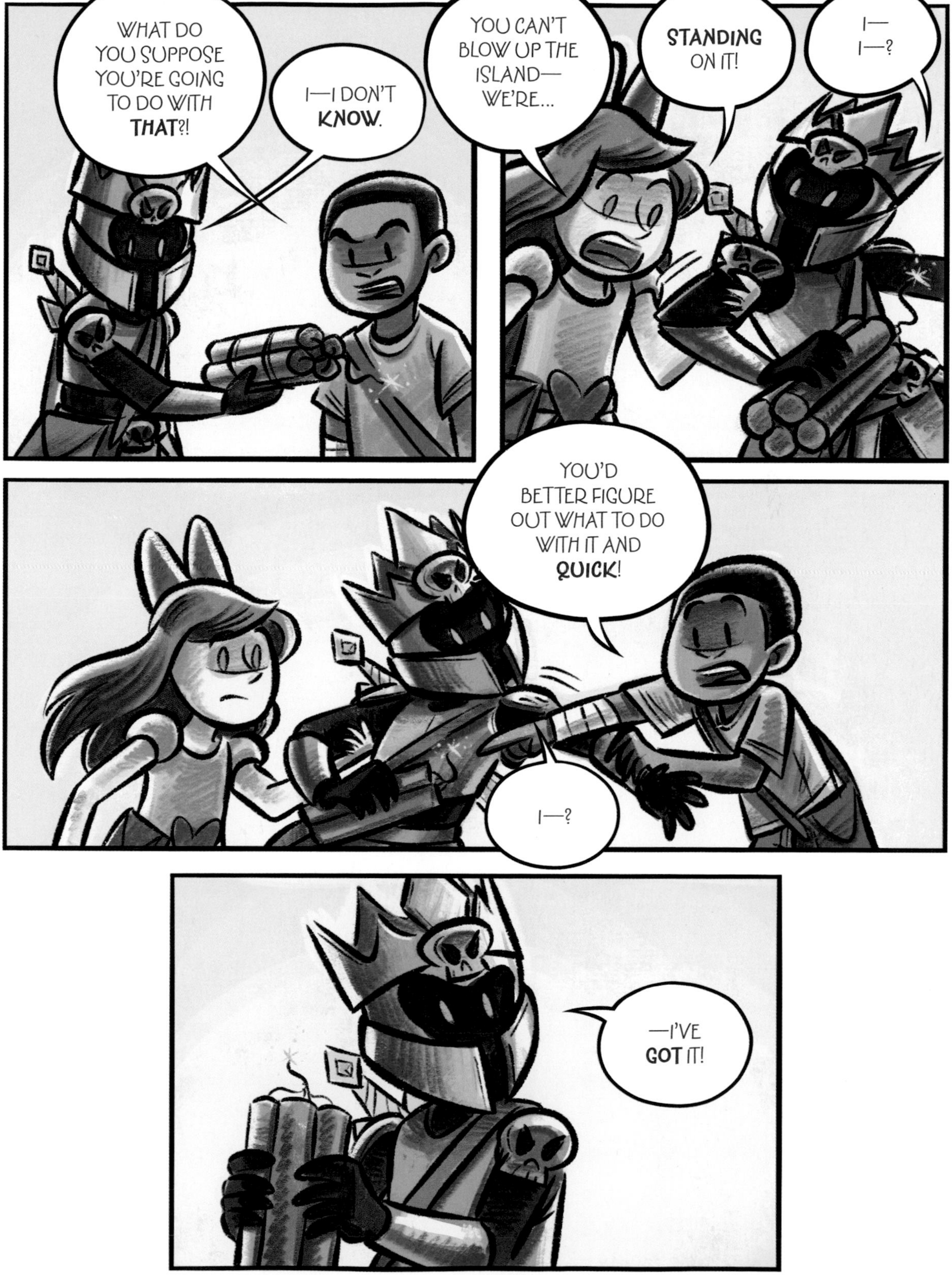
WHAT DO YOU SUPPOSE YOU'RE GOING TO DO WITH THAT?!
I—I DON'T KNOW.
YOU CAN'T BLOW UP THE ISLAND—WE'RE...
STANDING ON IT!
I—
I—?
YOU'D BETTER FIGURE OUT WHAT TO DO WITH IT AND QUICK!
I—?
—I'VE GOT IT!

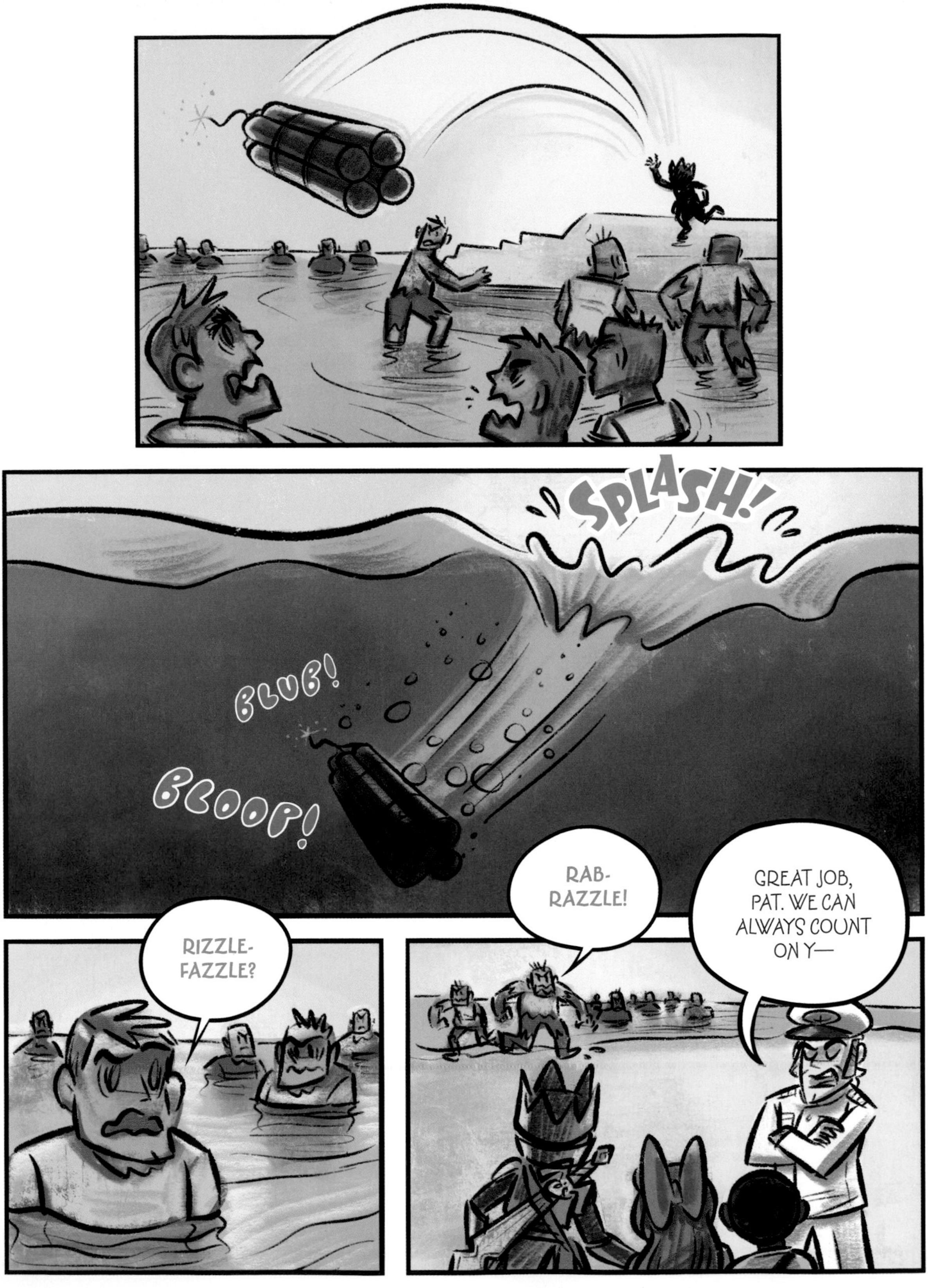
SPLASH!
BLUB!
BLOOP!
RIZZLE-FAZZLE?
RAB-RAZZLE!
GREAT JOB, PAT. WE CAN ALWAYS COUNT ON Y—

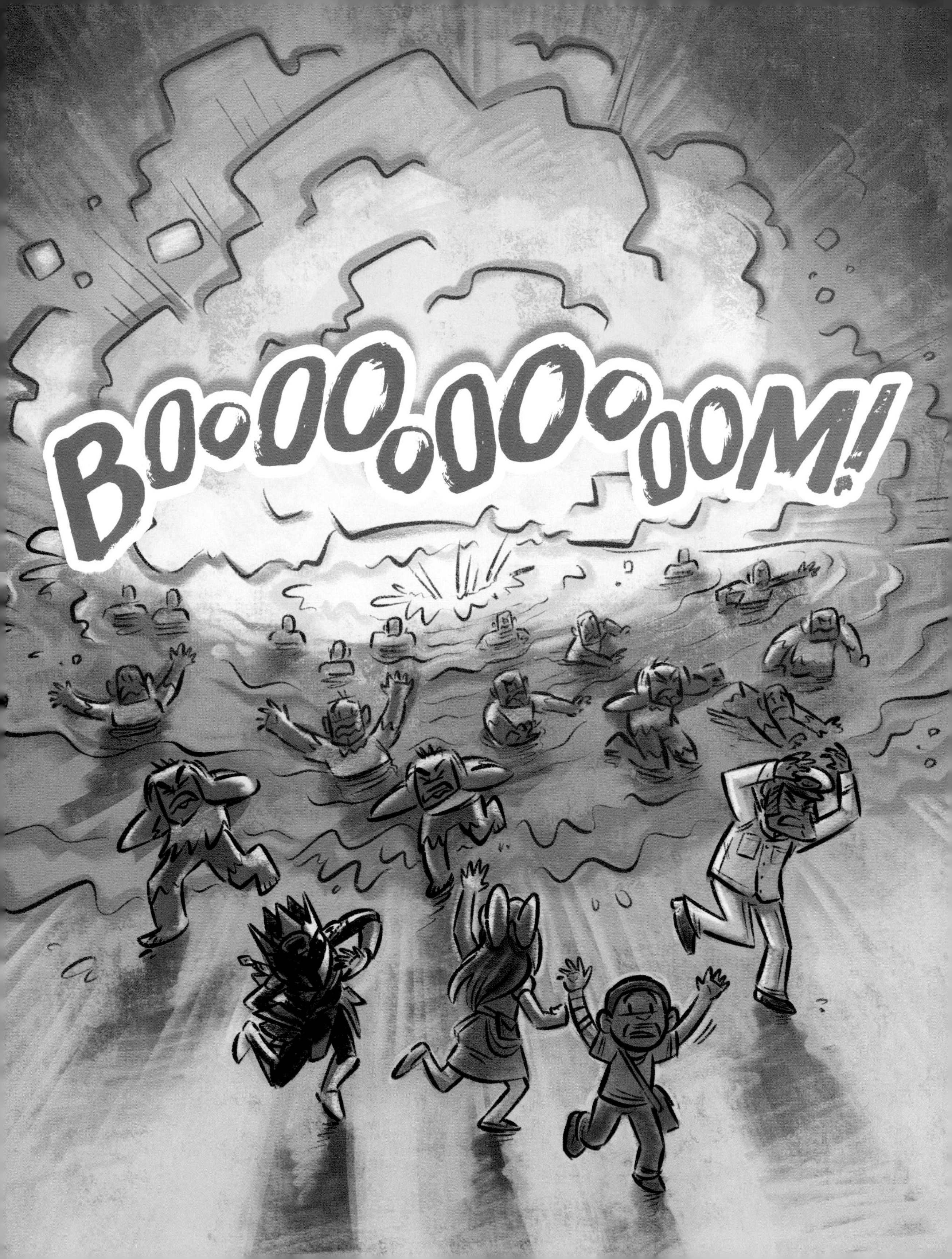
BOOOOOOOOOM!

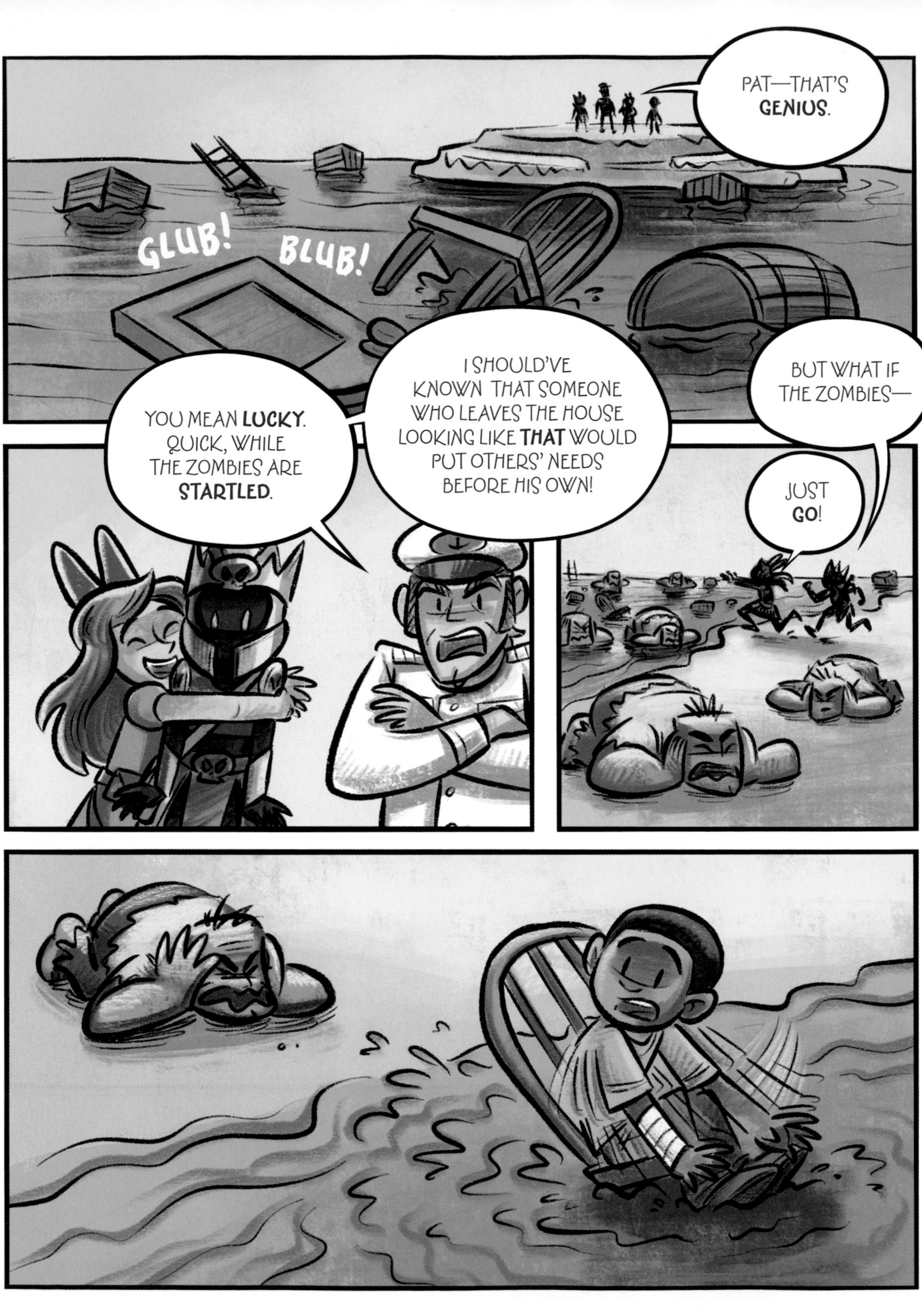
PAT—THAT'S **GENIUS**.
GLUB!
BLUB!
YOU MEAN **LUCKY**. QUICK, WHILE THE ZOMBIES ARE **STARTLED**.
I SHOULD'VE KNOWN THAT SOMEONE WHO LEAVES THE HOUSE LOOKING LIKE **THAT** WOULD PUT OTHERS' NEEDS BEFORE HIS OWN!
BUT WHAT IF THE ZOMBIES—
JUST **GO**!

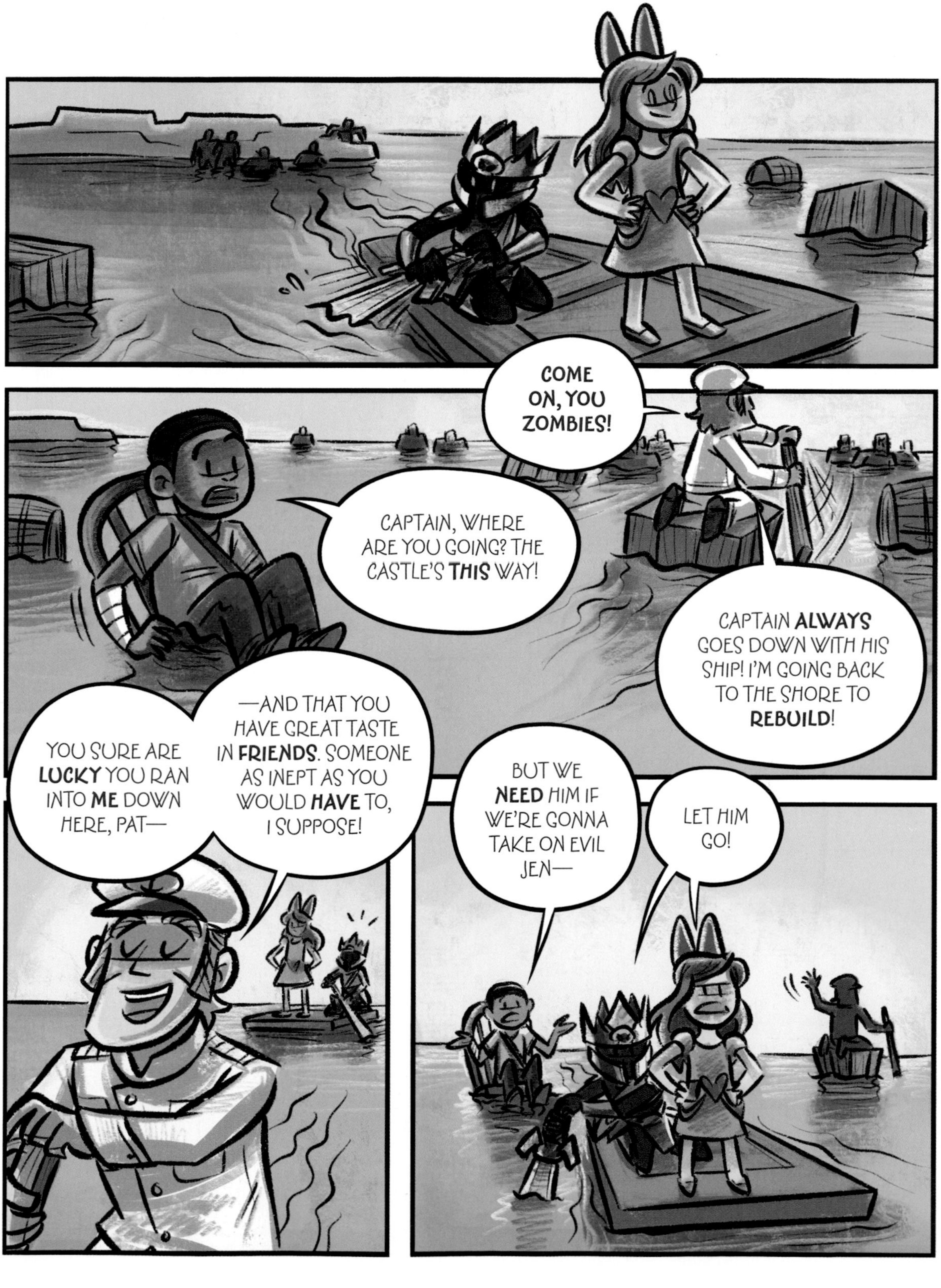
COME ON, YOU ZOMBIES!
CAPTAIN, WHERE ARE YOU GOING? THE CASTLE'S THIS WAY!
CAPTAIN ALWAYS GOES DOWN WITH HIS SHIP! I'M GOING BACK TO THE SHORE TO REBUILD!
YOU SURE ARE LUCKY YOU RAN INTO ME DOWN HERE, PAT—
—AND THAT YOU HAVE GREAT TASTE IN FRIENDS. SOMEONE AS INEPT AS YOU WOULD HAVE TO, I SUPPOSE!
BUT WE NEED HIM IF WE'RE GONNA TAKE ON EVIL JEN—
LET HIM GO!

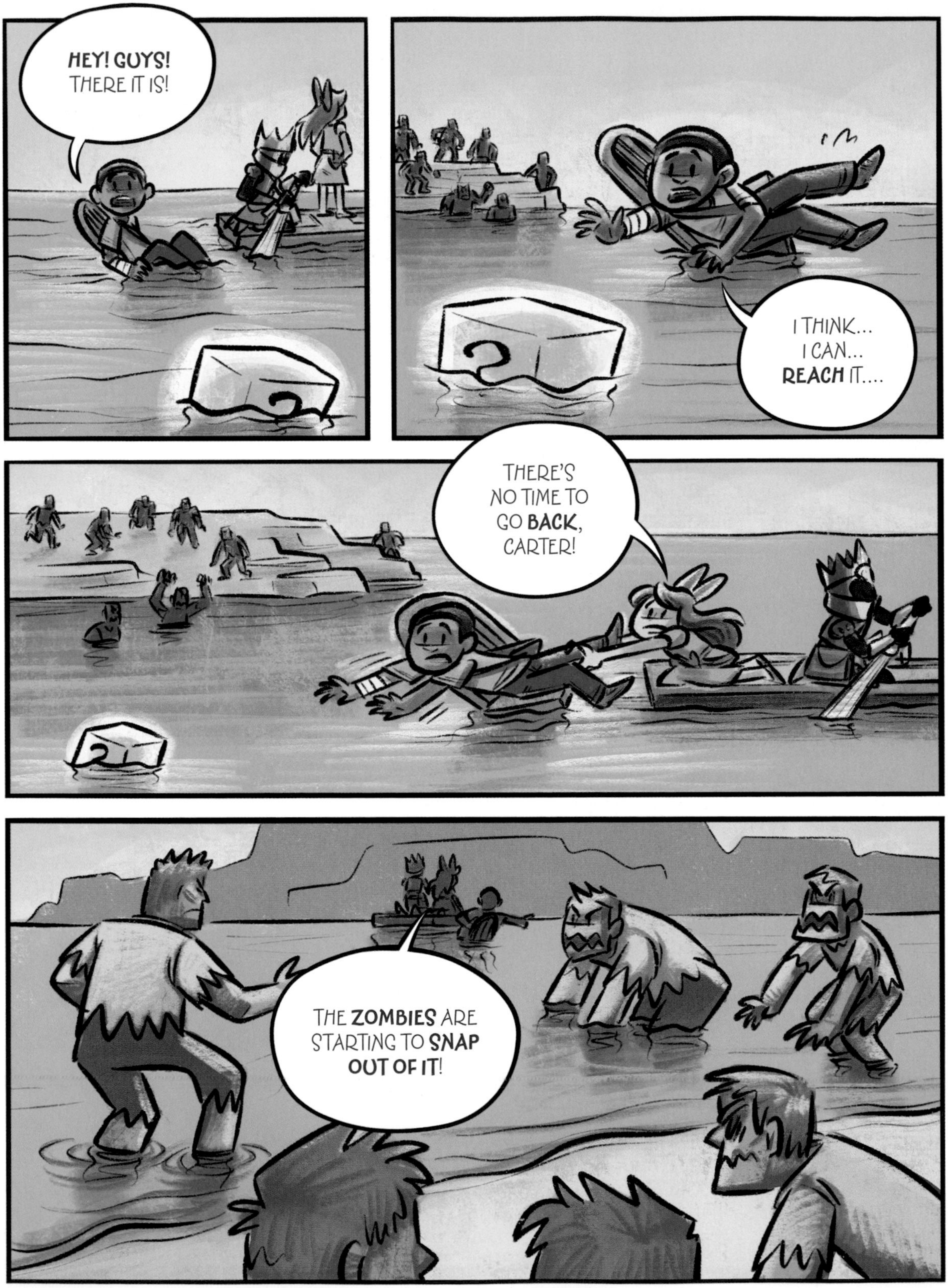
HEY! GUYS! THERE IT IS!
I THINK... I CAN... REACH IT....
THERE'S NO TIME TO GO BACK, CARTER!
THE ZOMBIES ARE STARTING TO SNAP OUT OF IT!

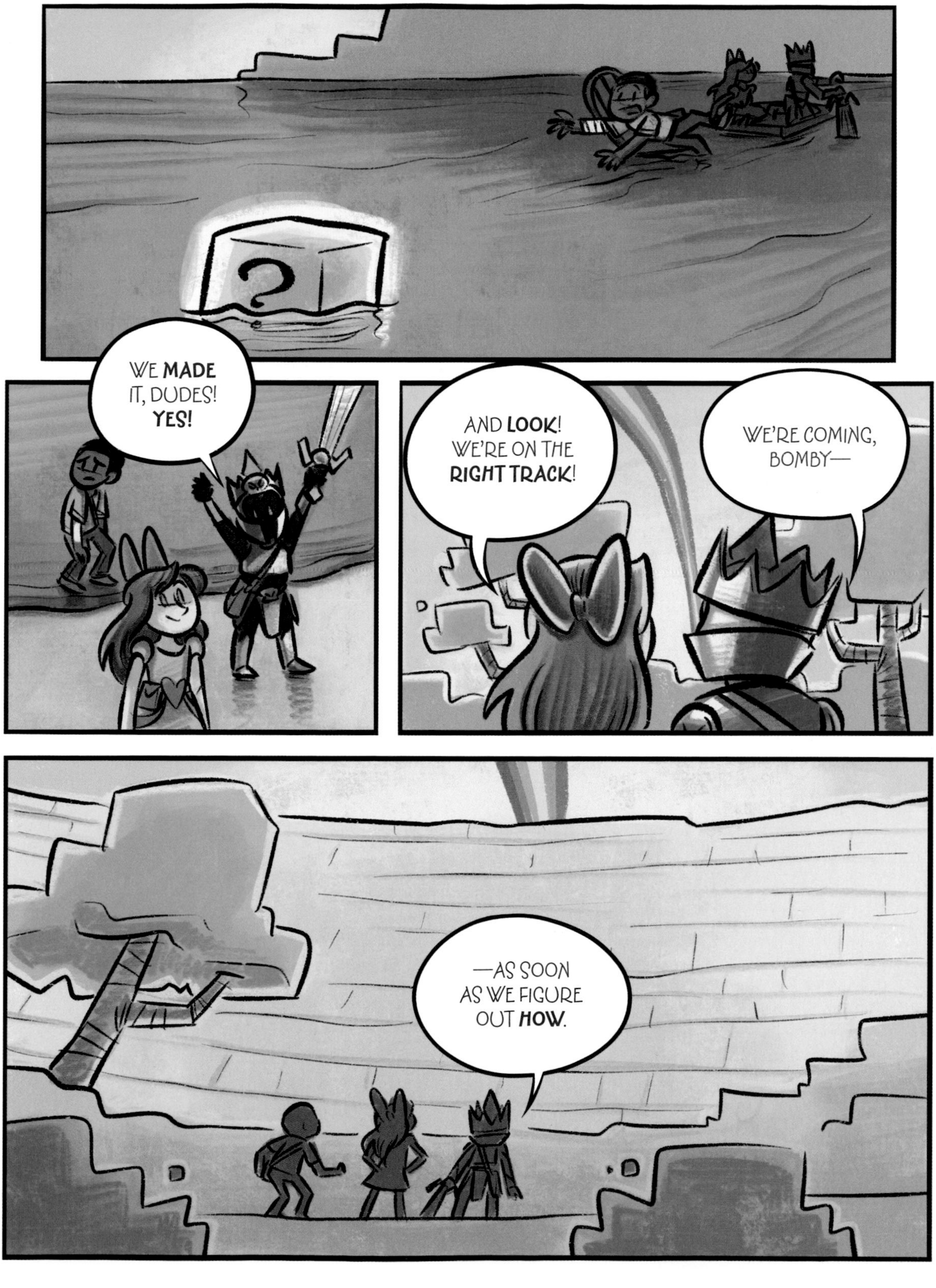
WE MADE IT, DUDES! YES!
AND LOOK! WE'RE ON THE RIGHT TRACK!
WE'RE COMING, BOMBY—
—AS SOON AS WE FIGURE OUT HOW.

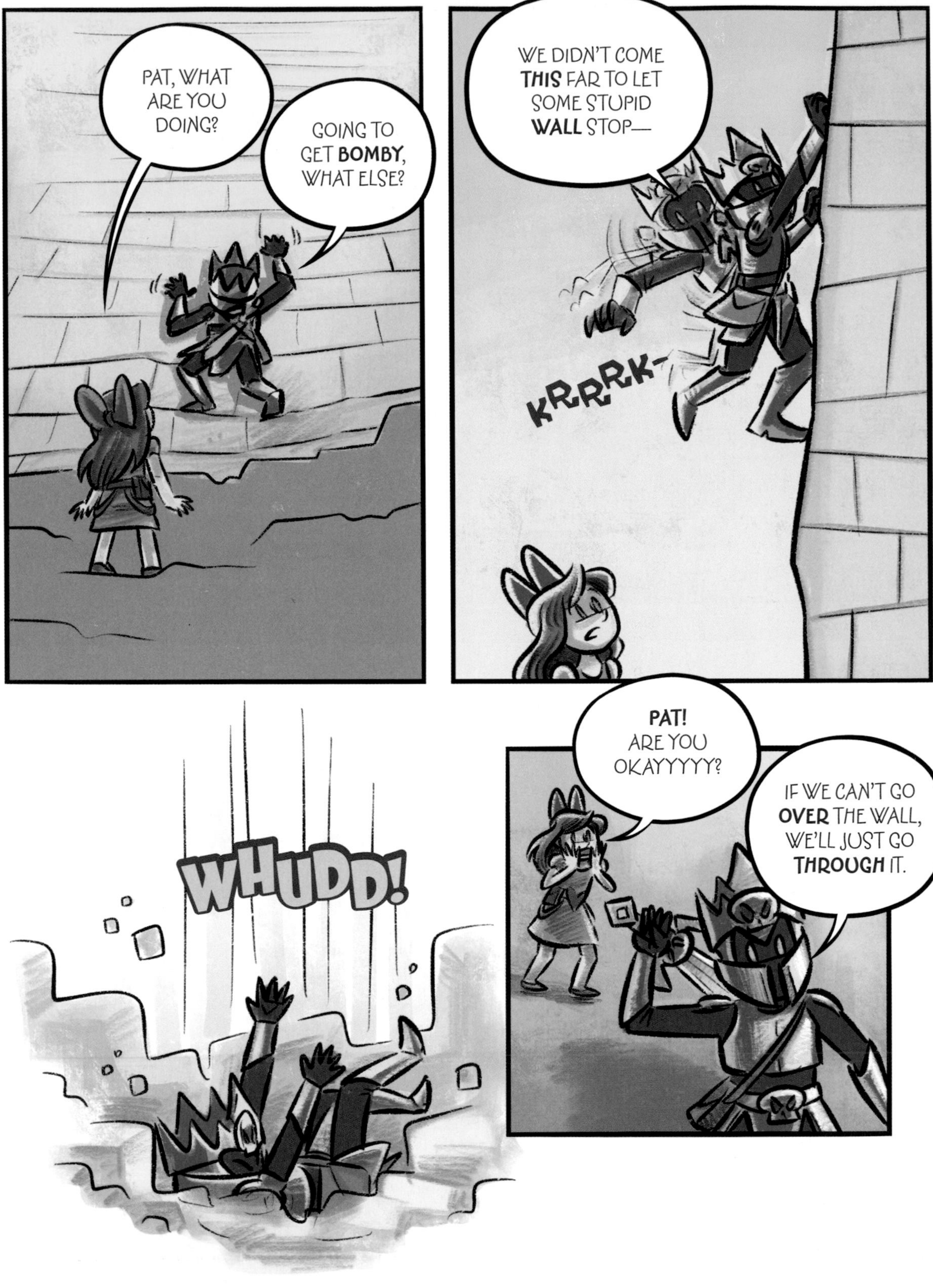
PAT, WHAT ARE YOU DOING?
GOING TO GET **BOMBY**, WHAT ELSE?
WE DIDN'T COME **THIS** FAR TO LET SOME STUPID **WALL** STOP—
KRRRK-
WHUDD!
PAT! ARE YOU OKAYYYYY?
IF WE CAN'T GO **OVER** THE WALL, WE'LL JUST GO **THROUGH** IT.

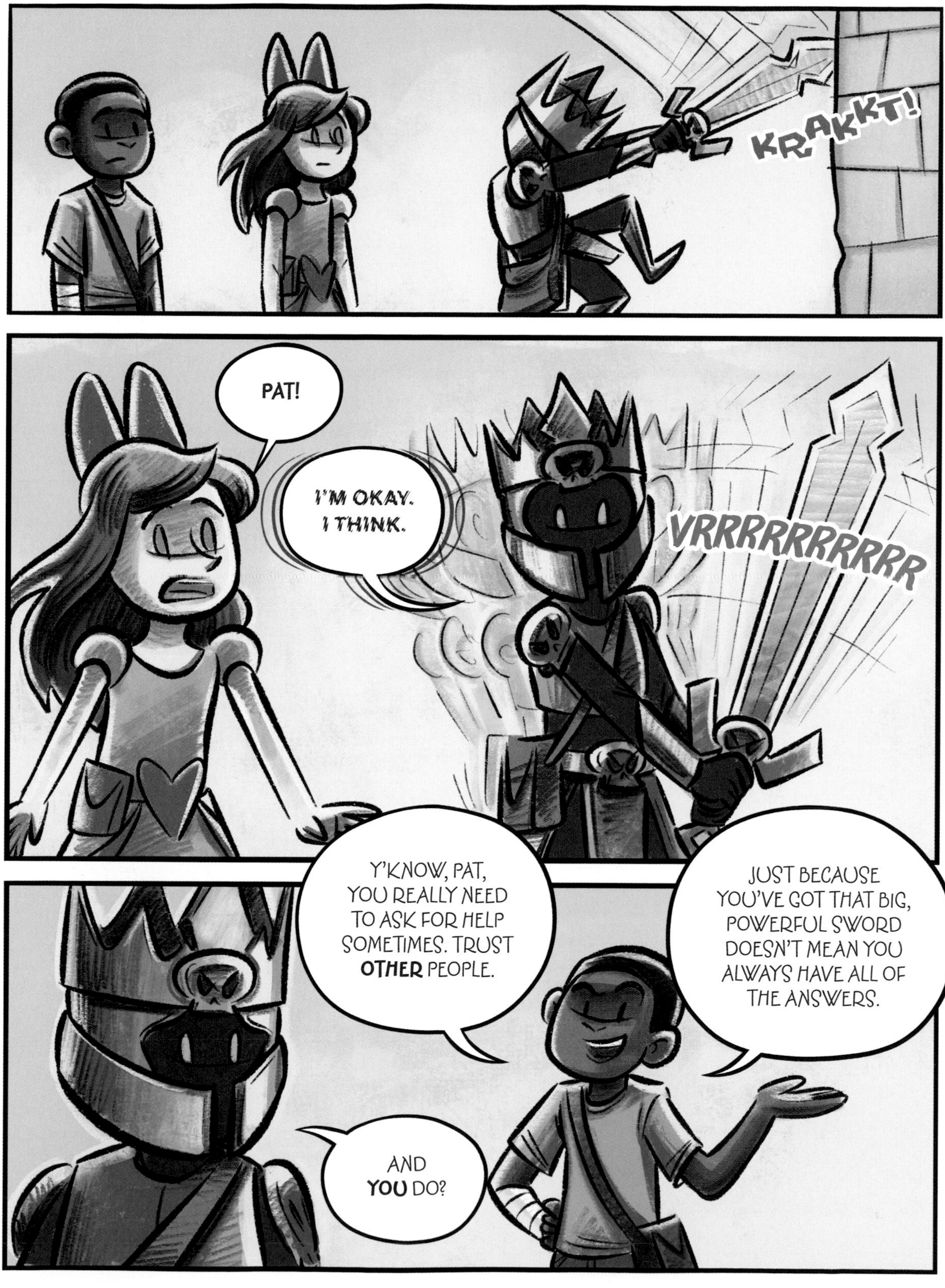
KRAKKT!
PAT!
I'M OKAY. I THINK.
VRRRRRRRRRRR
Y'KNOW, PAT, YOU REALLY NEED TO ASK FOR HELP SOMETIMES. TRUST **OTHER** PEOPLE.
JUST BECAUSE YOU'VE GOT THAT BIG, POWERFUL SWORD DOESN'T MEAN YOU ALWAYS HAVE ALL OF THE ANSWERS.
AND **YOU** DO?

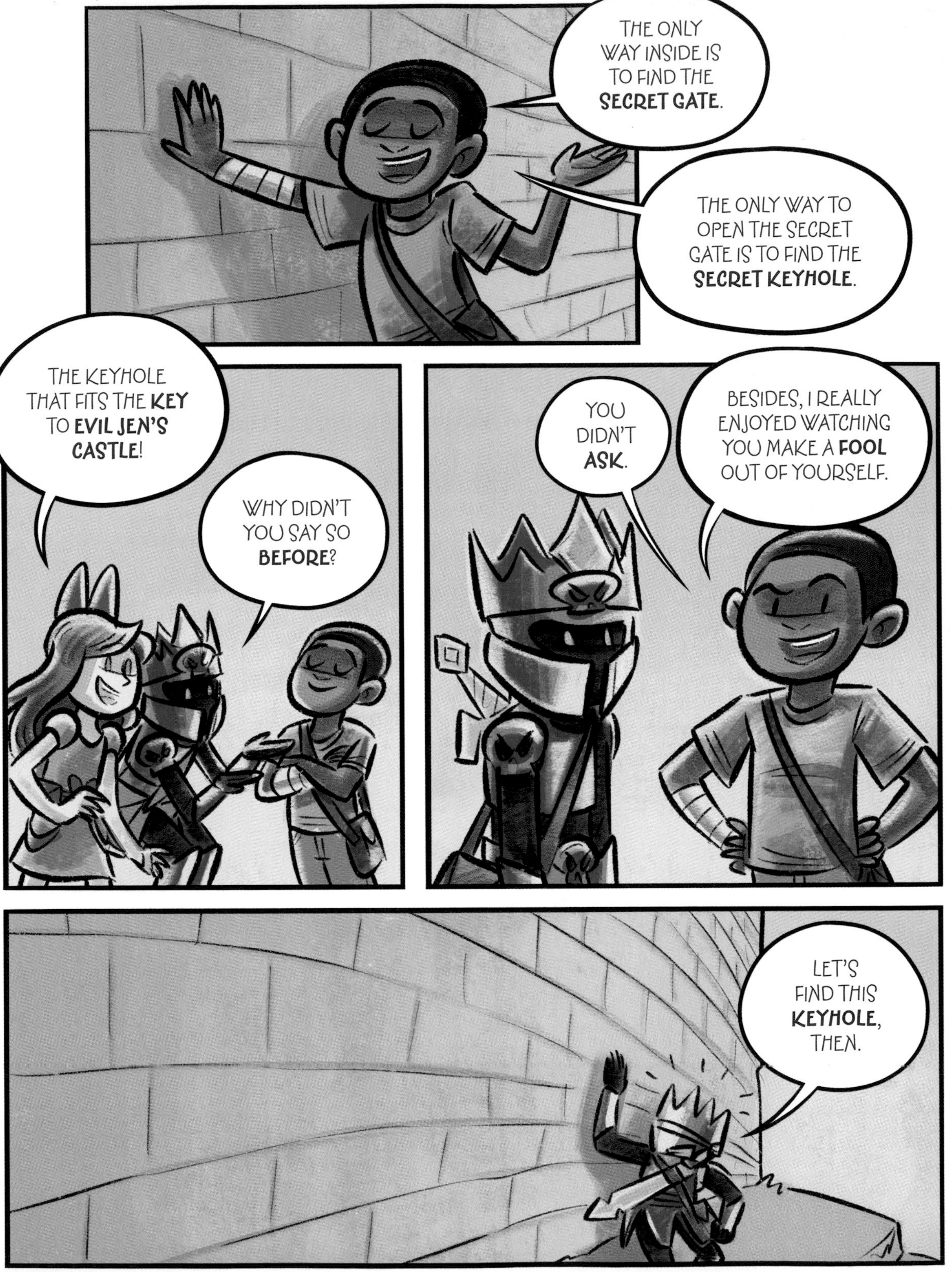
THE ONLY WAY INSIDE IS TO FIND THE **SECRET GATE**.
THE ONLY WAY TO OPEN THE SECRET GATE IS TO FIND THE **SECRET KEYHOLE**.
THE KEYHOLE THAT FITS THE **KEY** TO **EVIL JEN'S CASTLE**!
WHY DIDN'T YOU SAY SO **BEFORE**?
YOU DIDN'T **ASK**.
BESIDES, I REALLY ENJOYED WATCHING YOU MAKE A **FOOL** OUT OF YOURSELF.
LET'S FIND THIS **KEYHOLE**, THEN.

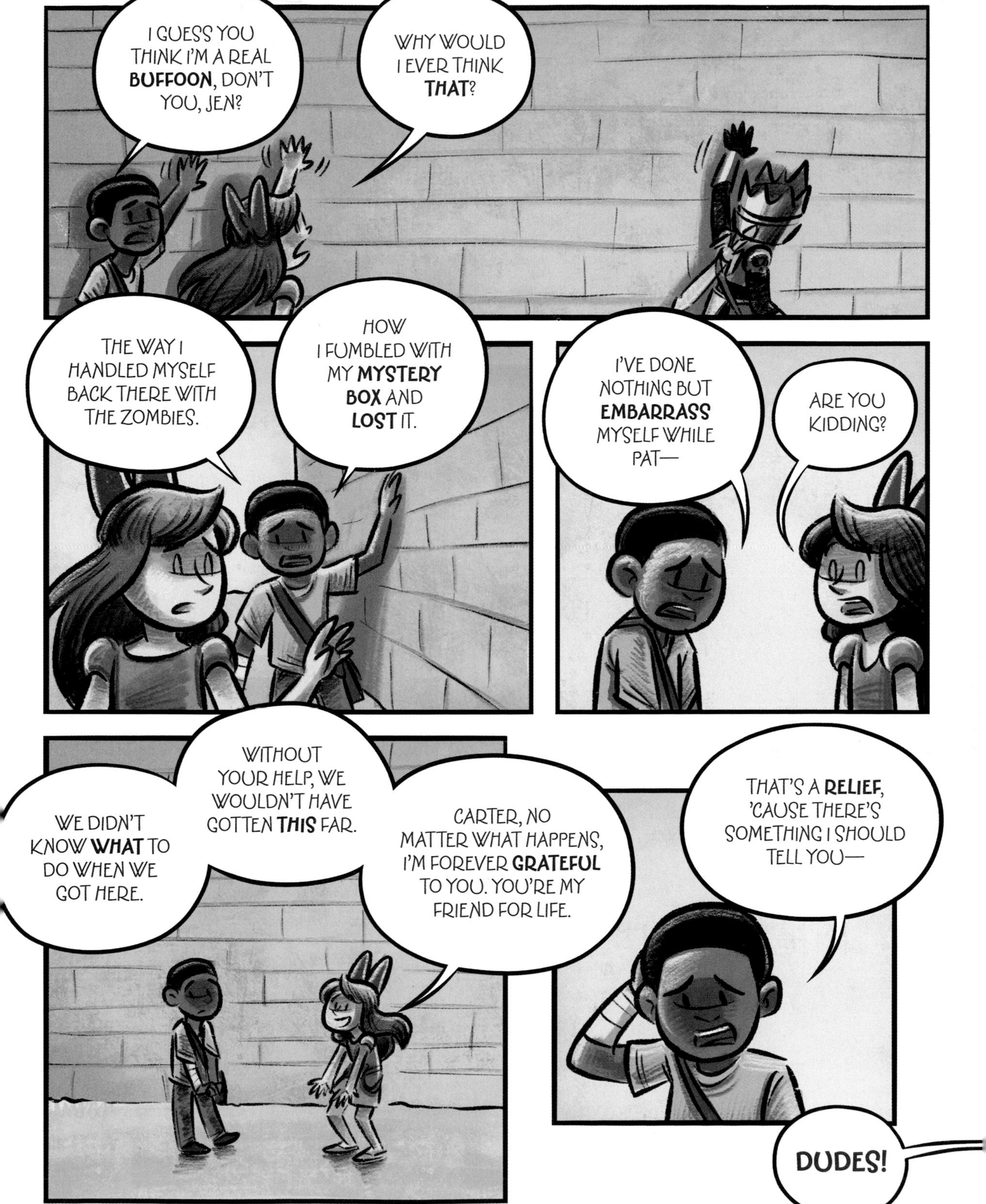
I GUESS YOU THINK I'M A REAL **BUFFOON**, DON'T YOU, JEN?
WHY WOULD I EVER THINK **THAT**?
THE WAY I HANDLED MYSELF BACK THERE WITH THE ZOMBIES.
HOW I FUMBLED WITH MY **MYSTERY BOX** AND **LOST** IT.
I'VE DONE NOTHING BUT **EMBARRASS** MYSELF WHILE PAT—
ARE YOU KIDDING?
WE DIDN'T KNOW **WHAT** TO DO WHEN WE GOT HERE.
WITHOUT YOUR HELP, WE WOULDN'T HAVE GOTTEN **THIS** FAR.
CARTER, NO MATTER WHAT HAPPENS, I'M FOREVER **GRATEFUL** TO YOU. YOU'RE MY FRIEND FOR LIFE.
THAT'S A **RELIEF**, 'CAUSE THERE'S SOMETHING I SHOULD TELL YOU—
DUDES!

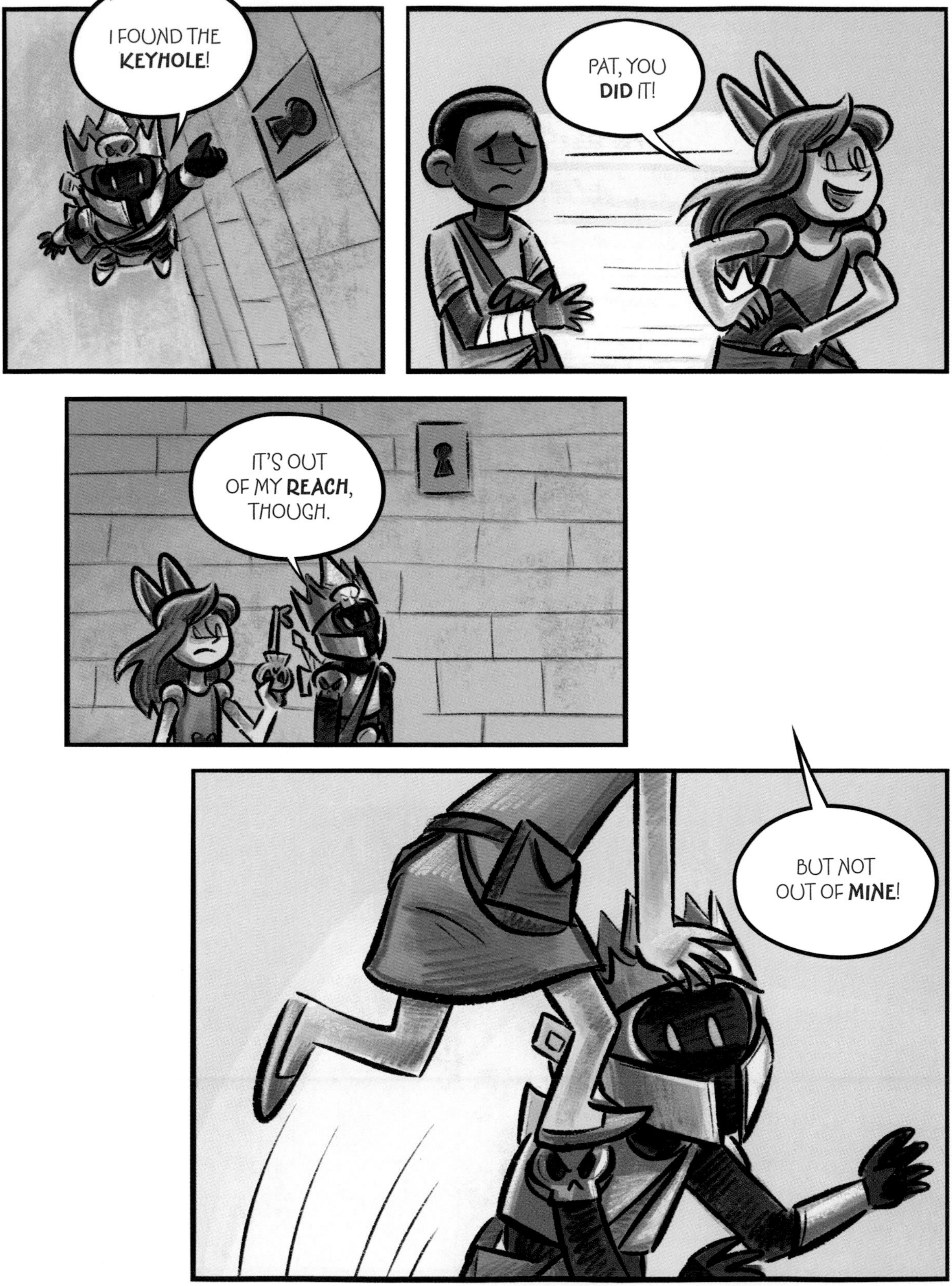
I FOUND THE **KEYHOLE**!
PAT, YOU **DID** IT!
IT'S OUT OF MY **REACH**, THOUGH.
BUT NOT OUT OF **MINE**!

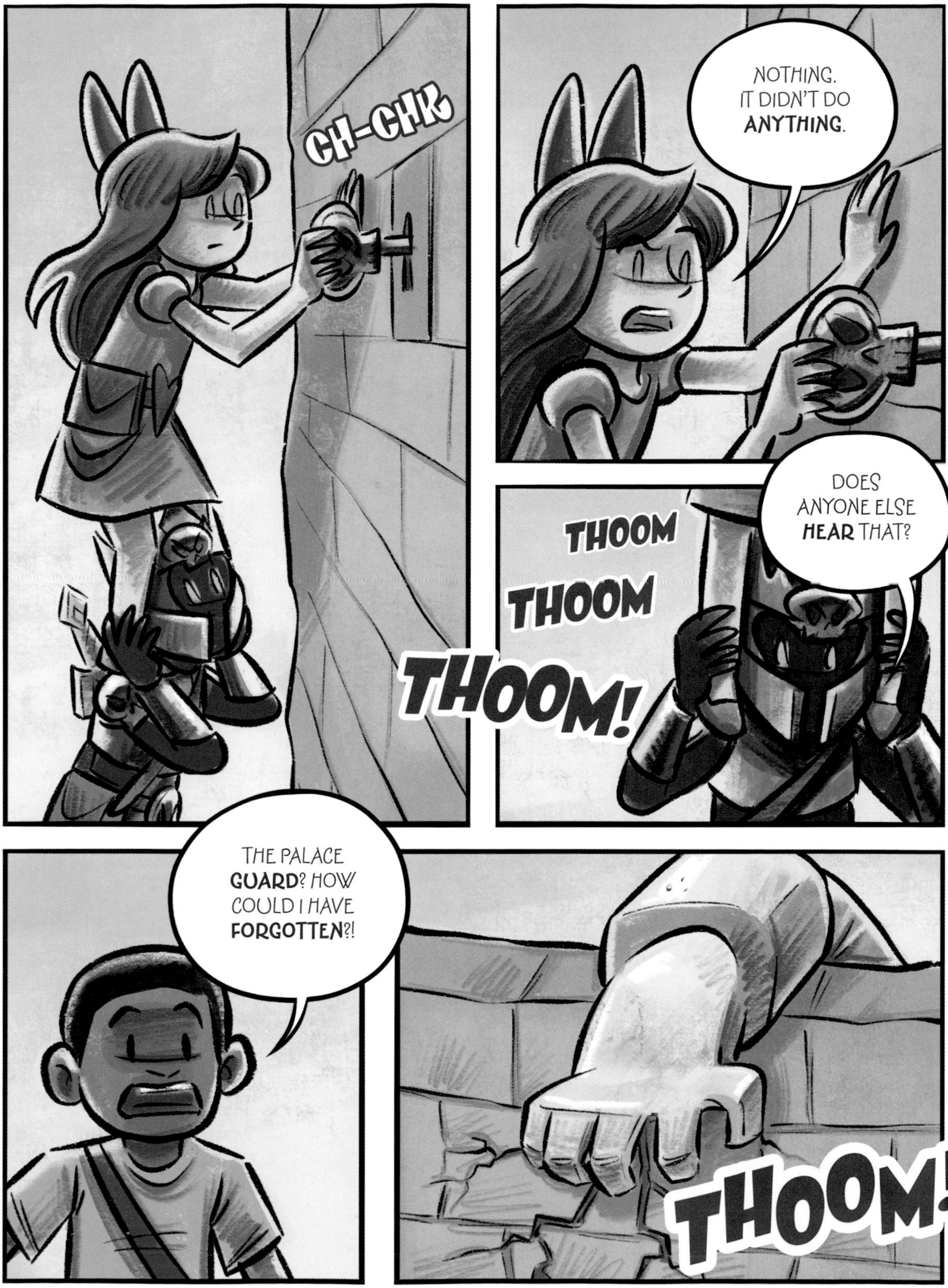
CH-CHR
NOTHING. IT DIDN'T DO **ANYTHING**.
THOOM
THOOM
THOOM!
DOES ANYONE ELSE **HEAR** THAT?
THE PALACE **GUARD**? HOW COULD I HAVE **FORGOTTEN**?!
THOOM!

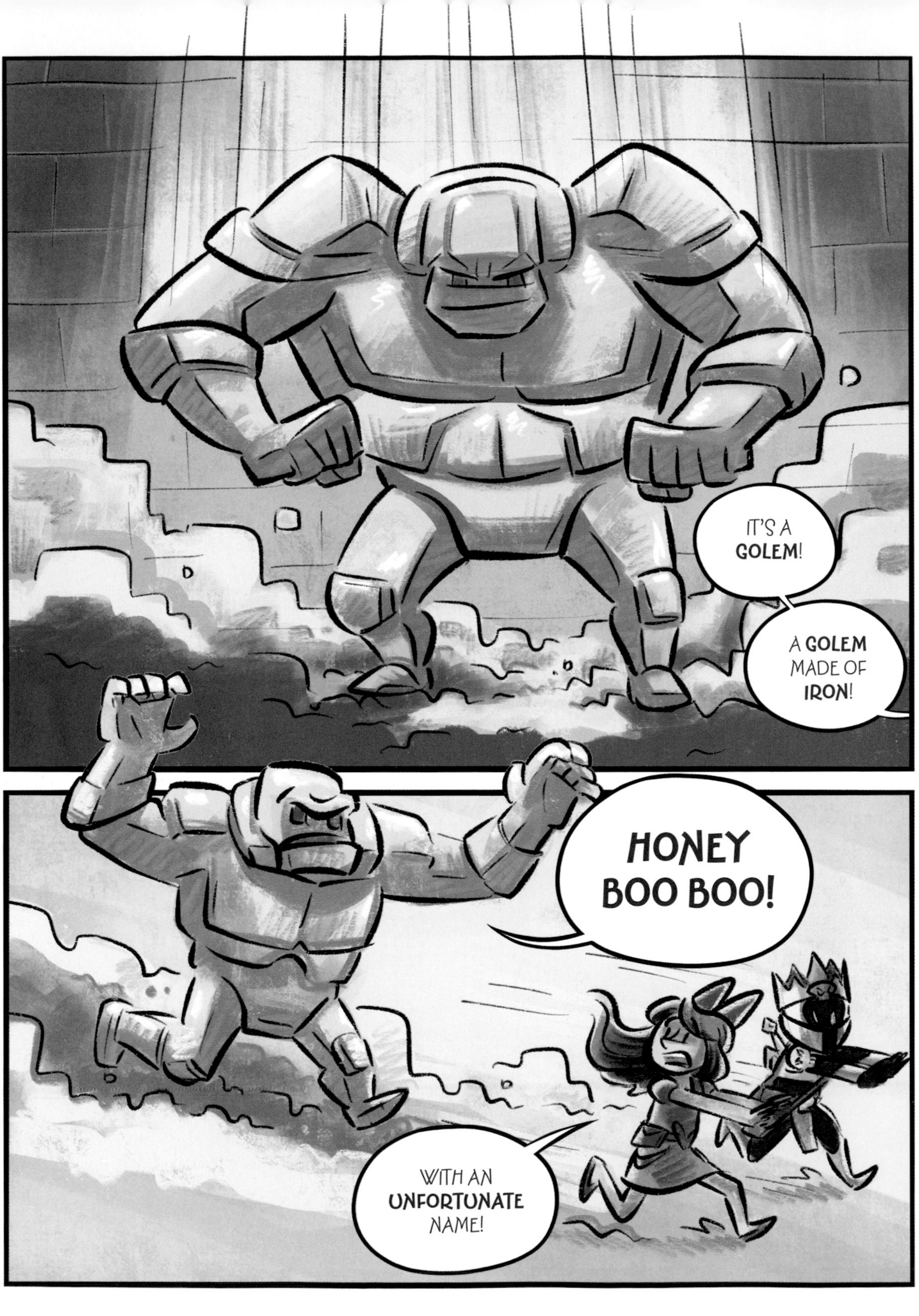
IT'S A GOLEM!
A GOLEM MADE OF IRON!
HONEY BOO BOO!
WITH AN UNFORTUNATE NAME!

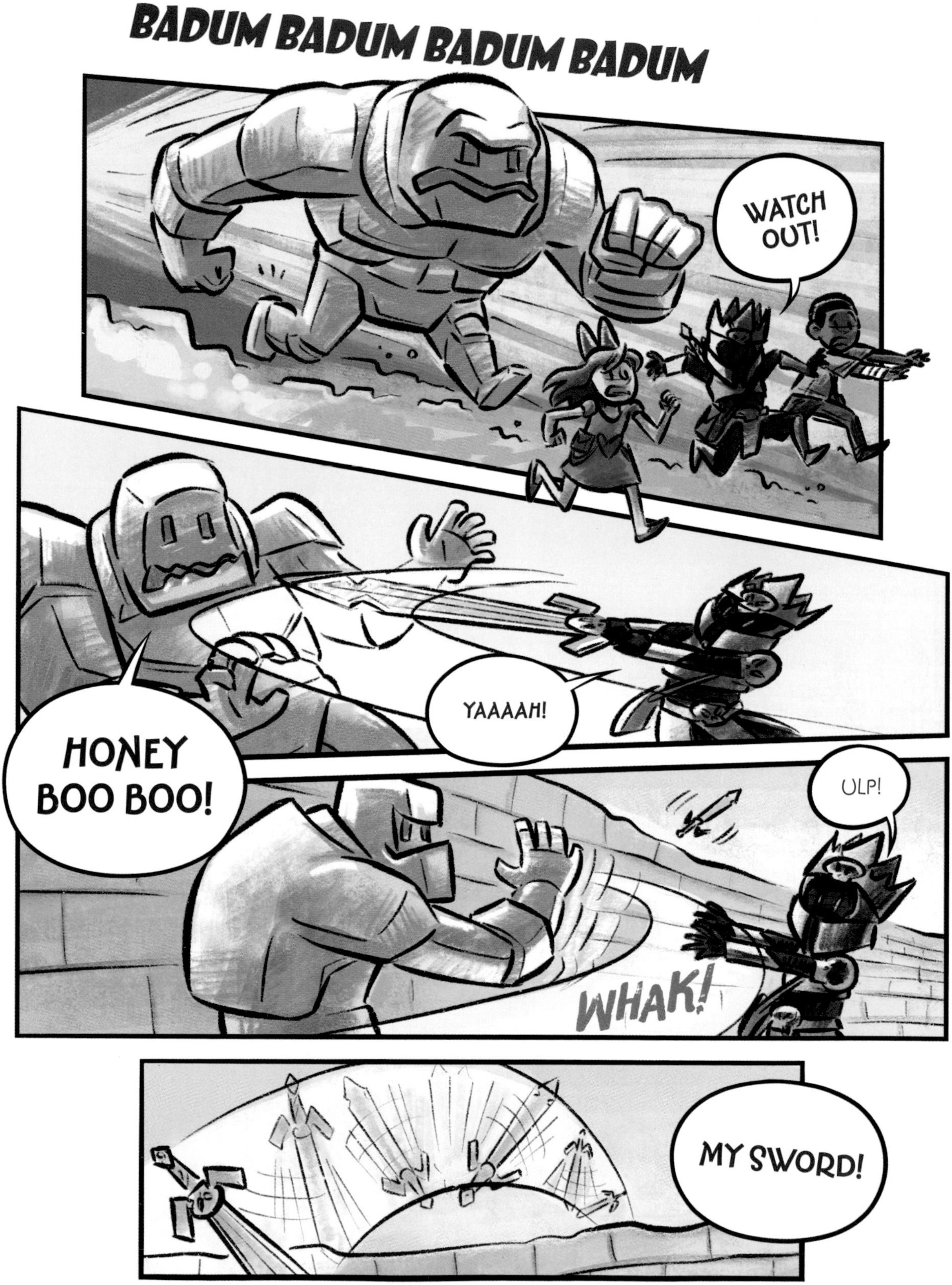
BADUM BADUM BADUM BADUM
WATCH OUT!
HONEY BOO BOO!
YAAAAH!
ULP!
WHAK!
MY SWORD!

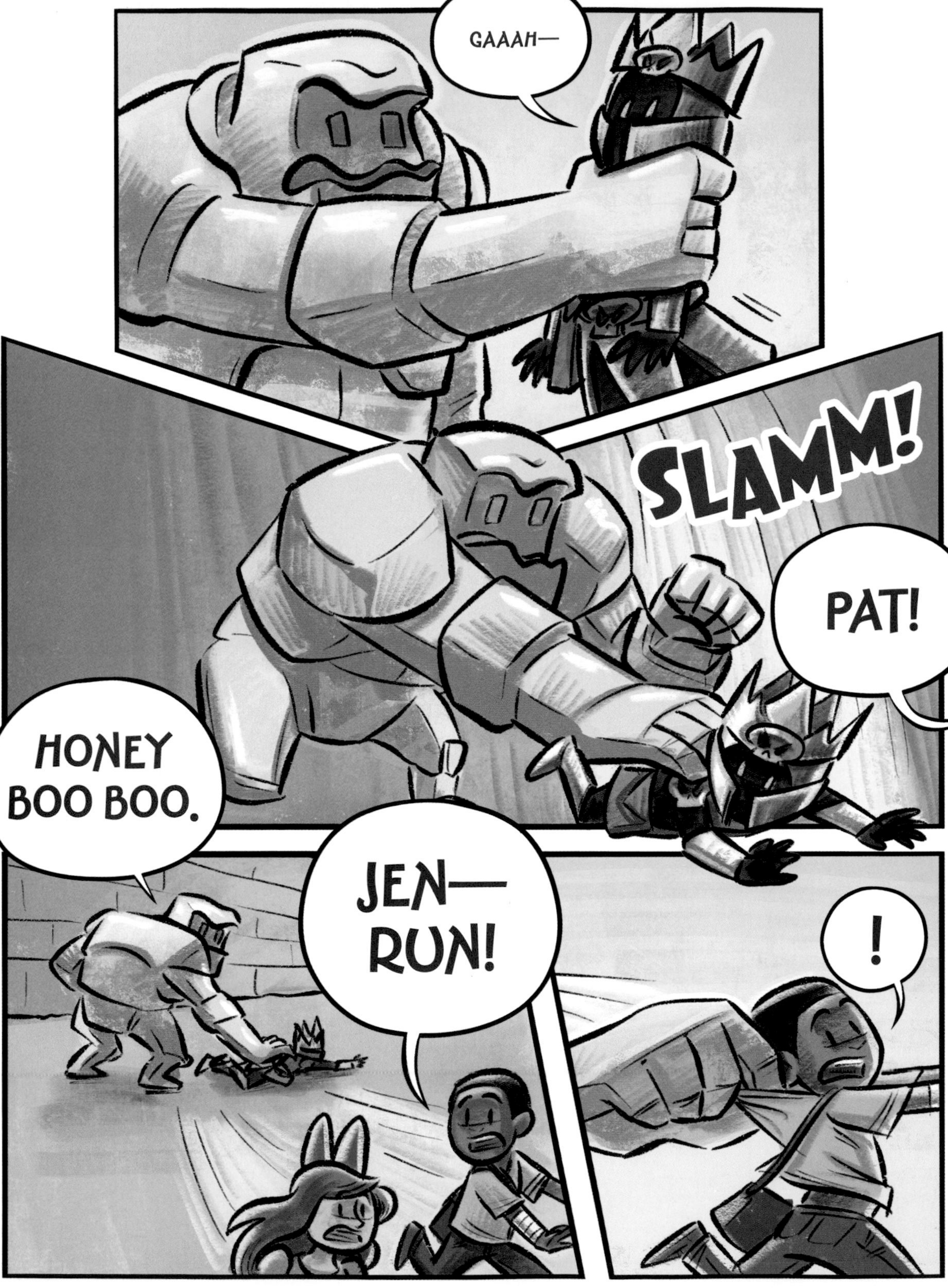
GAAAH—
SLAMM!
PAT!
HONEY BOO BOO.
JEN— RUN!
!

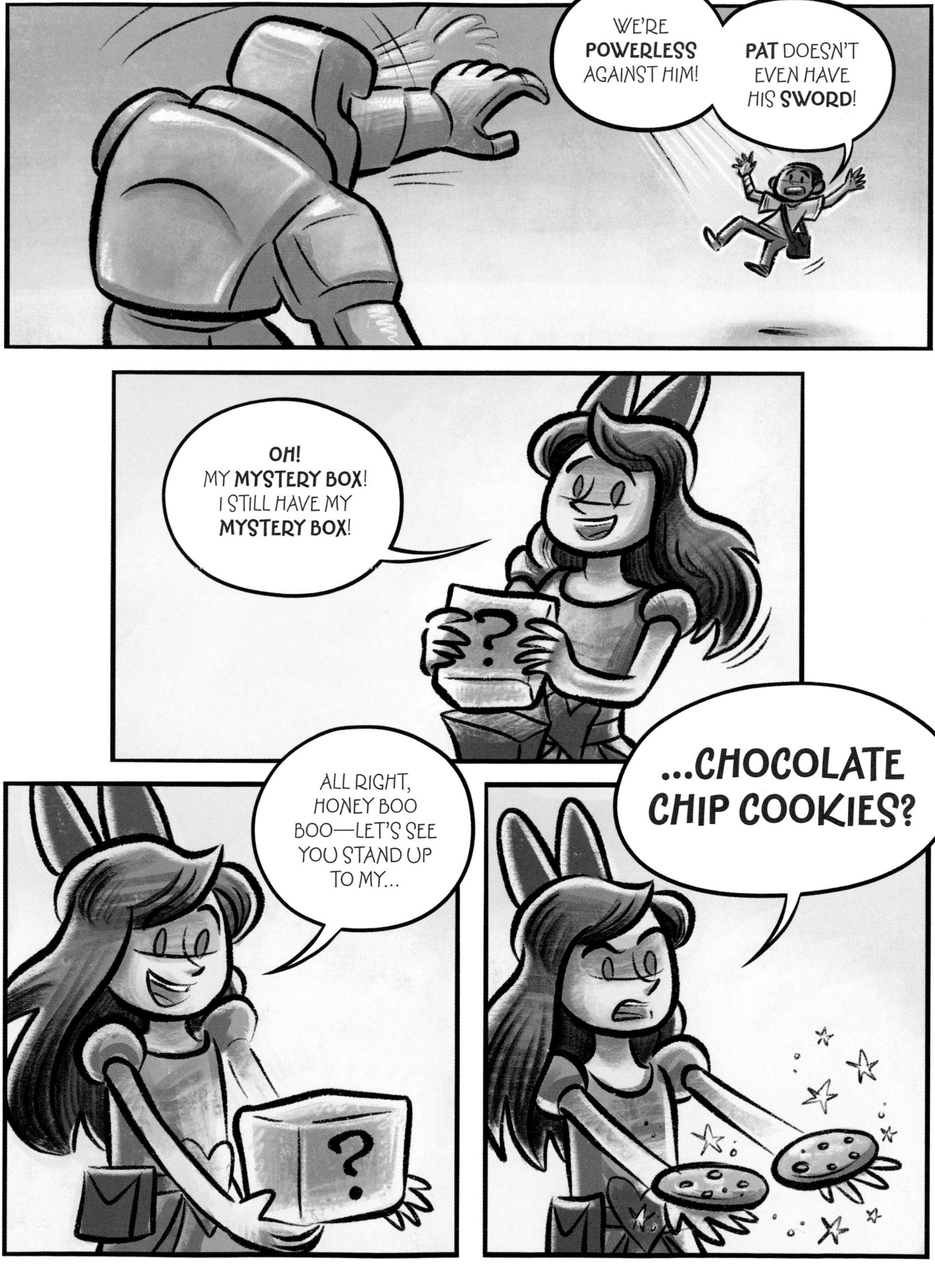
WE'RE POWERLESS AGAINST HIM!
PAT DOESN'T EVEN HAVE HIS SWORD!
OH! MY MYSTERY BOX! I STILL HAVE MY MYSTERY BOX!
ALL RIGHT, HONEY BOO BOO—LET'S SEE YOU STAND UP TO MY...
...CHOCOLATE CHIP COOKIES?

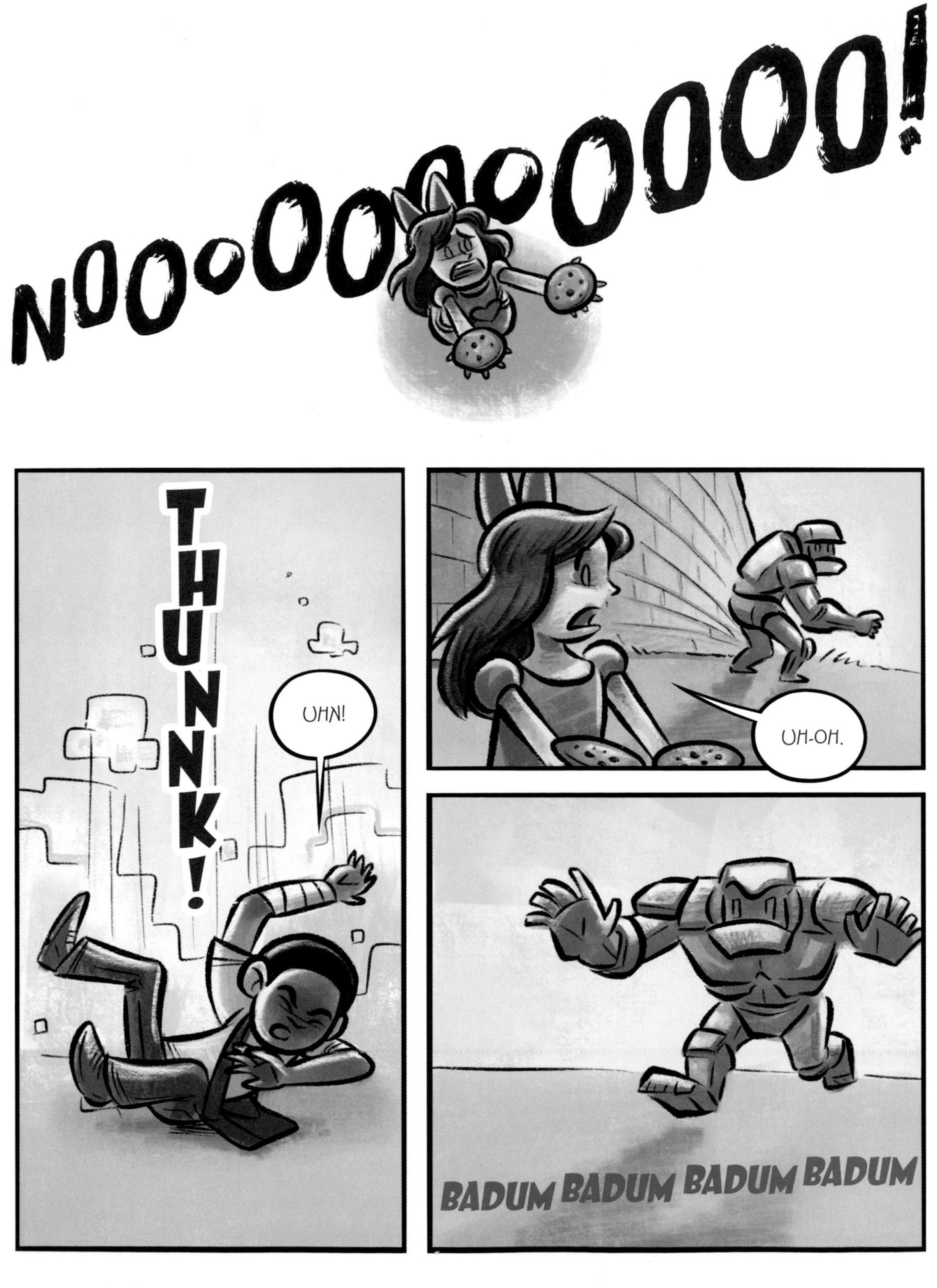
NOOOOOOOOOOOOO!
THUNK!
UHN!
UH-OH.
BADUM BADUM BADUM BADUM

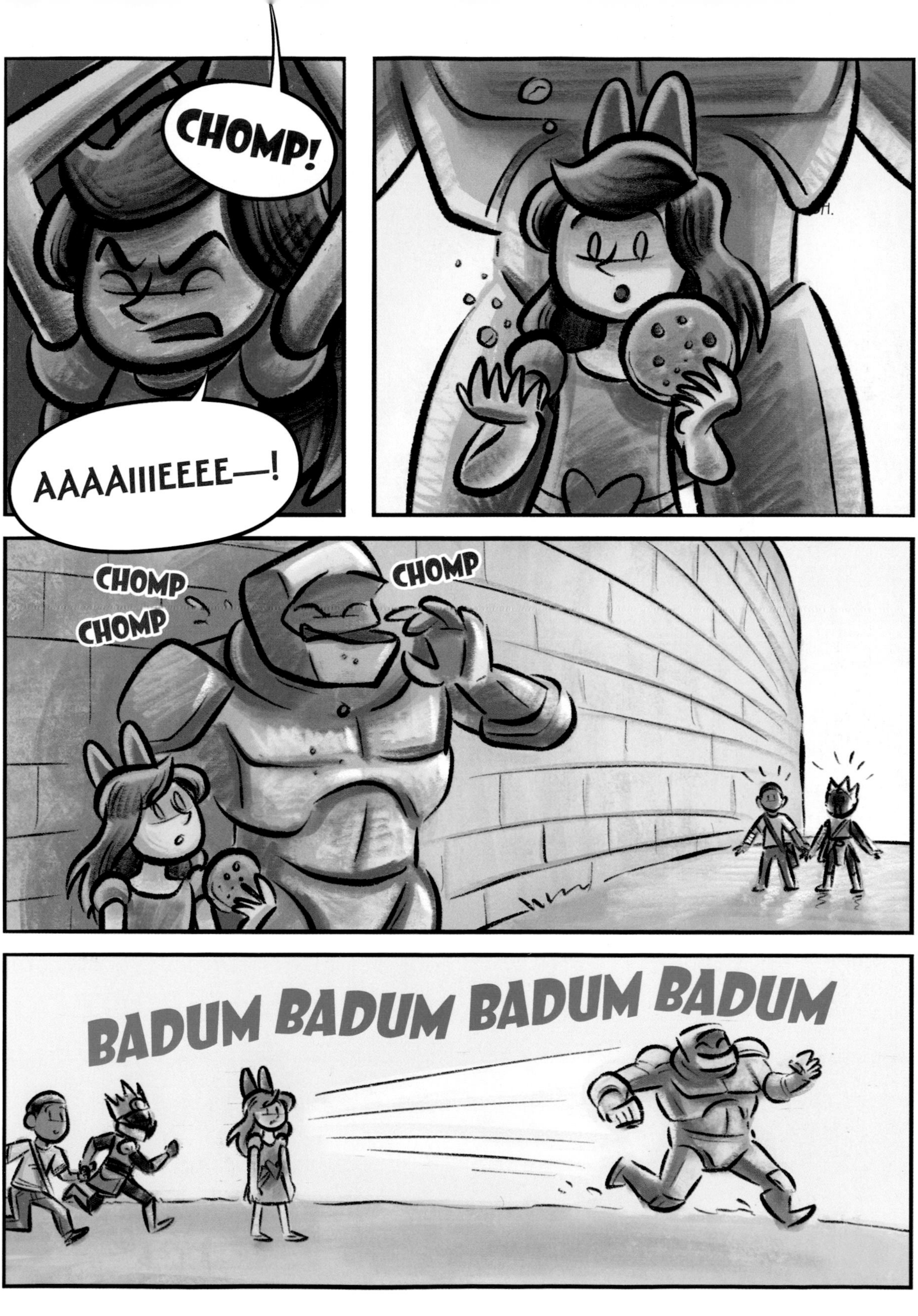
CHOMP!
AAAAIIIIEEEE—!
CHOMP
CHOMP
CHOMP
BADUM BADUM BADUM BADUM

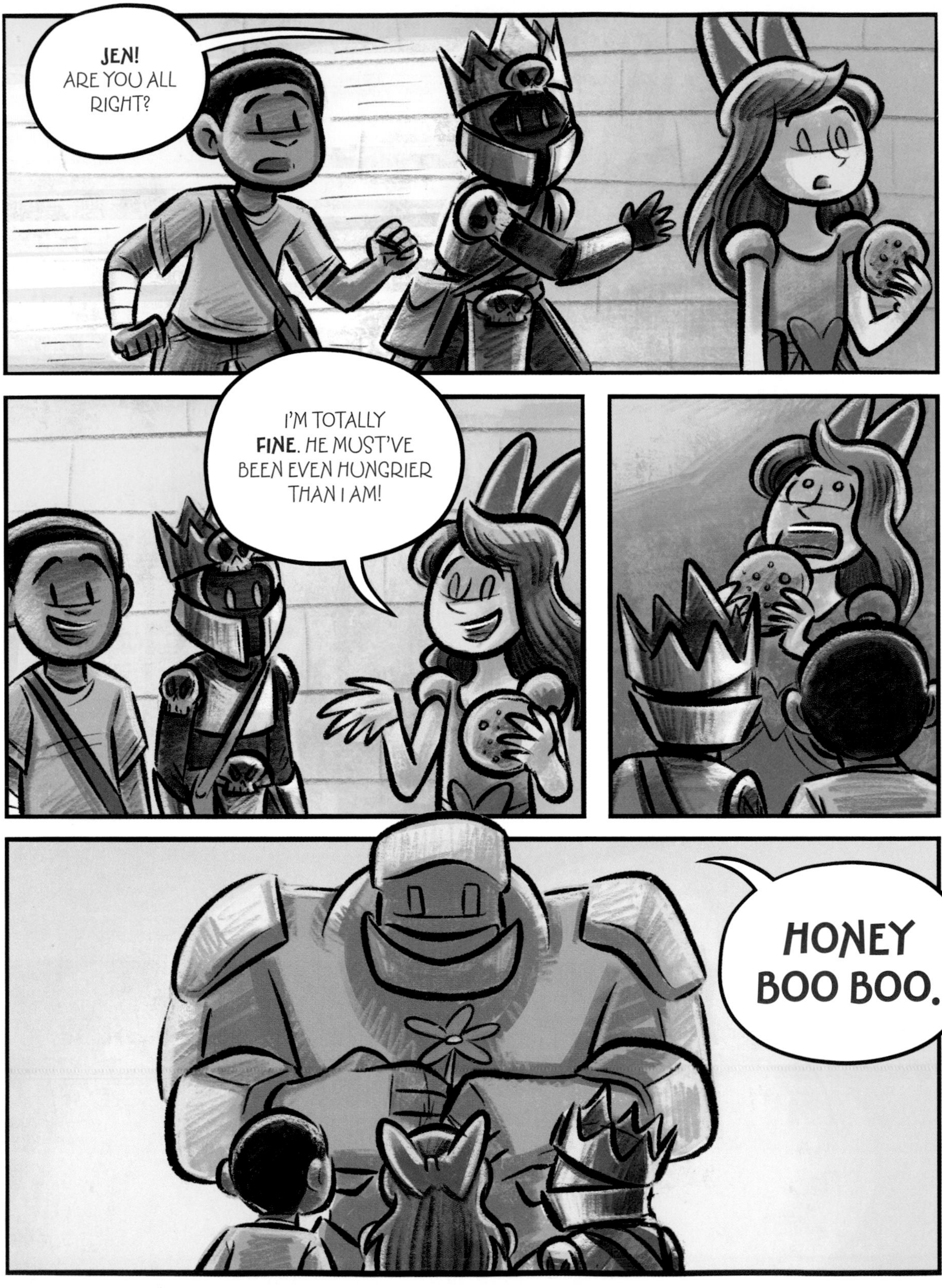
JEN! ARE YOU ALL RIGHT?
I'M TOTALLY FINE. HE MUST'VE BEEN EVEN HUNGRIER THAN I AM!
HONEY BOO BOO.

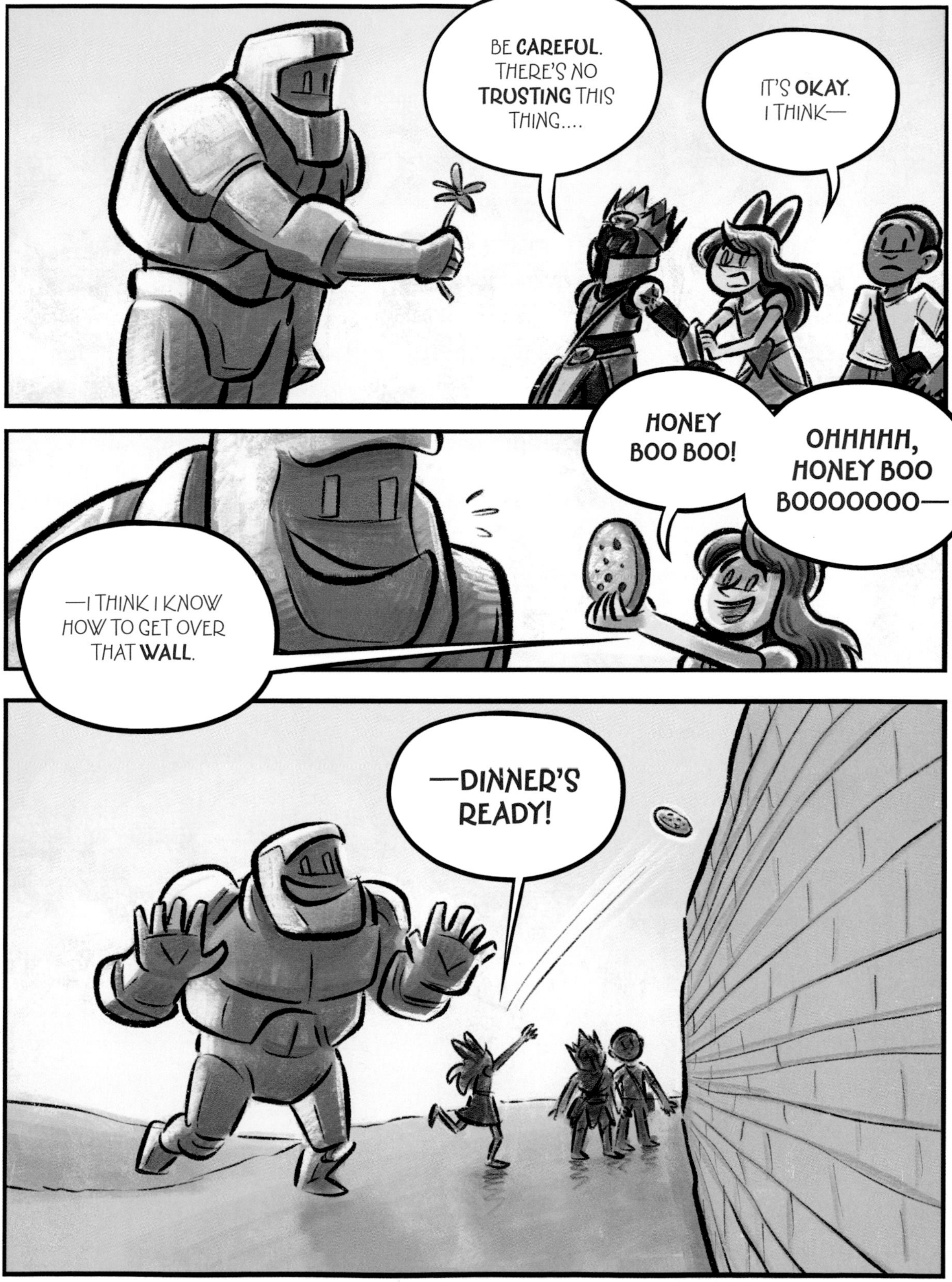
BE **CAREFUL**. THERE'S NO **TRUSTING** THIS THING....
IT'S **OKAY**. I THINK—
HONEY BOO BOO!
OHHHHH, HONEY BOO BOOOOOOO—
—I THINK I KNOW HOW TO GET OVER THAT **WALL**.
—DINNER'S READY!

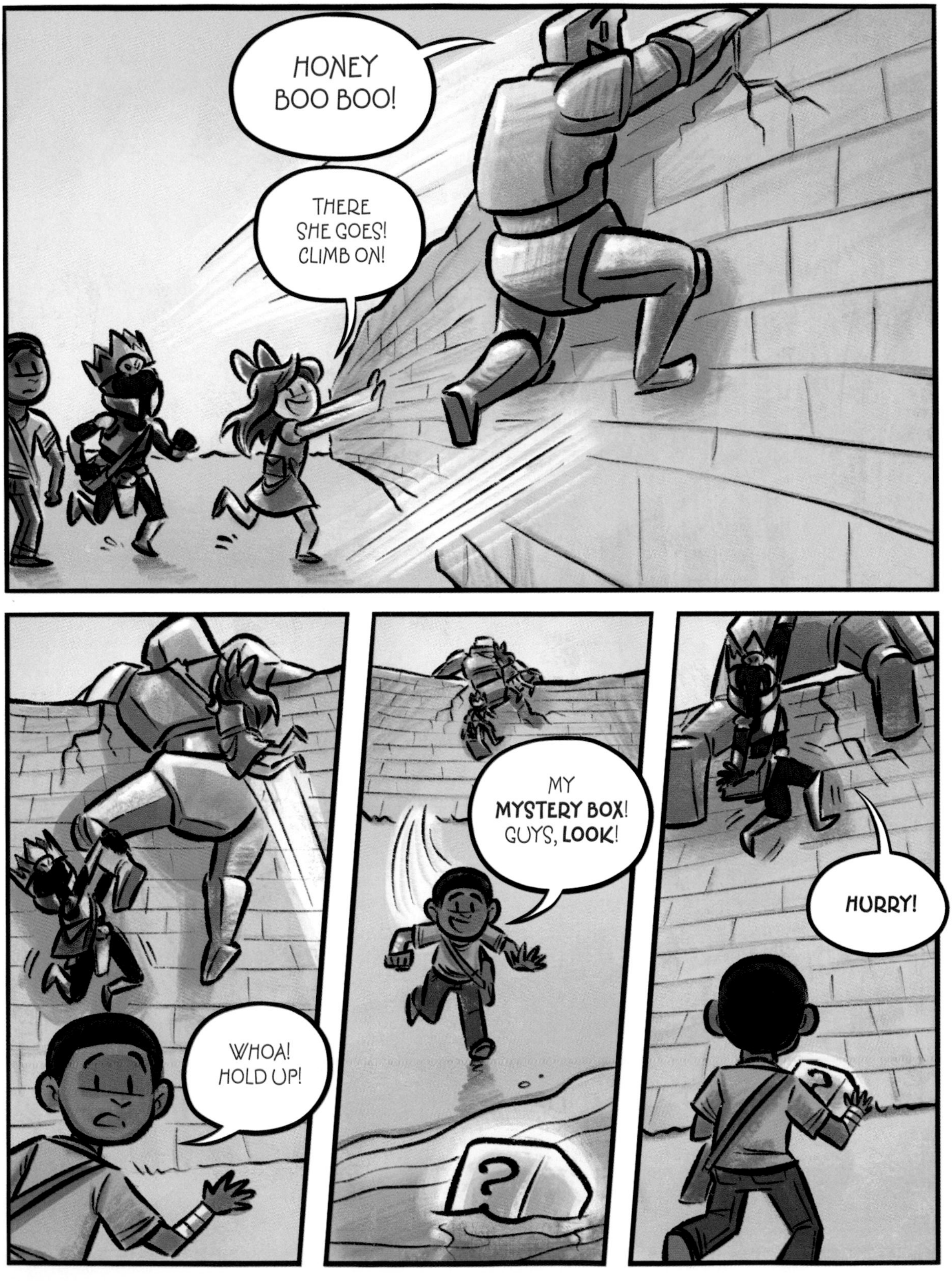
HONEY BOO BOO!
THERE SHE GOES! CLIMB ON!
WHOA! HOLD UP!
MY **MYSTERY BOX**! GUYS, **LOOK**!
HURRY!

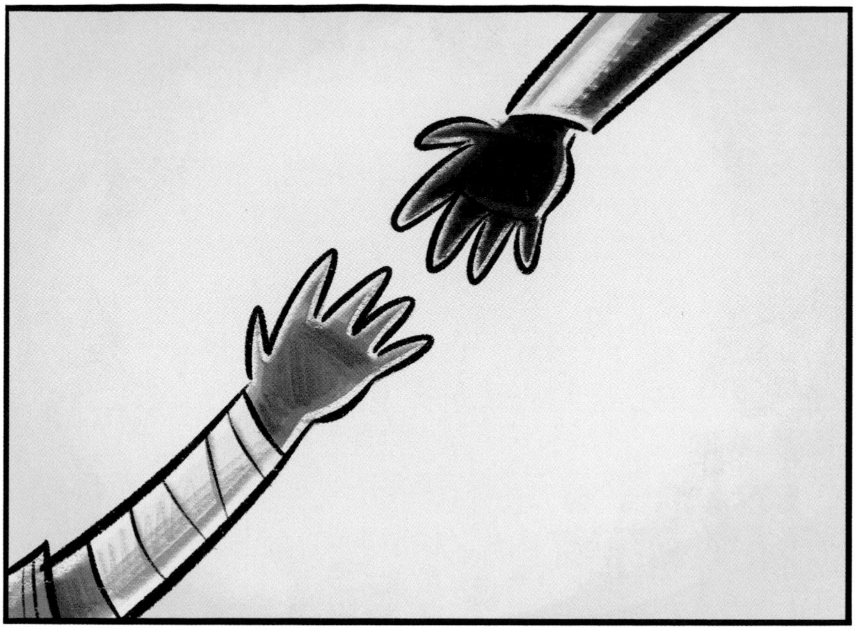

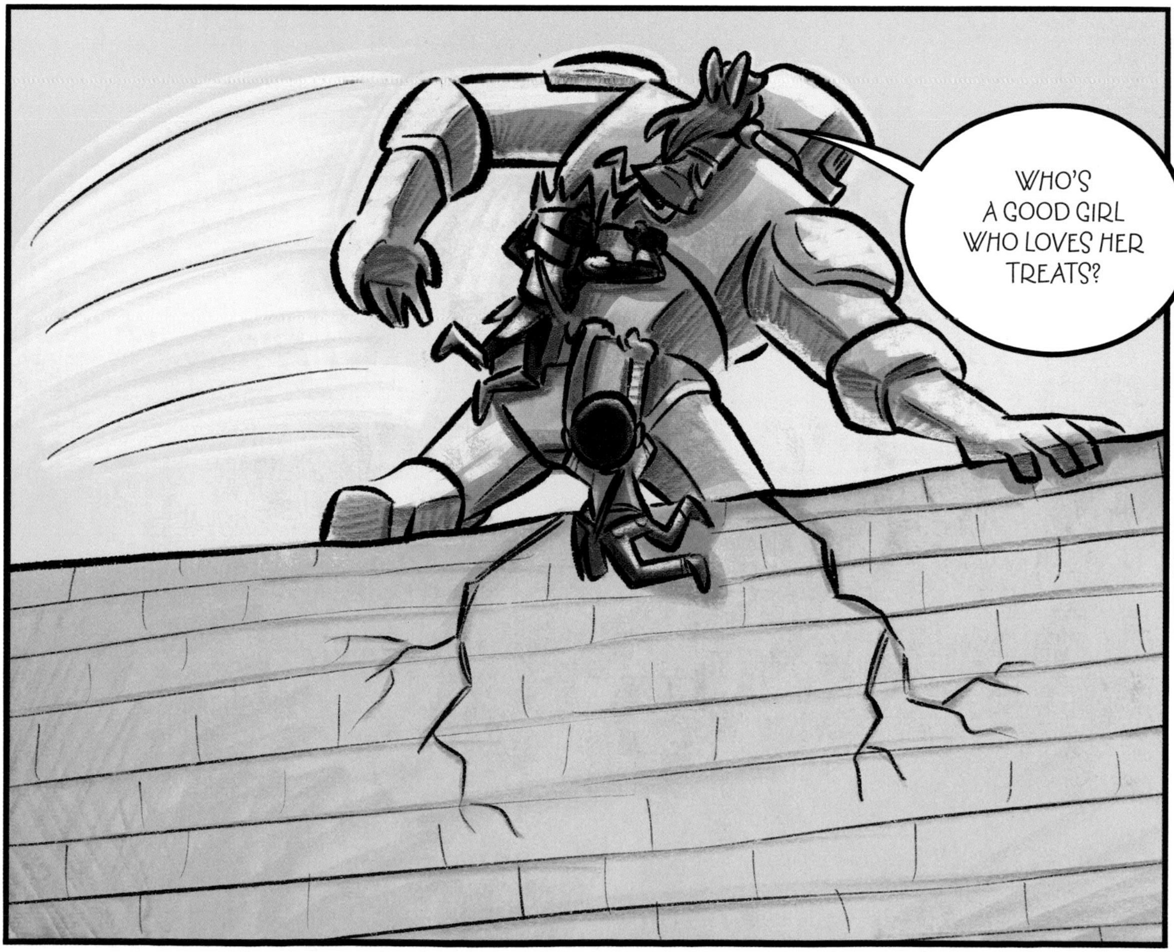
WHO'S A GOOD GIRL WHO LOVES HER TREATS?

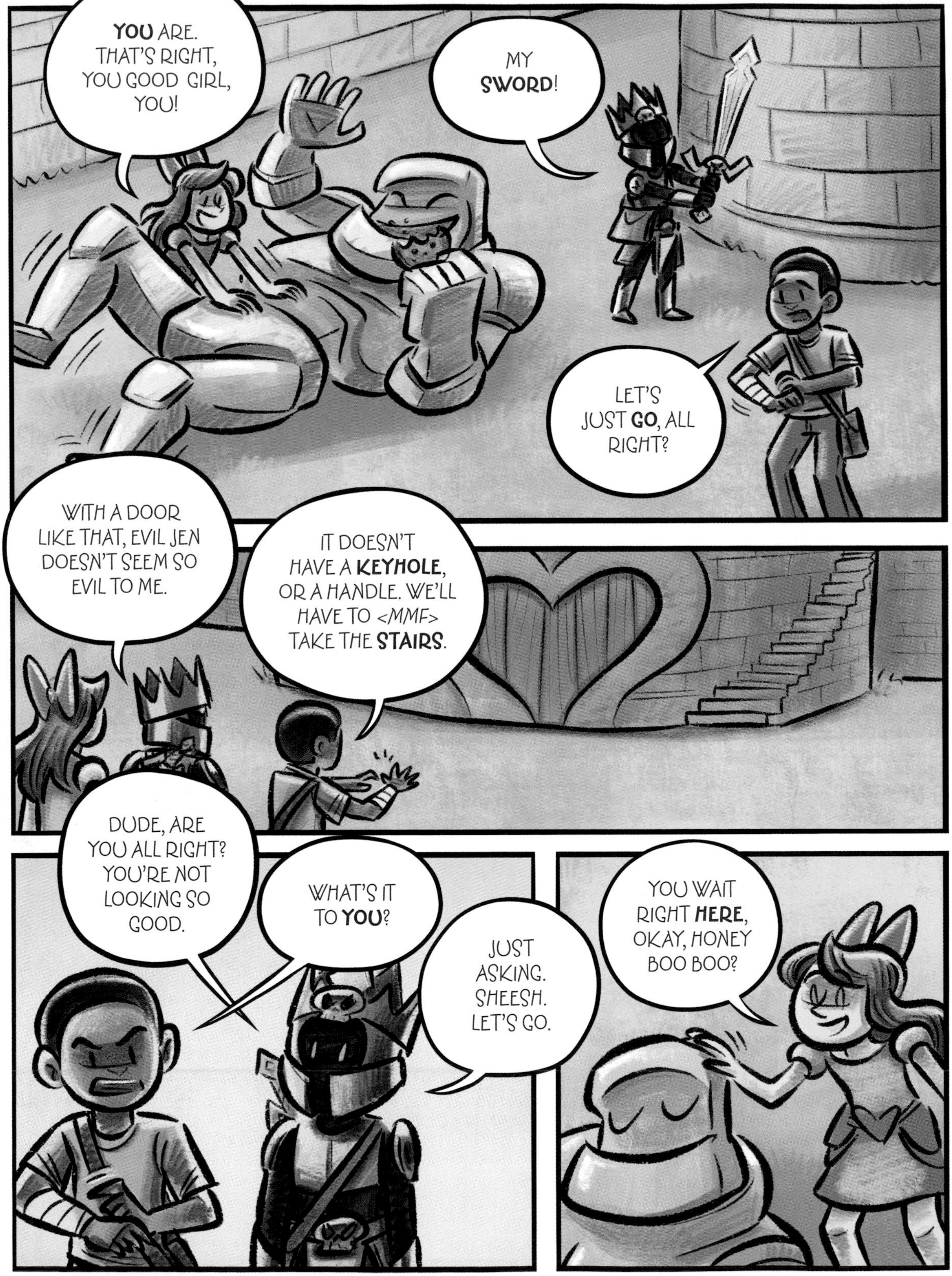
YOU ARE. THAT'S RIGHT, YOU GOOD GIRL, YOU!
MY SWORD!
LET'S JUST GO, ALL RIGHT?
WITH A DOOR LIKE THAT, EVIL JEN DOESN'T SEEM SO EVIL TO ME.
IT DOESN'T HAVE A KEYHOLE, OR A HANDLE. WE'LL HAVE TO <MMF> TAKE THE STAIRS.
DUDE, ARE YOU ALL RIGHT? YOU'RE NOT LOOKING SO GOOD.
WHAT'S IT TO YOU?
JUST ASKING. SHEESH. LET'S GO.
YOU WAIT RIGHT HERE, OKAY, HONEY BOO BOO?

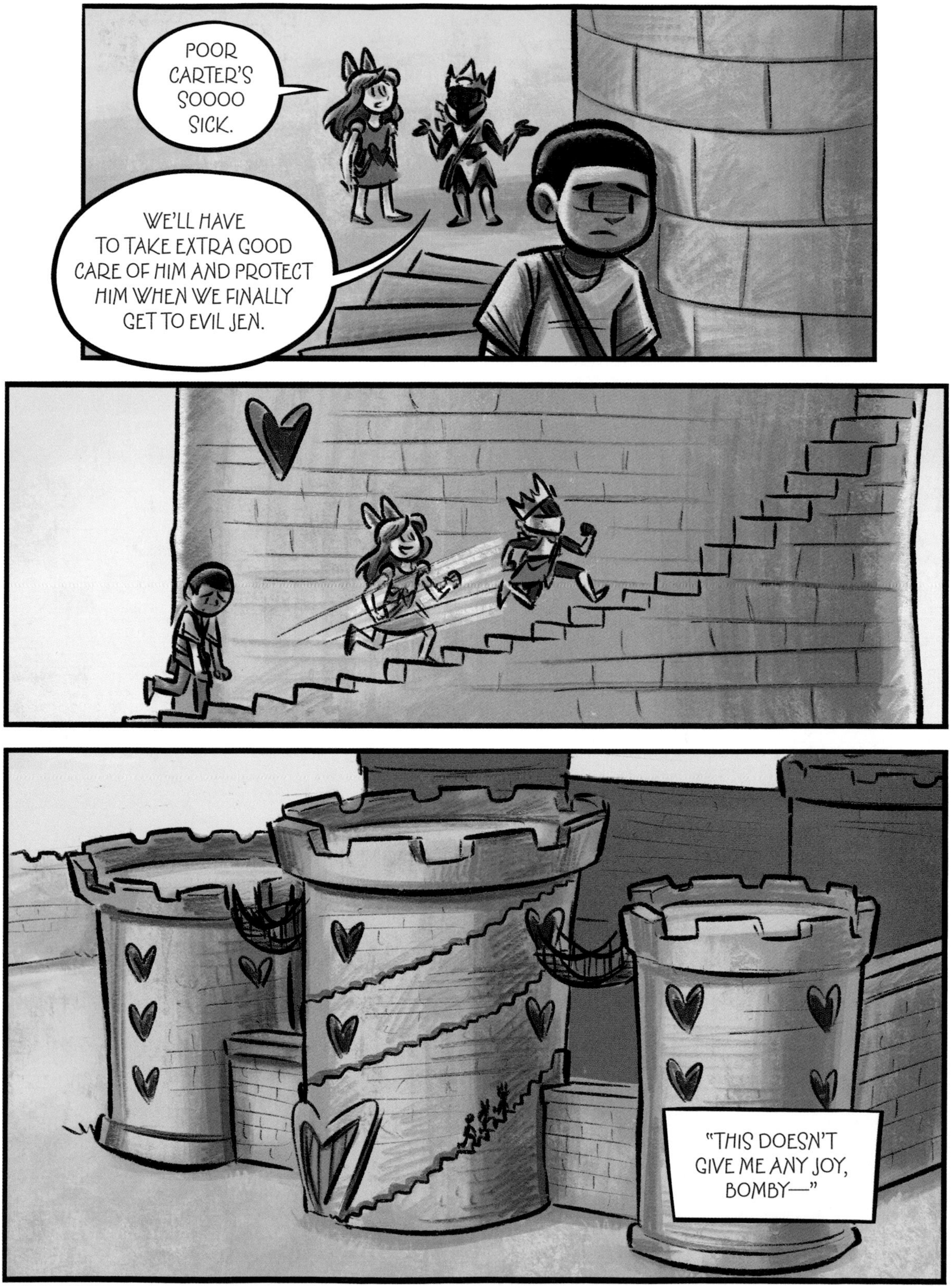
POOR CARTER'S SOOOO SICK.
WE'LL HAVE TO TAKE EXTRA GOOD CARE OF HIM AND PROTECT HIM WHEN WE FINALLY GET TO EVIL JEN.
"THIS DOESN'T GIVE ME ANY JOY, BOMBY—"

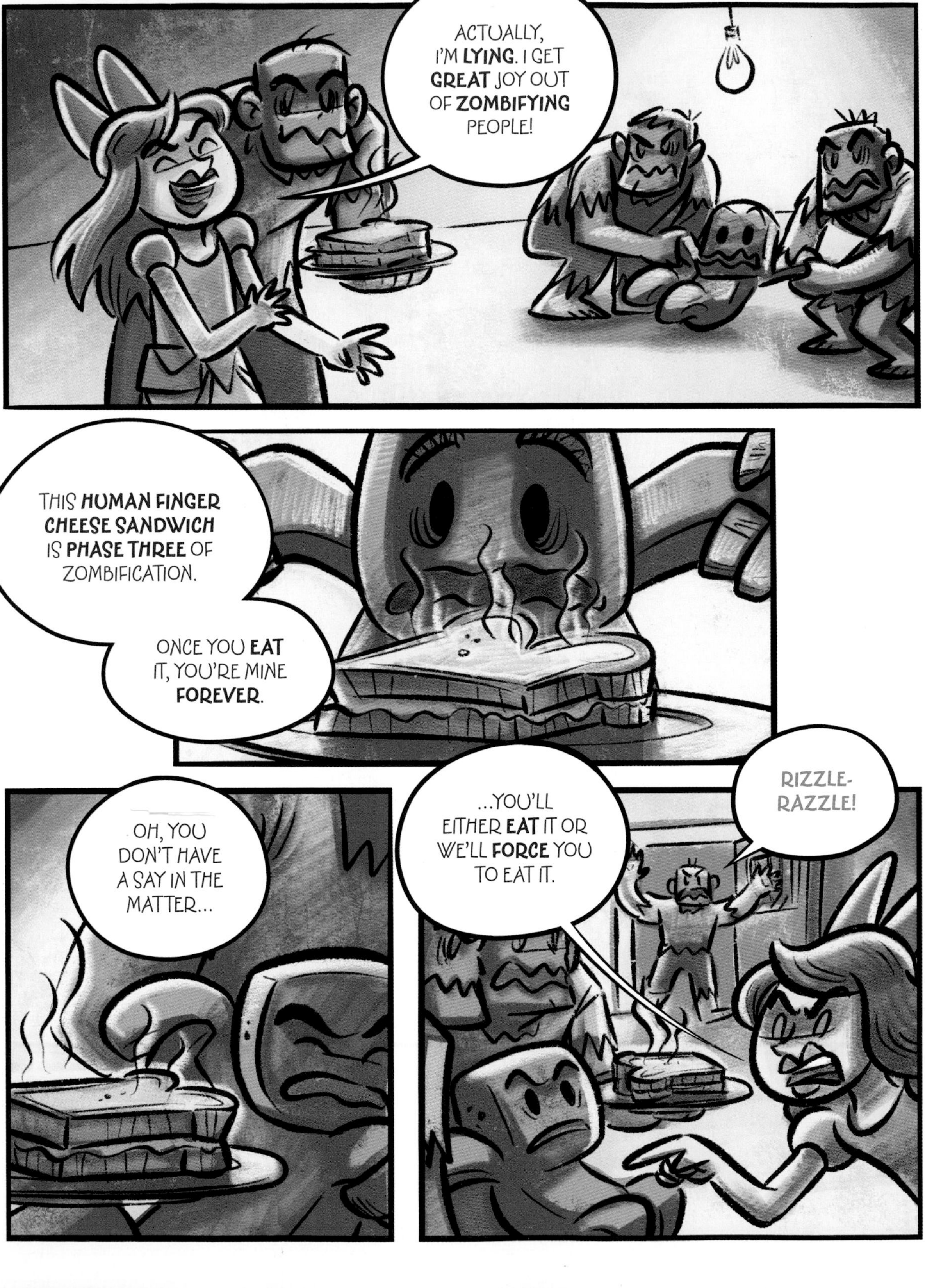
ACTUALLY, I'M LYING. I GET GREAT JOY OUT OF ZOMBIFYING PEOPLE!
THIS HUMAN FINGER CHEESE SANDWICH IS PHASE THREE OF ZOMBIFICATION.
ONCE YOU EAT IT, YOU'RE MINE FOREVER.
OH, YOU DON'T HAVE A SAY IN THE MATTER...
...YOU'LL EITHER EAT IT OR WE'LL FORCE YOU TO EAT IT.
RIZZLE-RAZZLE!

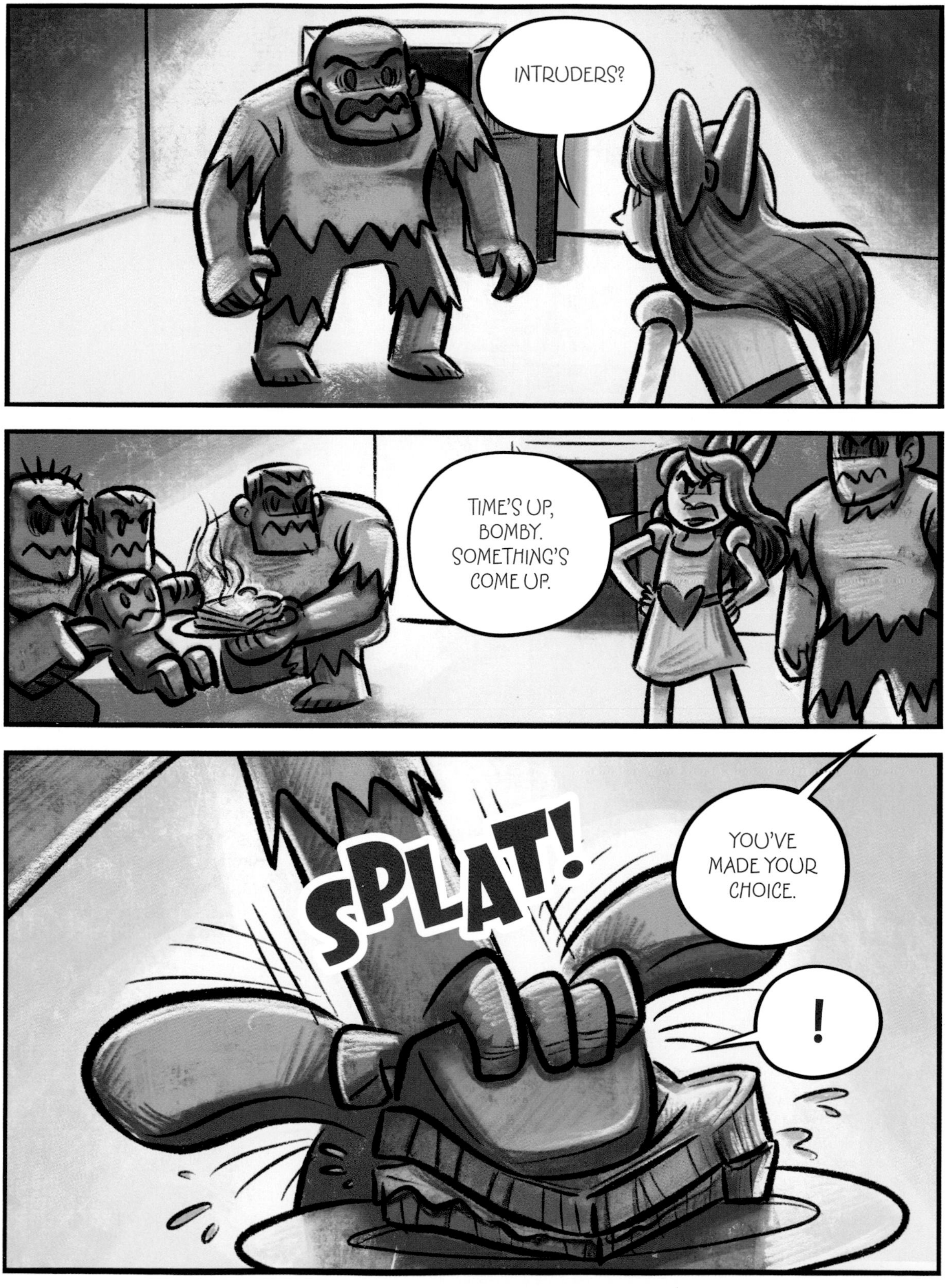
INTRUDERS?
TIME'S UP, BOMBY. SOMETHING'S COME UP.
SPLAT!
YOU'VE MADE YOUR CHOICE.
!

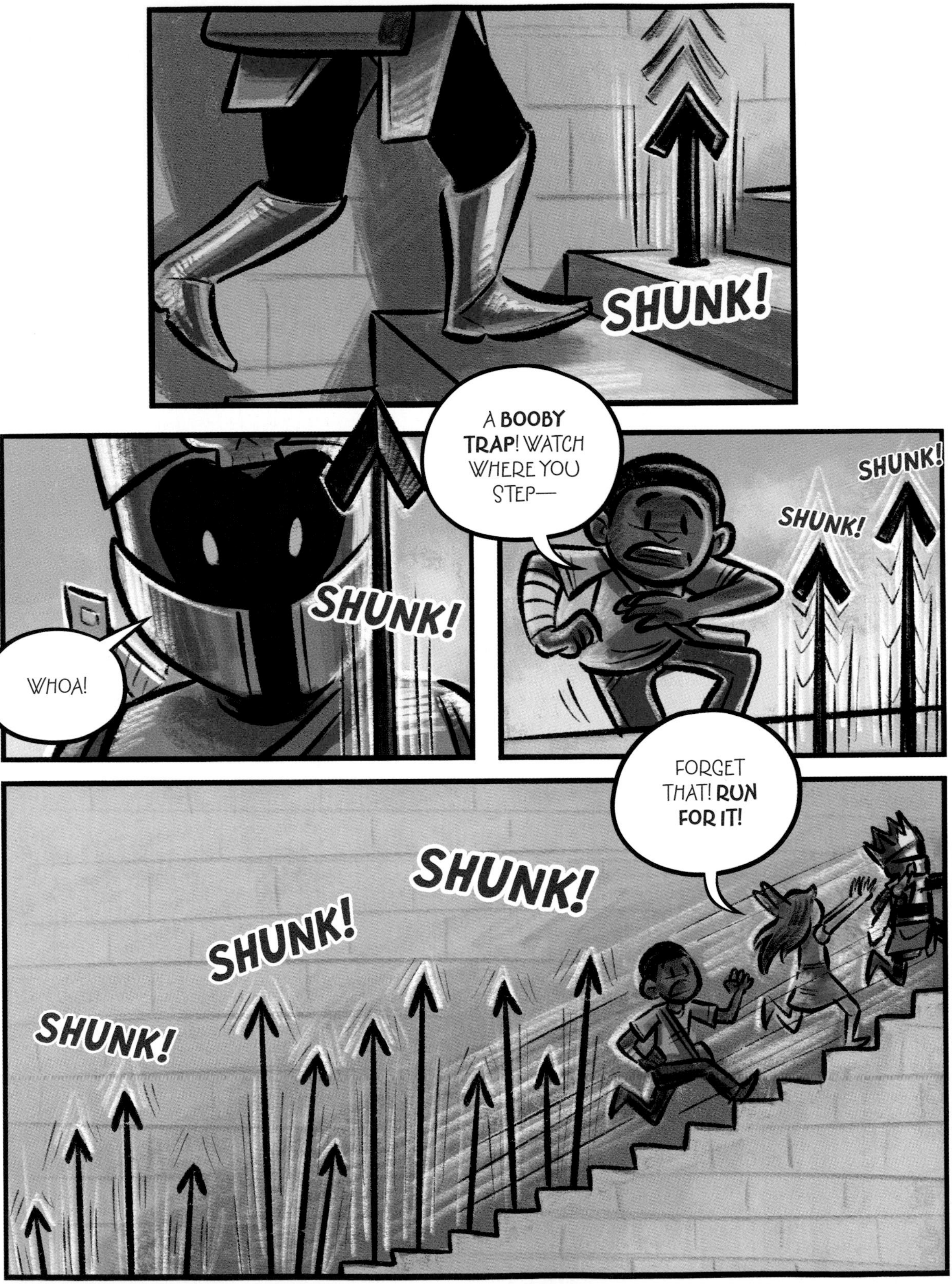
SHUNK!
SHUNK!
WHOA!
A BOOBY TRAP! WATCH WHERE YOU STEP—
SHUNK!
SHUNK!
FORGET THAT! RUN FOR IT!
SHUNK!
SHUNK!
SHUNK!

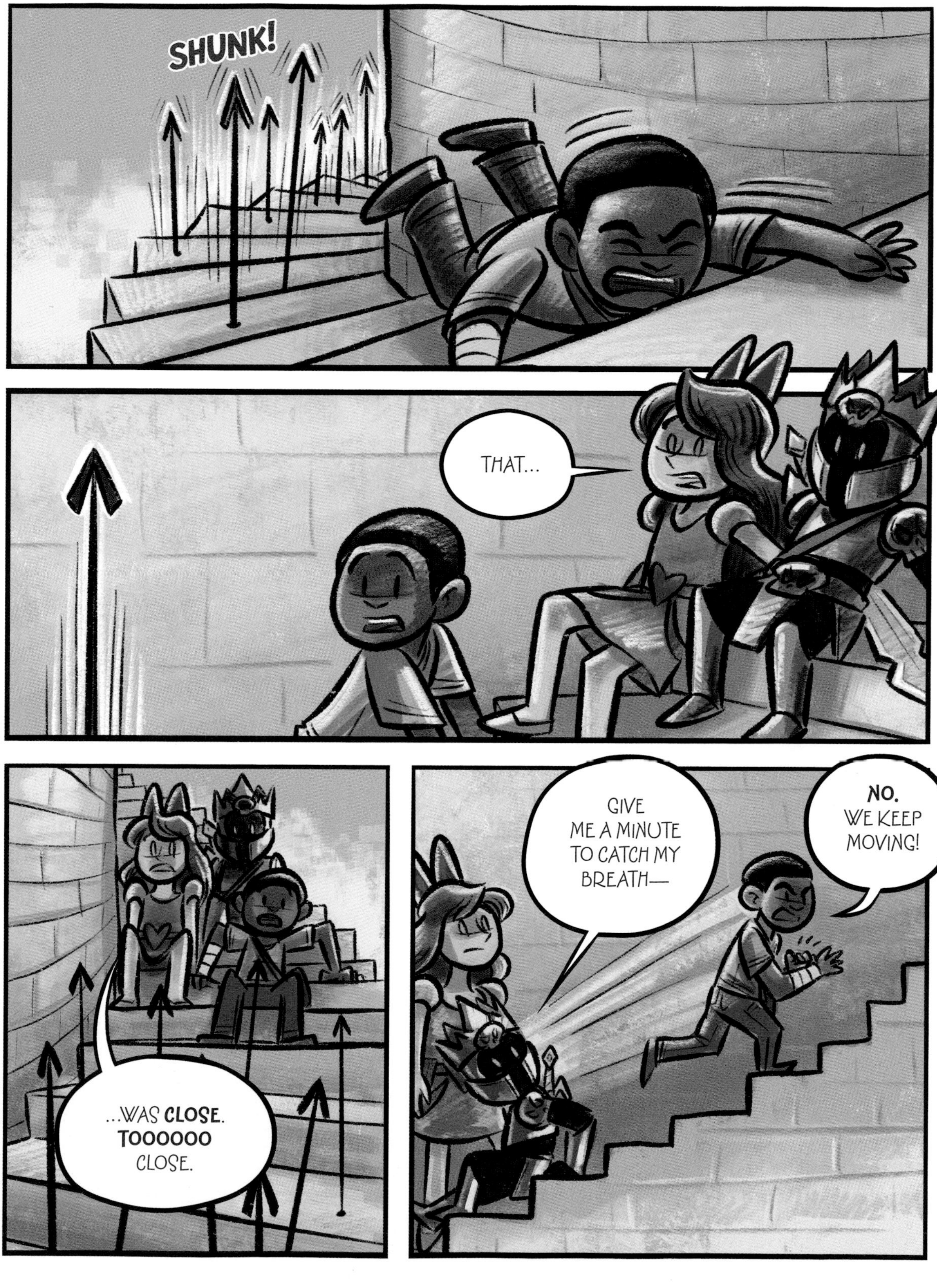
SHUNK!
THAT...
...WAS **CLOSE**. **TOOOOOO** CLOSE.
GIVE ME A MINUTE TO CATCH MY BREATH—
NO. WE KEEP MOVING!

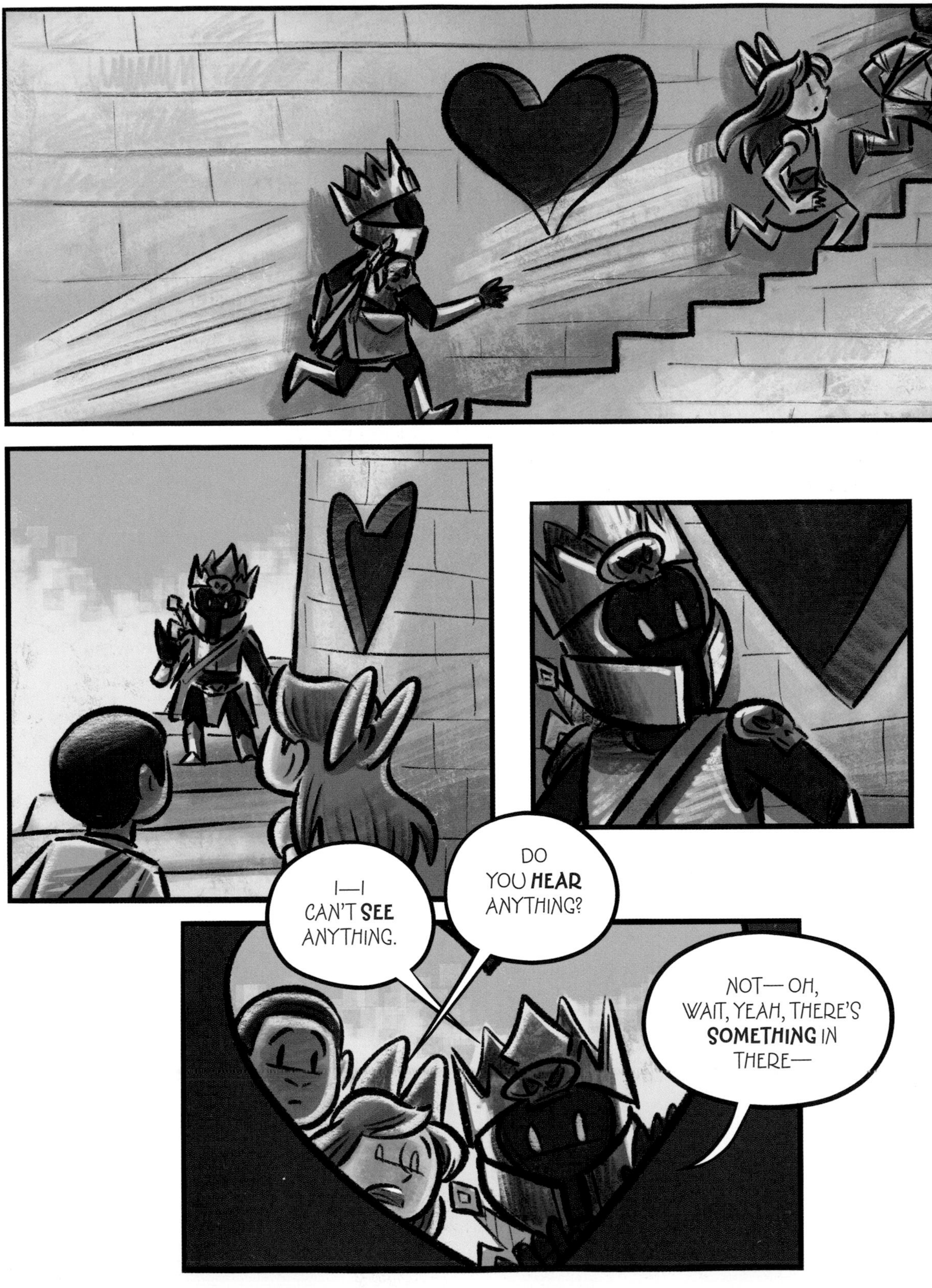
I—I CAN'T **SEE** ANYTHING.
DO YOU **HEAR** ANYTHING?
NOT— OH, WAIT, YEAH, THERE'S **SOMETHING** IN THERE—

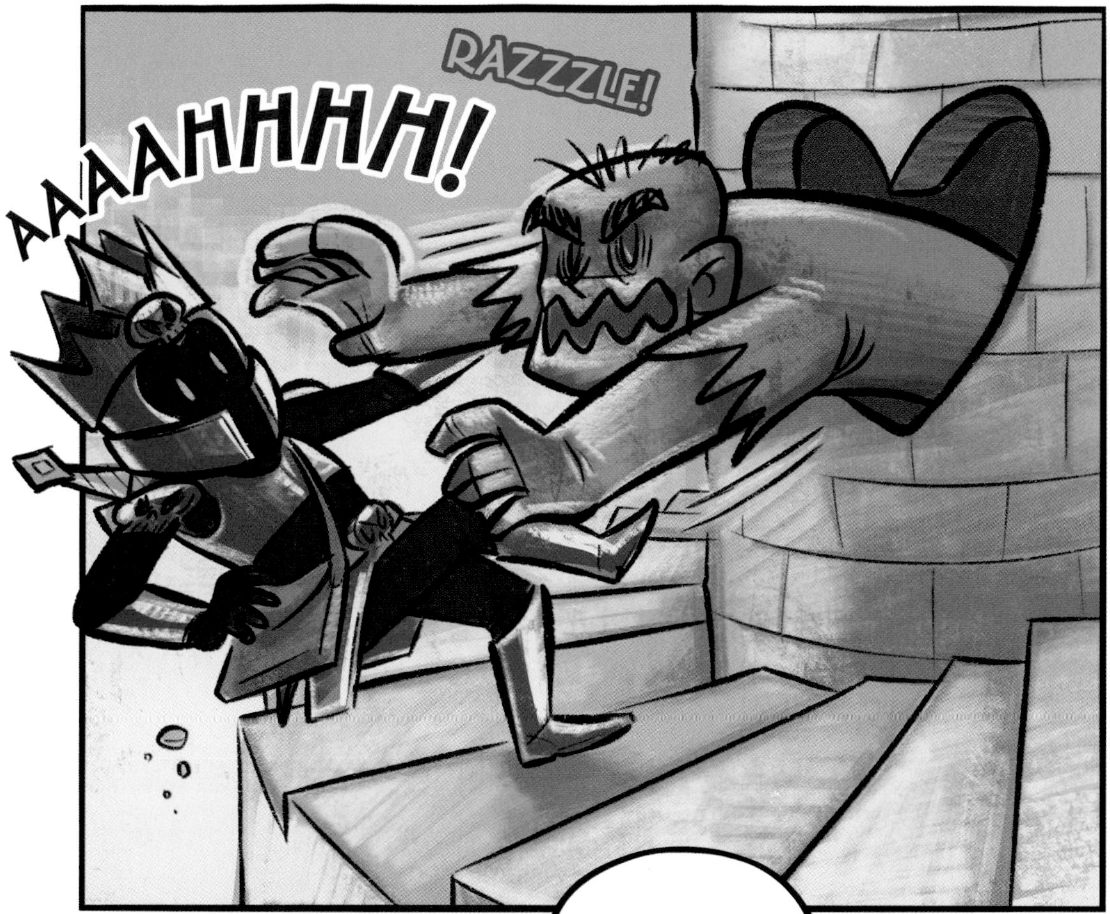
AAAAHHHH!
RAZZZLE!

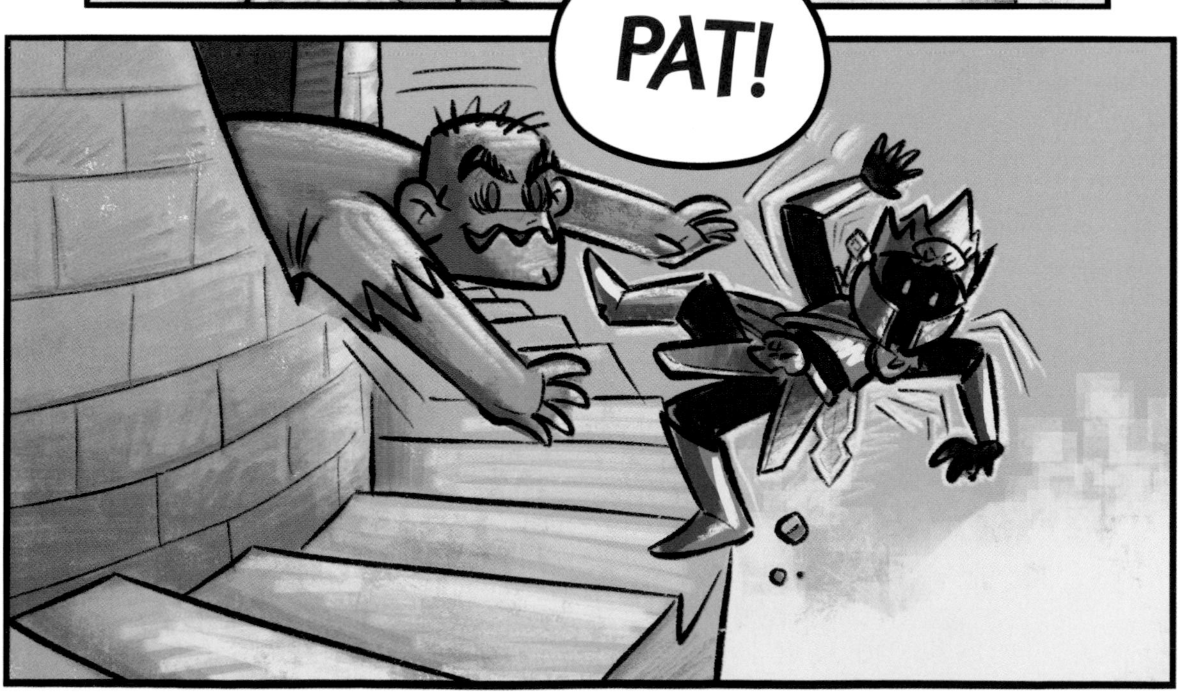
PAT!

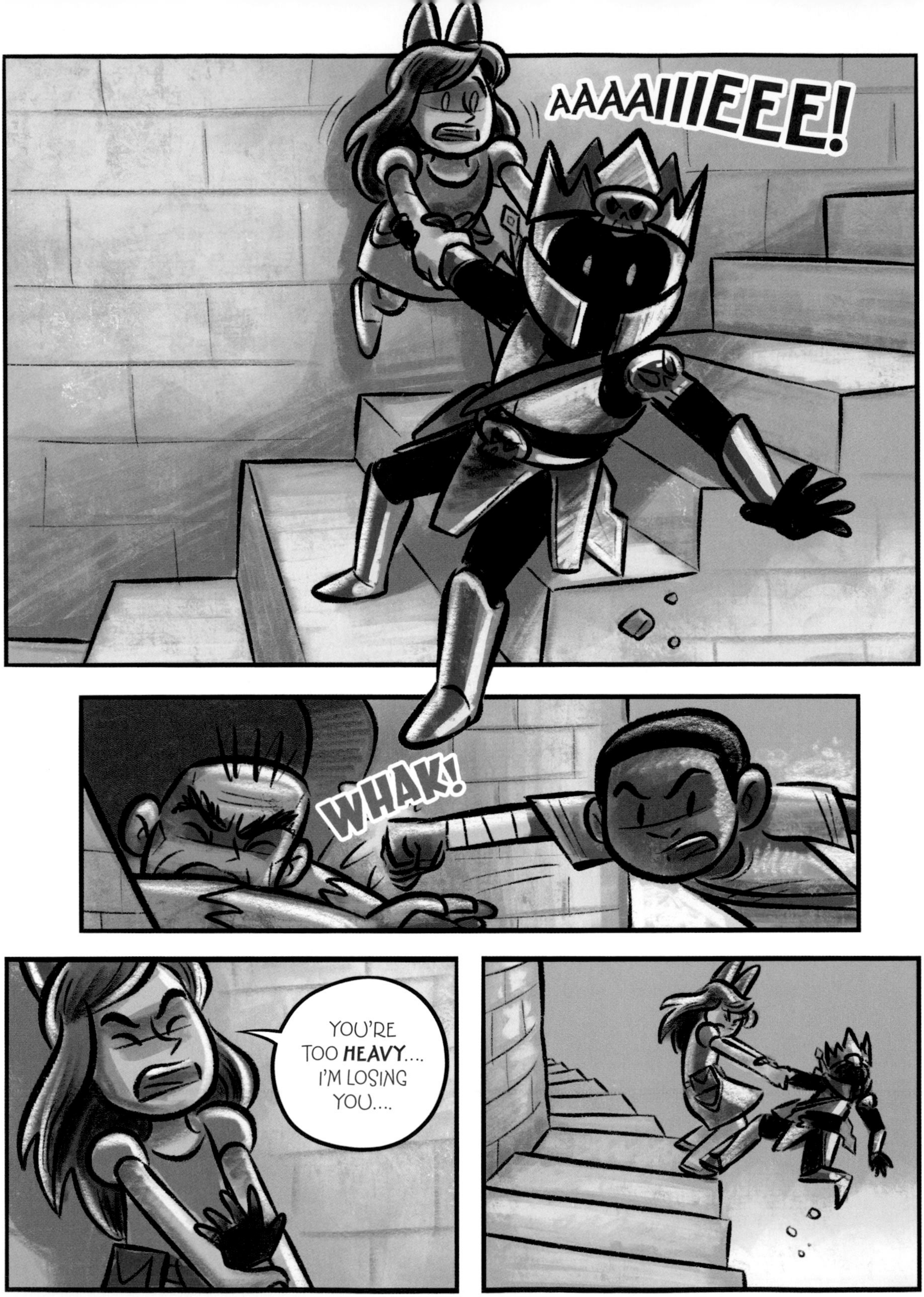
AAAAIIIEEE!
WHAK!
YOU'RE TOO **HEAVY**.... I'M LOSING YOU....

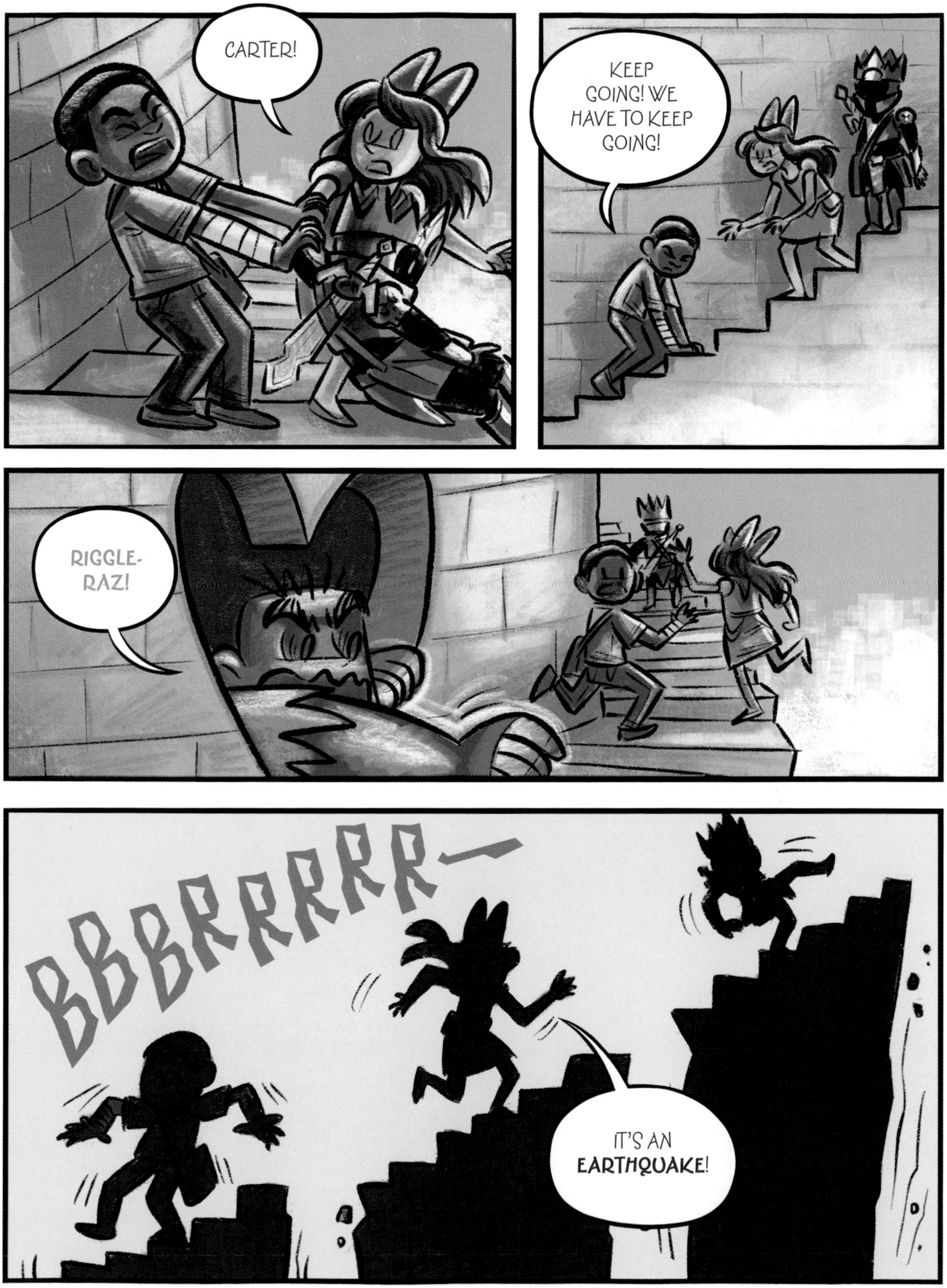
CARTER!
KEEP GOING! WE HAVE TO KEEP GOING!
RIGGLE-RAZ!
BBBRRRRRR—
IT'S AN **EARTHQUAKE**!

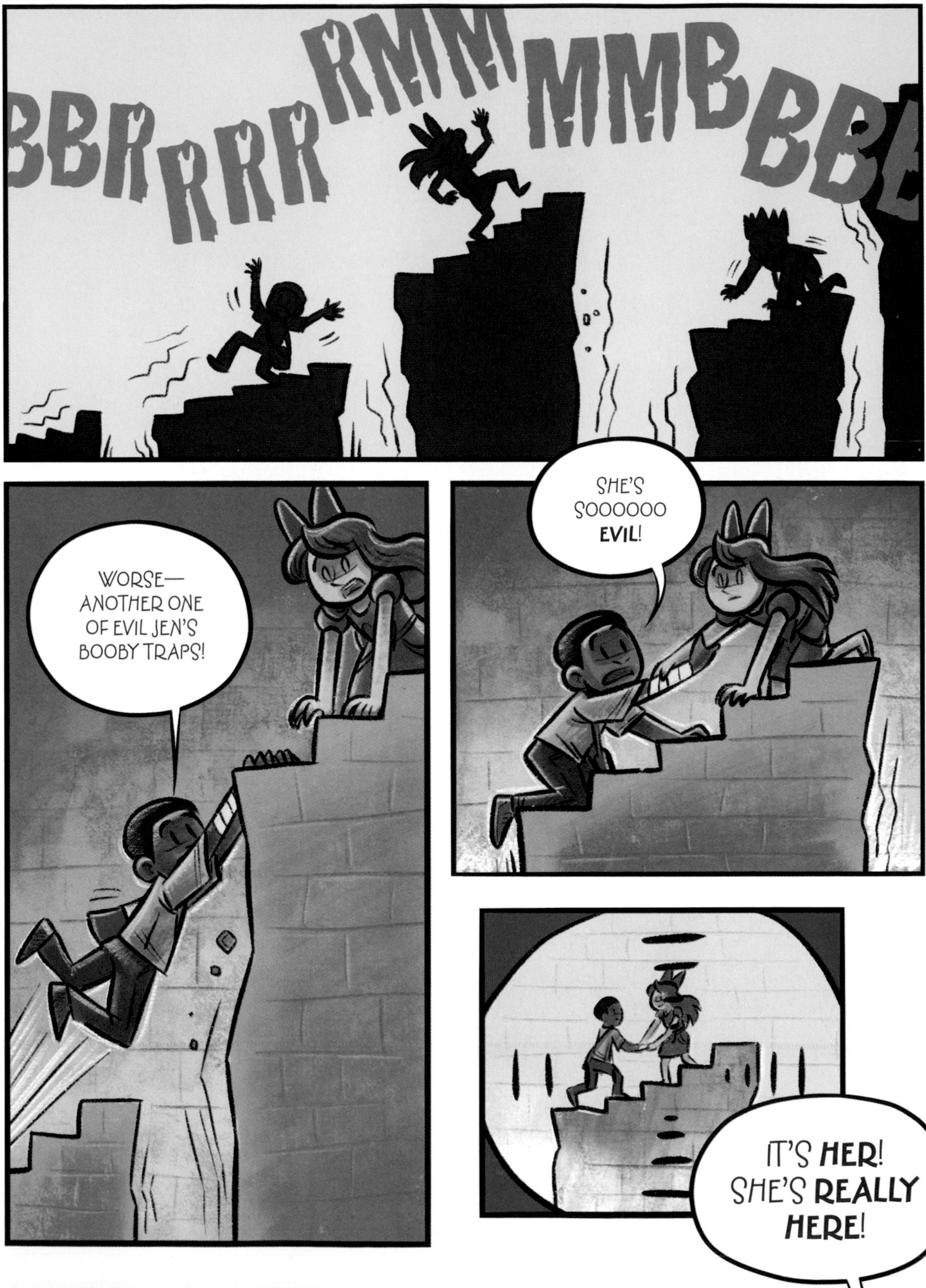
BBRRRRRRMMMMMBBBB
WORSE—ANOTHER ONE OF EVIL JEN'S BOOBY TRAPS!
SHE'S SOOOOOO **EVIL**!
IT'S **HER**! SHE'S **REALLY HERE**!

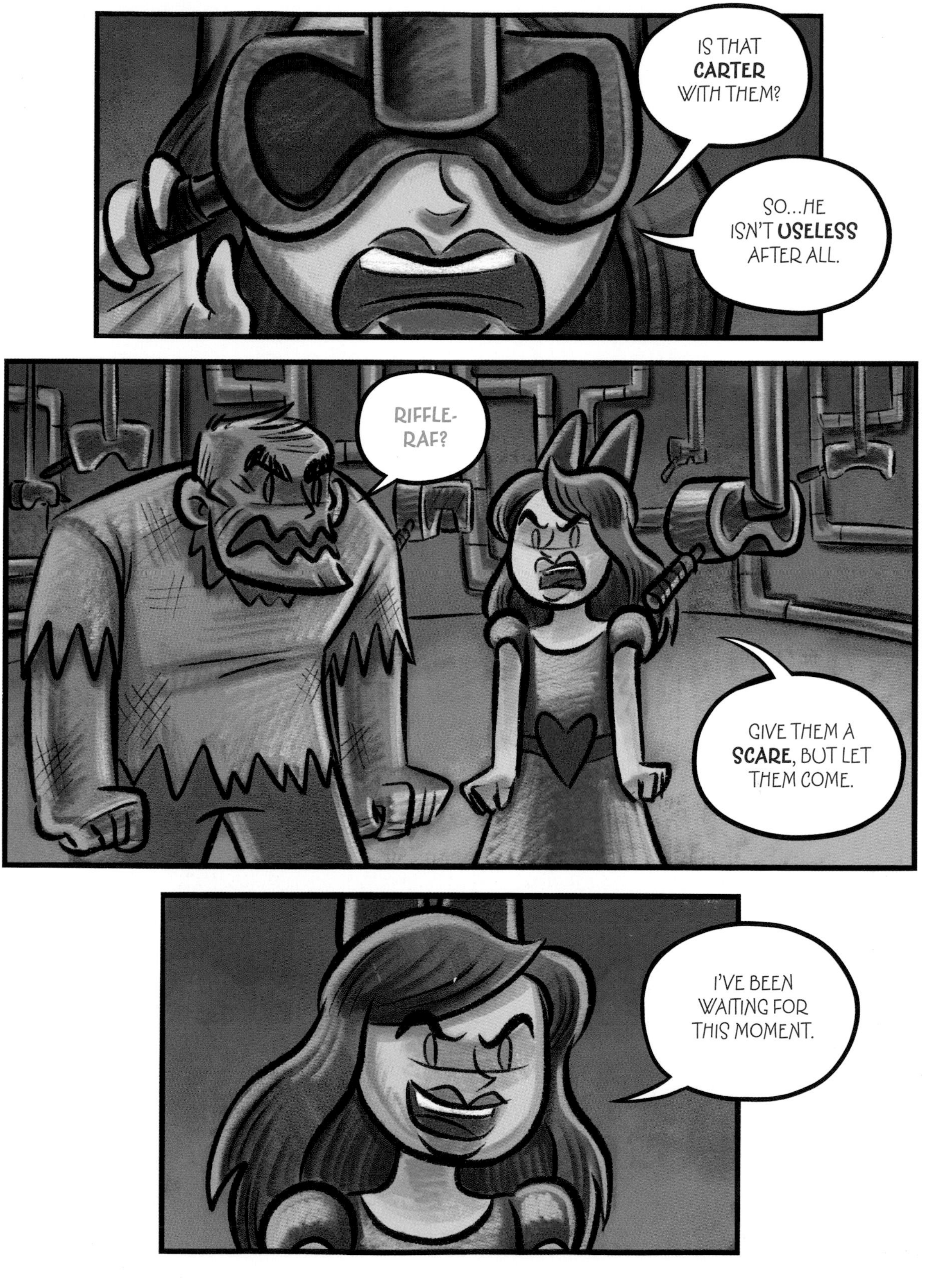
IS THAT **CARTER** WITH THEM?
SO...HE ISN'T **USELESS** AFTER ALL.
RIFFLE-RAF?
GIVE THEM A **SCARE**, BUT LET THEM COME.
I'VE BEEN WAITING FOR THIS MOMENT.

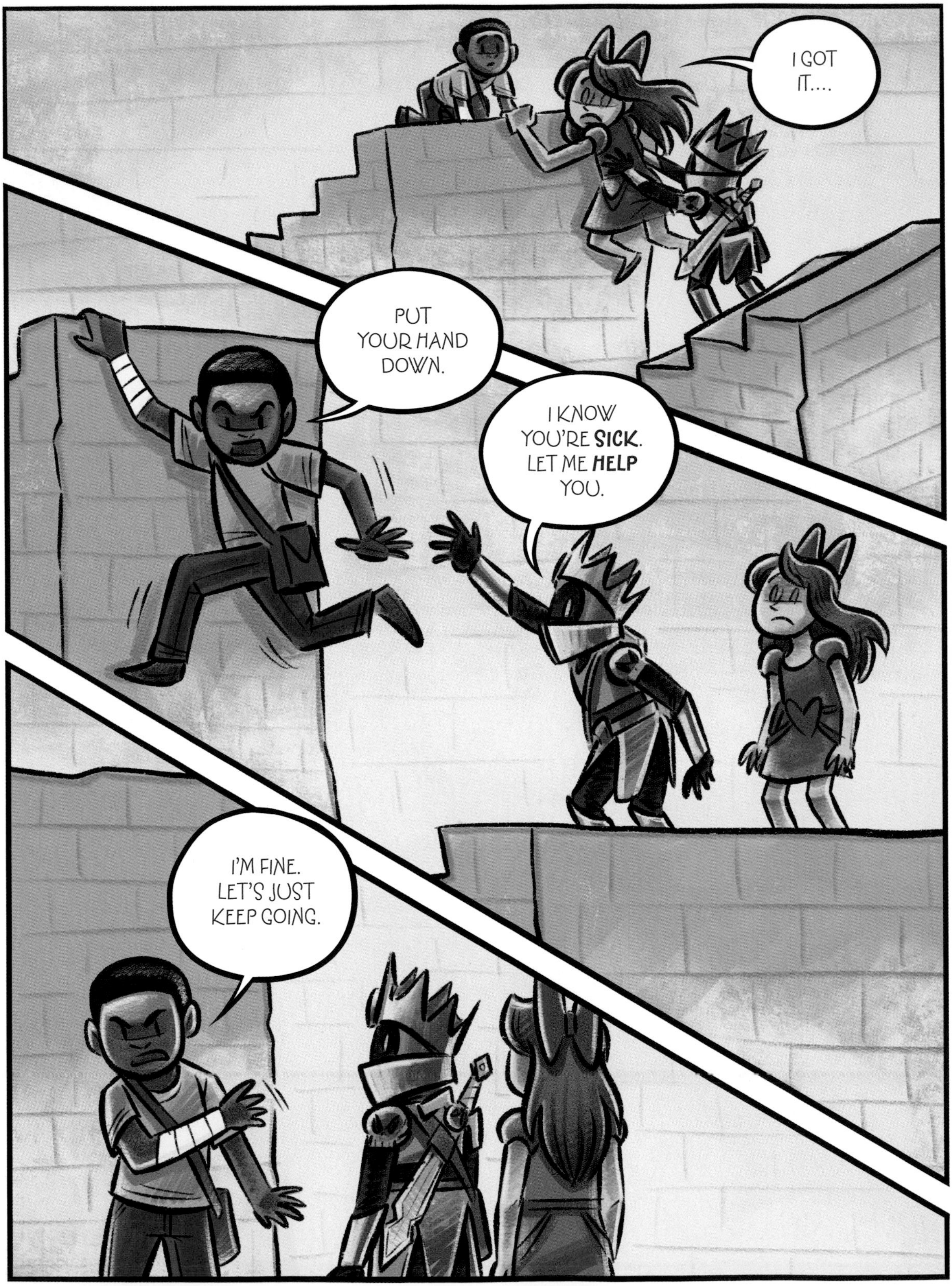
I GOT IT....
PUT YOUR HAND DOWN.
I KNOW YOU'RE **SICK**. LET ME **HELP** YOU.
I'M FINE. LET'S JUST KEEP GOING.

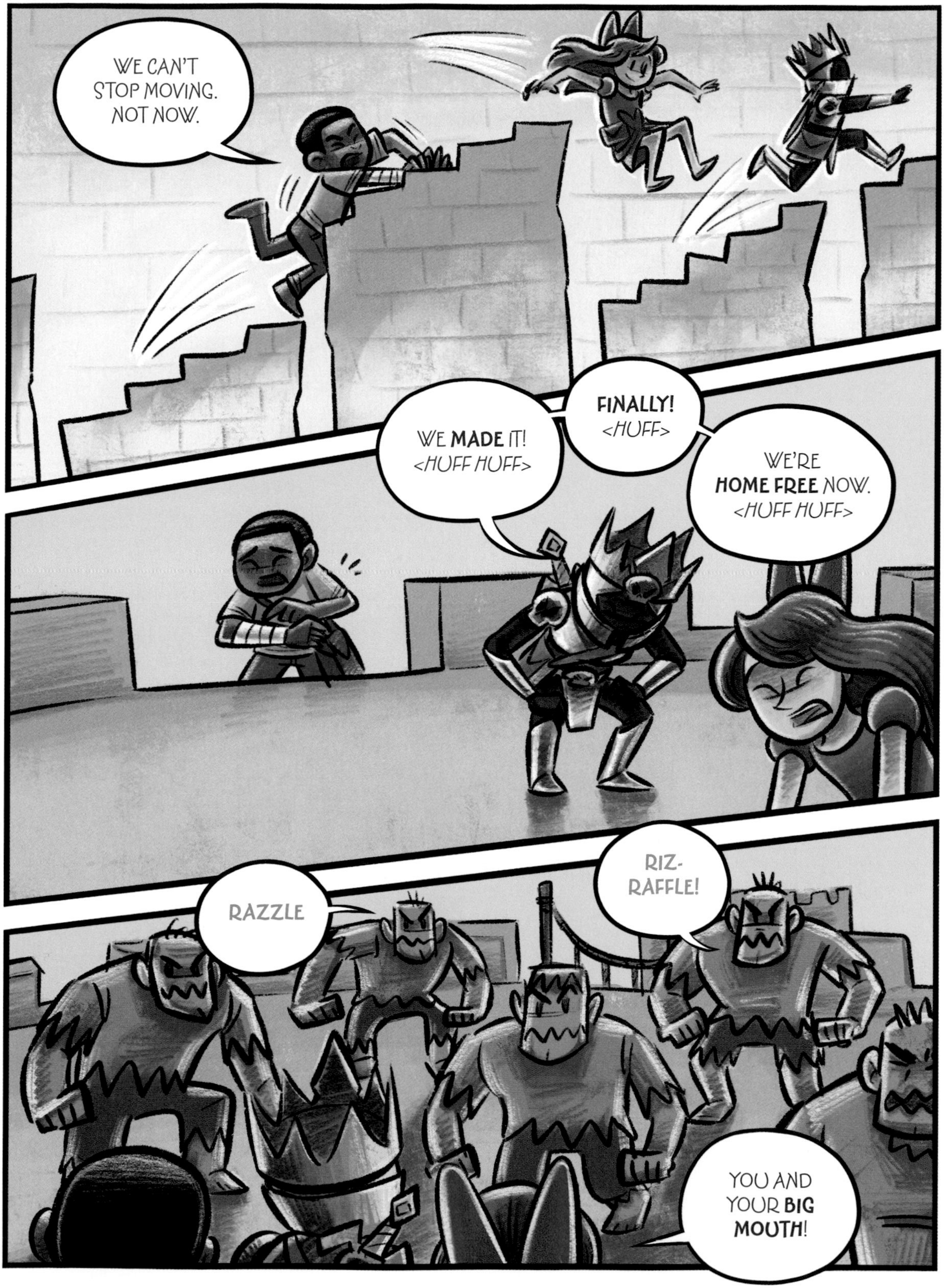
WE CAN'T STOP MOVING. NOT NOW.
WE MADE IT! <HUFF HUFF>
FINALLY! <HUFF>
WE'RE HOME FREE NOW. <HUFF HUFF>
RAZZLE
RIZ-RAFFLE!
YOU AND YOUR BIG MOUTH!

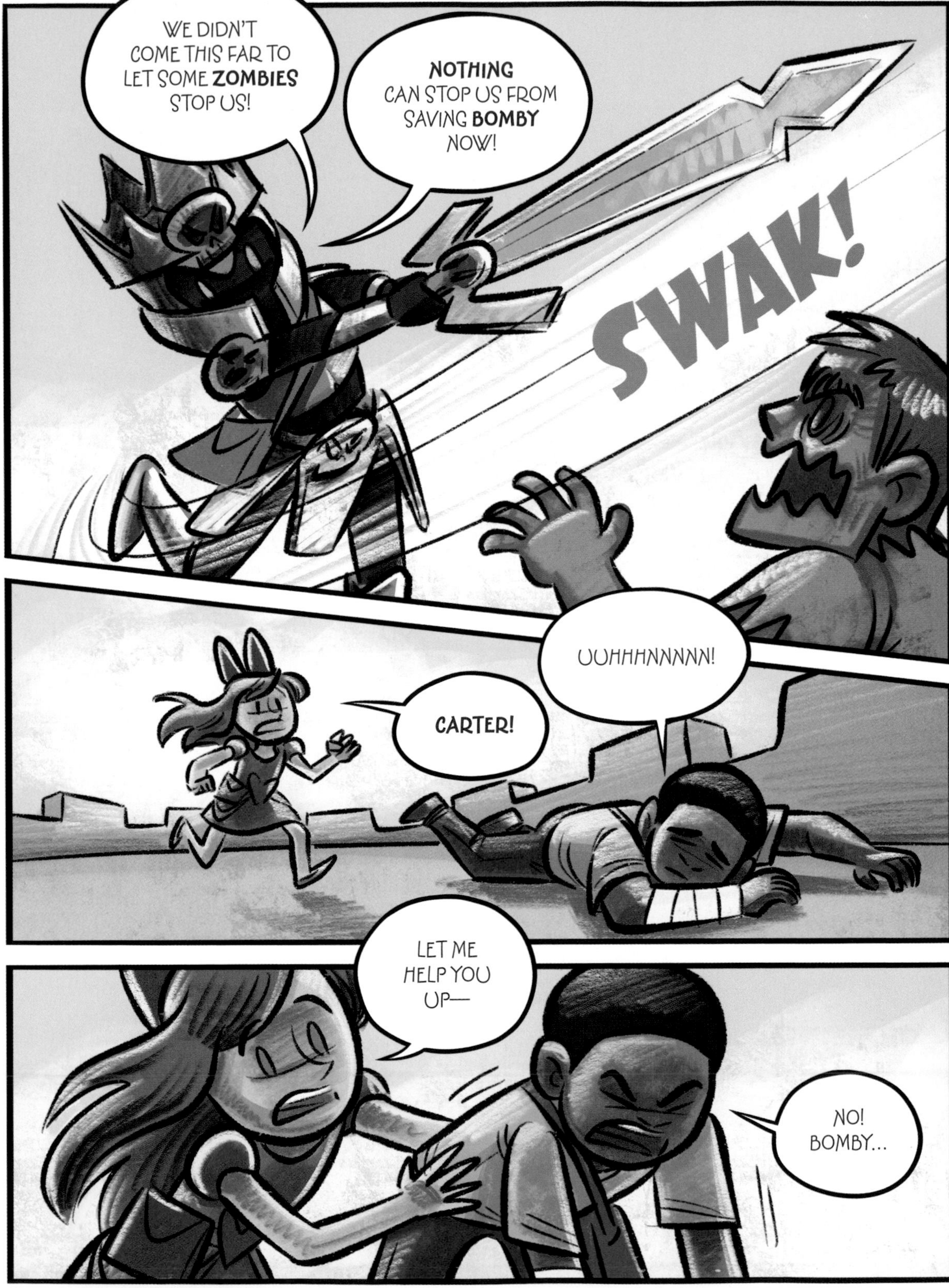
WE DIDN'T COME THIS FAR TO LET SOME **ZOMBIES** STOP US!
NOTHING CAN STOP US FROM SAVING **BOMBY** NOW!
SWAK!
UUHHHNNNNN!
CARTER!
LET ME HELP YOU UP—
NO! BOMBY...

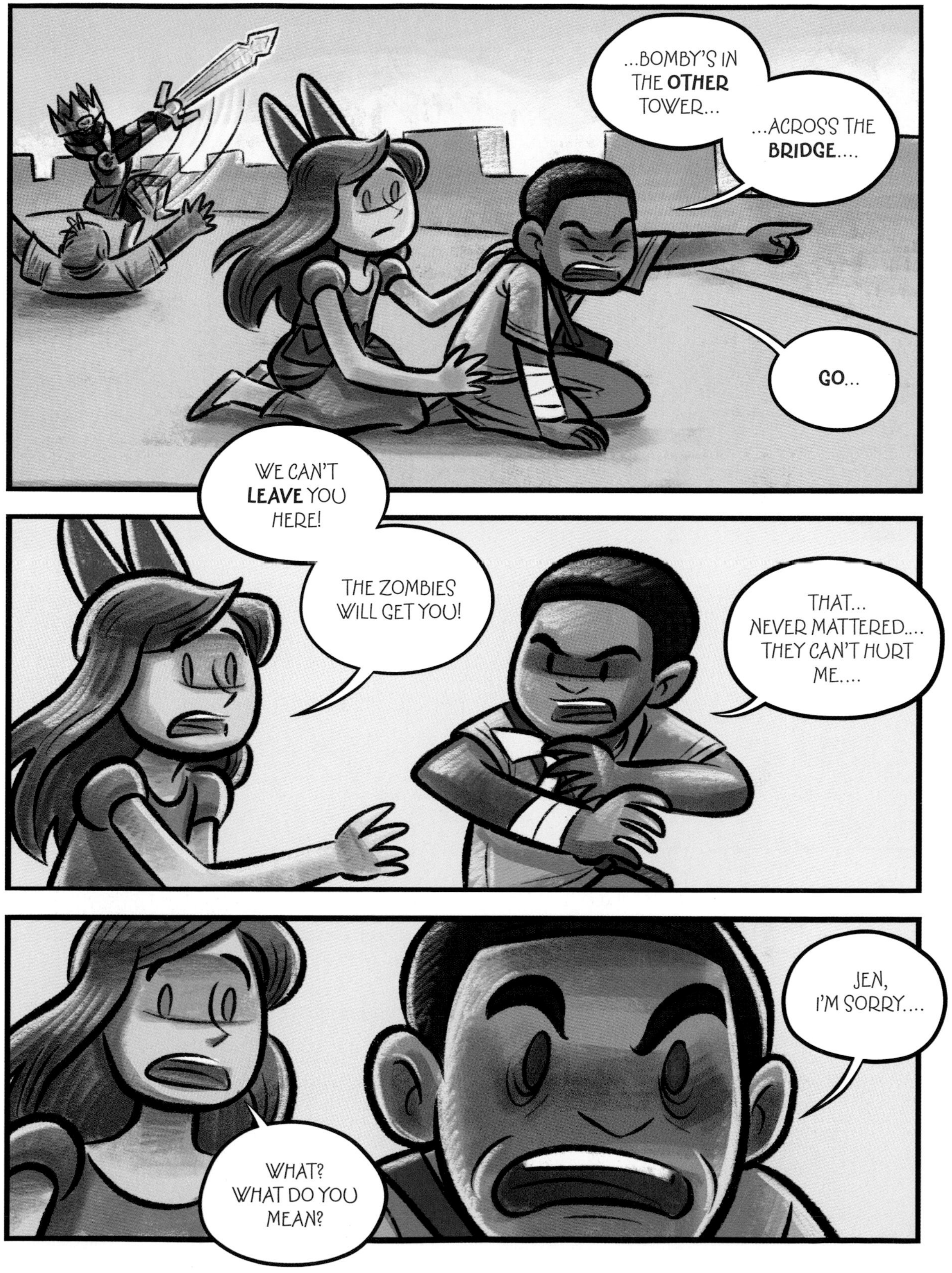
...BOMBY'S IN THE **OTHER** TOWER...
...ACROSS THE **BRIDGE**....
GO...
WE CAN'T **LEAVE** YOU HERE!
THE ZOMBIES WILL GET YOU!
THAT... NEVER MATTERED.... THEY CAN'T HURT ME....
JEN, I'M SORRY....
WHAT? WHAT DO YOU MEAN?

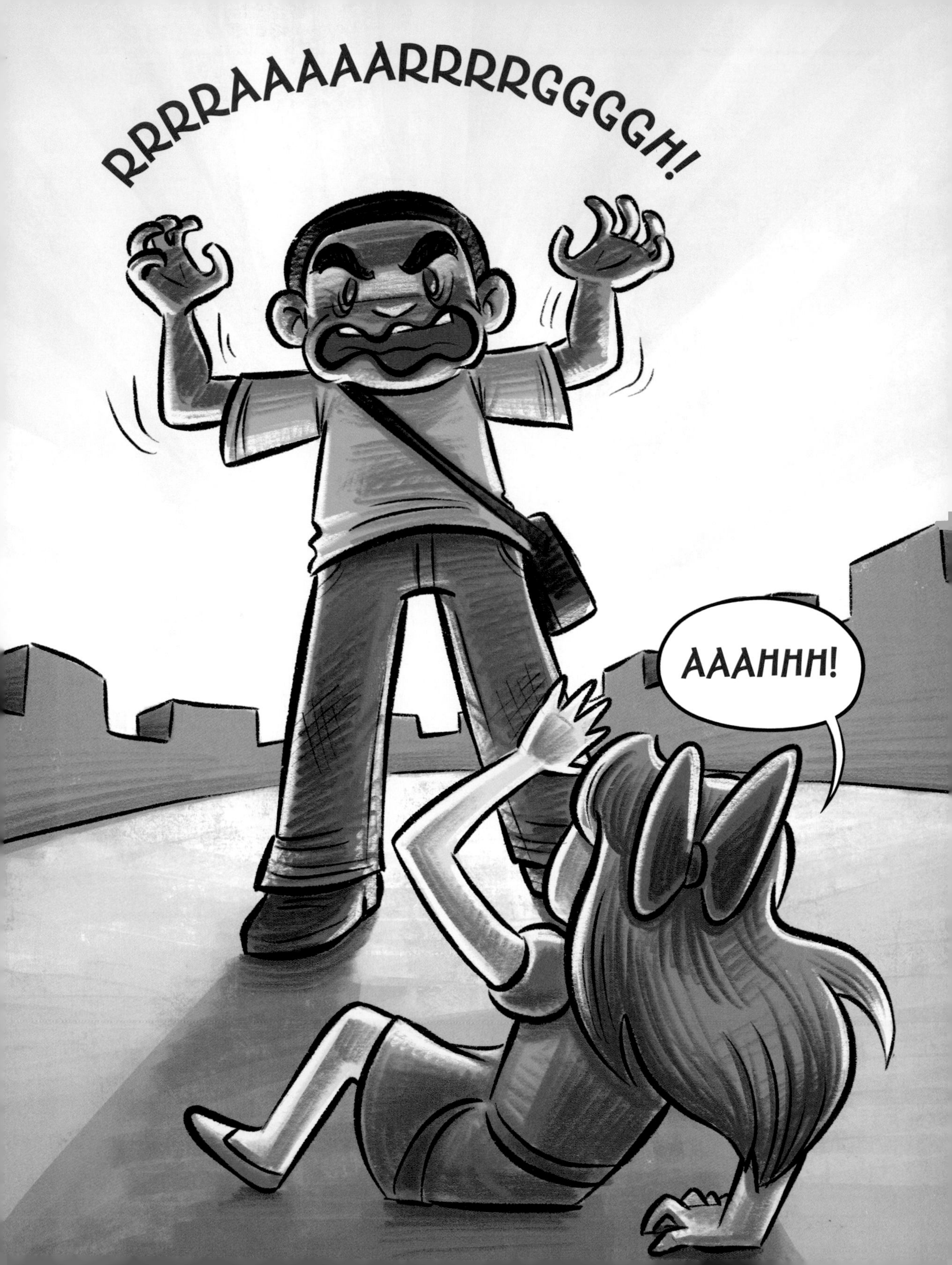
RRRRAAAAAARRRRRGGGGGH!
AAAHHH!

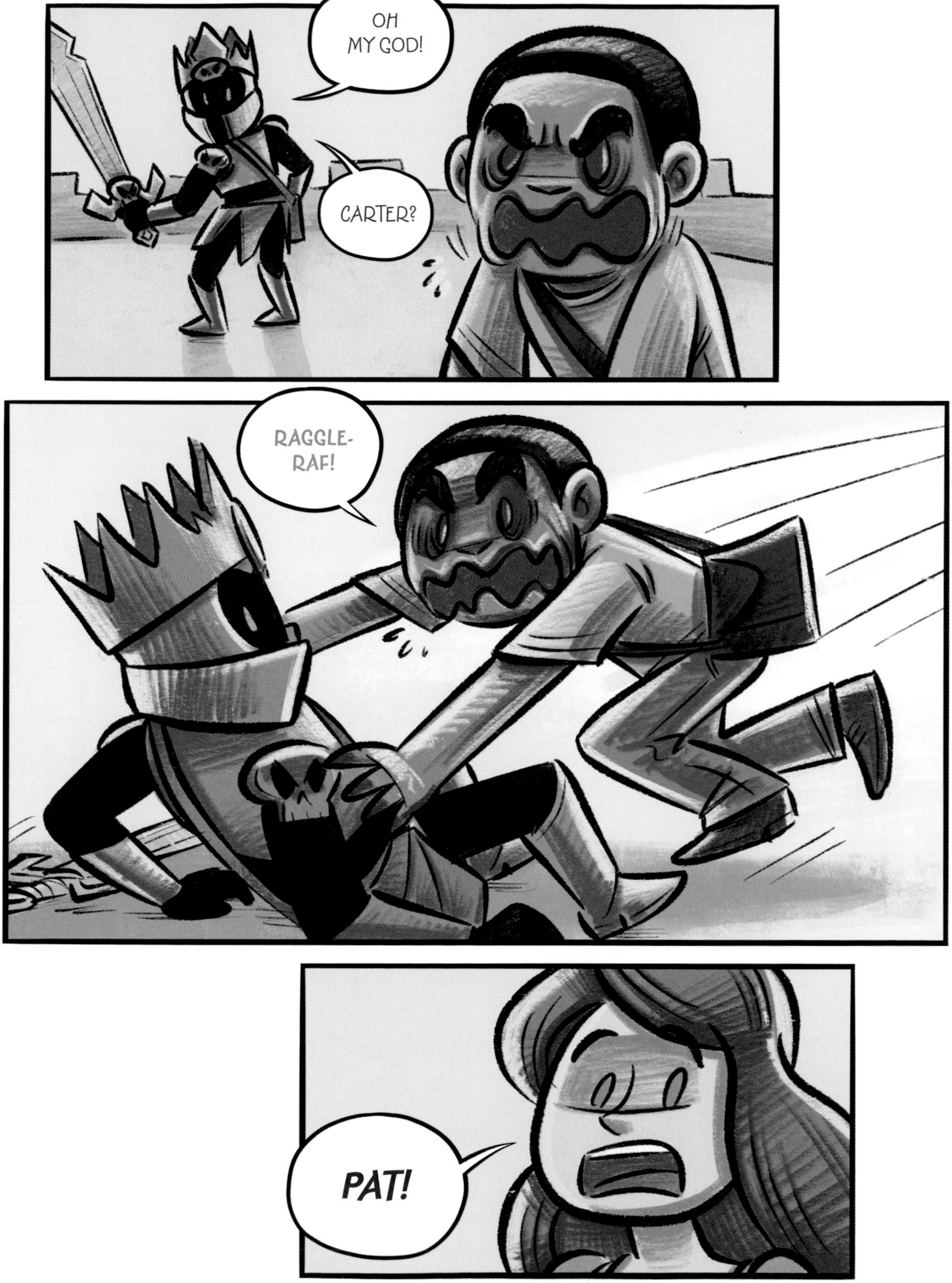
OH MY GOD!
CARTER?
RAGGLE-RAF!
PAT!

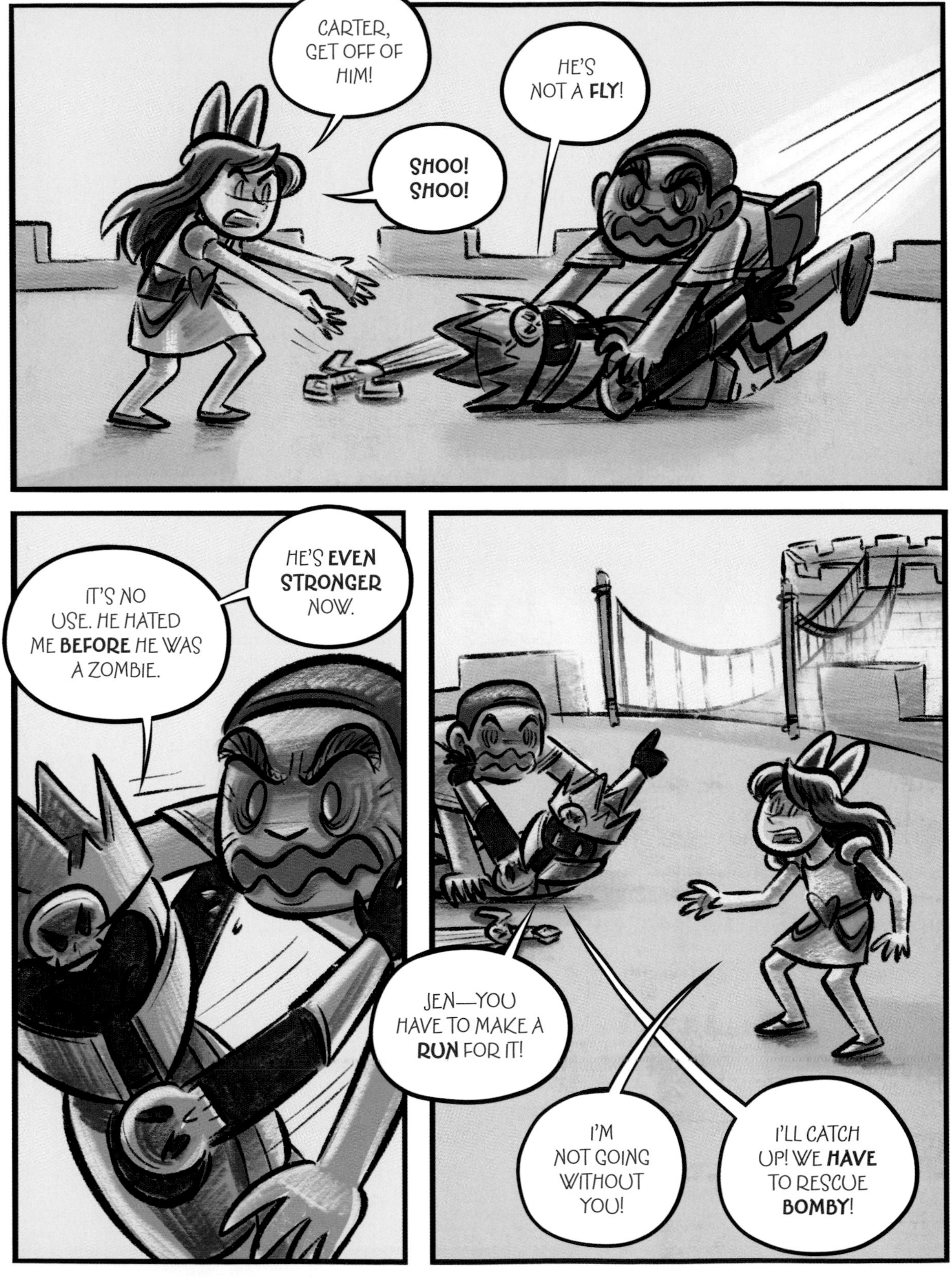

CARTER, GET OFF OF HIM!
SHOO! SHOO!
HE'S NOT A **FLY**!
IT'S NO USE. HE HATED ME **BEFORE** HE WAS A ZOMBIE.
HE'S **EVEN STRONGER** NOW.
JEN—YOU HAVE TO MAKE A **RUN** FOR IT!
I'M NOT GOING WITHOUT YOU!
I'LL CATCH UP! WE **HAVE** TO RESCUE **BOMBY**!

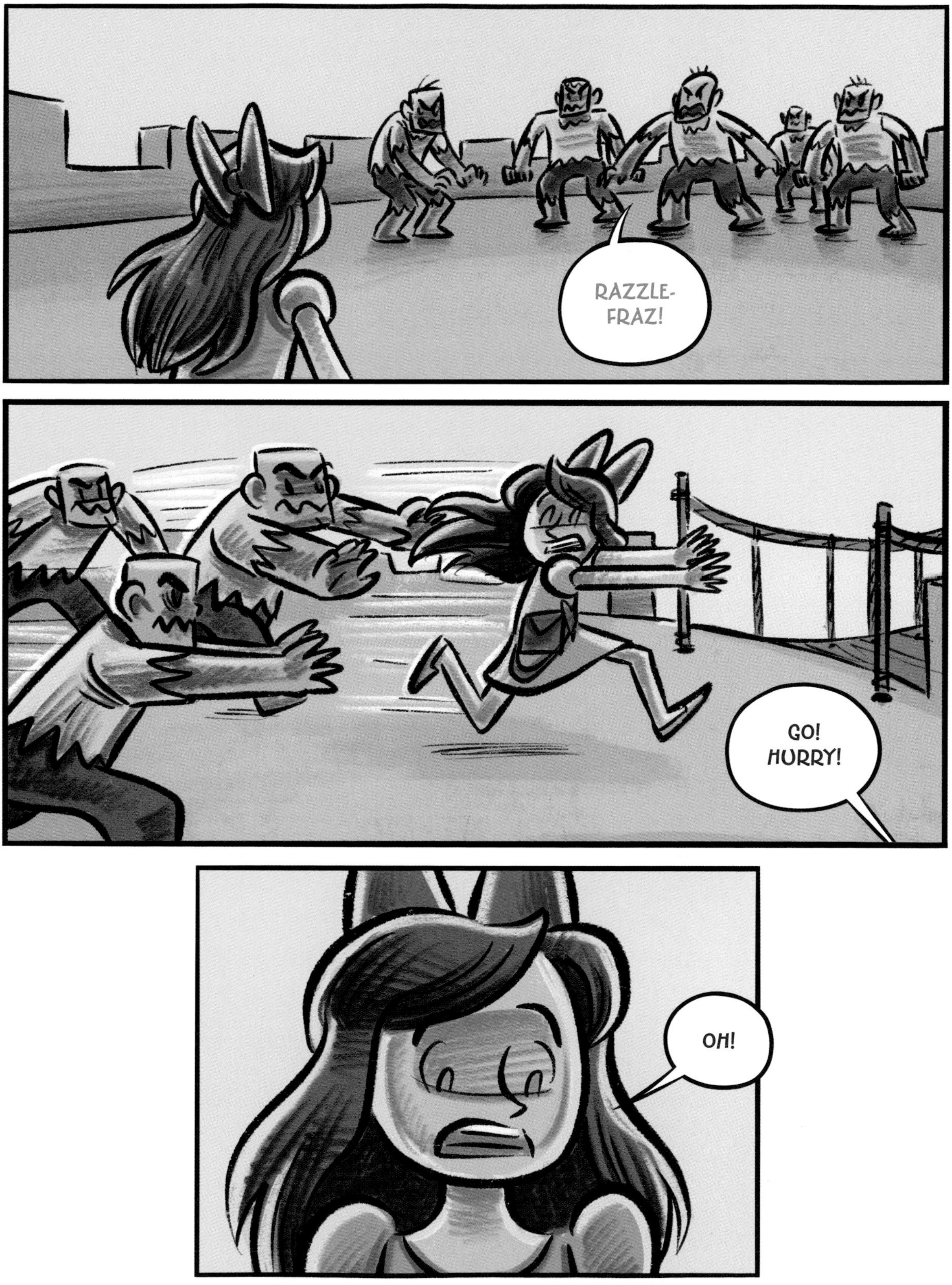
RAZZLE-FRAZ!
GO! HURRY!
OH!

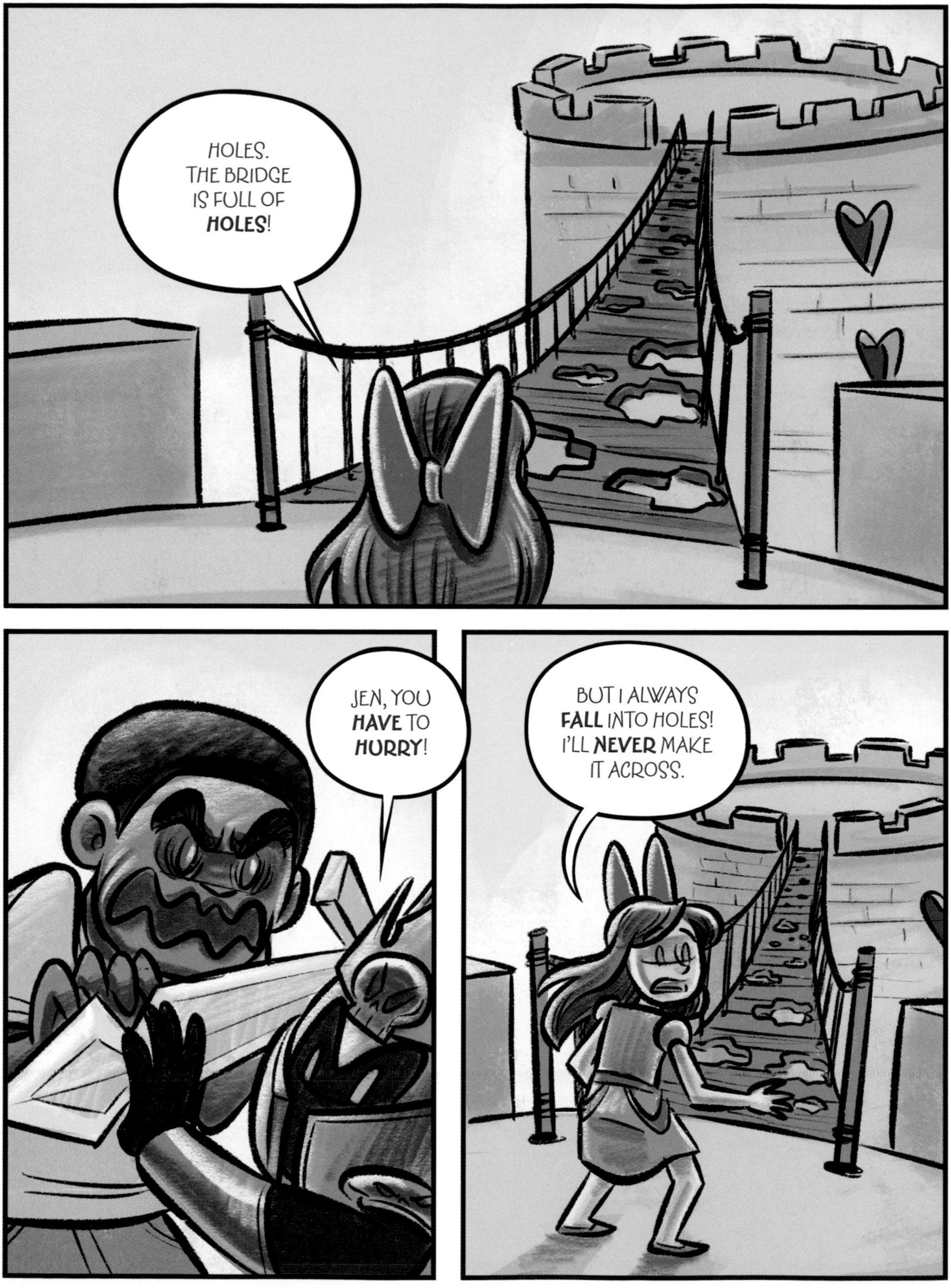
HOLES. THE BRIDGE IS FULL OF **HOLES**!
JEN, YOU **HAVE** TO **HURRY**!
BUT I ALWAYS **FALL** INTO HOLES! I'LL **NEVER** MAKE IT ACROSS.

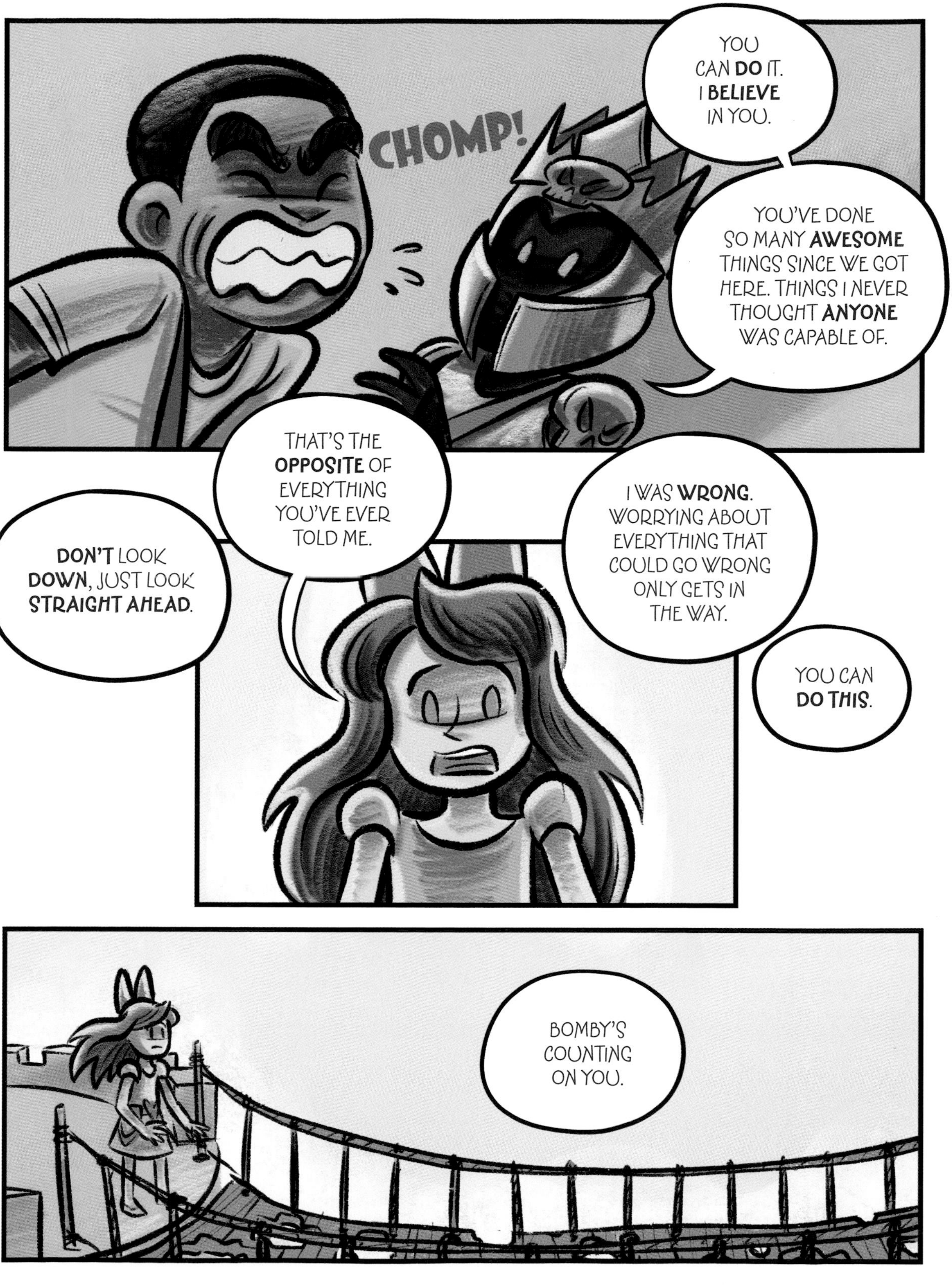
CHOMP!
YOU CAN DO IT. I BELIEVE IN YOU.
YOU'VE DONE SO MANY AWESOME THINGS SINCE WE GOT HERE. THINGS I NEVER THOUGHT ANYONE WAS CAPABLE OF.
DON'T LOOK DOWN, JUST LOOK STRAIGHT AHEAD.
THAT'S THE OPPOSITE OF EVERYTHING YOU'VE EVER TOLD ME.
I WAS WRONG. WORRYING ABOUT EVERYTHING THAT COULD GO WRONG ONLY GETS IN THE WAY.
YOU CAN DO THIS.
BOMBY'S COUNTING ON YOU.

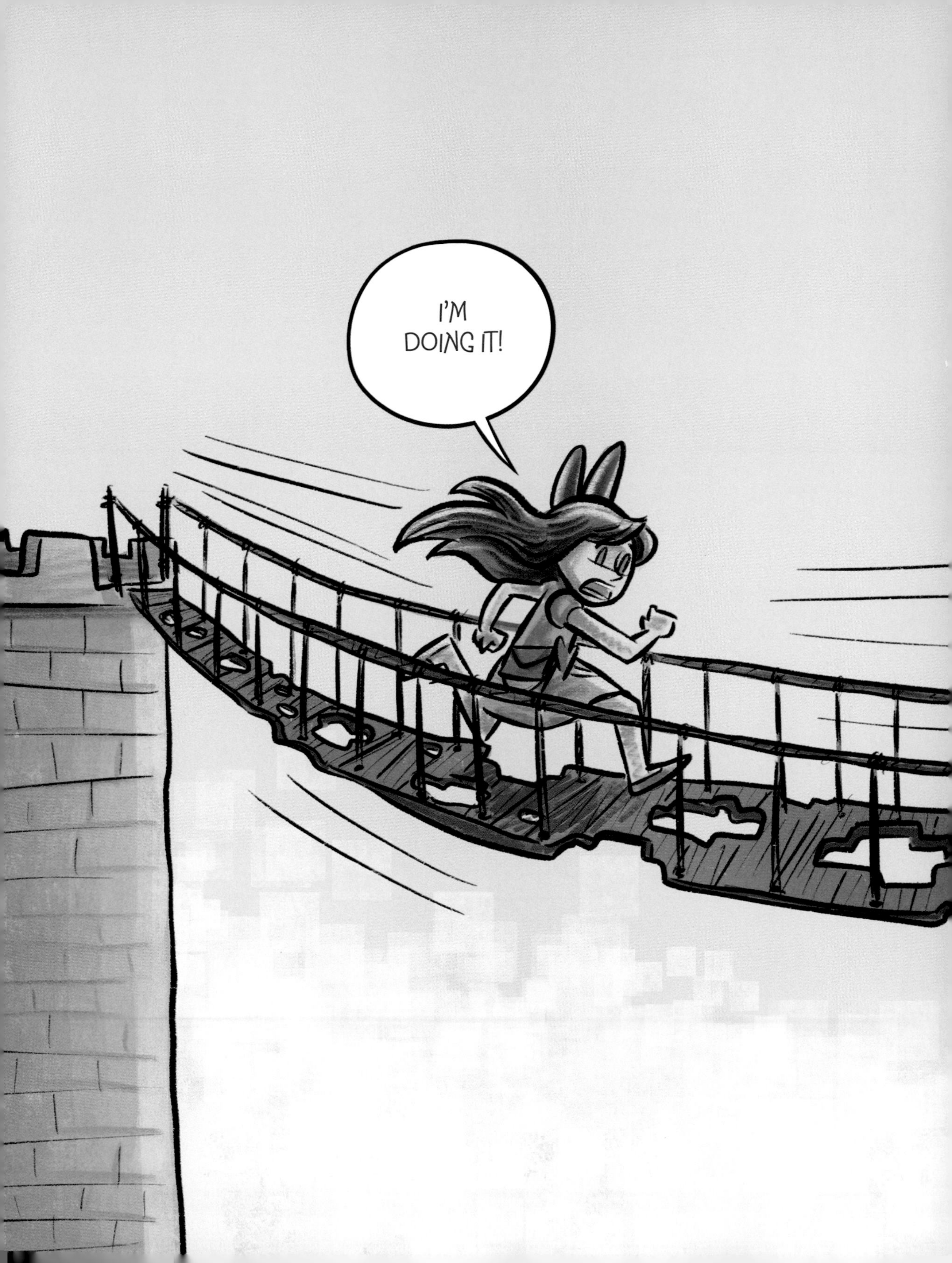
I'M DOING IT!

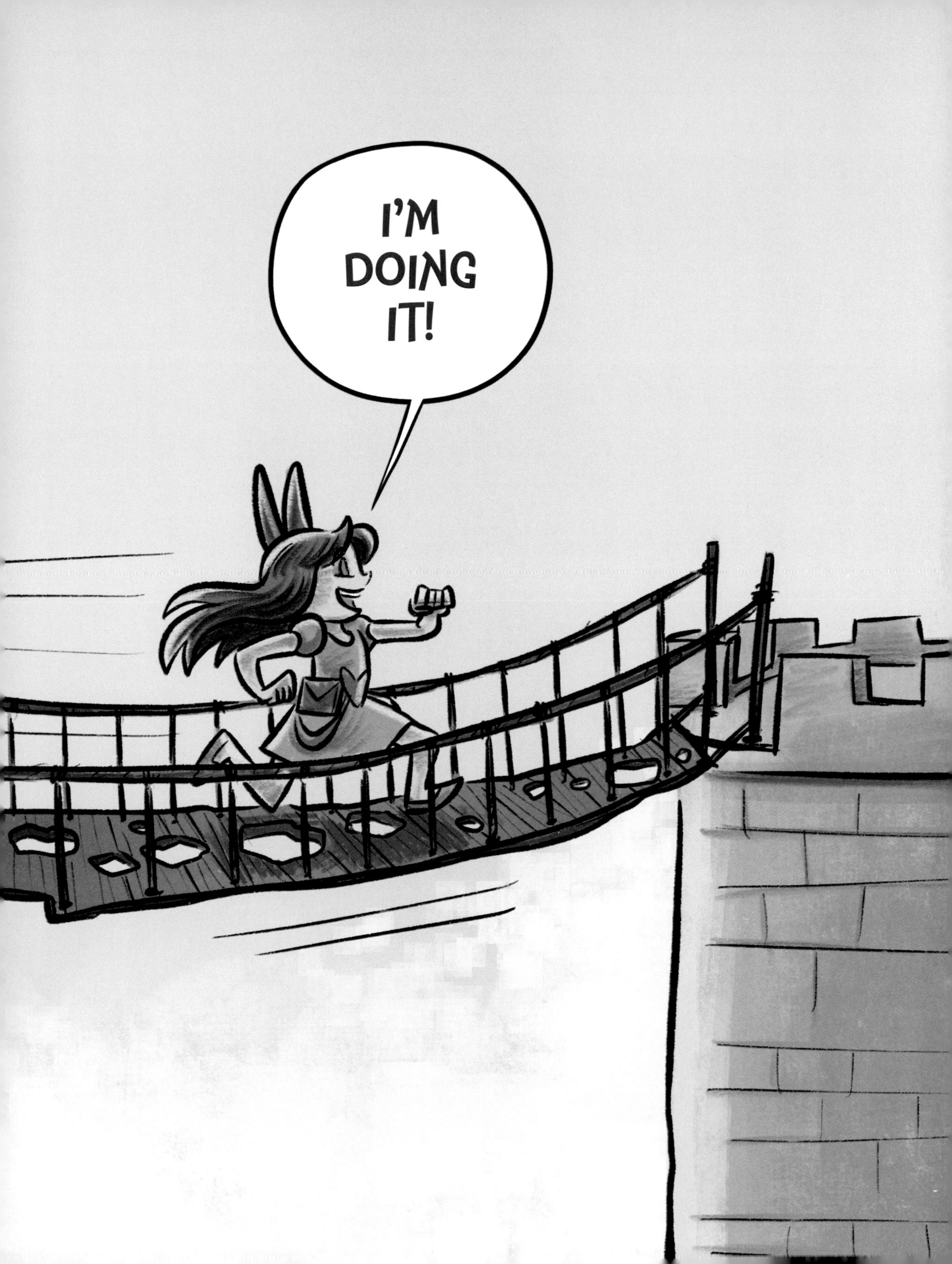
I'M DOING IT!

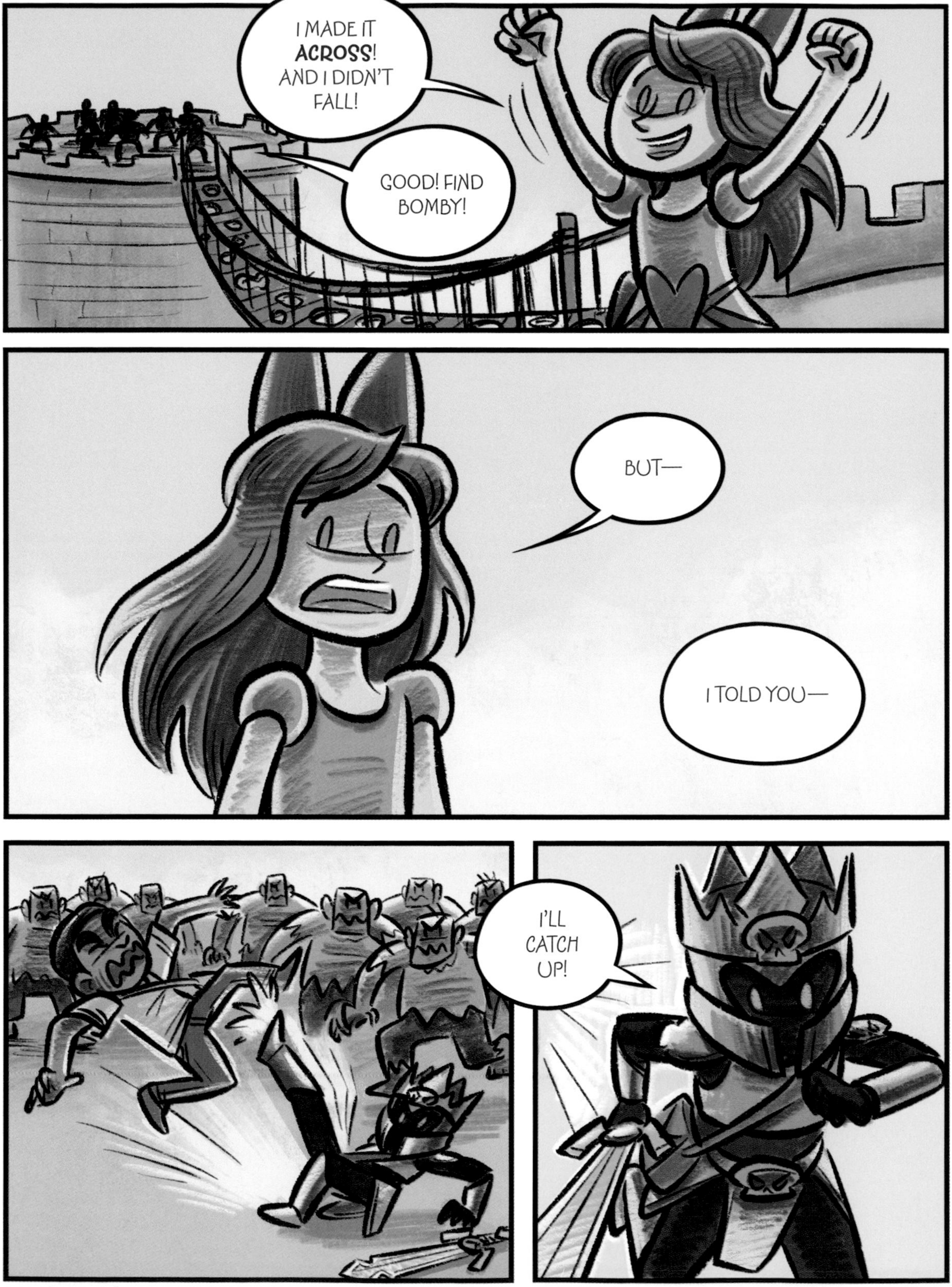
I MADE IT **ACROSS**! AND I DIDN'T FALL!
GOOD! FIND BOMBY!
BUT—
I TOLD YOU—
I'LL CATCH UP!

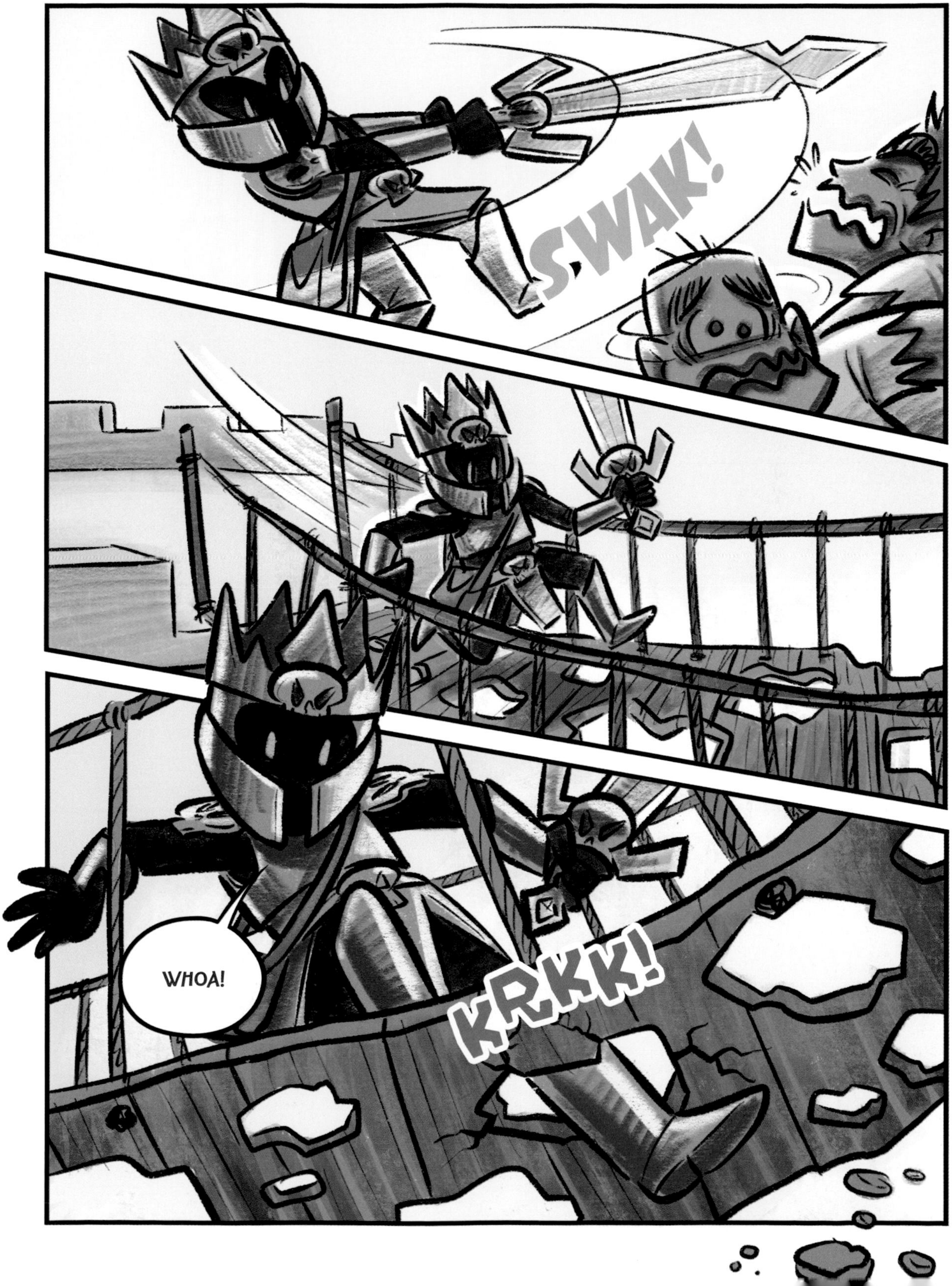

SWAK!
WHOA!
KRKK!

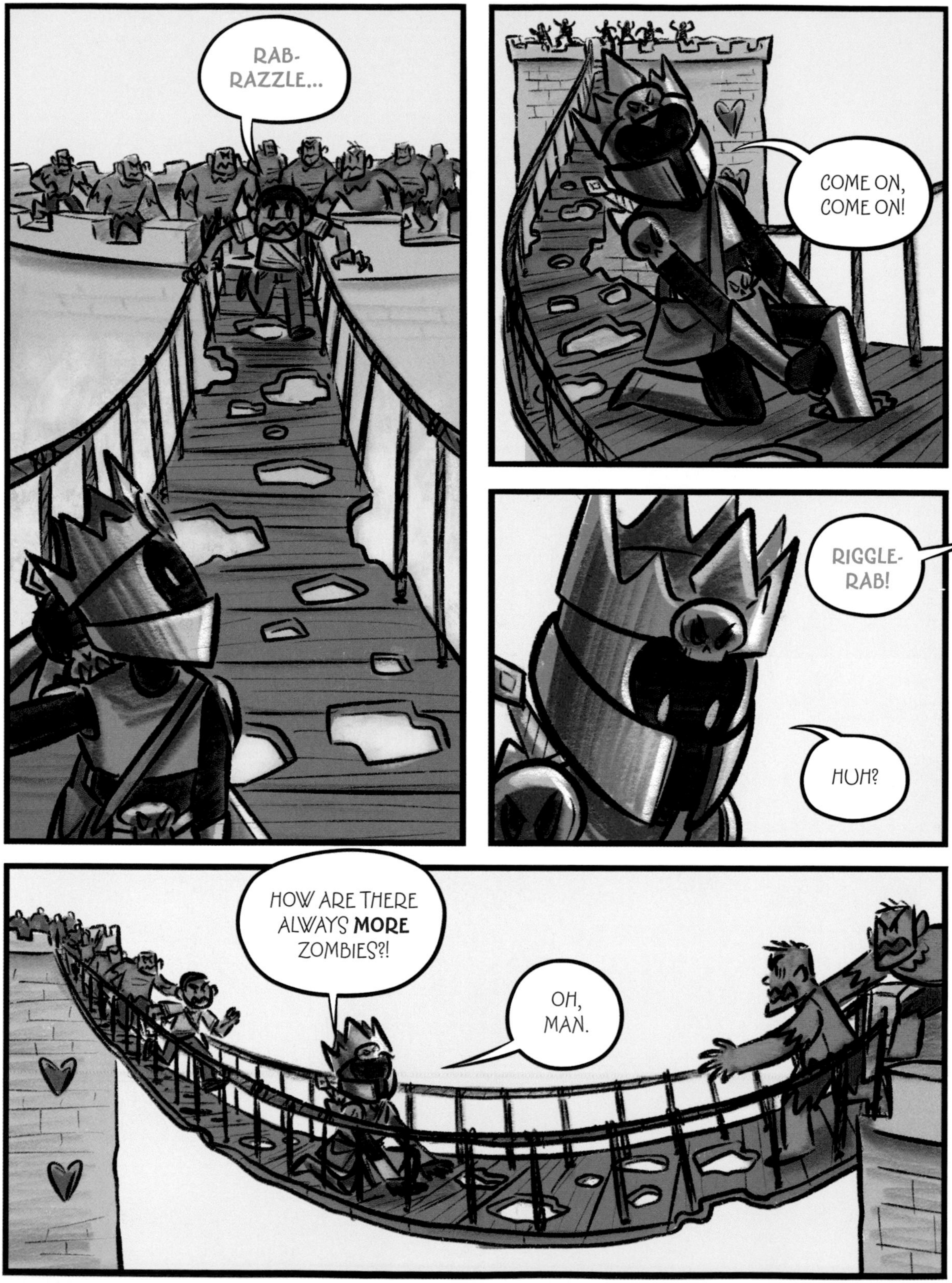
RAB-
RAZZLE...
COME ON,
COME ON!
RIGGLE-
RAB!
HUH?
HOW ARE THERE ALWAYS **MORE** ZOMBIES?!
OH, MAN.

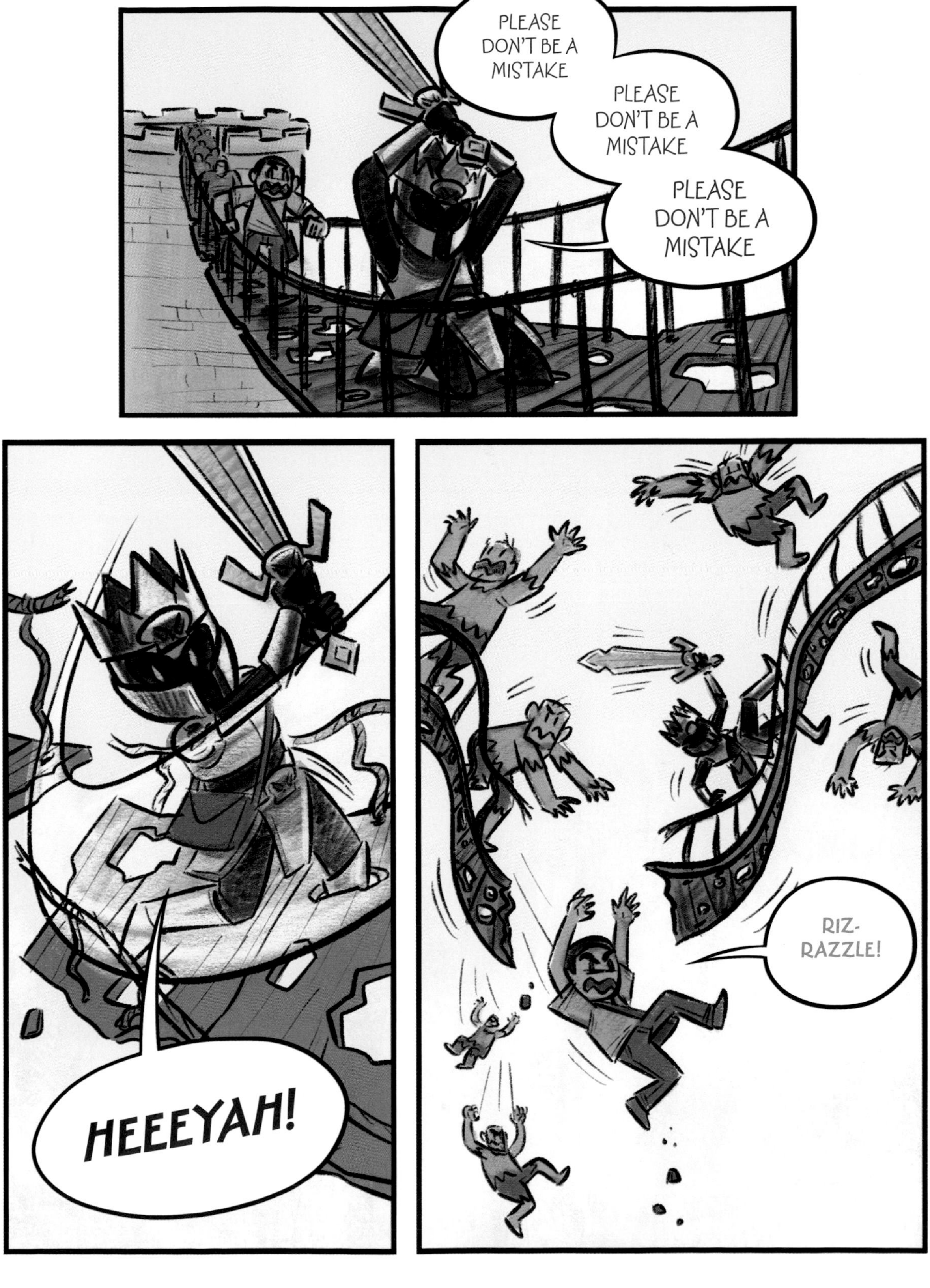
PLEASE DON'T BE A MISTAKE
PLEASE DON'T BE A MISTAKE
PLEASE DON'T BE A MISTAKE
HEEEYAH!
RIZ-RAZZLE!

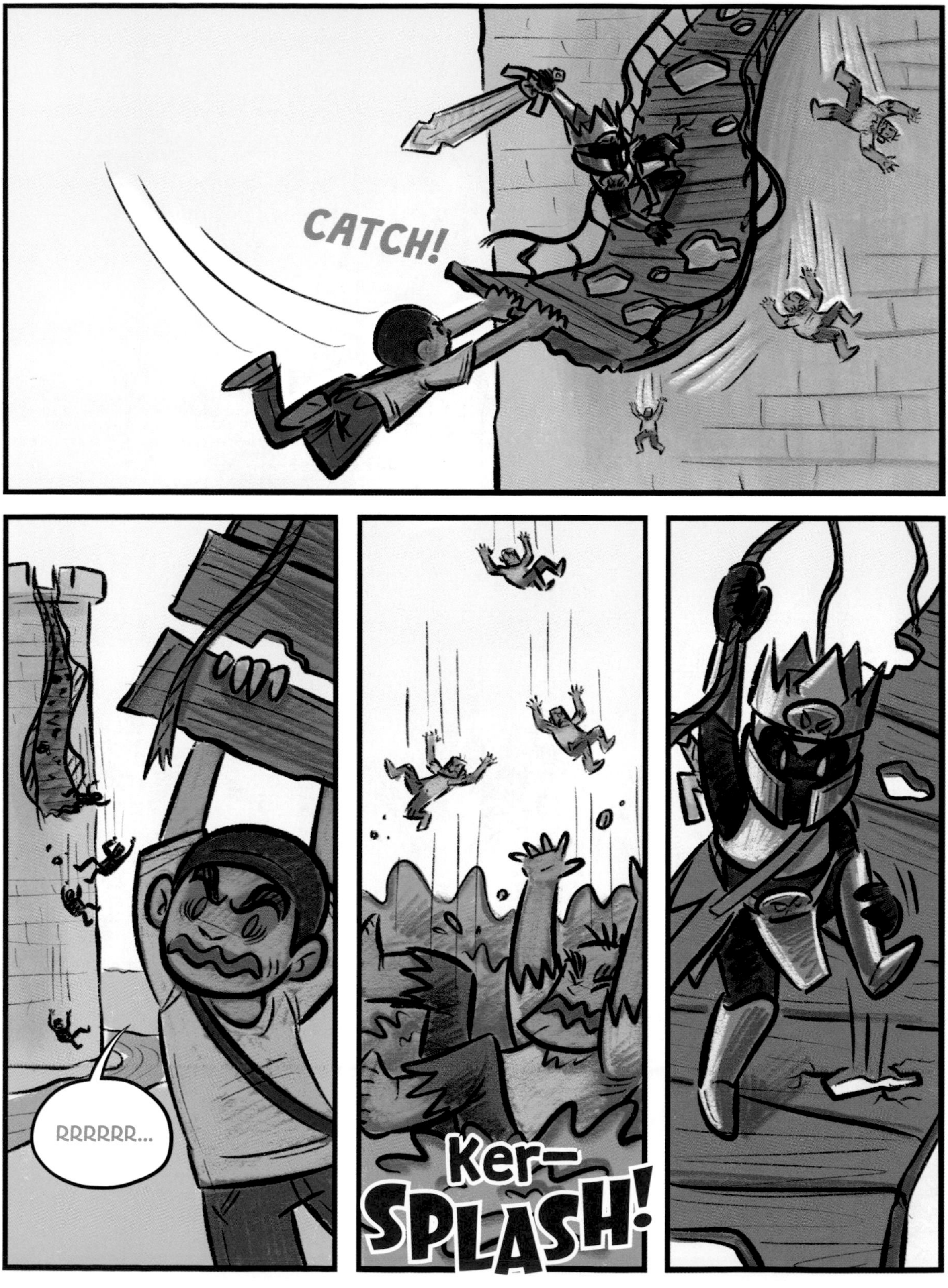
CATCH!
RRRRRR...
Ker-
SPLASH!

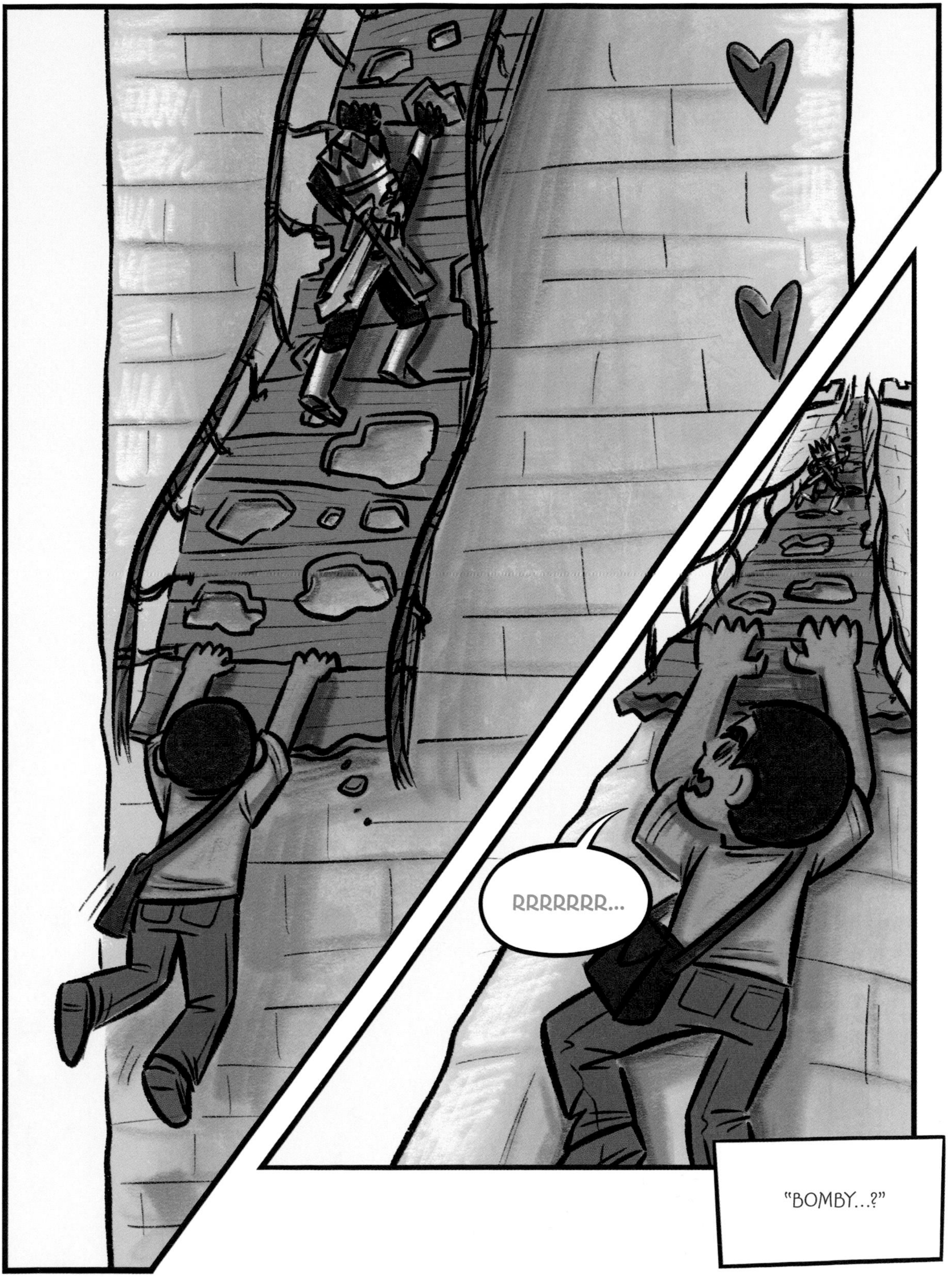
RRRRRRR...
"BOMBY...?"

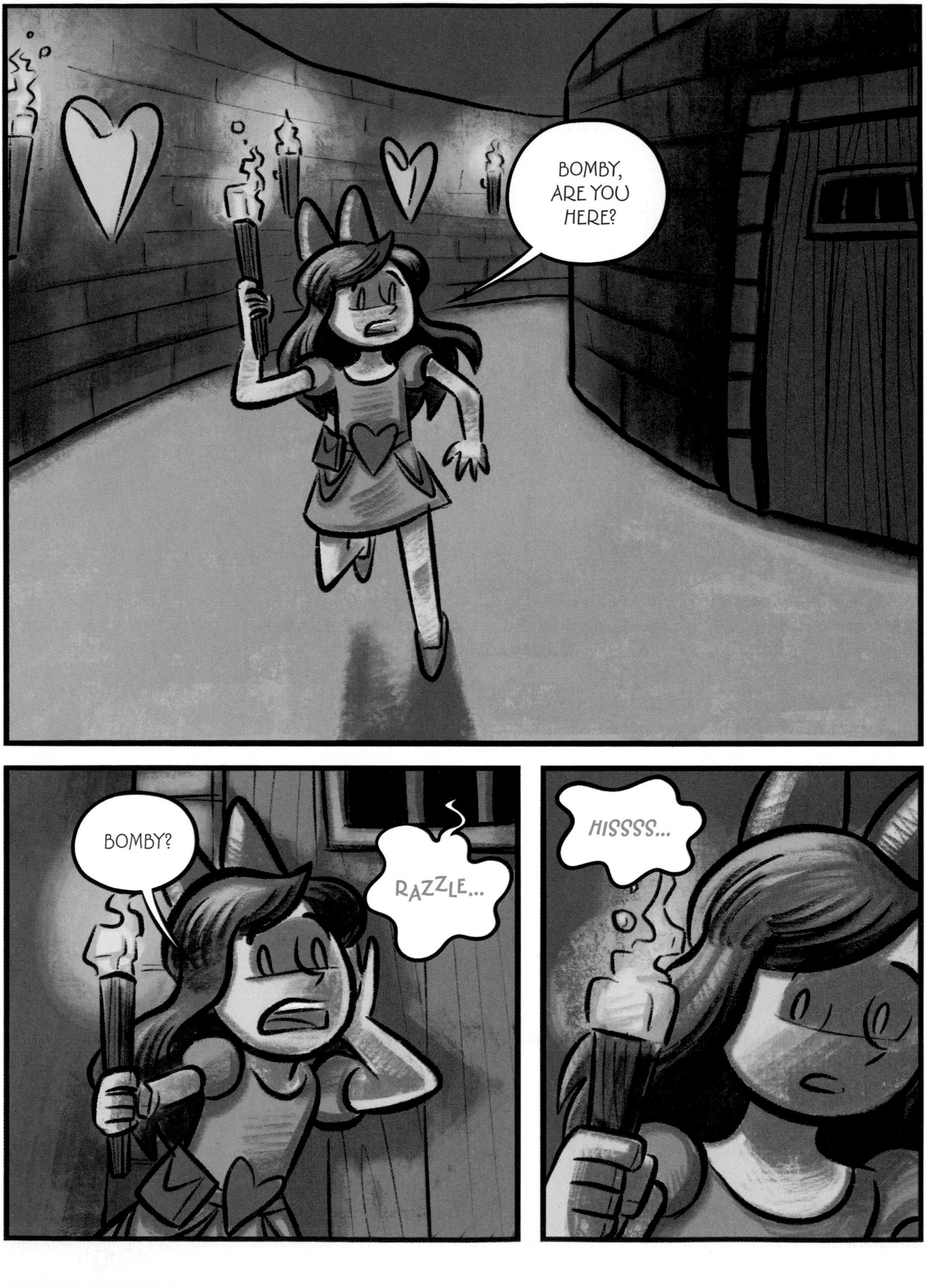
BOMBY, ARE YOU HERE?
BOMBY?
RAZZLE...
HISSSS...

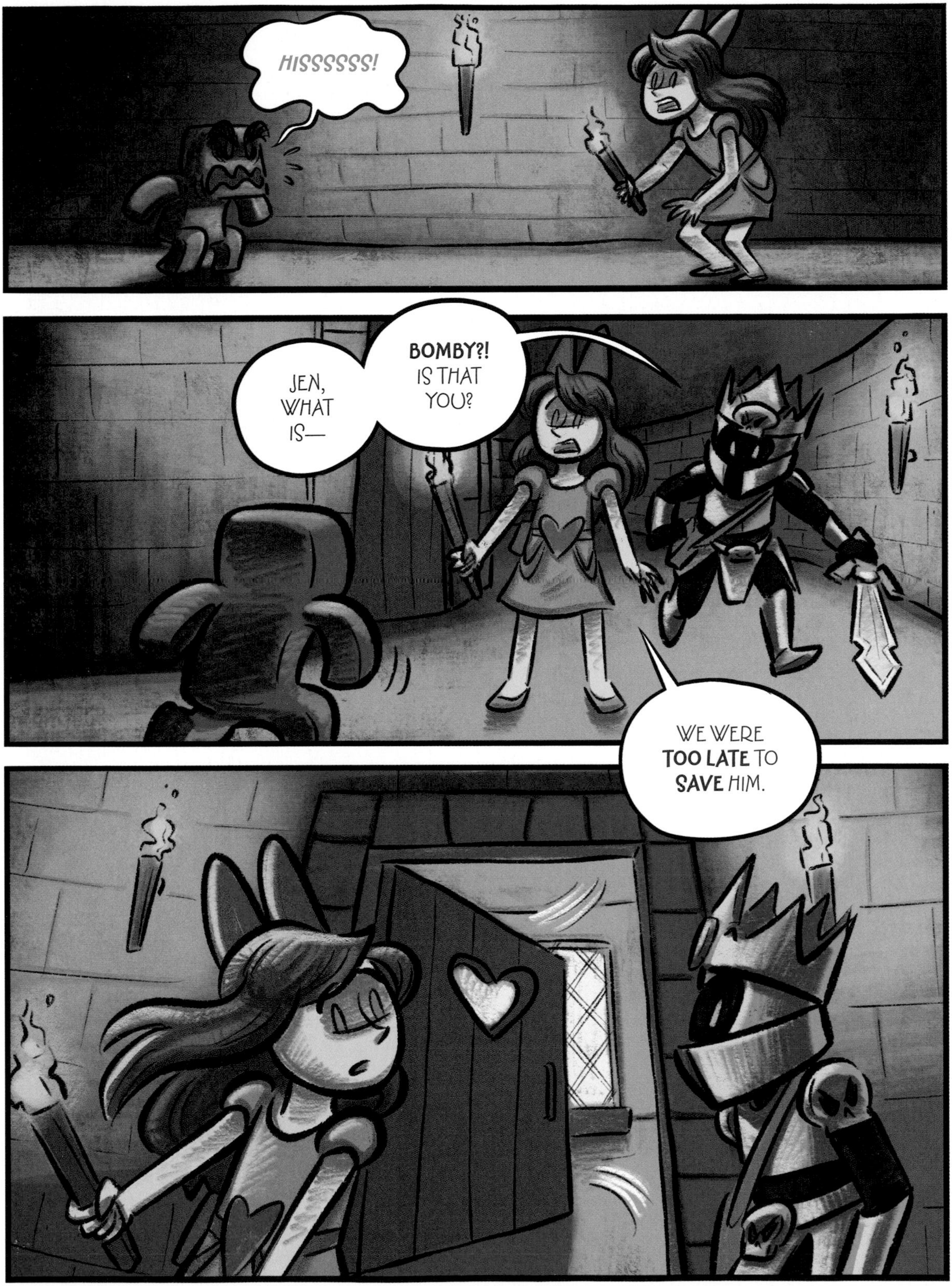
HISSSSSS!
JEN, WHAT IS—
BOMBY?! IS THAT YOU?
WE WERE TOO LATE TO SAVE HIM.

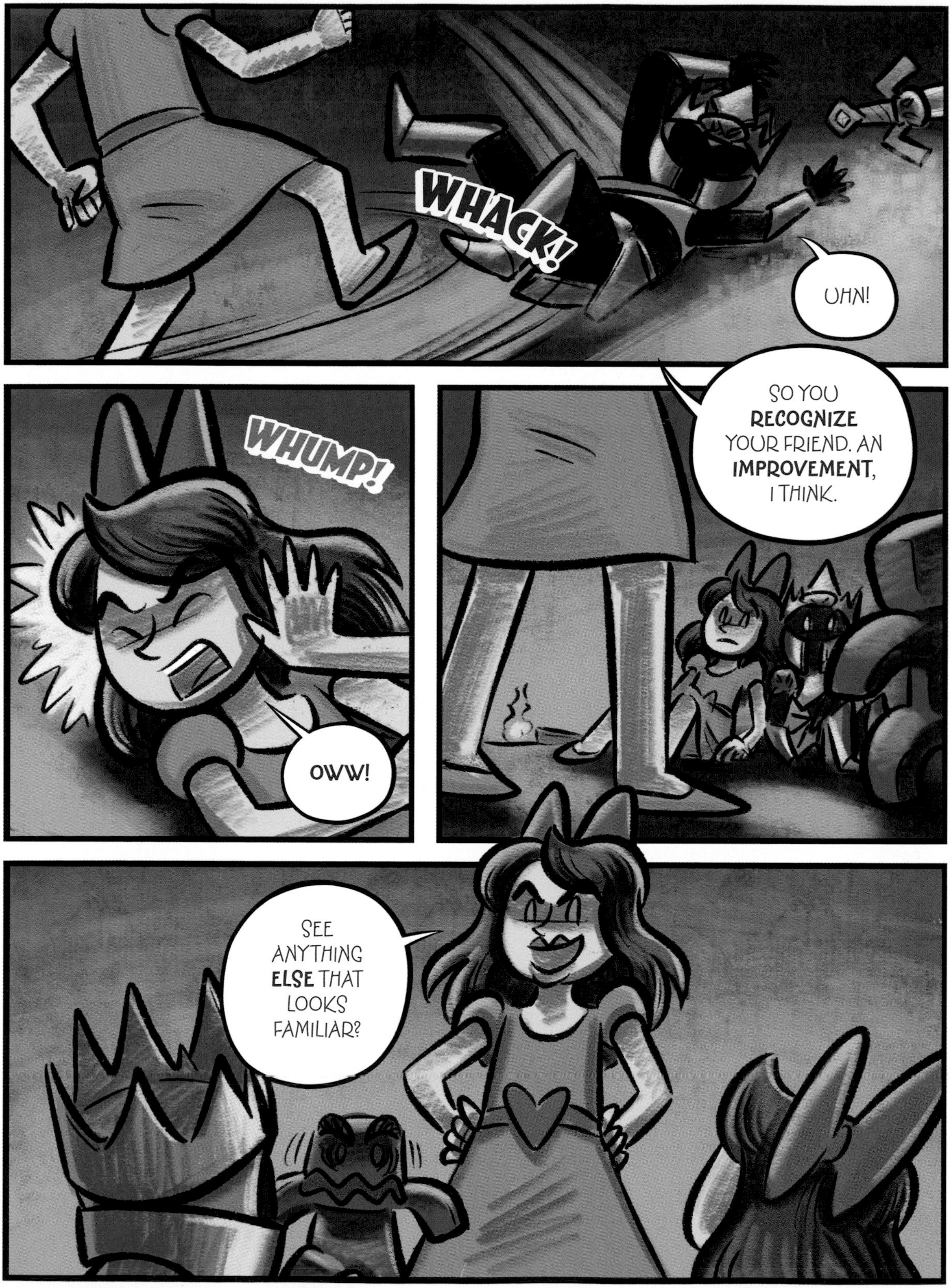
WHACK!
UHN!
WHUMP!
OWW!
SO YOU **RECOGNIZE** YOUR FRIEND. AN **IMPROVEMENT**, I THINK.
SEE ANYTHING **ELSE** THAT LOOKS FAMILIAR?

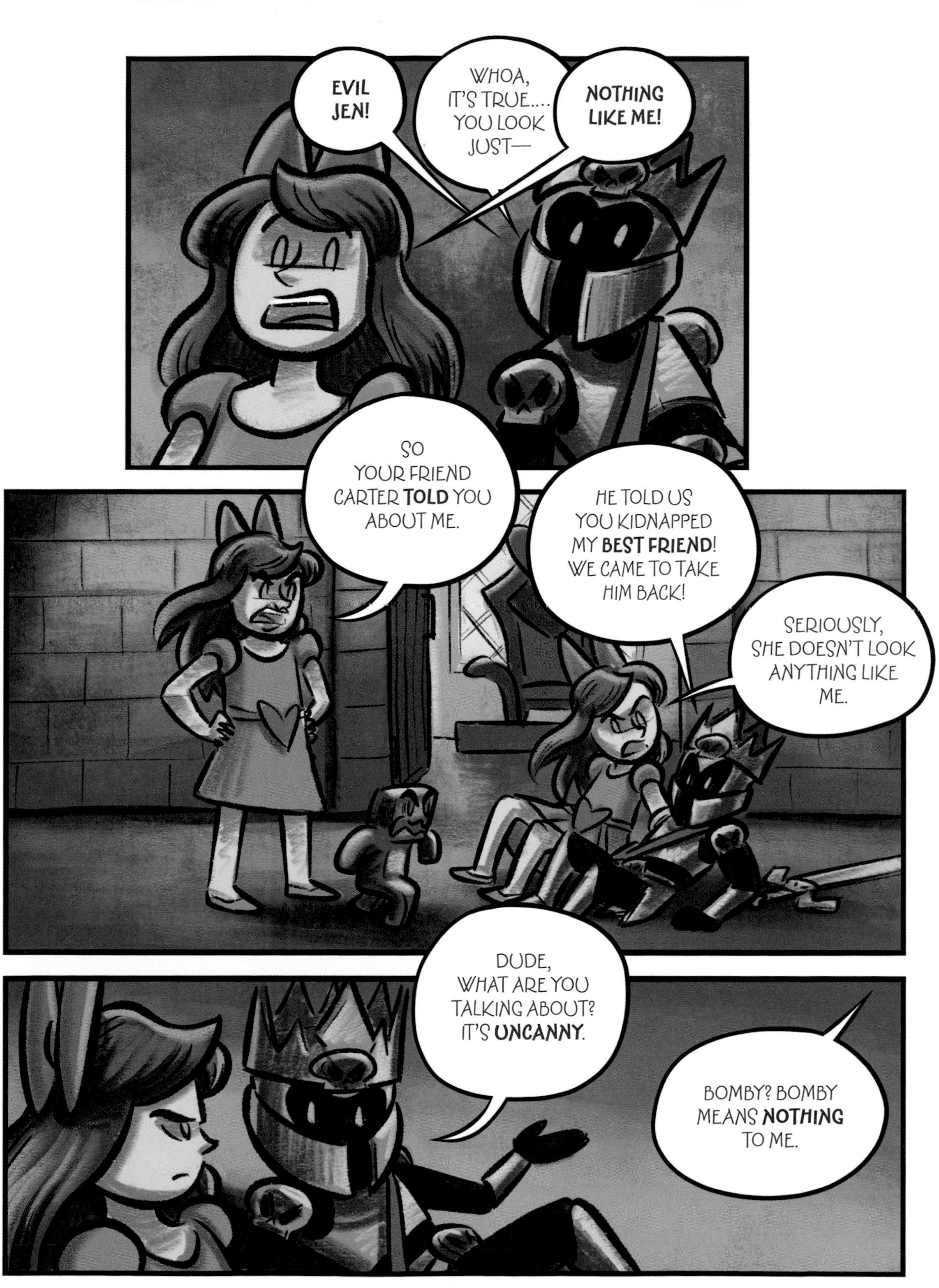
EVIL JEN!
WHOA, IT'S TRUE.... YOU LOOK JUST—
NOTHING LIKE ME!
SO YOUR FRIEND CARTER **TOLD** YOU ABOUT ME.
HE TOLD US YOU KIDNAPPED MY **BEST FRIEND**! WE CAME TO TAKE HIM BACK!
SERIOUSLY, SHE DOESN'T LOOK ANYTHING LIKE ME.
DUDE, WHAT ARE YOU TALKING ABOUT? IT'S **UNCANNY**.
BOMBY? BOMBY MEANS **NOTHING** TO ME.

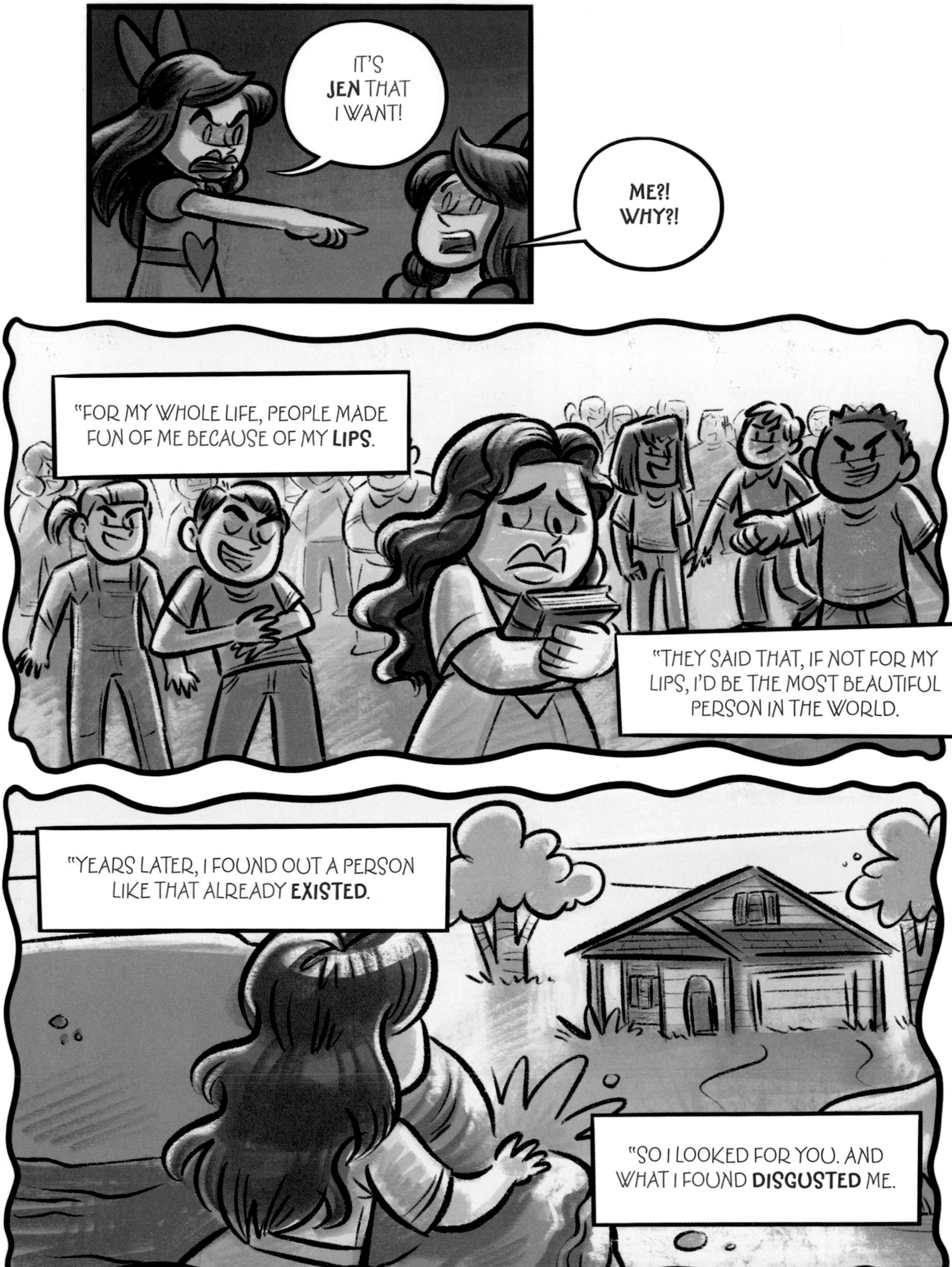
IT'S **JEN** THAT I WANT!
ME?! WHY?!
"FOR MY WHOLE LIFE, PEOPLE MADE FUN OF ME BECAUSE OF MY **LIPS**.
"THEY SAID THAT, IF NOT FOR MY LIPS, I'D BE THE MOST BEAUTIFUL PERSON IN THE WORLD.
"YEARS LATER, I FOUND OUT A PERSON LIKE THAT ALREADY **EXISTED**.
"SO I LOOKED FOR YOU. AND WHAT I FOUND **DISGUSTED** ME.

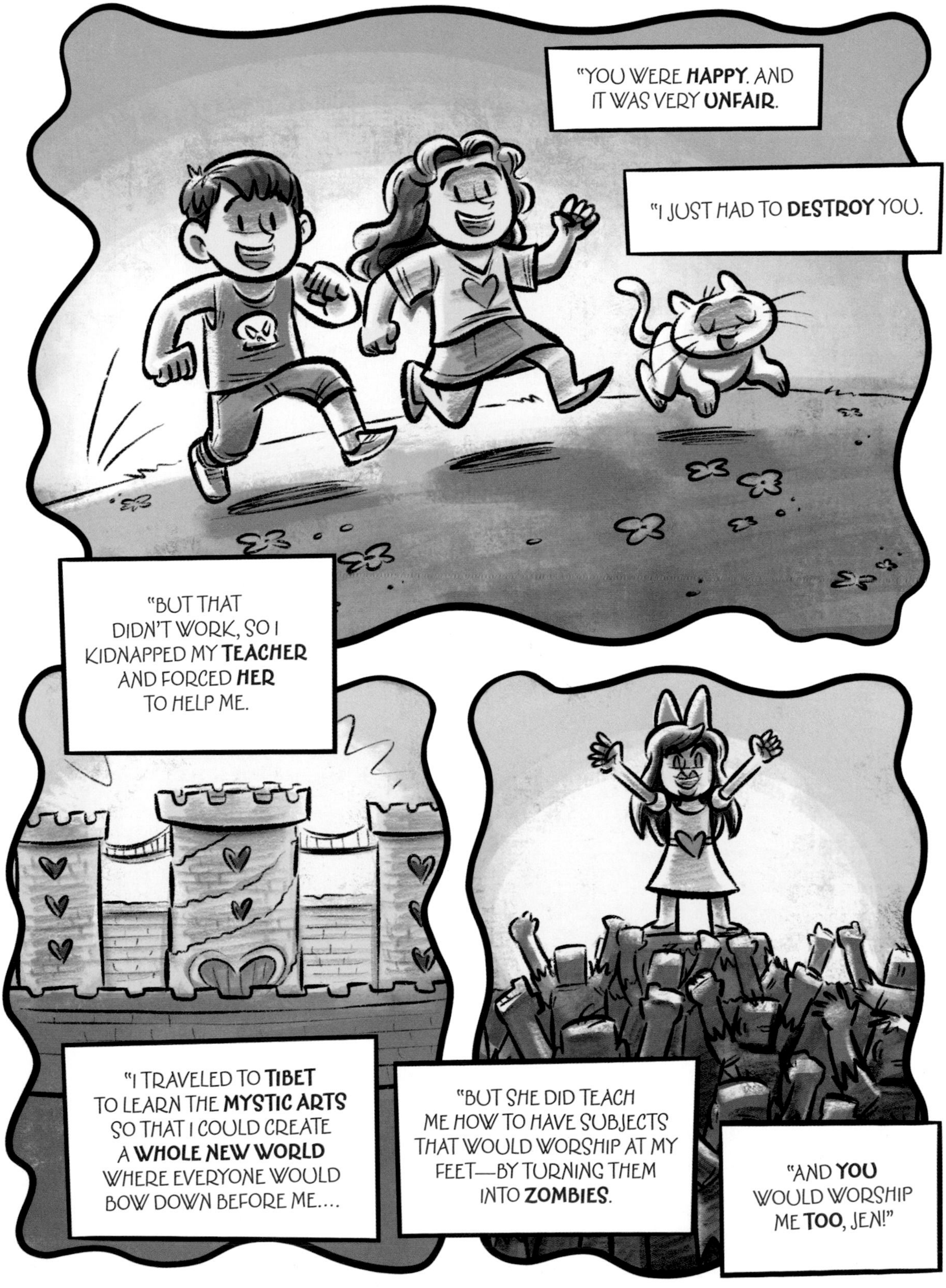
"YOU WERE HAPPY. AND IT WAS VERY UNFAIR.
"I JUST HAD TO DESTROY YOU.
"BUT THAT DIDN'T WORK, SO I KIDNAPPED MY TEACHER AND FORCED HER TO HELP ME.
"I TRAVELED TO TIBET TO LEARN THE MYSTIC ARTS SO THAT I COULD CREATE A WHOLE NEW WORLD WHERE EVERYONE WOULD BOW DOWN BEFORE ME....
"BUT SHE DID TEACH ME HOW TO HAVE SUBJECTS THAT WOULD WORSHIP AT MY FEET—BY TURNING THEM INTO ZOMBIES.
"AND YOU WOULD WORSHIP ME TOO, JEN!"

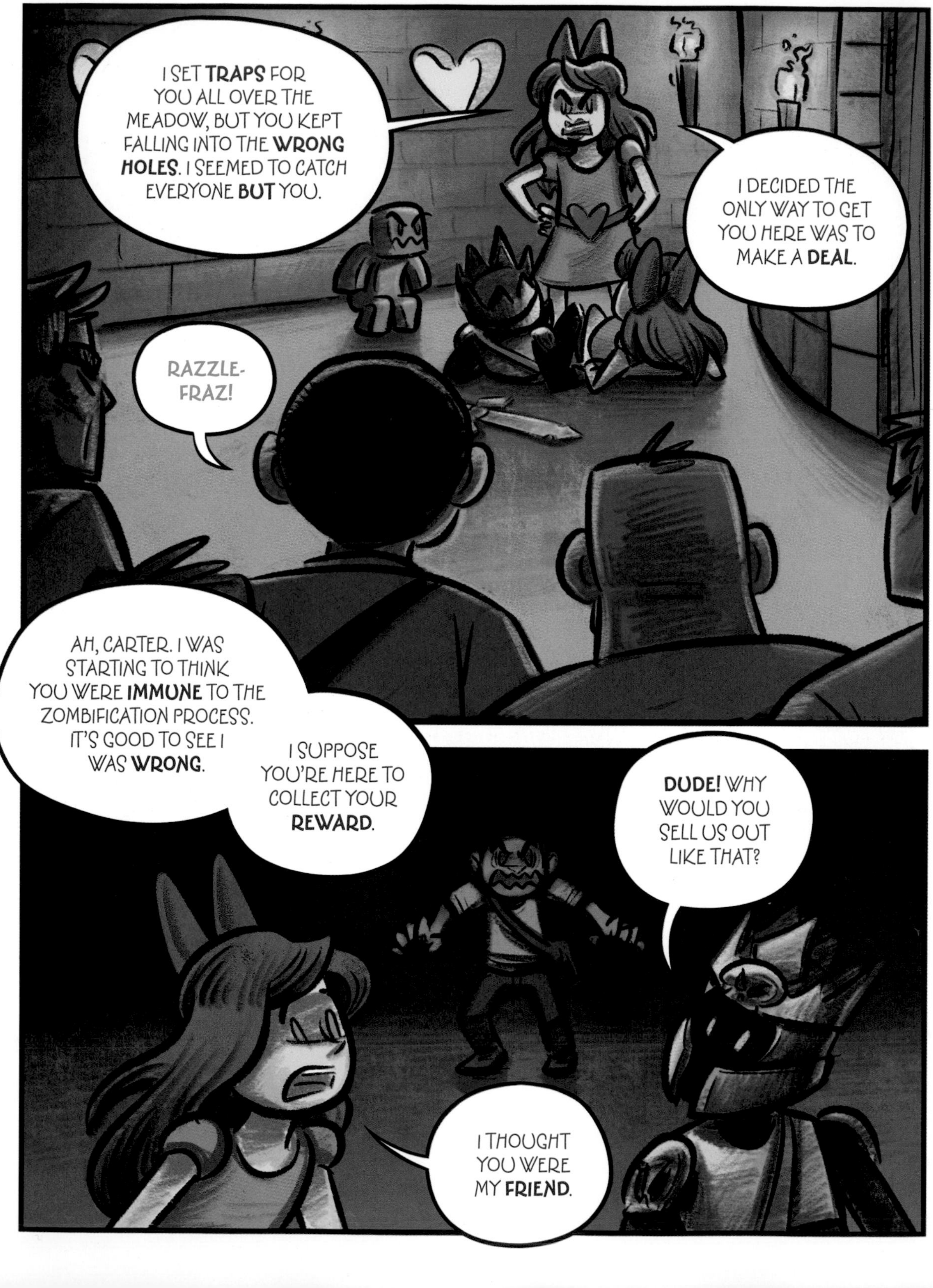
I SET TRAPS FOR YOU ALL OVER THE MEADOW, BUT YOU KEPT FALLING INTO THE WRONG HOLES. I SEEMED TO CATCH EVERYONE BUT YOU.
I DECIDED THE ONLY WAY TO GET YOU HERE WAS TO MAKE A DEAL.
RAZZLE-FRAZ!
AH, CARTER. I WAS STARTING TO THINK YOU WERE IMMUNE TO THE ZOMBIFICATION PROCESS. IT'S GOOD TO SEE I WAS WRONG.
I SUPPOSE YOU'RE HERE TO COLLECT YOUR REWARD.
DUDE! WHY WOULD YOU SELL US OUT LIKE THAT?
I THOUGHT YOU WERE MY FRIEND.

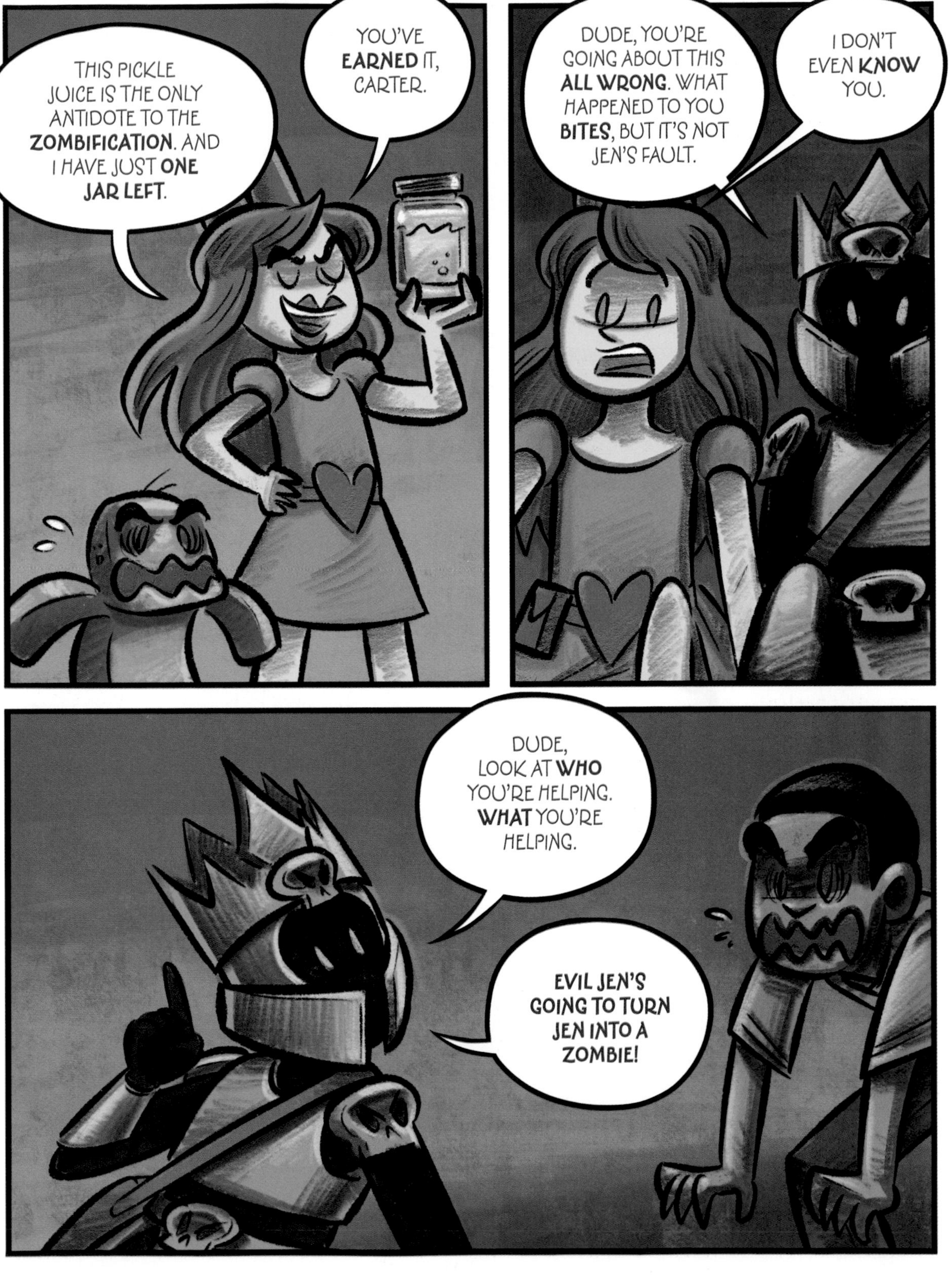
THIS PICKLE JUICE IS THE ONLY ANTIDOTE TO THE **ZOMBIFICATION**. AND I HAVE JUST **ONE JAR LEFT**.
YOU'VE **EARNED** IT, CARTER.
DUDE, YOU'RE GOING ABOUT THIS **ALL WRONG**. WHAT HAPPENED TO YOU **BITES**, BUT IT'S NOT JEN'S FAULT.
I DON'T EVEN **KNOW** YOU.
DUDE, LOOK AT **WHO** YOU'RE HELPING. **WHAT** YOU'RE HELPING.
EVIL JEN'S GOING TO TURN JEN INTO A ZOMBIE!

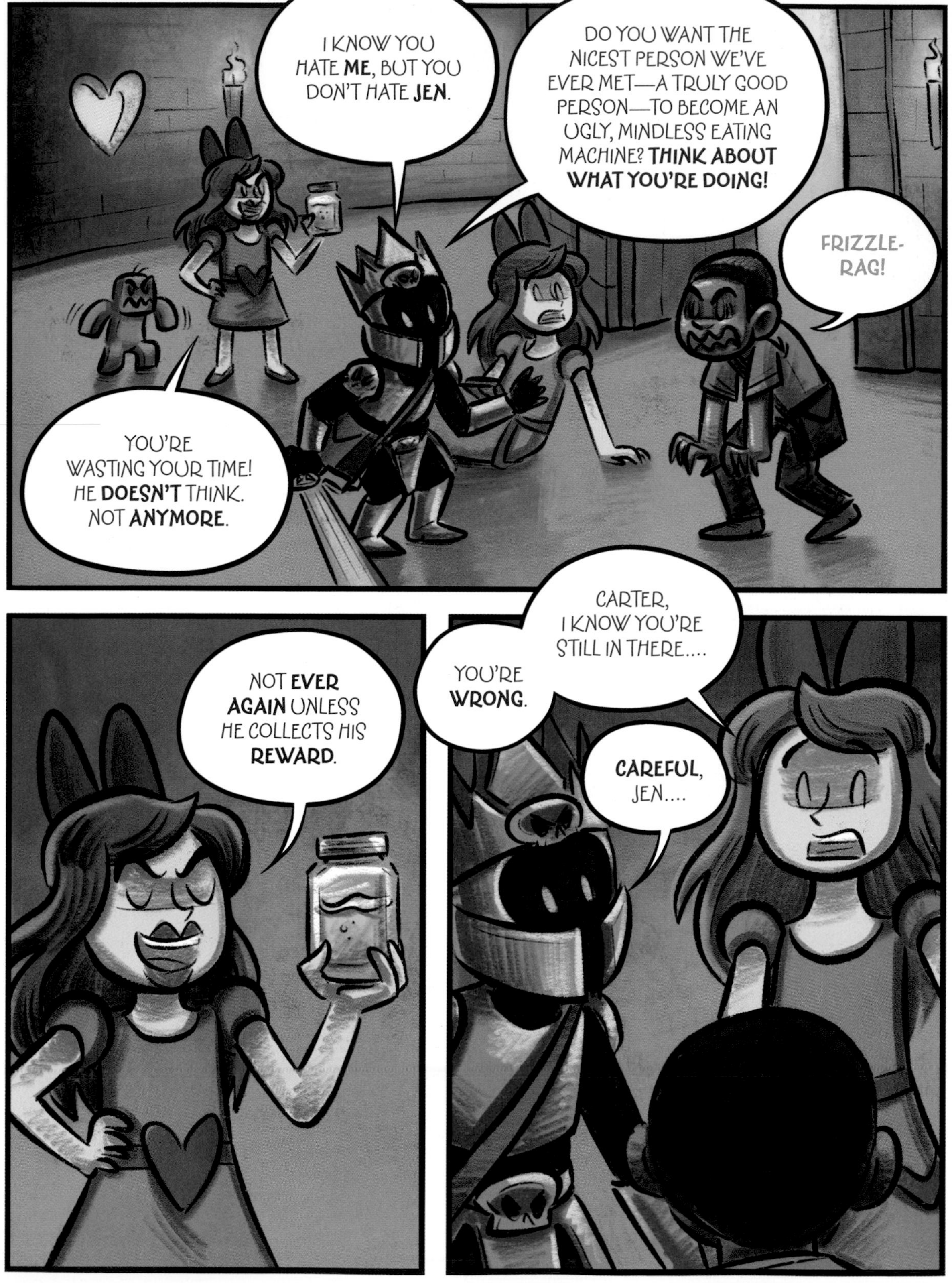
I KNOW YOU HATE **ME**, BUT YOU DON'T HATE **JEN**.
DO YOU WANT THE NICEST PERSON WE'VE EVER MET—A TRULY GOOD PERSON—TO BECOME AN UGLY, MINDLESS EATING MACHINE? **THINK ABOUT WHAT YOU'RE DOING!**
FRIZZLE-RAG!
YOU'RE WASTING YOUR TIME! HE **DOESN'T** THINK. NOT **ANYMORE**.
NOT **EVER AGAIN** UNLESS HE COLLECTS HIS **REWARD**.
YOU'RE **WRONG**.
CARTER, I KNOW YOU'RE STILL IN THERE....
CAREFUL, JEN....

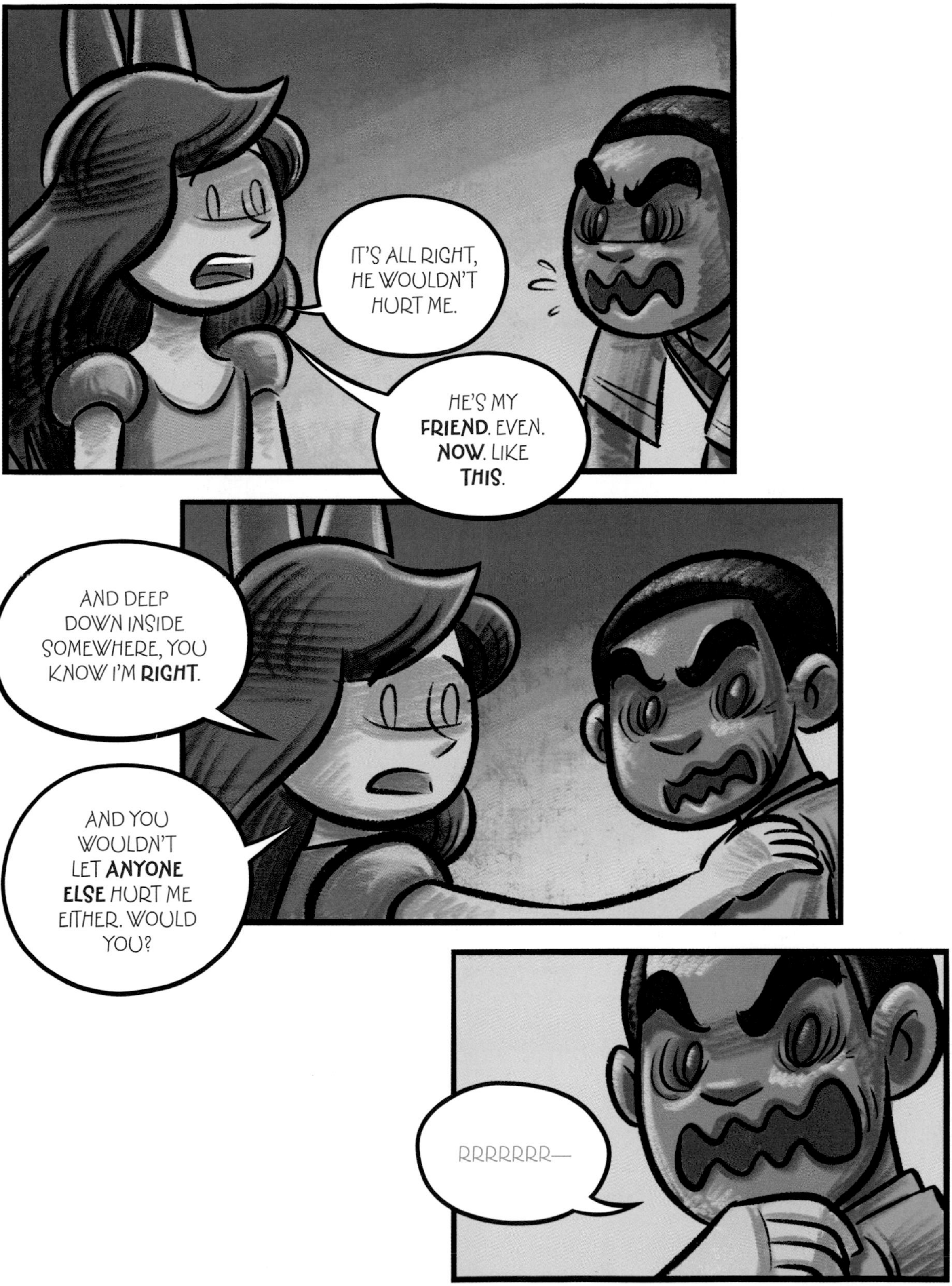
IT'S ALL RIGHT, HE WOULDN'T HURT ME.
HE'S MY **FRIEND**. EVEN. **NOW**. LIKE **THIS**.
AND DEEP DOWN INSIDE SOMEWHERE, YOU KNOW I'M **RIGHT**.
AND YOU WOULDN'T LET **ANYONE ELSE** HURT ME EITHER. WOULD YOU?
RRRRRRR—

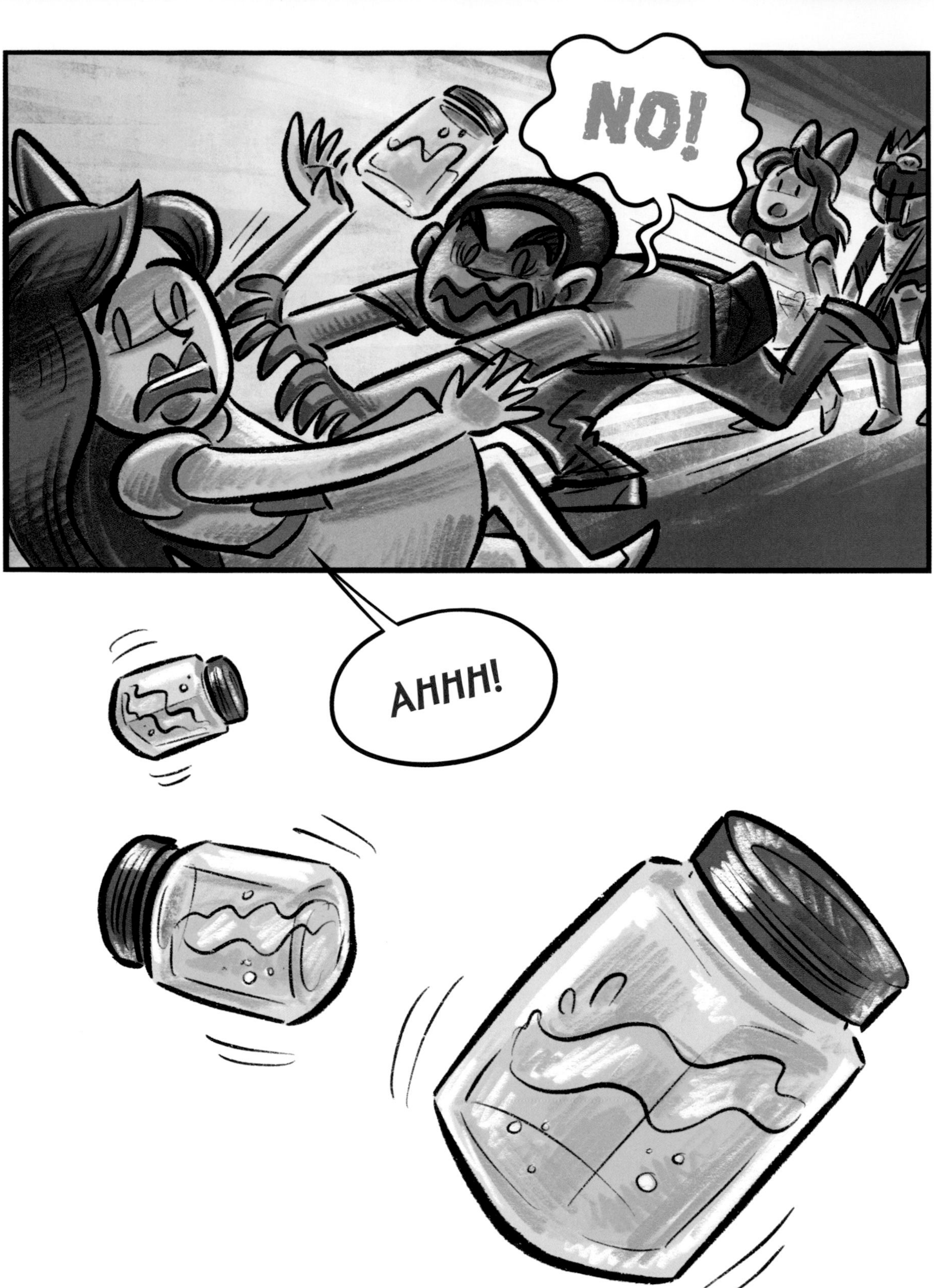
NO!
AHHH!

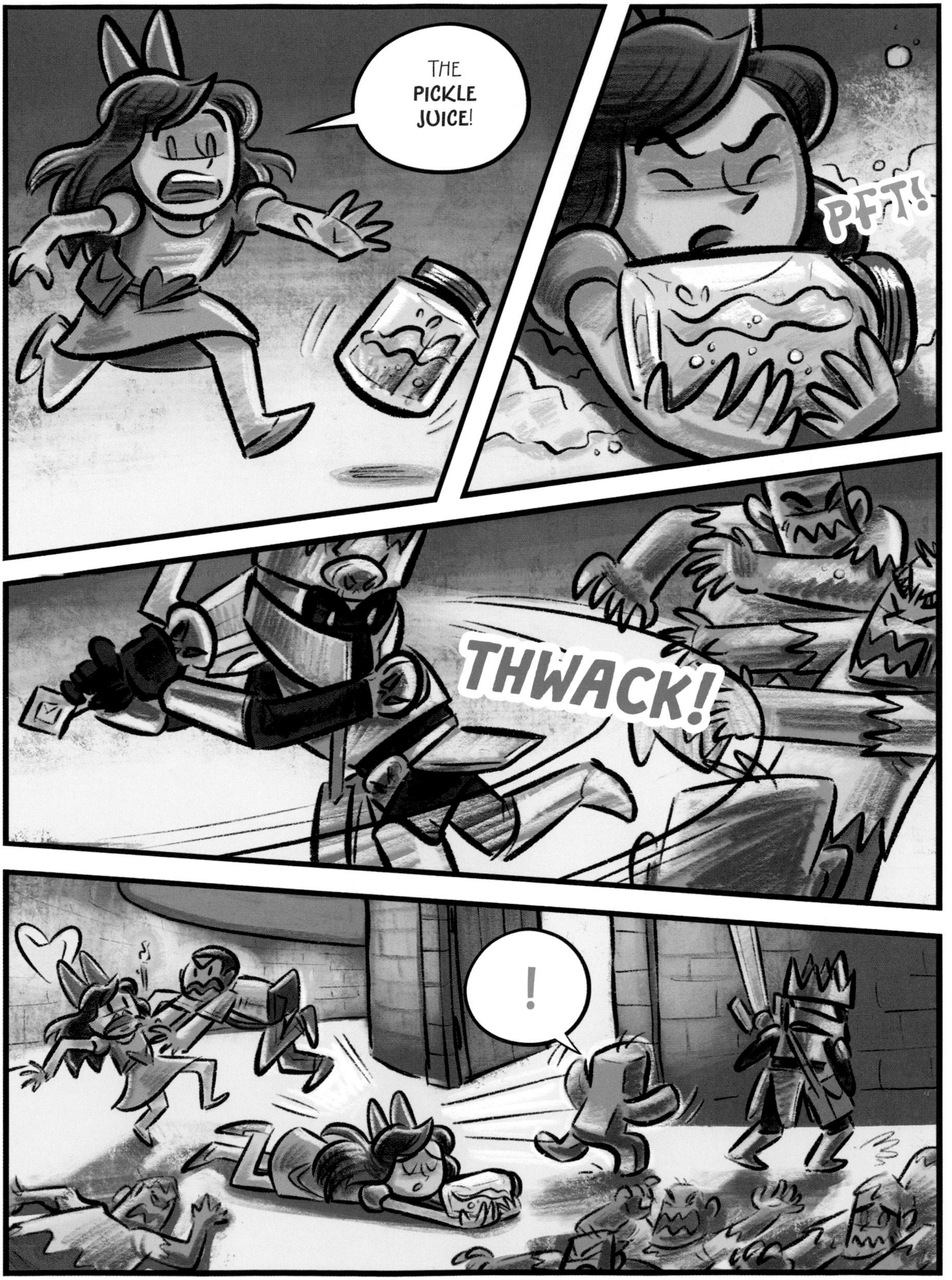
THE PICKLE JUICE!
PFT!
THWACK!
!

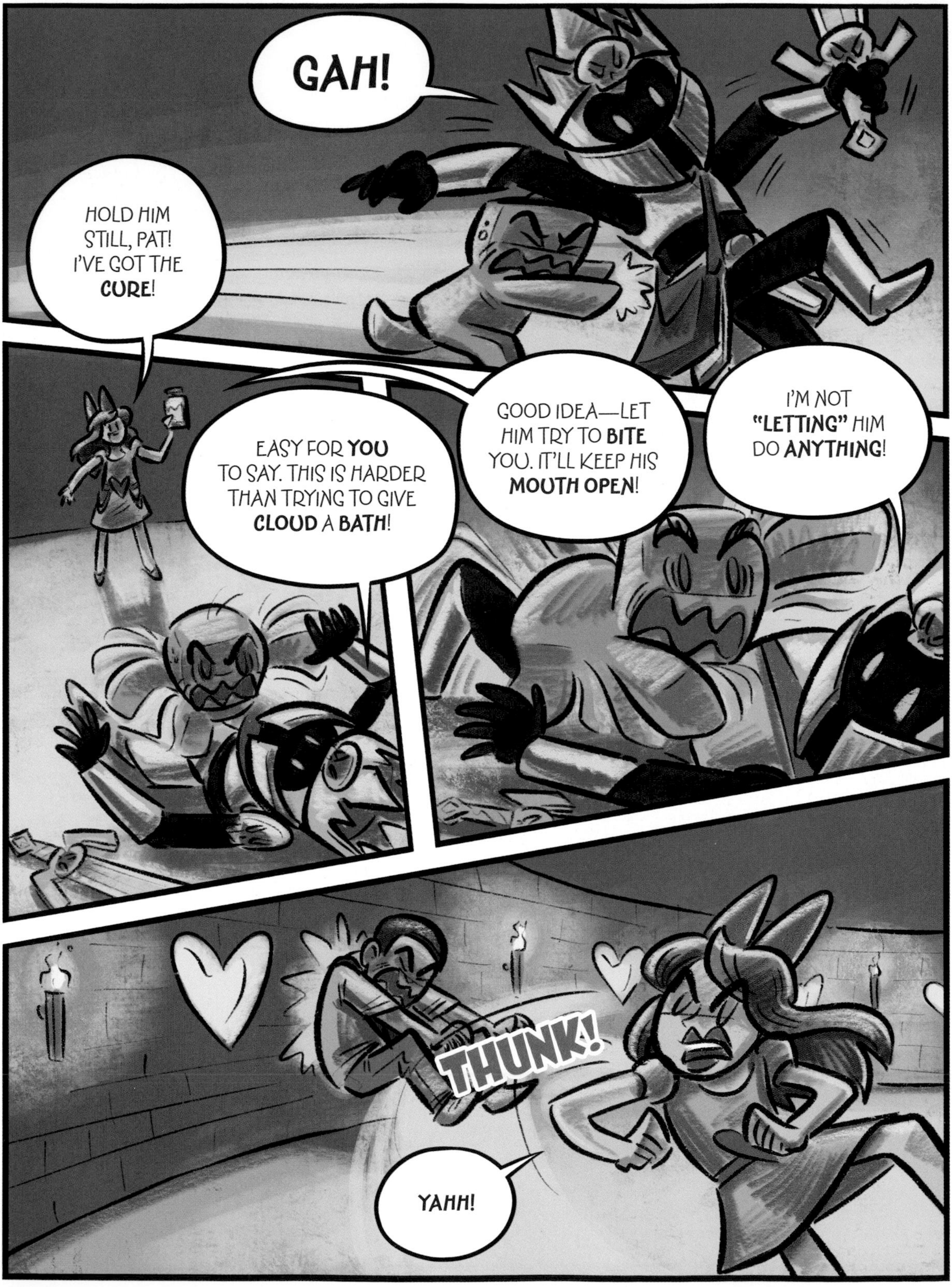
GAH!
HOLD HIM STILL, PAT! I'VE GOT THE CURE!
EASY FOR YOU TO SAY. THIS IS HARDER THAN TRYING TO GIVE CLOUD A BATH!
GOOD IDEA—LET HIM TRY TO BITE YOU. IT'LL KEEP HIS MOUTH OPEN!
I'M NOT "LETTING" HIM DO ANYTHING!
THUNK!
YAHH!

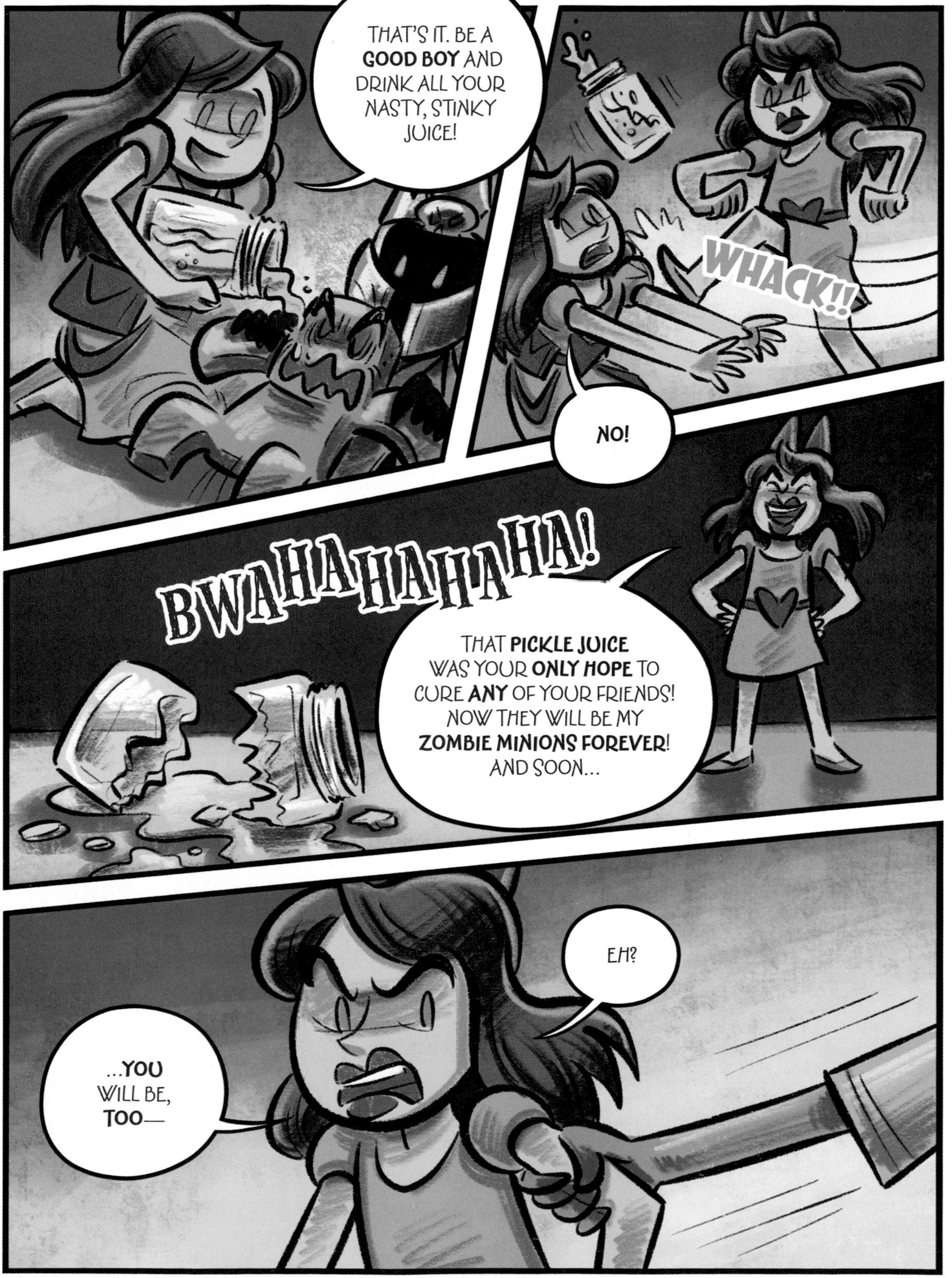
THAT'S IT. BE A **GOOD BOY** AND DRINK ALL YOUR NASTY, STINKY JUICE!
WHACK!!
NO!
BWAHAHAHAHAHA!
THAT **PICKLE JUICE** WAS YOUR **ONLY HOPE** TO CURE **ANY** OF YOUR FRIENDS! NOW THEY WILL BE MY **ZOMBIE MINIONS FOREVER**! AND SOON...
EH?
...**YOU** WILL BE, **TOO**—

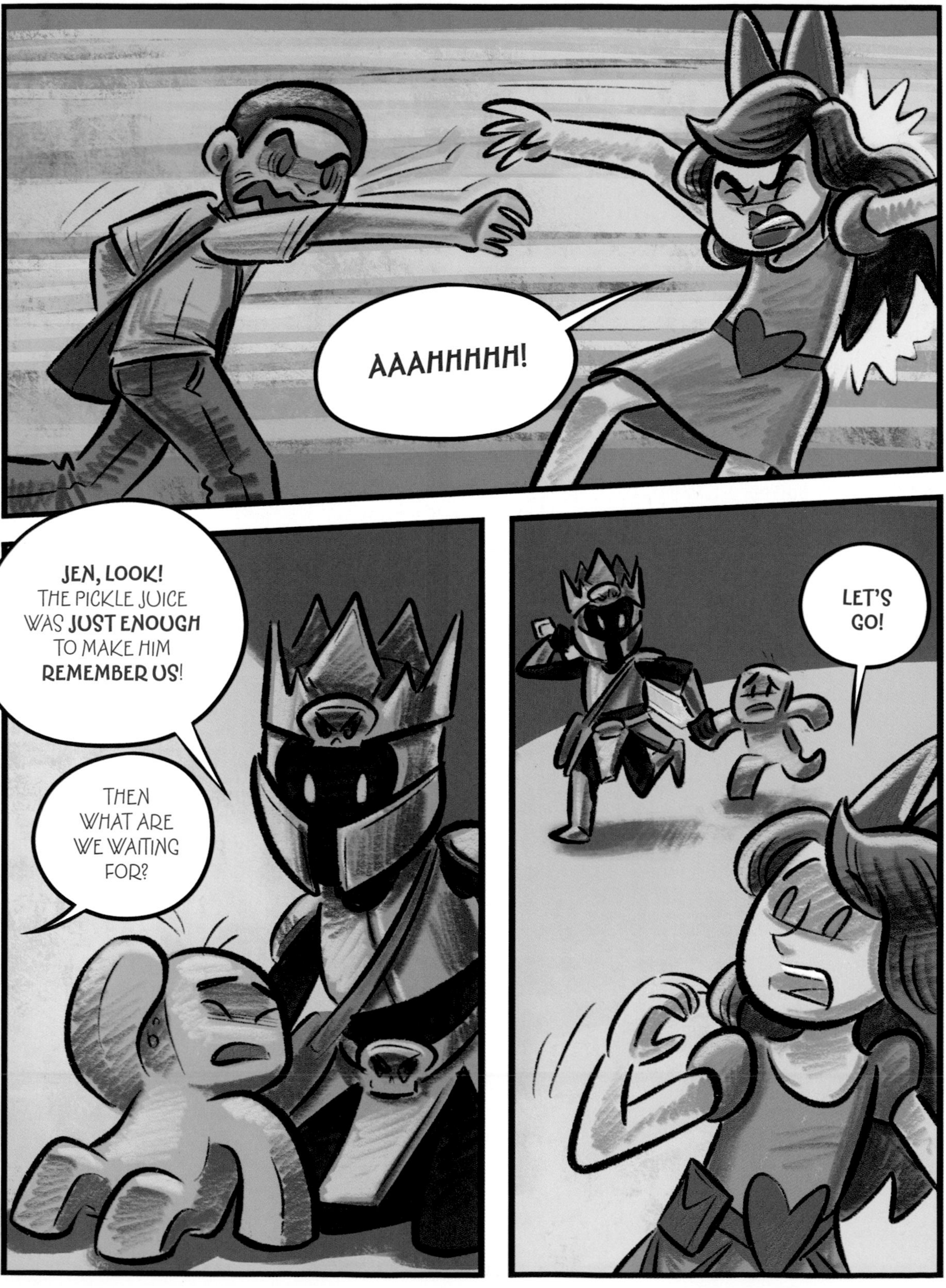
AAAHHHHH!
JEN, LOOK! THE PICKLE JUICE WAS JUST ENOUGH TO MAKE HIM REMEMBER US!
THEN WHAT ARE WE WAITING FOR?
LET'S GO!

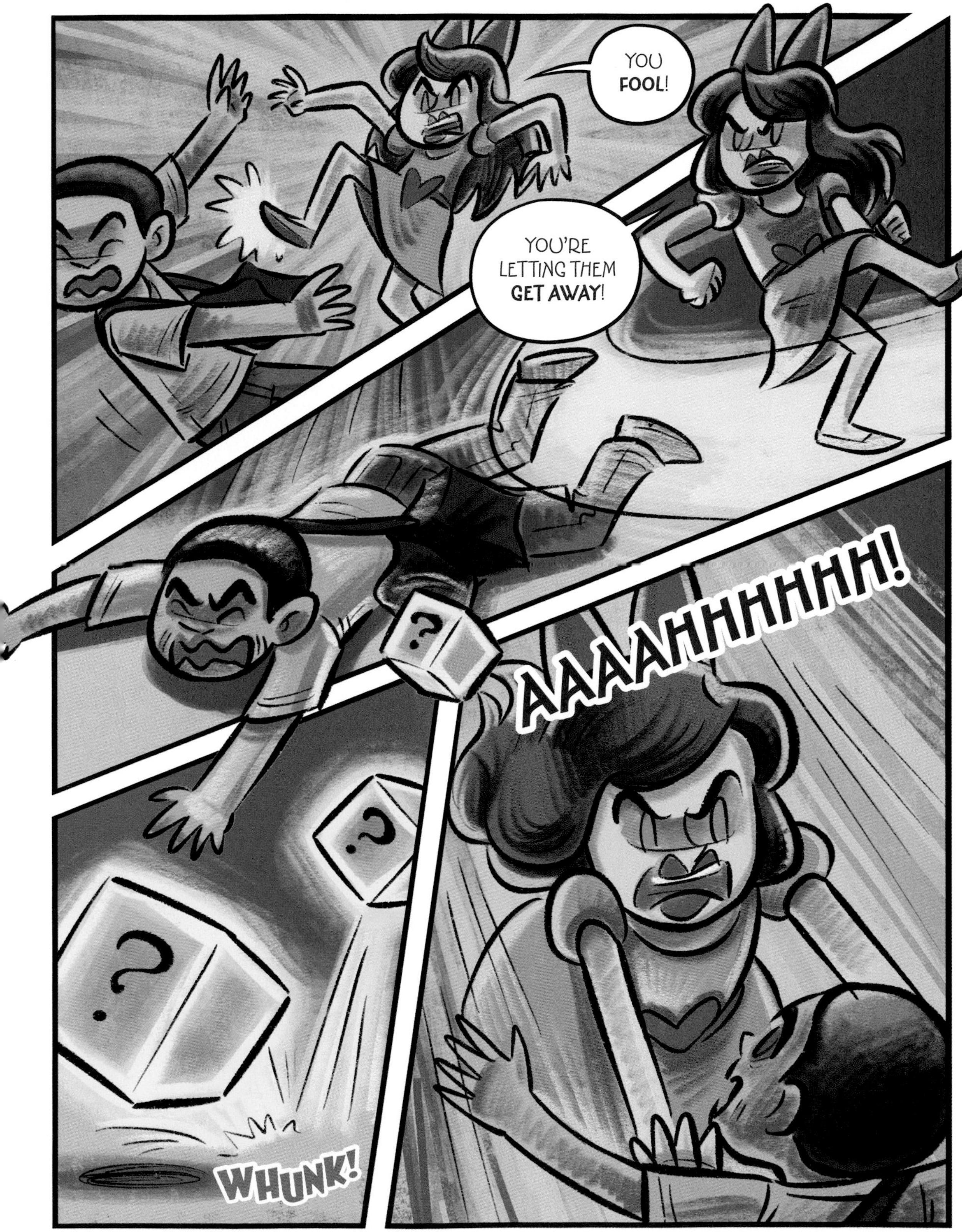
YOU **FOOL**!
YOU'RE LETTING THEM **GET AWAY**!
AAAAHHHHHH!
WHUNK!

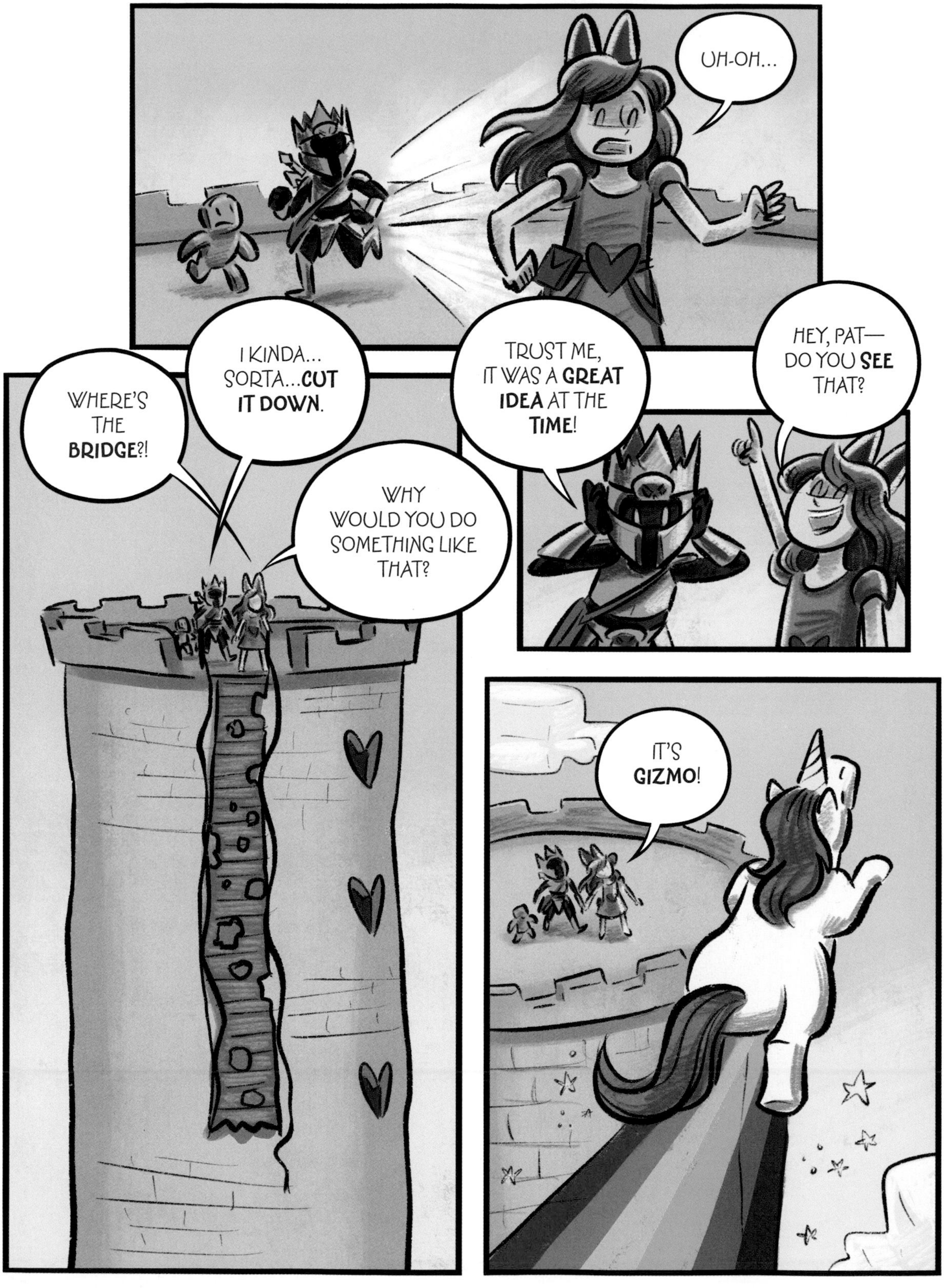
UH-OH...
WHERE'S THE BRIDGE?!
I KINDA... SORTA...CUT IT DOWN.
WHY WOULD YOU DO SOMETHING LIKE THAT?
TRUST ME, IT WAS A GREAT IDEA AT THE TIME!
HEY, PAT— DO YOU SEE THAT?
IT'S GIZMO!

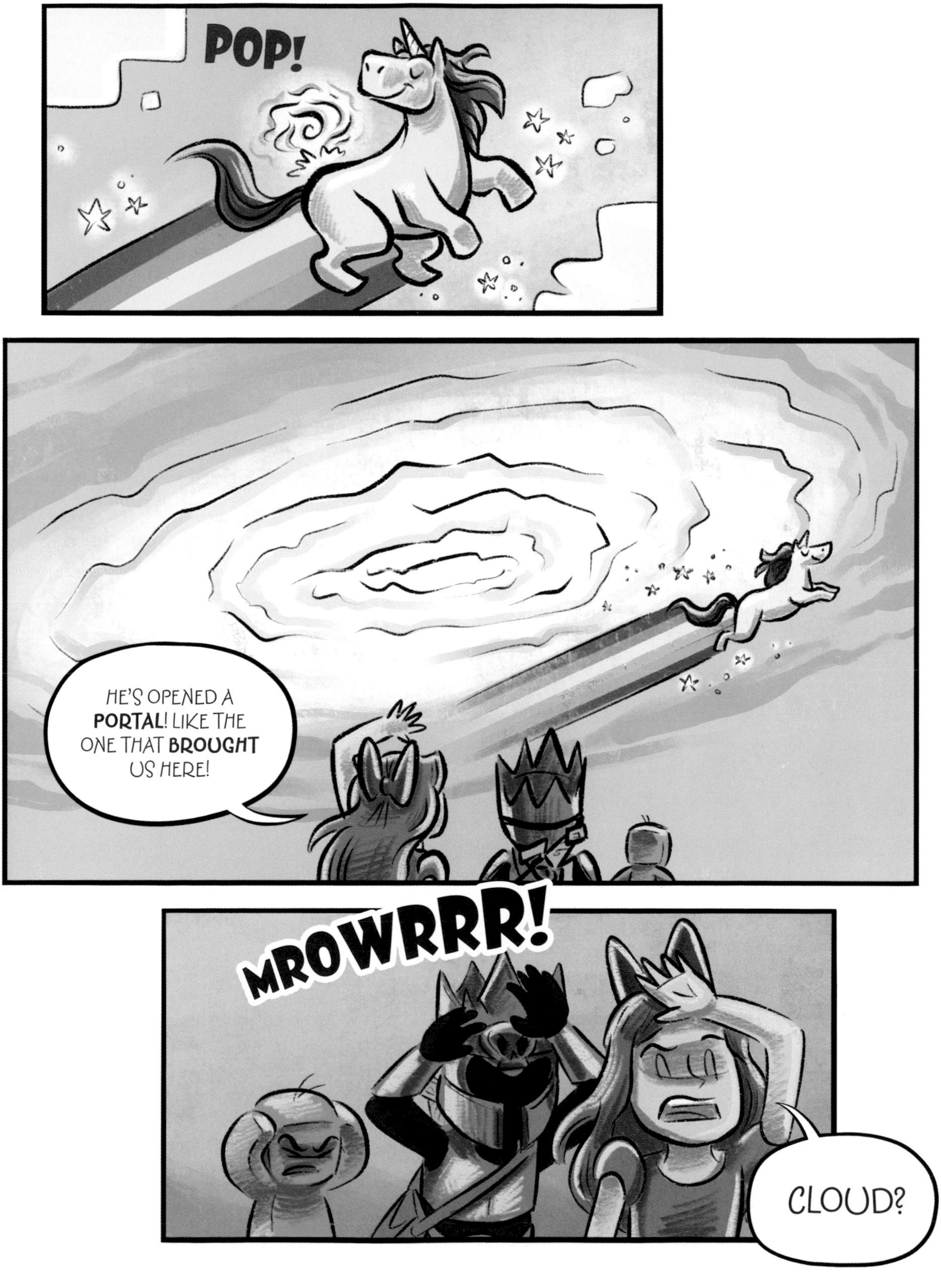
POP!
HE'S OPENED A PORTAL! LIKE THE ONE THAT BROUGHT US HERE!
MROWRRR!
CLOUD?

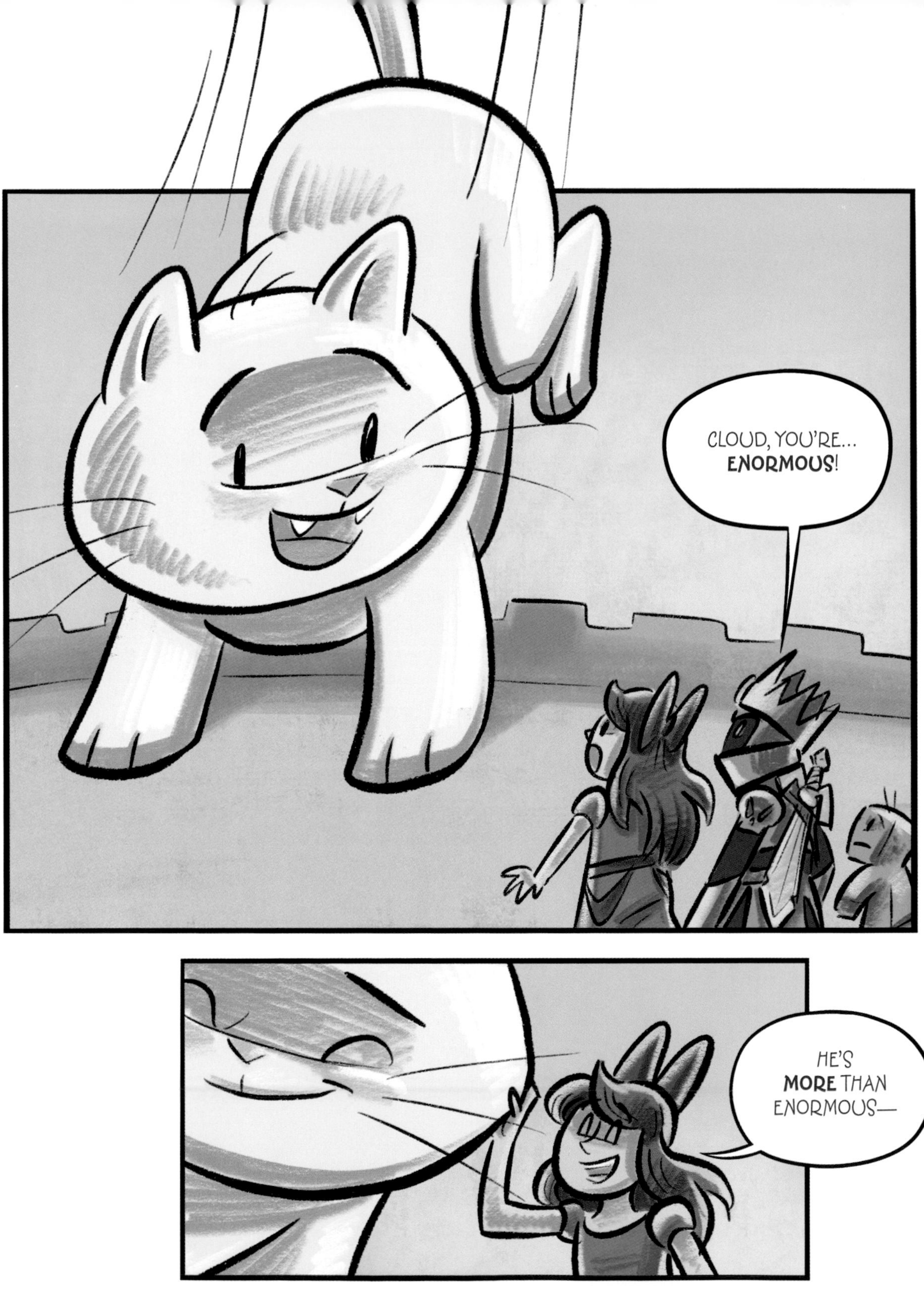
CLOUD, YOU'RE... **ENORMOUS**!
HE'S **MORE** THAN ENORMOUS—

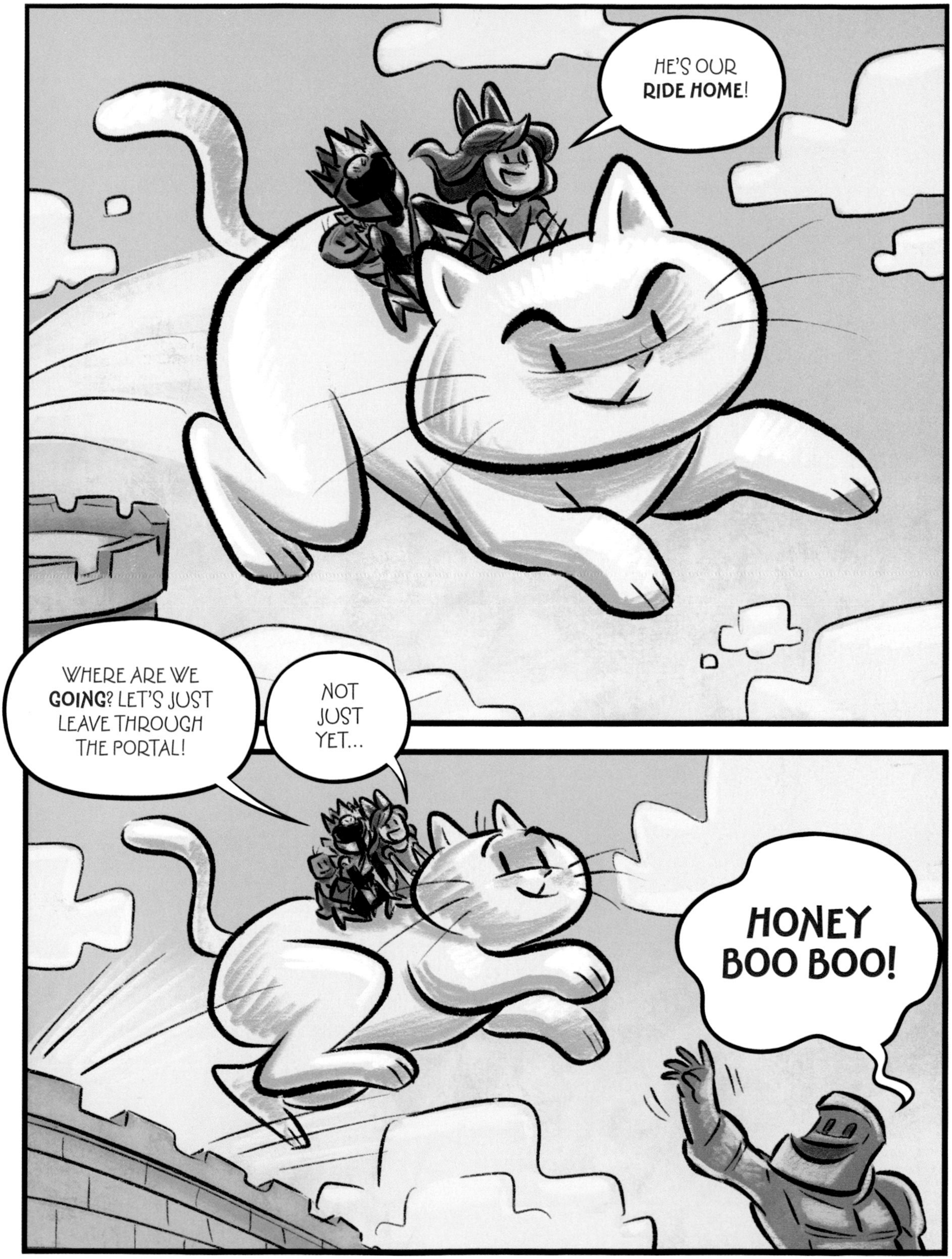
HE'S OUR **RIDE HOME**!
WHERE ARE WE **GOING**? LET'S JUST LEAVE THROUGH THE PORTAL!
NOT JUST YET...
HONEY BOO BOO!

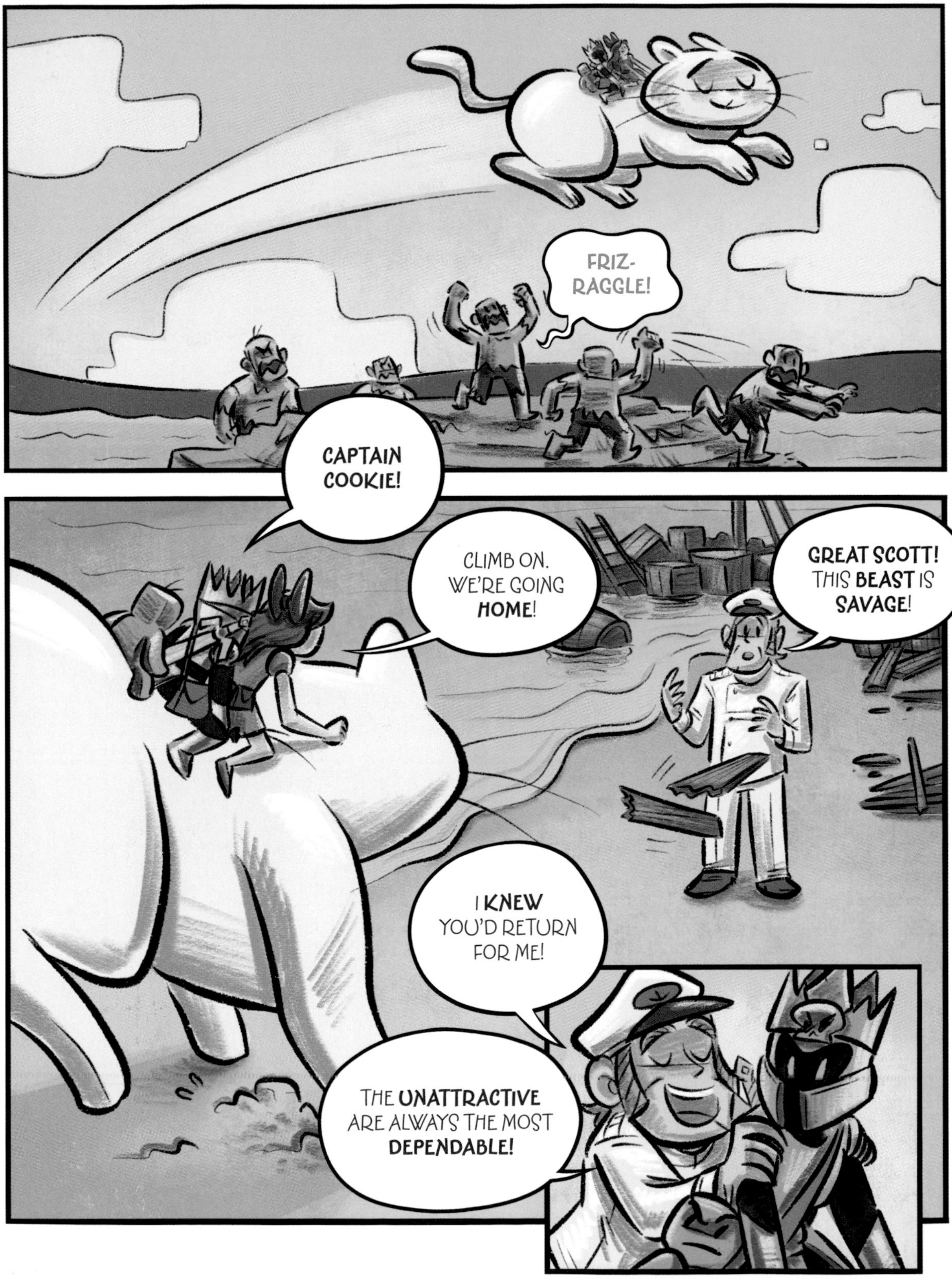
FRIZ-RAGGLE!
CAPTAIN COOKIE!
CLIMB ON. WE'RE GOING HOME!
GREAT SCOTT! THIS BEAST IS SAVAGE!
I KNEW YOU'D RETURN FOR ME!
THE UNATTRACTIVE ARE ALWAYS THE MOST DEPENDABLE!

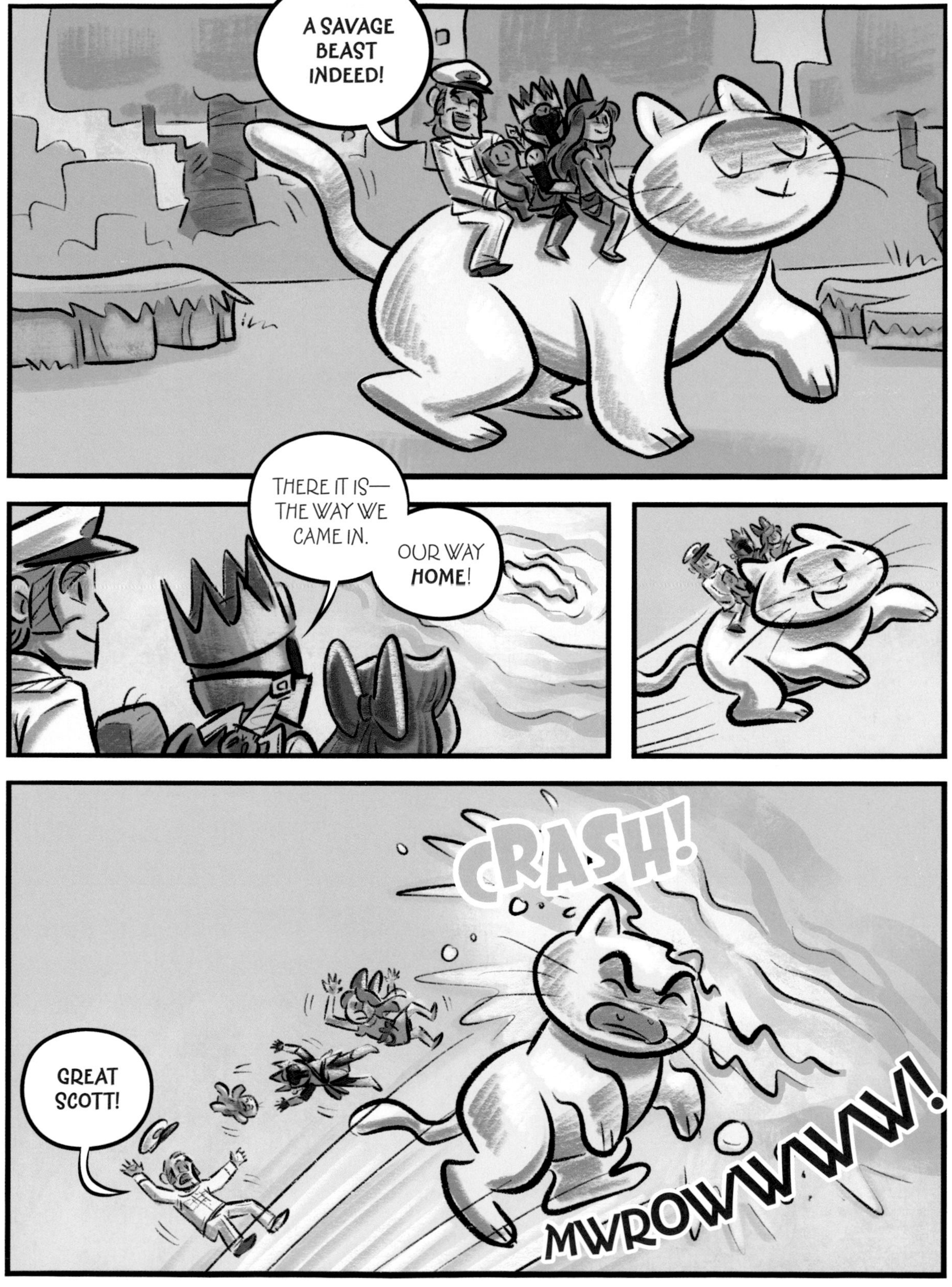
A SAVAGE BEAST INDEED!
THERE IT IS— THE WAY WE CAME IN.
OUR WAY HOME!
CRASH!
GREAT SCOTT!
MWROWWWW!

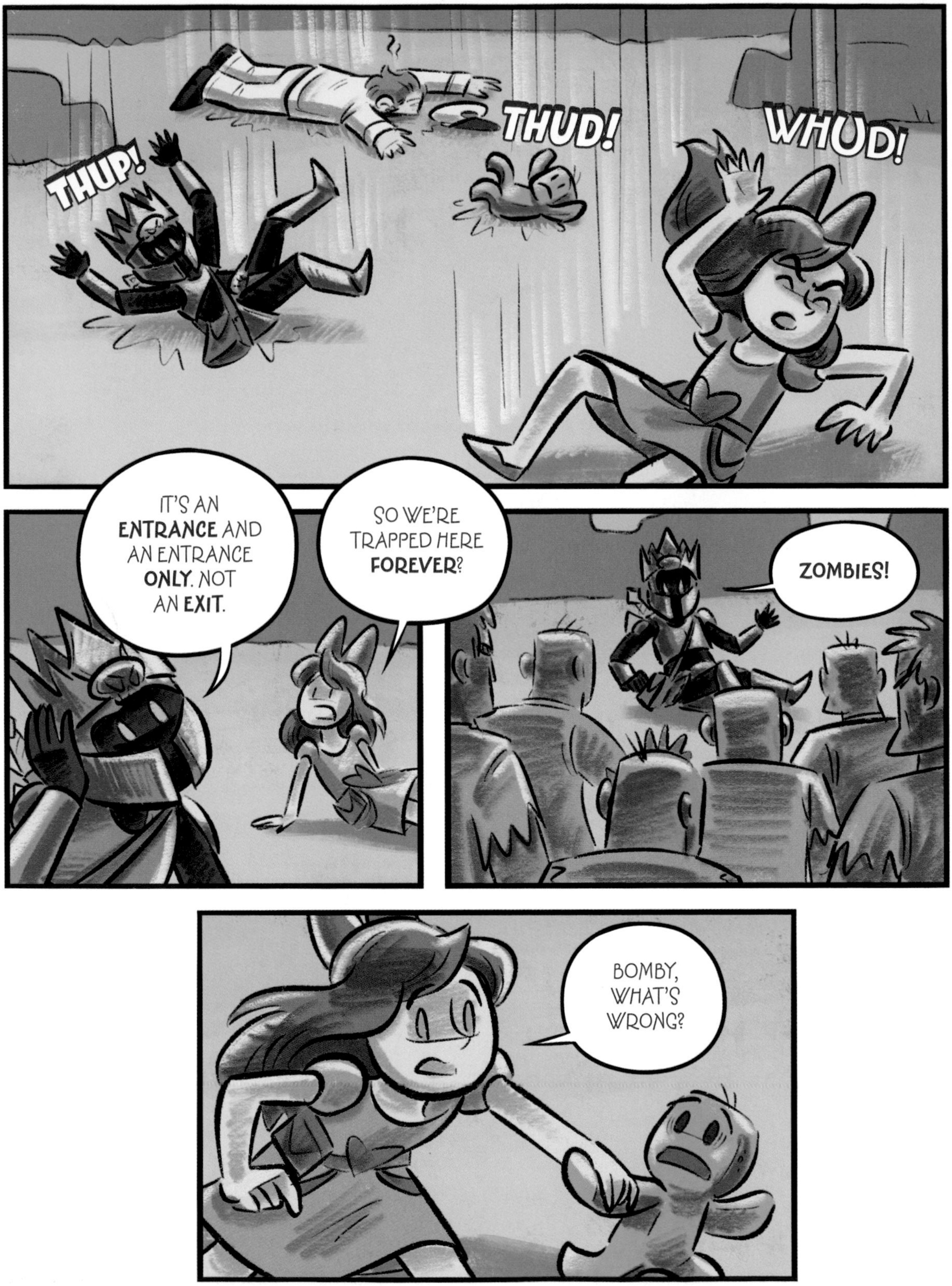
THUP!
THUD!
WHUD!
IT'S AN **ENTRANCE** AND AN ENTRANCE **ONLY**. NOT AN **EXIT**.
SO WE'RE TRAPPED HERE **FOREVER**?
ZOMBIES!
BOMBY, WHAT'S WRONG?

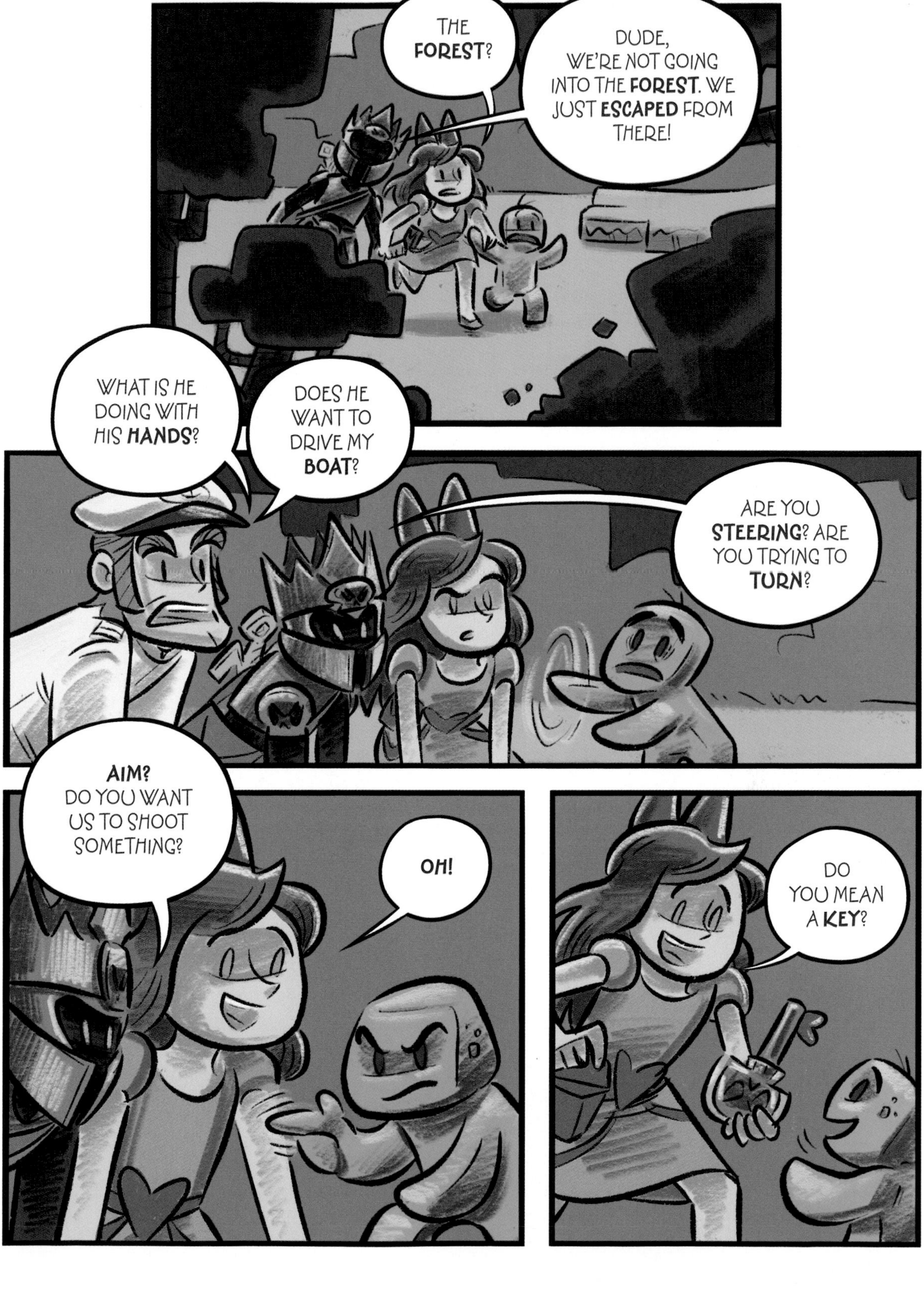
THE FOREST?
DUDE, WE'RE NOT GOING INTO THE FOREST. WE JUST ESCAPED FROM THERE!
WHAT IS HE DOING WITH HIS HANDS?
DOES HE WANT TO DRIVE MY BOAT?
ARE YOU STEERING? ARE YOU TRYING TO TURN?
AIM? DO YOU WANT US TO SHOOT SOMETHING?
OH!
DO YOU MEAN A KEY?

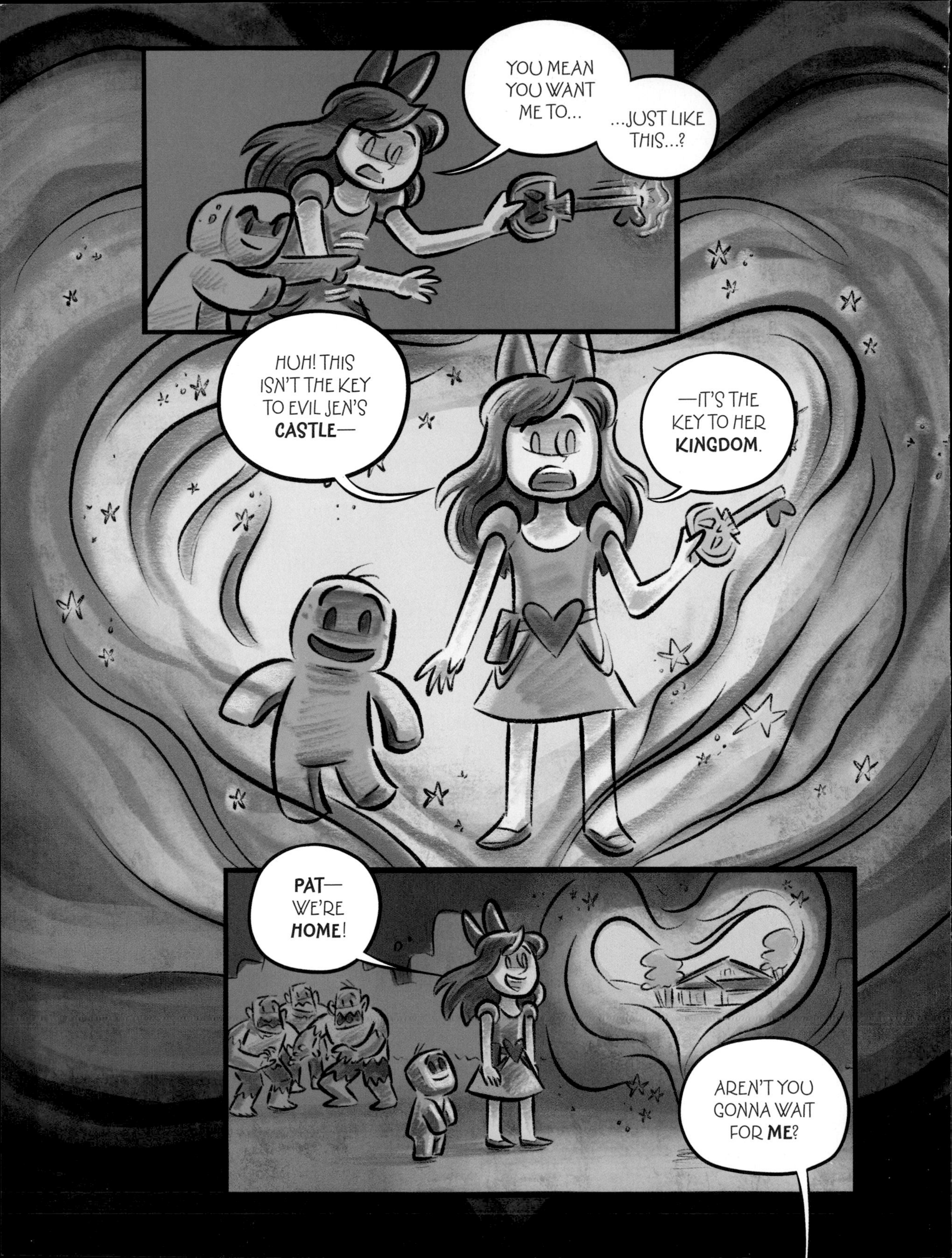

YOU MEAN YOU WANT ME TO...
...JUST LIKE THIS...?
HUH! THIS ISN'T THE KEY TO EVIL JEN'S CASTLE—
—IT'S THE KEY TO HER KINGDOM.
PAT— WE'RE HOME!
AREN'T YOU GONNA WAIT FOR ME?

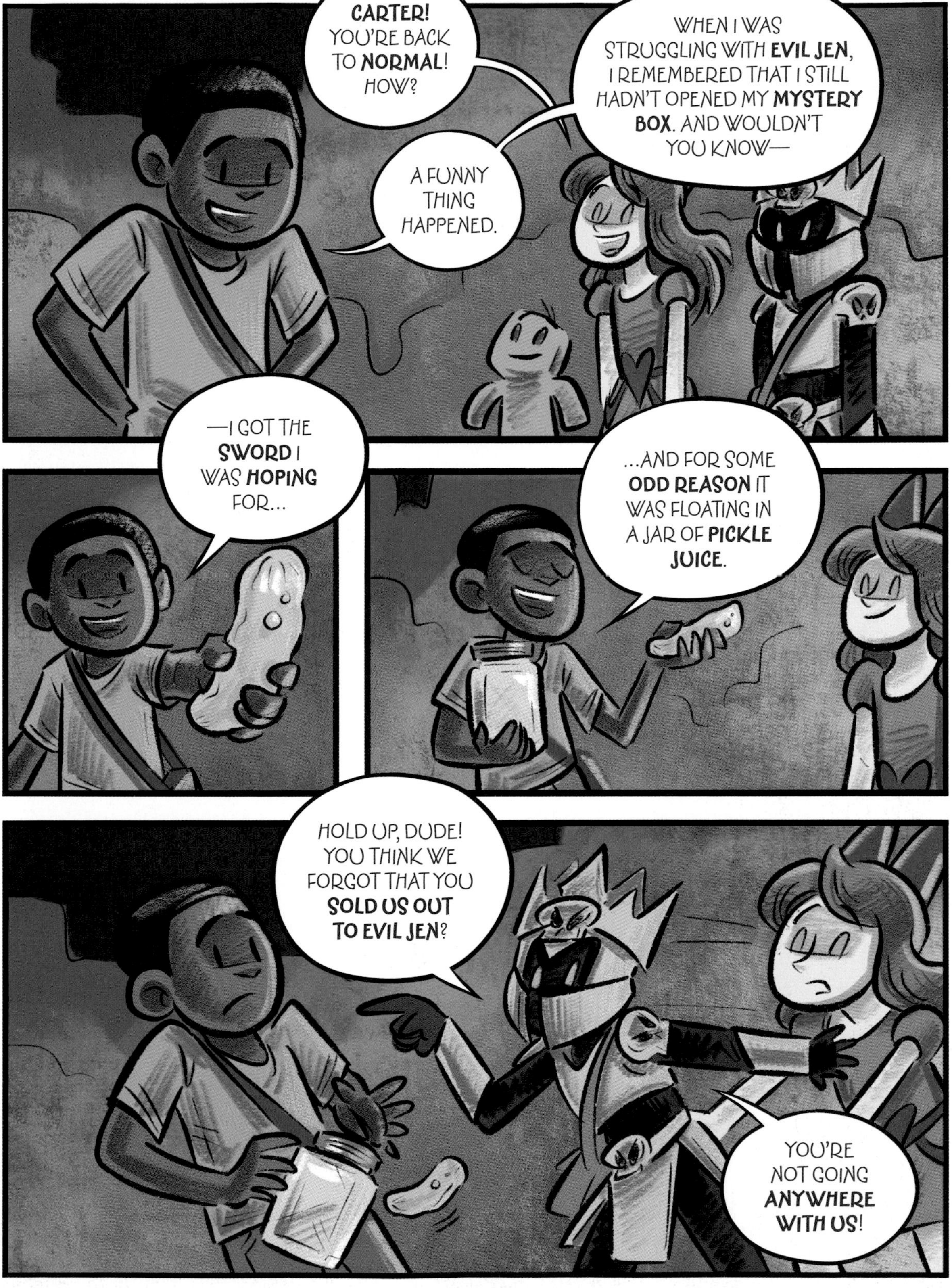
CARTER! YOU'RE BACK TO NORMAL! HOW?
A FUNNY THING HAPPENED.
WHEN I WAS STRUGGLING WITH EVIL JEN, I REMEMBERED THAT I STILL HADN'T OPENED MY MYSTERY BOX. AND WOULDN'T YOU KNOW—
—I GOT THE SWORD I WAS HOPING FOR...
...AND FOR SOME ODD REASON IT WAS FLOATING IN A JAR OF PICKLE JUICE.
HOLD UP, DUDE! YOU THINK WE FORGOT THAT YOU SOLD US OUT TO EVIL JEN?
YOU'RE NOT GOING ANYWHERE WITH US!

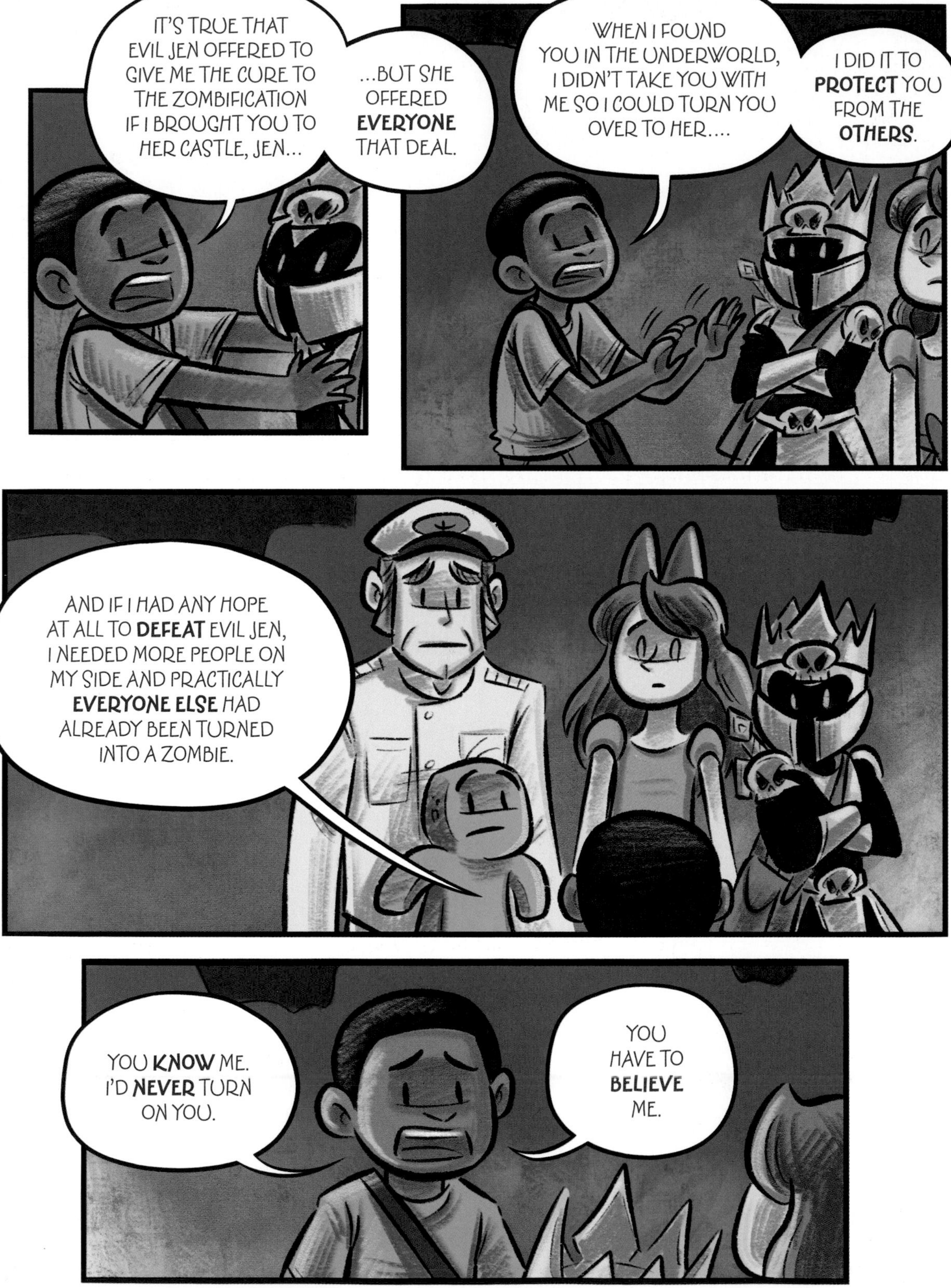
IT'S TRUE THAT EVIL JEN OFFERED TO GIVE ME THE CURE TO THE ZOMBIFICATION IF I BROUGHT YOU TO HER CASTLE, JEN...
...BUT SHE OFFERED **EVERYONE** THAT DEAL.
WHEN I FOUND YOU IN THE UNDERWORLD, I DIDN'T TAKE YOU WITH ME SO I COULD TURN YOU OVER TO HER....
I DID IT TO **PROTECT** YOU FROM THE **OTHERS**.
AND IF I HAD ANY HOPE AT ALL TO **DEFEAT** EVIL JEN, I NEEDED MORE PEOPLE ON MY SIDE AND PRACTICALLY **EVERYONE ELSE** HAD ALREADY BEEN TURNED INTO A ZOMBIE.
YOU **KNOW** ME. I'D **NEVER** TURN ON YOU.
YOU HAVE TO **BELIEVE** ME.

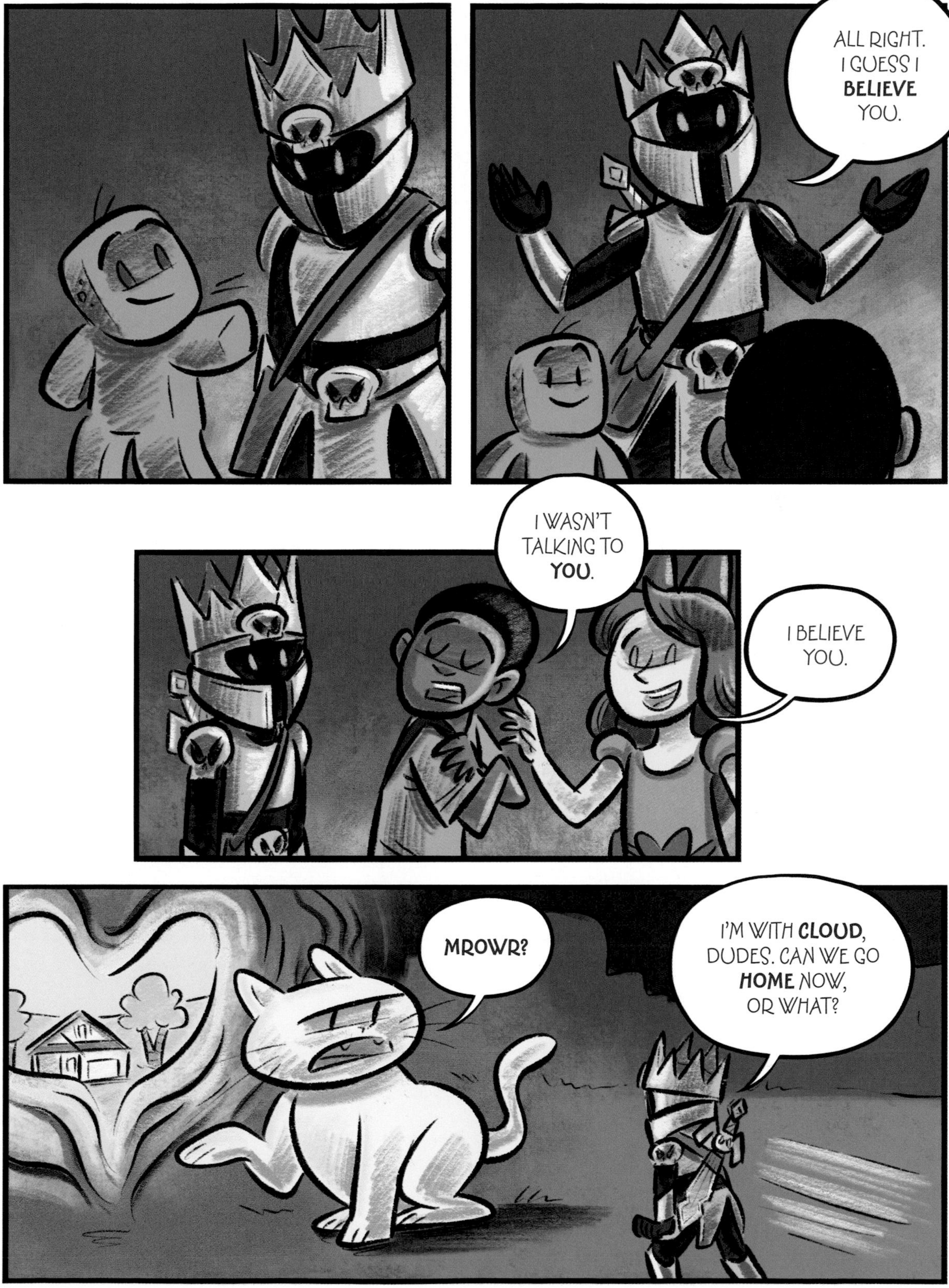
ALL RIGHT. I GUESS I **BELIEVE** YOU.
I WASN'T TALKING TO **YOU**.
I BELIEVE YOU.
MROWR?
I'M WITH **CLOUD**, DUDES. CAN WE GO **HOME** NOW, OR WHAT?

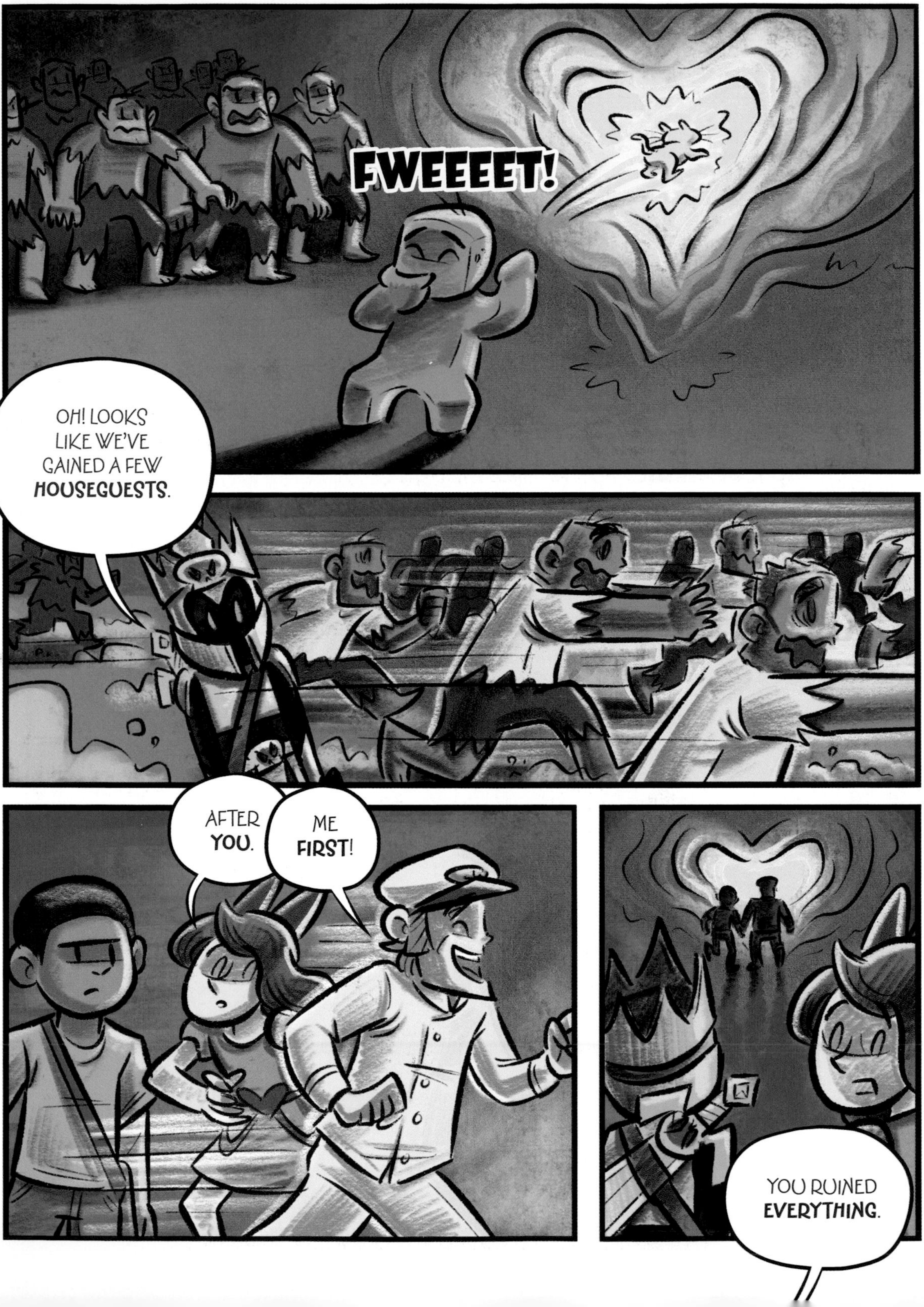
FWEEEET!
OH! LOOKS LIKE WE'VE GAINED A FEW HOUSEGUESTS.
AFTER YOU.
ME FIRST!
YOU RUINED EVERYTHING.

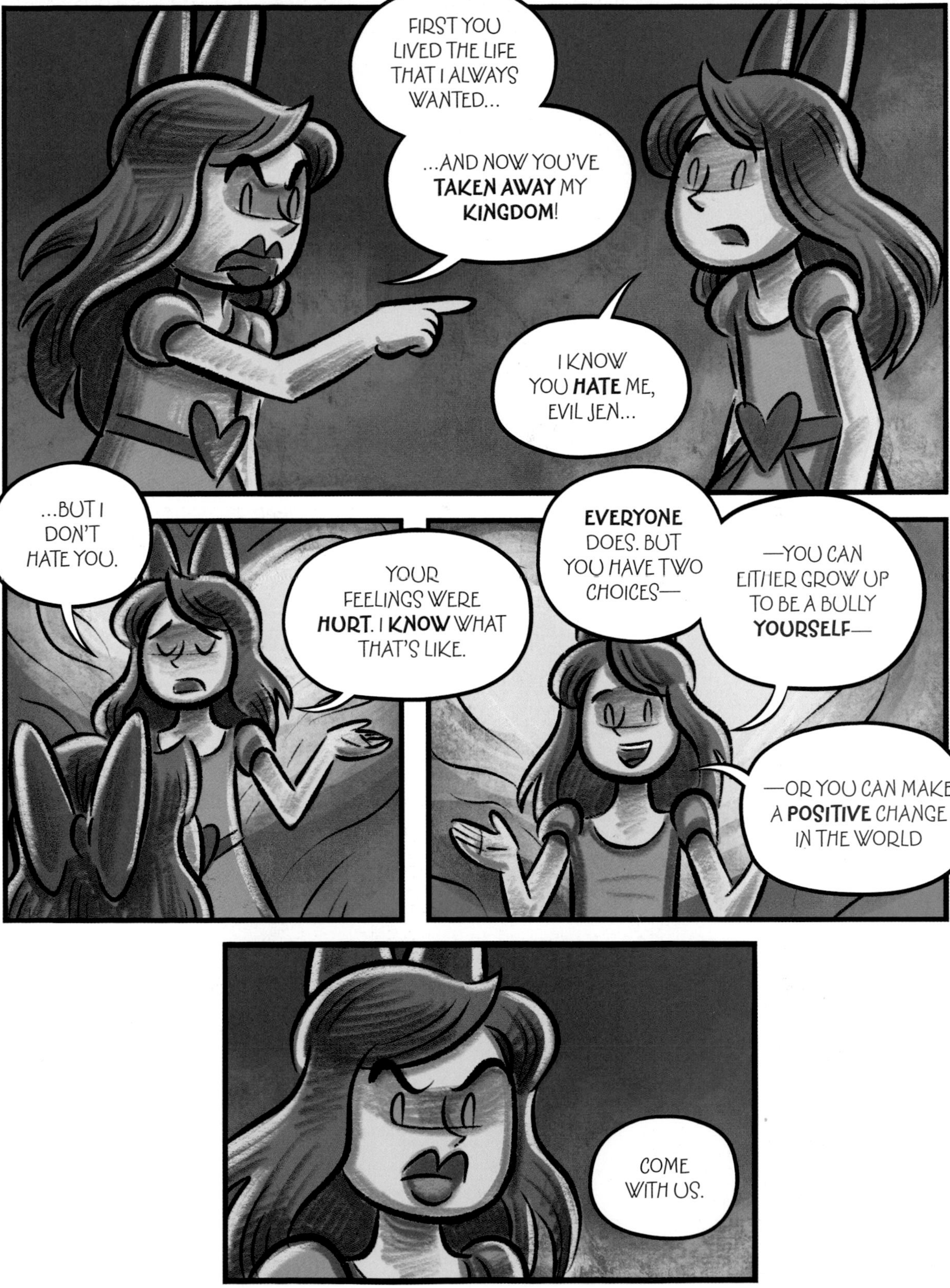
FIRST YOU LIVED THE LIFE THAT I ALWAYS WANTED...
...AND NOW YOU'VE **TAKEN AWAY** MY **KINGDOM**!
I KNOW YOU **HATE** ME, EVIL JEN...
...BUT I DON'T HATE YOU.
YOUR FEELINGS WERE **HURT**. I **KNOW** WHAT THAT'S LIKE.
EVERYONE DOES. BUT YOU HAVE TWO CHOICES—
—YOU CAN EITHER GROW UP TO BE A BULLY **YOURSELF**—
—OR YOU CAN MAKE A **POSITIVE** CHANGE IN THE WORLD
COME WITH US.

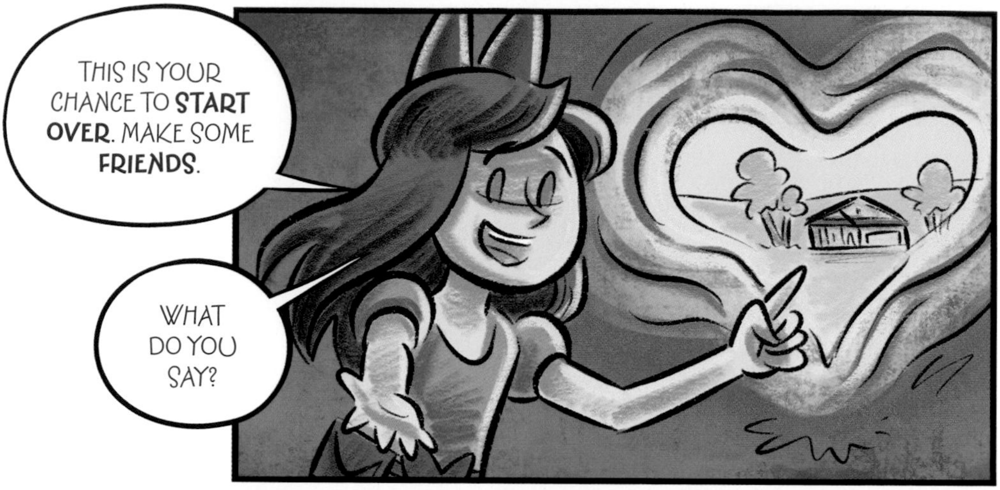
THIS IS YOUR CHANCE TO **START OVER**. MAKE SOME **FRIENDS**.
WHAT DO YOU SAY?

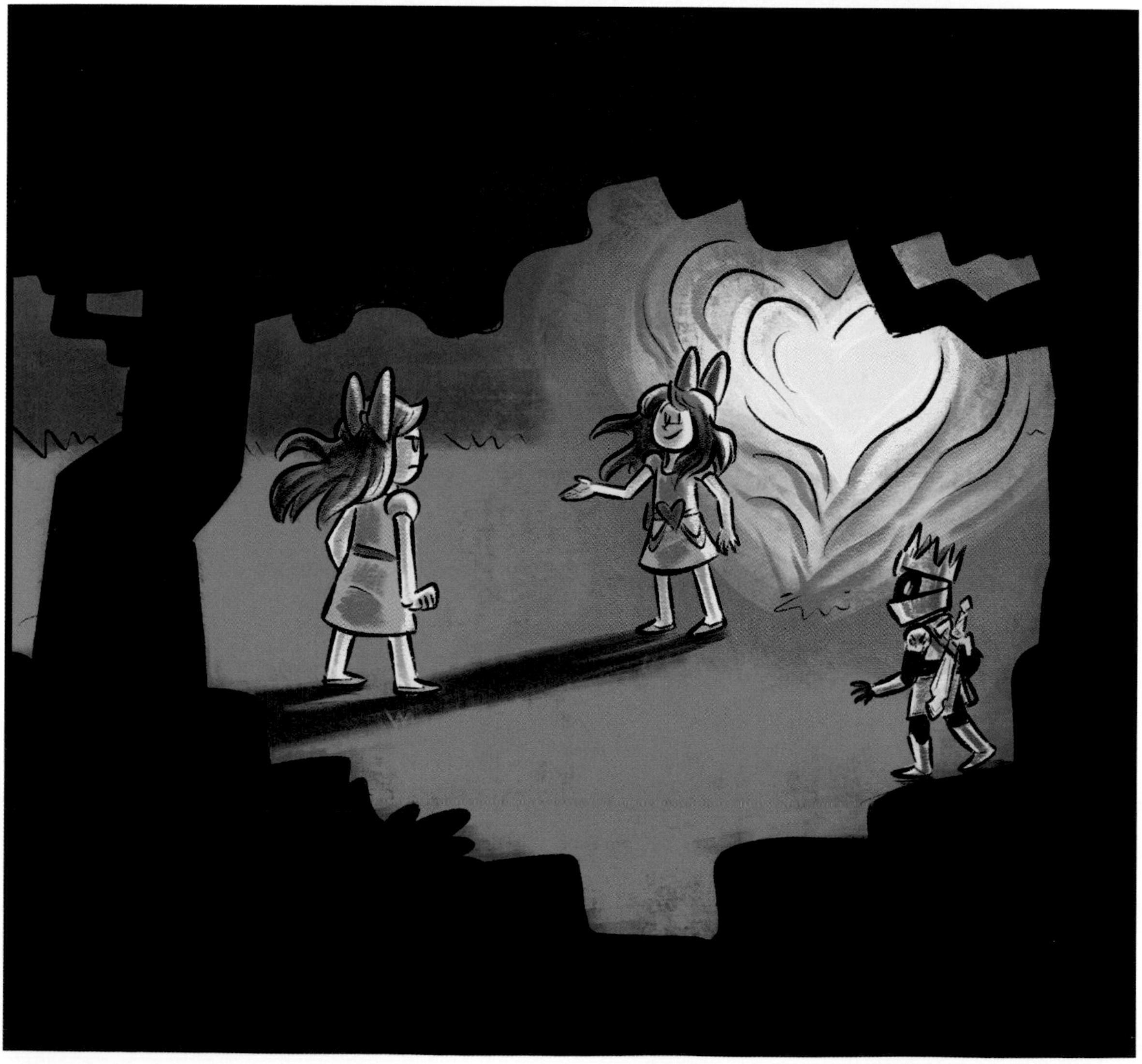

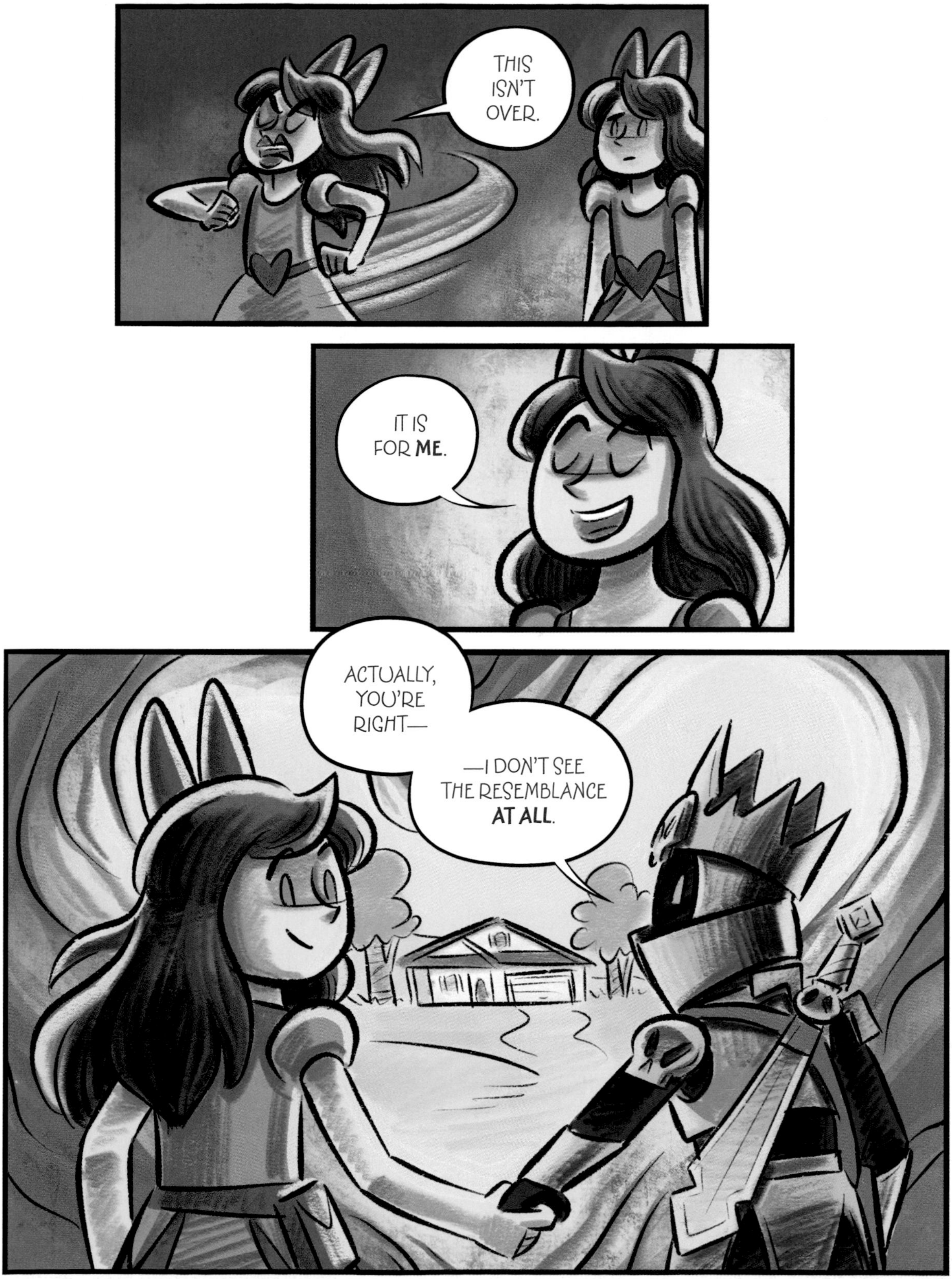
THIS ISN'T OVER.
IT IS FOR **ME**.
ACTUALLY, YOU'RE RIGHT—
—I DON'T SEE THE RESEMBLANCE **AT ALL**.

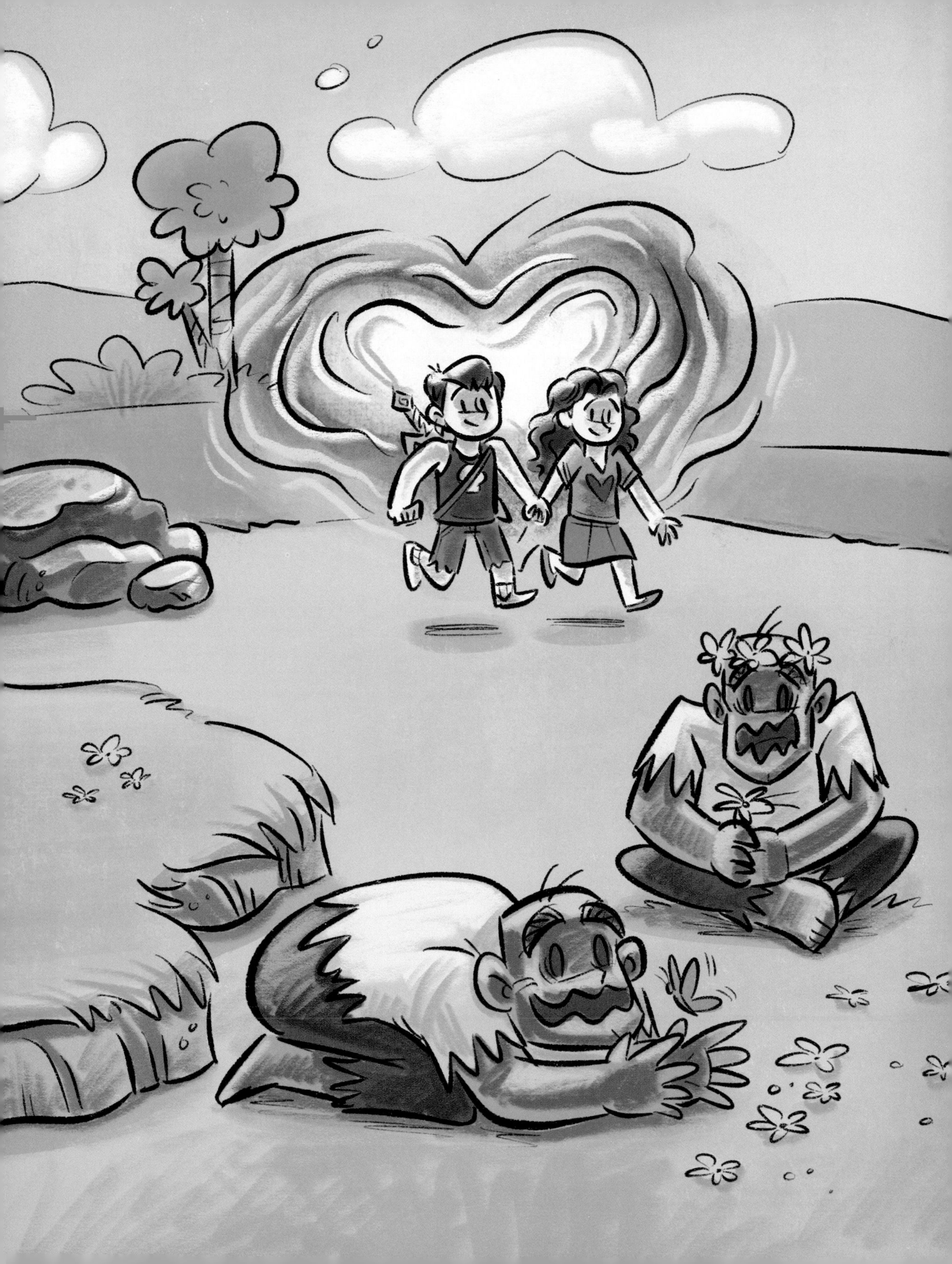

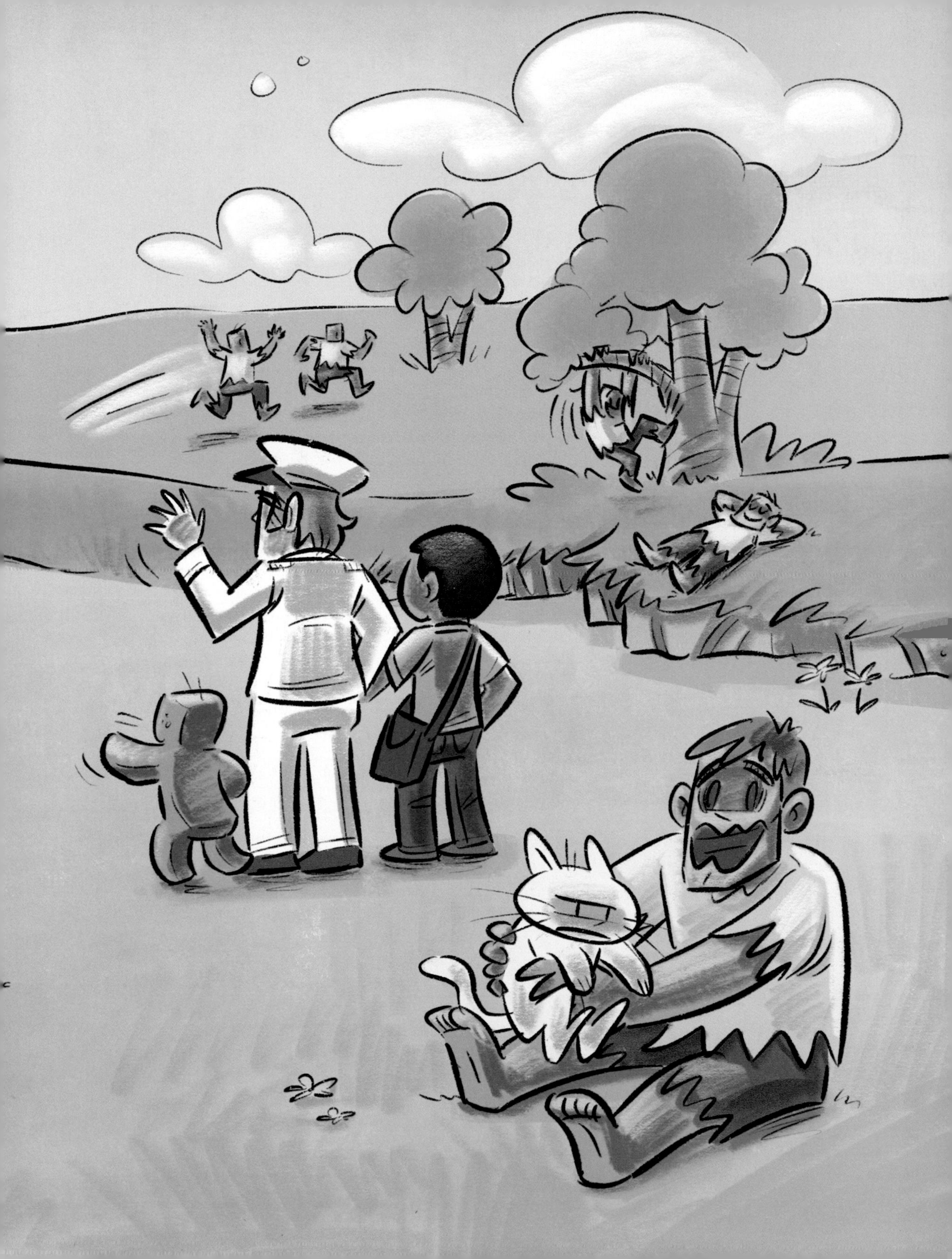

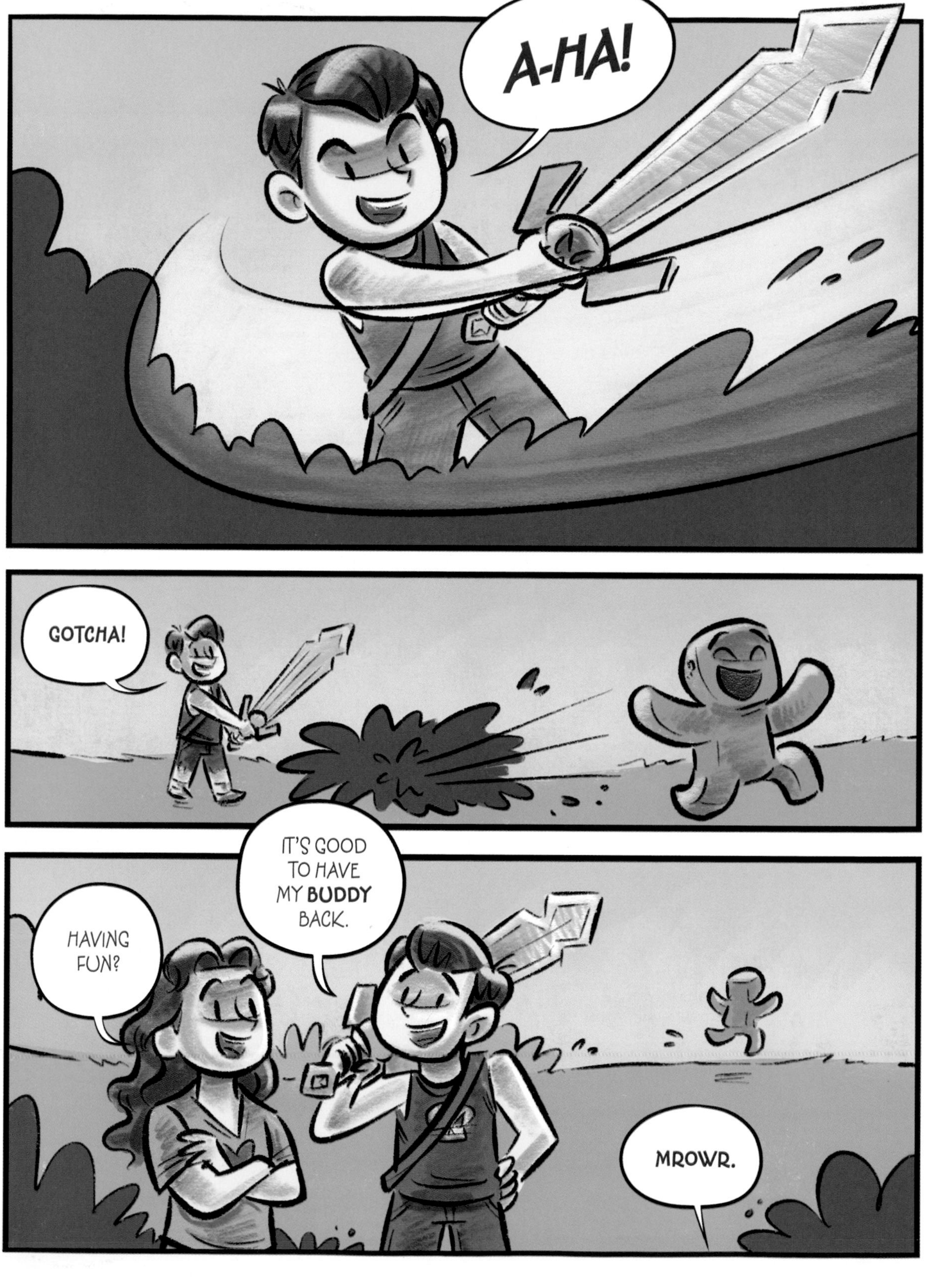
A-HA!
GOTCHA!
HAVING FUN?
IT'S GOOD TO HAVE MY **BUDDY** BACK.
MROWR.

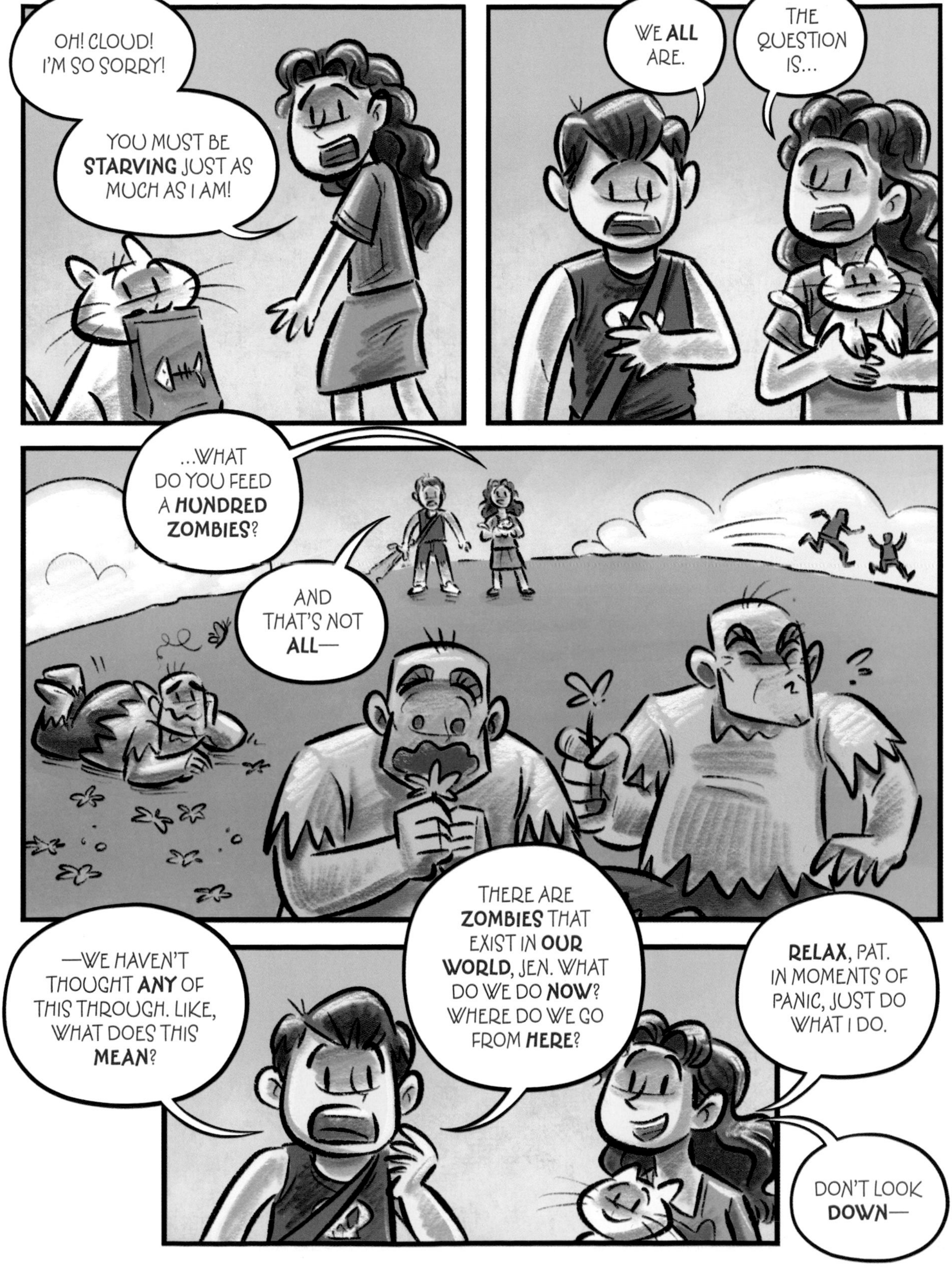
OH! CLOUD! I'M SO SORRY!
YOU MUST BE **STARVING** JUST AS MUCH AS I AM!
WE **ALL** ARE.
THE QUESTION IS...
...WHAT DO YOU FEED A **HUNDRED ZOMBIES**?
AND THAT'S NOT **ALL**—
—WE HAVEN'T THOUGHT **ANY** OF THIS THROUGH. LIKE, WHAT DOES THIS **MEAN**?
THERE ARE **ZOMBIES** THAT EXIST IN **OUR WORLD**, JEN. WHAT DO WE DO **NOW**? WHERE DO WE GO FROM **HERE**?
RELAX, PAT. IN MOMENTS OF PANIC, JUST DO WHAT I DO.
DON'T LOOK **DOWN**—

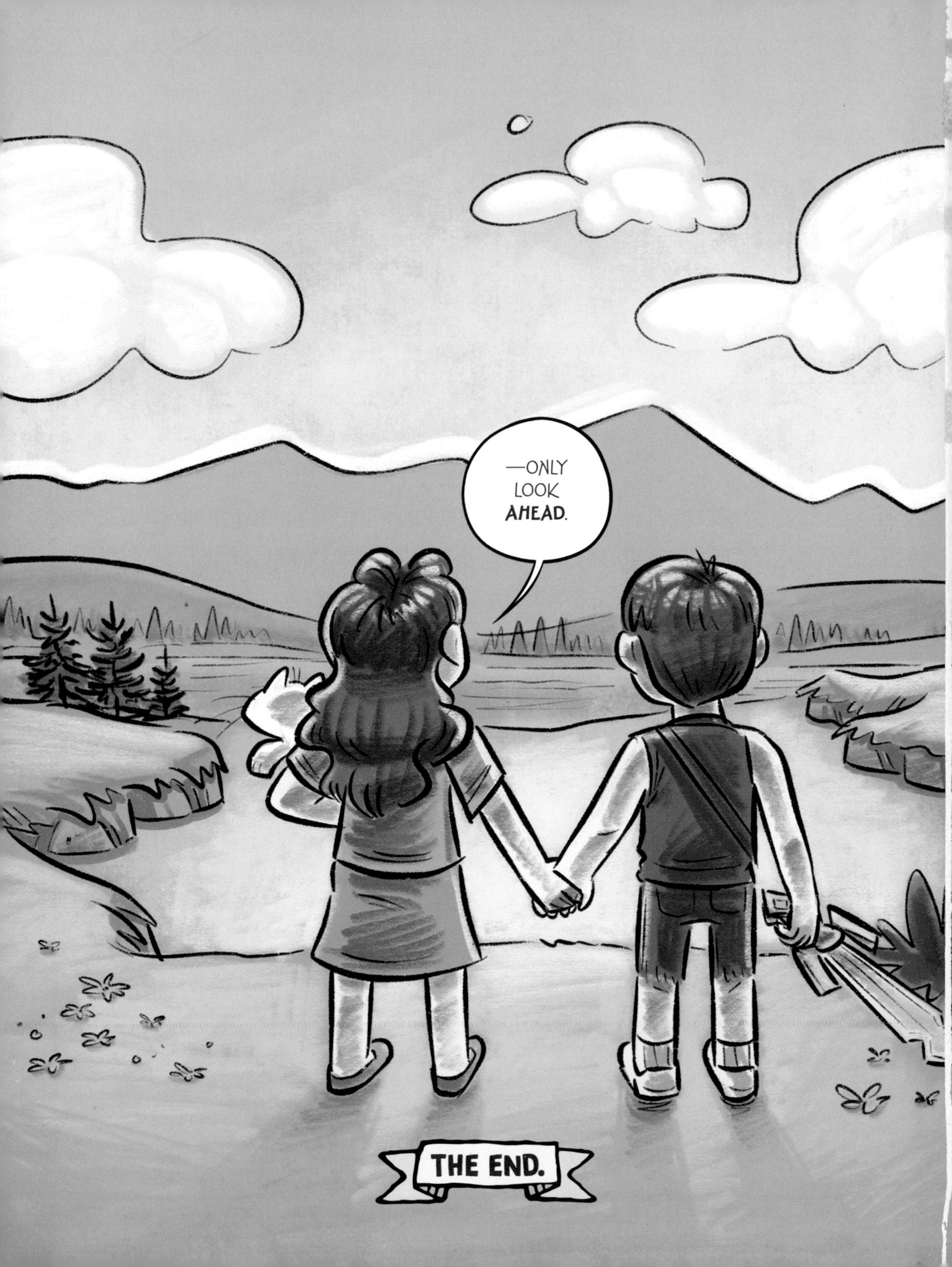
—ONLY LOOK AHEAD.
THE END.